An avid reader since childhood, **Beverly Barton** wrote her first book at the age of nine. She wrote short stories, poetry, plays and novels throughout high school and college, and is now a *New York Times* bestselling author, having written over sixty books since she was first published in 1990. Beverly lives in Alabama with her husband.

BEVERLY BARTON

A TIME TO DIE

MIRA

MIRA is a registered trademark of Harlequin Enterprises Limited,
used under licence.

Published in Great Britain 2009
MIRA Books, Eton House, 18-24 Paradise Road,
Richmond, Surrey, TW9 1SR

ISBN 978 0 7783 0260 5

58-0109

Harlequin Mills & Boon policy is to use papers that are
natural, renewable and recyclable products and made from
wood grown in sustainable forests. The logging and
manufacturing processes conform to the legal environmental
regulations of the country of origin.

Printed and bound in Spain
by Litografia Rosés S.A., Barcelona

ACKNOWLEDGEMENTS

A special thank-you for invaluable technical
and medical research assistance.
Roger Waldrep
Steven L Romiti, MD

In loving memory of Wilhelimena "Willie" Wood, who lived her religious beliefs, setting an example for family and friends. You left this life much too soon, but your deep faith in a heavenly eternity comforts those you left behind.

PROLOGUE

THIS ASSIGNMENT sucked big-time. Lexie would rather be just about anywhere than here in Gadi covering the presidential inauguration ceremonies. Newly elected President Tum was an evil, arrogant son of a bitch who had massacred a hundred thousand of his own citizens in an ethnic cleansing. And the world had turned a blind eye. Even UBC, United Broadcasting Center, for whom she worked as a TV journalist had thought this man's official takeover of power was so insignificant that they had sent only her—a rookie reporter—and a lone cameraman to cover the event. Their escort/bodyguard, Mr. Kele, was here somewhere in the crowd, a moth-eaten-looking rogue who made Lexie's skin crawl. But at least the guy carried a gun and spoke the language.

"There he is. President Tum. Get as many close-ups of the cocky little bastard as possible," Lexie told Marty Bearn, her cameraman.

Marty and she had met for the first time on their recent plane ride from Atlanta, the home base for UBC. She had bellyached to him about this crap assignment until she'd vented as much frustration as she could, and he had shown her photos of his bride, a cute little brunette with big doe eyes. She had wondered what a cutie like his Sherry saw in a big, hefty oaf like Marty, with his shock of auburn red hair, hee-haw laugh and oversize teeth. But by the time they arrived on the Dark Continent, Lexie understood Marty's appeal. He possessed a laid-back, easy-going nature, an appealing personality and a caring attitude. Not to mention that he was hog-wild, crazy in love with his wife. What woman could resist a man who loved her that much?

"Look at him strutting up to the podium like a little bantam rooster," Marty said. "I bet he's not more than five-six without those high-heel boots he's wearing. He's definitely got a Napoleon complex."

"He's a monster, if you ask me," Lexie said off-camera. Then she returned to reporter mode, keeping her voice low as Marty began filming again.

Prior to Babu Tum's arrival, she had commented on the outdoor event being held in an open courtyard half the size of a football field. As Marty had cinematically scanned the area and the large crowd of citizens who had been herded into place like mindless cattle, she had considered how she would present this news event to her audience. Later, once back at the studio in the U.S., she would create a voiceover to describe today's farce. A fake election. A dictator president. A subjugated people. She supposed it was possible that UBC would use the entire piece Marty and she created, but she seriously doubted it. The "powers that be" would cut it down to a two- or three-minute segment and put their own spin on the soon-to-be forgotten event. One more African dictator assuming official power was hardly newsworthy, was he?

Unfortunately, Lexie was not proficient in the native language, so she managed to pick up only a word here and there, occasionally piecing words together to figure out a sentence. Where was their guide when she needed him? Lost in the crowd, not worth the two hundred dollars a day UBC was paying him.

Oh, well, it probably didn't matter that she couldn't understand every word of Tum's speech. Overall, the man was simply blowing his own horn.

Less than five minutes into Tum's speech, which had been interrupted half a dozen times by shouts Lexie *did* understand—*Long live President Tum*—a ripple of apprehension tapped up her spine just as droplets of perspiration trickled between her breasts. In one life-altering moment, she instinctively knew something horrible was about to happen.

A single rifle shot rang out—the long-range weapon hitting its mark. Babu Tum's dark eyes widened in shock and realization as the bullet entered his forehead.

"My God!" Marty Bearn gasped. "Tum's been assassinated."

Tum's guards, whose presence on the podium with him had apparently not deterred the assassin, aimed their weapons, searching the crowd for the killer. One by one, three of Tum's six-man advisory council dropped as shot after shot rang out. While the other three men took cover, the crowd went wild, screaming and running, everyone hysterical with fear. Caught up in the frenzy, Tum's guards began firing into the crowd, killing at random, taking down unarmed civilians.

"Let's get out of here!" Marty called to Lexie.

"No way in hell!" she yelled back. "This is history in the making. Keep rolling. We don't want to miss a thing."

"Damn it, Lexie, we'll get ourselves killed."

"Keep rolling!" Being on the scene for this story could make her career as a journalist. Once she got this footage back to Atlanta, her face and name would become famous overnight.

As if from out of nowhere, a group of armed warriors surrounded the courtyard, returning fire in an attempt to protect the crowd by taking on Tum's guards. While the gunfire continued, Lexie described what was happening and Marty filmed the scene as it continued to unfold. What appeared to be a four-man team, all wearing black, their faces masked by some sort of camouflage paint, each carrying a rifle, stormed forward, waging war on three times their number. One man in particular stood out, at least in Lexie's mind. Towering a good six-four, his sheer size distinguished him from the others.

"They're not Gadian," she said into her microphone. "From what I can tell, these soldiers are all Caucasian, except one. Apparently they're either mercenaries or special agents of some type who were sent to assassinate President Tum or—"

Marty Bearn grunted loudly, then clamped his left hand over his chest and went down on his knees, all the while clutching his camera in his right hand. Bright-red blood stained his shirt and seeped between the fingers of his left hand.

"Marty!" Lexie screamed.

She dropped down beside him as he crumpled into a heap at her feet. Oh, God. Oh, God! "How bad is it?" she asked as she tried to pull his hand away from the wound.

He tried to speak, but couldn't. A gurgle of bloody saliva erupted from his mouth.

"Marty! Don't you dare die. Do you hear me?"

His hand clutching his chest went limp. Lexie's heartbeat drummed inside her head. *Please, God, help him. Don't let him die.* She lifted his hand from the wound, then gasped when she saw the damage a single shot had done, the entry wound almost directly over his heart. Then she looked into Marty's face. She knew he was dead.

Just to make sure, she felt for a pulse.

Nothing.

This was all her fault. He had wanted them to run, to get away, but she'd insisted they stay and keep filming. *I'm sorry, Marty. I'm so sorry.*

She loosened the camera from his hand and rose to her feet. She had to find a way out of this nightmare. There was nothing she could do for Marty. Not now. It was too late for anything except remorse.

Doing her best to avoid getting caught in the cross-fire, Lexie tried to make her way out of the courtyard, but too many dead bodies blocked her path, men and women cut down by Tum's retaliating guardsmen. Keeping low, pressing the camera to her breasts, she visually scanned in a circular motion, seeking an escape route. She spied an open gateway directly to the left of the podium, where several guards remained. In her survey, she had noted that only a handful of Tum's soldiers were still standing. Whoever the hell this elite squad of assassins were, they were good. Very good. Good enough to eliminate seventy-five percent of their foes in record time.

The gunfire overrode the screams, which seemed like a rumble beneath the roar. The scent of sweat mixed with the metallic odor of blood as the sweltering African sun blasted down on the dead and wounded.

The taste of fear coated Lexie's dry mouth.

What should she do? Stay here and risk being killed?

Or run for her life? Neither option appealed to her, but what other choice did she have?

Going strictly on gut instinct, she made a mad dash for the one escape hatch open to her. She crawled halfway there, then stood and ran as if the devil were chasing her.

Almost there. Almost there. Just a few more feet.

Wham! The bullet hit her in the back with thundering force, knocking her flat as pain shot through her like a wildfire raging along every muscle and nerve.

She had come so close, had almost escaped.

Her body floated downward, as if in slow motion. She tried to make sense of what had happened and why. She lifted her gaze as she fell and saw three of Tum's guards go down in rapid succession, blood spurting from their splintered heads. When she hit the stone floor of the courtyard, her tight grip on the camera holding the footage of the day's events loosened. Try as she might, she could not stop the camera from skidding out of her reach. She had risked her life and Marty's for nothing. He was dead, and she was probably dying.

Slipping in and out of consciousness, Lexie had no idea how long she lay on the hot, bloody stone floor. Five minutes? Fifty minutes? Five hours?

"You can't take her with us," a man's voice said, his accent decidedly British.

"If I don't, she'll die," a deeper, harsher voice replied. American, Lexie thought somewhere in the deepest recesses of her addled brain.

Seconds later, she felt a pair of large, strong arms lift her as if she weighed no more than a child. He crushed her wounded, agonized body against his hard chest.

She managed to focus on his face for half a second, not long enough to really see him, catching only a glimpse of smoky-gray eyes before passing out.

GEOFF MONDAY, the SAS officer who had been second in command on their secret assignment, which had sent a select group of American and British soldiers into Gadi, came up to Deke. He nodded toward the closed door across the hall from where Deke was waiting to speak to Lexie Murrough's doctor.

"Any change in her condition?" Monday asked.

Deke shook his head.

"It wasn't your fault, you know," Monday told him. "She was just in the wrong place at the wrong time."

"Yeah, I know." It wasn't as if this UBC reporter had been the first innocent civilian he'd wounded or killed, but she was the only American. Civilians died in wars every day, casualties of hatred, revenge or sheer madness. So why was Lexie Murrough any different? Because she was a woman? Because she was a fellow American?

"You risked your career, not to mention your neck and mine, to save her," Monday told him. "She's going to live, thanks to you."

"She's paralyzed because of me, because my bullet hit her spine."

The closed door opened, and two military doctors emerged. One walked away down the hall, while the other approached Deke.

"Captain Bronson?"

Deke nodded.

"Ms. Murrough is awake and asking questions," the doctor said. "She wants to know the name of the soldier who rescued her."

Every nerve in Deke's body tensed.

"You can go in to see her, if you'd like."

Deke shook his head. "Tell her you don't know who the soldier was."

The doctor gave Deke a quizzical look, then said, "If that's what you want, but I'm sure she'd like to thank you."

"I don't want her thanks." Deke turned and walked away. How could he face the woman—a girl really, only twenty-four—and accept her thanks, when he knew it had been his bullet that hit her and probably paralyzed her for the rest of her life?

CHAPTER ONE

Ten years later...

LEXIE MURROUGH gazed out of her office window overlooking the Market Street Bridge, which was now a pedestrian-only crossing. When arranging the furniture in her office, she had made certain the beautiful view was available to her throughout the workday. For the past two years, she had called Chattanooga home, ever since she'd joined forces with billionaire heiress Cara Bedell to found a charitable organization to help the underprivileged worldwide. Although Lexie was listed as the group's president and was the person who oversaw the day-to-day running of the charity, Cara not only provided the bulk of the funds for Helping Hands, she often took an active role in the decision-making. Since joining forces for such a worthwhile cause, Lexie and Cara had become good friends.

There had been a time when Lexie had taken friendship for granted, when she'd taken many things for granted. But that had been another Lexie, the young and very foolish rookie reporter who had thought the world revolved around her. In the span of five minutes, her entire life had changed forever. The cute, feisty college cheerleader who'd been voted Most Likely to Succeed and had reigned as homecoming queen her senior year at the University of Georgia had died in a godforsaken African country on a sweltering June day ten years ago. But unlike her cameraman, Marty Bearn, Lexie had been reborn, given a second chance at life.

"Daydreaming again?" a female voice inquired, breaking into Lexie's thoughts.

Lexie sighed, then turned and smiled at her assistant, Toni Wells. "I was just enjoying the view." Lexie didn't discuss her past with her friends and associates. Her therapist had helped her understand that in order to move forward, she had to let go of the past. Not only of the lost hopes and dreams, but of the guilt and the anger.

"I come bearing gifts." Toni placed a lidded foam cup on Lexie's desk. "Fat-free mocha, no whipped cream."

"Thanks. You're a sweetie." Lexie picked up the cup, snapped back the plastic lip of the lid and took a sip of the hot coffee. "This is just what I needed."

Toni sat in a chair across from Lexie's antique desk—a gift from Cara—crossed her long, jeans-clad legs and relaxed as she sipped her own drink, no doubt something sinfully rich and loaded with calories. Toni was one of those fortunate women who never gained an ounce and ate like a lumberjack.

Years ago, when she'd been in her early twenties, Lexie had never worried about her weight. But inactivity and overeating had added a good thirty pounds to her five-five, medium-boned frame. It had taken her years to shed twenty of those pounds, and she now had to watch every bite she ate in order to maintain her weight.

Lexie studied her young assistant. Antoinette Wells was twenty-five, tall, slender and exotically lovely, with curly black hair, a café-au-lait complexion and striking hazel eyes. Her mother, an African-American poet, and her father, a white third-generation Georgia politician and now a state representative, had divorced when Toni was twelve.

"Don't look at me that way," Toni said. "I didn't bring any doughnuts or Danish today. And I can't help it if I inherited skinny genes from both parents, can I?"

Lexie laughed. "Heredity can be a bitch sometimes, but in your case, it was a blessing."

"Only in the looks department," Toni said. "At least you don't have the complications I do, dealing with a mixed heritage."

"You're right. Life isn't perfect for any of us, is it?"

"Ooh, you're in one of those moods, huh?"

Lexie scooted back her chair and turned it so that she faced the window instead of the room. With her back to Toni, she said, "I went for my six-month checkup yesterday, and the news was pretty much what I expected."

"No change?" Toni's voice held just a hint of pity.

Lexie shook her head. "No change. And after all this time, there isn't likely to be any further improvement." Emotion welled up inside her, tightening her throat. But she didn't cry. Wouldn't cry. At this point in her life, tears would be a waste.

Toni came across the room and stood behind Lexie. "Do you want the pep talk now, or should I save it for later?"

"Now would be good." Lexie heaved a deep sigh.

"You're young, beautiful, have a job you love and friends who adore you, and even if you can't run, you can walk." Toni let her hands drift down from where she'd been gripping the back of the chair to touch

Lexie's shoulders. She gave her a reassuring squeeze, then grabbed the chair again and whirled Lexie around to face her. "And the only reason you don't have a man in your bed is because you won't make the effort. How many times has Lieutenant Desmond asked you out on a date this past year?"

"You could have stopped before bringing up Bain Desmond. From now on, he's off limits during any pep talk."

"Why?" Easing her hips against the side of Lexie's desk, Toni sat on the edge.

"Why? You know why."

"Explain it to me again."

"Because Bain Desmond isn't the type of man I want as a boyfriend," Lexie said. "He's a police detective. He carries a gun. He shoots people." She had an aversion to guns and to the men who carried them, especially in a professional capacity. "Besides that, actually dating Bain would ruin our friendship."

"What's wrong with Farris Richardson? He wouldn't know one end of a gun from the other."

Lexie wrinkled her nose. "If you like our accountant so much, why don't you date him?"

"I have Jafari now. Why would I ever want anyone else? But you, on the other hand, have no one warming your bed at night."

"When did finding a man for me become your goal in life?"

Toni sighed dreamily. "Since I've fallen in love. I suppose I think all my best friends should be as happy as I am." She looked Lexie right in the eyes. "Of course, you might not find a guy as wonderful as Jafari. He's definitely one of a kind."

"I'll make you a deal. If you can put Jafari out of your mind for a few hours, I'll do my best to forget my visit with Dr. Burns yesterday. Then we can actually get some work done before lunch. I'm meeting with Cara at one. Would you order lunch in for the three of us? I want you to sit in on this meeting and tell her some of your ideas about the charity auction she's hosting to raise funds."

"I have a lunch date with Jafari, but since we're having dinner together this evening, he won't mind if I cancel." Toni eased off Lexie's desk and headed for the door. "Want me to order something now and then pick it up around noon?"

"That would be great. Thanks." Just as Toni opened the office door, Lexie called, "Let Robert, Vega and Malik know that I'm going to bring Ms. Bedell by today to say hello to everyone."

"Will do. I'll forewarn the workers that the Queen Bee will be buzzing through on her way in and out this afternoon."

"Look, Toni, despite your personal feelings about the human rights policies of some of Bedell, Inc.'s worldwide business partners, you need to remember that Cara Bedell signs your paycheck and mine. And she only took over her father's business two years ago. She can't change everything overnight. Give her credit where credit is due. Okay?"

Toni shrugged. "Okay."

Alone again in her office, Lexie reached over to where her cane leaned against the edge of her desk. Using the cane to brace herself, she lifted her body slowly and stood. Discomfort, but no pain. Pain was in the past, as was the struggle to relearn how to walk.

After several operations and five years of physical therapy, she had gone from being an invalid to a partial invalid to completely mobile. Except for a decided limp and the use of a cane, Lexie was for all intents and purposes normal. As Toni had pointed out, she couldn't run, but she could walk. Considering how close the bullet had come to severing her spine, she was damn lucky she wasn't paralyzed from the waist down.

Just as she took a couple of steps, her cell phone rang. During working hours, she kept it on her desk, just in case she received any personal calls. Leaning on the cane with one hand, she reached out with the other, picked up the phone and checked the caller ID.

Smiling, she flipped open the phone and said, "Hello, Lieutenant Desmond."

"Hello, beautiful."

"Thank you, sir. You certainly know how to make a girl's day."

"I should hope so." He chuckled. "Look, the reason I'm calling is…well, I need to do some of my Christmas shopping, and I thought you might help me get started tonight. What do you say?"

"Only if you buy me supper first."

"It's a small price to pay for your assistance."

"This is not a date," she warned him. "It's just two friends getting together."

"That's right. You and me. Just buddies." Bain chuckled again. "You really don't have to go over the same territory every time we go out. No matter how charming and persuasive I am, you're not going to have sex with me."

Ignoring his last comment completely, she said, "And you won't wear your gun."

"I'll be off duty tonight, so that won't be a problem."

"Good. Then pick me up here around six and we'll grab burgers at Steak and Shake before we hit Hamilton Place Mall."

"You got it."

After they ended their conversation, Lexie made her way across the room slowly, carefully, until she reached the row of file cabinets on the opposite wall. As much as she liked Bain, they really were just friends and nothing more. She didn't know why she felt compelled to keep reminding him of that fact. Although they'd never talked about it, they each knew the other was in love with someone else. He with a woman he wouldn't admit he loved and she with a man she didn't know— a man with smoky-gray eyes.

She had met Bain through a chance encounter. About eighteen months ago, she and Cara had run into the CPD lieutenant and his date one evening at a local restaurant. Bain Desmond had been the lead detective during the investigation into Cara's half sister's death, which had turned out to be the responsibility, albeit accidental, of her own father. And, unable to cope with what had happened to his daughter Audrey, Edward Bedell had committed suicide. As his only remaining child, Cara had inherited the vast Bedell, Inc. conglomerate and all the responsibilities that entailed. Lexie would have had to be blind to have missed the sexual vibes radiating between Cara and Bain. And she would have had to be an idiot not to realize that both of them were pretending—to each other and to themselves— that there were no vibes.

After propping her cane against the wall, Lexie opened the middle file cabinet and flipped through until she found the *G*s. Gadi. The country where she had met

death head-on and survived had become her pet project.
Of all the people in the world who needed help, her
heart went out to those in the small African nation
steeped in poverty and ignorance. But at least they were
no longer under a vicious dictator's rule. Ever since
President Tum's death ten years ago, the country had
undergone numerous changes, and after a four-year
civil war, they were now reemerging as a democracy.

Lexie had brought several Gadians into the Helping
Hands organization, with three working here at the
Chattanooga headquarters. Robert would complete his
internship with the organization and return home by
year's end. Another young Gadian would take his place.
Malik and Vega were permanent employees now and
had applied for U.S. citizenship.

Just as Lexie lifted the file from the cabinet, a thun-
derous boom rocked the building, shaking the walls
and shattering the windows. Losing her balance, she
toppled over, hitting her hip against the carpeted floor
and her forehead against the edge of a filing cabinet. Her
cane sailed across the room and struck the side of her
desk.

My God! What had happened? Could it have been
an earthquake? Surely not one of such magnitude here
in Chattanooga. But if not an earthquake, then what?

HE TOSSED the detonator into the Dumpster in the alley
beside the building across the street from the four-story
structure occupied by Helping Hands. Then he removed
his gloves, stuffed them into his coat pocket and emerged
onto the sidewalk. A small crowd of onlookers had already
congregated, so he simply joined them, just one more
curious, concerned person wondering what had happened.

He had constructed the bomb in the laundry room of his apartment complex late last night, putting it together with the expertise he'd gained during his year of instruction by the Majeed. The small explosive would harm only those within a twenty-five-foot radius and was not intended to kill or create extensive damage. It was nothing more than a first warning of the terror yet to come.

Within minutes, sirens shrilled through downtown Chattanooga: the police, firefighters and paramedics racing to the scene. Now, before the situation escalated, he slipped away from the crowd and entered the building, going straight to the men's restroom on the ground level.

After checking the room to make certain he was alone, he pulled the prepaid cell phone from his pocket and dialed hurriedly. The phone rang several times, then went to voice mail. He waited, redialed and got her voice mail again.

Pick up the phone, bitch. The bomb didn't explode in your office. You're all right. I wouldn't kill you so easily. You have to suffer greatly before you die.

After his third attempt to reach her, she answered. "Hello?"

Her voice was shaky. Good. She was unnerved, at least.

Placing a folded handkerchief over the phone, he deliberately disguised his voice as best he could and said in a raspy whisper, "This is only the beginning of the end for you and Cara Bedell and Helping Hands. I warn you now that there is a special time for you to die, a time I have chosen."

"What? Who is this? Did you—"

He ended the call, leaving her asking questions he did not intend to answer. Not now. Not yet. Let her worry. Let her learn the true meaning of fear.

WHENEVER he was between assignments for the Dundee Private Security and Investigation Agency, Deke Bronson made a point of being at the downtown Atlanta office on Wednesdays because office manager Daisy Holbrook always brought a homemade meal for the employees' lunch on that day. The agents had nicknamed Daisy Ms. Efficiency, because she seemed to be able to juggle a dozen different things at once, do each extremely well and accomplish them all on time. Daisy wasn't the matronly type, as one would expect from a "mother hen." She was young, cute as a button and slightly plump, with big brown eyes and a warm, outgoing personality. Everyone adored Daisy, even Dundee's CEO, Sawyer McNamara, who was a stern, by-the-book, don't-mix-with-employees kind of guy.

"Is that chili I smell?" Lucie Evans asked as she entered the employees' lounge, better known as the break room.

"Chili and corn bread," Deke replied as he ladled a huge helping of Daisy's famous homemade chili into a deep bowl.

"And apple-dapple cake for dessert," Geoff Monday added.

"There's vanilla ice cream in the freezer to top off the cake," Daisy said as she sliced the two large skillets of corn bread into pie-shaped pieces. "One of these is Mexican corn bread and the other is plain."

Geoff Monday placed his arm around Daisy's shoulders and kissed her on the cheek. "Ms. Holbrook, you certainly know the way to a man's heart."

Daisy blushed. Everyone at Dundee's—everyone except Geoff—knew that Daisy had a major crush on the former SAS officer. Deke had wondered if maybe he should clue his clueless British friend in on the obvious, but not being the type of man who interfered in other people's lives, he'd kept quiet. Besides, if Geoff knew how Daisy felt about him, he would probably stop casually flirting with her, and that would end all of Daisy's hopes and dreams. Poor Daisy. She had to know that a guy like Monday would never settle down, especially not with a sweet kid like her.

Deke chose the smaller of the two round tables in the break room, set down his bowl filled high with chili and topped with a huge slice of Mexican corn bread, and settled comfortably into the cushioned chair. He was officially off today, but no way would he miss one of Daisy's meals if he was in town. Noting that Geoff and Lucie were the only other two agents there, he assumed everyone else was on assignment.

"Just us today?" Geoff asked, apparently thinking along the same lines as Deke.

"Ty's supposed to come in later," Daisy replied.

"I leave first thing tomorrow for another boring, nobody-else-wants-it assignment," Lucie said.

Geoff rolled his eyes. Deke grunted. Daisy gave Lucie a commiserating half smile. They all knew that Sawyer deliberately chose the worst jobs for Lucie. Why he did, no one other than Sawyer and Lucie knew. And why he didn't just fire her, and why she kept taking everything that Sawyer dished out, was something else only the two of them knew. Everyone who worked at Dundee's was aware of the ongoing feud between the CEO and the Amazonian redheaded agent, but no one knew when or why it had started. Years ago, the two had been FBI agents, so the most logical explanation was that something had happened between them back then.

Lucie and Geoff joined Deke. Instead of sitting down with them, Daisy prepared a tray of food and headed toward the door.

"Where are you going with that?" Lucie asked.

"Mr. McNamara has requested lunch in his office," she replied.

"Too good to eat with the peasants." Lucie shoved back her chair, stood and held out her hands. "Here, let me take it to him."

Grinning, Daisy shook her head. "I believe Mr. McNamara wants to eat his lunch, not wear it. Don't think I'm not aware of what would happen if you served him."

With that said, Daisy balanced the tray with one hand and opened the door with the other. Just as she crossed the threshold, she stopped abruptly, coming face-to-face with the big boss himself.

"I was on my way to your office with lunch," Daisy said.

"It'll have to wait," Sawyer replied. Not unpleasant, but not friendly. And certainly all business. He eased past her and entered the break room. His gaze traveled to the table where his three available agents had begun devouring Daisy's delicious chili. "Good, you're all here."

Deke knew what that meant. Either a delayed lunch or no lunch at all. Sawyer was about to give one or more of them a new assignment.

"I'm not going anywhere until I've eaten lunch," Lucie said, not even glancing at their boss.

Sawyer bristled. Deke noticed only because he possessed an uncanny ability to read people. That intuitive instinct had given him an advantage as a member of the Delta Force and later as a mercenary. Sawyer's jaw tightened, his gaze narrowing as he took a deep breath. The guy was reining in his impulse to tell Lucie Evans to go straight to hell.

"Daisy?" Sawyer motioned to the office manager. "Bring that tray in here. We'll eat lunch while we discuss the new assignment."

After Daisy placed the tray on the table where the others had congregated, she hurried out of the room, closing the door quietly behind her.

Sawyer glanced from one agent to another, then eyed the meal in front of him. "I just got off the phone with Cara Bedell of Bedell, Inc.," he told them.

"Someone hasn't killed that worthless brother-in-law of hers, have they?" Deke asked. He'd met Grayson Perkins when he'd been called in as a backup agent for Domingo Shea the last time Bedell, Inc. had used Dundee's services.

"As far as I know, Mr. Perkins is alive and well," Sawyer said. "But it seems there was a bombing at the headquarters of Helping Hands, one of Cara Bedell's pet charities. The building is in downtown Chattanooga. The bomb exploded on the first floor and seriously injured three employees, one of whom has since died."

"And Ms. Bedell wants Dundee's involved because…?" Geoff asked.

"Because the president of Helping Hands received a threatening phone call shortly after the explosion."

"Was the threat directed at him?" Geoff asked.

"Her," Sawyer corrected. "Yes, the threat was directed at the president as well as at Ms. Bedell and the organization itself."

"Why would anyone threaten a charity organization?" Lucie shook her head, bouncing her copper-red curls. "You know, we're living in a really screwed-up world."

"How astute of you, Ms. Evans," Sawyer said sarcastically. "Bronson, I want you and Monday to drive over to Chattanooga as soon as you finish lunch and can go home to pack your bags. I'll leave it up to the two of you to choose who guards Ms. Bedell and who guards the Helping Hands president."

"Who's going to head up the investigation?" Deke asked.

"The Chattanooga PD," Sawyer replied. "Lieutenant Bain Desmond is in charge. As for who will be Dundee's investigator—"

"You could send me," Lucie suggested.

"I could, but won't. You already have an assignment that starts tomorrow. I'm calling in Ty Garrett to handle the investigation for Dundee's." Sawyer looked from Deke to Geoff. "You two have worked with Ty before. You know he's good at what he does."

Geoff reached in his pants pocket, pulled out a quarter and grinned at Deke. "Flip you for the heiress. You call it." He tossed the coin.

"Tails," Deke said.

Geoff caught the quarter in his palm. Grinning broadly, he said, "Heads. Sorry, old chap, but I get Ms. Bedell."

Deke shrugged. It didn't matter to him. One client was the same as the other. One woman no different than any other.

"I'll have Daisy put together some preliminary info and e-mail it to both of you. You should have the report by the time you arrive in Chattanooga," Sawyer said.

BAIN DESMOND met the two Dundee agents at three-thirty that afternoon, when they arrived at Helping Hands' headquarters. The CSI team was working the scene when Geoff and Deke arrived.

"What can you tell us?" Geoff asked as they rode up in the elevator with the police detective.

"The bomb was placed in a storage room. If the maintenance man hadn't been in there getting some supplies, he'd be alive. The bomb probably wasn't intended to kill anyone. The area of destruction was limited, so we surmise it was detonated as a warning."

"A warning to Helping Hands, its president and Ms. Bedell. Is that right?" Deke asked.

"From what the caller said, yeah, that's right."

When the elevator doors opened on the fourth floor, Lieutenant Desmond emerged first. "The ladies are pretty shook up. I told Cara…Ms. Bedell, that hiring around-the-clock bodyguards probably wasn't neces-sary, but she insisted. And what Ms. Bedell wants, she gets. Money talks," Desmond grumbled.

"Her money shouts over at Dundee's," Geoff said.

Desmond nodded. They followed him down the hall to where one of the office doors stood wide open, re-vealing three women. When they entered, one woman turned and faced them, one glanced over her shoulder at them, and the other remained seated, partially blocked from Deke's view by the other two.

He recognized Cara Bedell immediately: tall, stat-uesque and redheaded. Although not as pretty as Lucie Evans, there was something about Ms. Bedell that reminded him of the Dundee agent. They were approximately the same height and size, but Lucie was a few years older and her hair a deeper, darker shade of red.

Ms. Bedell moved forward, her hand outstretched. "You're from Dundee Security?"

"Yes, ma'am." Deke shook her hand. "I'm Deke Bronson." He hitched his thumb in Geoff's direction. "This is Geoff Monday."

"I assume that Sawyer explained the situation, and you understand that I want you two on the job until we find the person behind today's bombing," Cara said.

"Yes, ma'am," Deke replied.

She turned to Desmond. "I expect daily updates from the police department. And I want any information you can legally share with Dundee Security to be shared with Mr. Bronson and Mr. Monday. Understood?"

"Yeah, I understand," Desmond said, a flash of irritation in his gaze.

Cara Bedell turned to the tall, slender African-American woman with curly black hair and striking hazel eyes. "Take tomorrow off, Toni. I don't want anyone coming to work here until we get heavier security in place."

"No problem, Ms. Bedell. After what happened, I'm not eager to come back." Toni turned to the seated woman. "Jafari is waiting for me downstairs. I'll call you at home later. Are you're sure you're all right? You don't need to go to the ER or…?"

"The medics checked me out," the woman said. "I've got a bruise on one knee and a slight bump on my forehead. I'm fine. Go home. Call me tomorrow. I should know by then if we can return to work Friday."

Deke and Geoff watched Toni as she exited the office, both quite aware of how attractive she was. Then

Deke faced the seated woman. *Beautiful* didn't quite describe her. *Exquisite* might come close. Blond hair hung below her shoulders in soft, loose curls. Blue eyes were framed by thick, dark lashes. A peaches-and-cream complexion was touched with a fading summer tan. He blinked once, twice and then closed his eyes for a couple of seconds, certain his vision was playing tricks on him.

When he reopened his eyes, his gaze connected with the lady's. Momentarily robbed of breath, he stared at her. It had been ten years, but seeing her again, he felt as if it had been only yesterday. Hers was the face that had haunted his dreams ever since that bloody day in the capital of Gadi when she had gotten caught in the crossfire between his team and Babu Tum's guards.

She rose from the chair, leaning heavily on a decorative wooden cane with a bronze handle. He didn't move. Didn't speak. She took a step toward him, then held out her free hand.

"I'm Lexie Murrough, the president of Helping Hands."

CHAPTER TWO

LEXIE GAZED at the big, dark man standing in front of her, and an involuntary shiver rippled along her nerve endings. Sexual awareness, plain and simple. Although not actually handsome—he was far too rugged to be good-looking—he possessed a raw, masculine magnetism that overwhelmed her senses. She couldn't remember ever having had such a strong reaction to a man.

Before Mr. Bronson could shake her hand, the stoutly built blond guy stepped between them and grinned at her. "I'm Geoff Monday. I believe I'm your bodyguard, Ms. Murrough."

Deke Bronson grasped his co-worker's shoulder and urged him aside. "No, you've got that wrong. I'll be guarding Ms. Murrough." He nodded toward Cara. "Ms. Bedell is your assignment."

"Are you sure about this?" Mr. Monday said.

"Positive," Mr. Bronson replied, a look of certainty and determination in his dark gray eyes.

Lexie's heart skipped a beat. Heaven help her! She instinctively understood that Deke Bronson had claimed her, and his possessive attitude felt oddly personal. If this was some sort of one-upmanship between the two Dundee agents, she really didn't understand why either would consider her the prize. After all, Cara Bedell was the billionaire heiress.

"Look, whichever one of you is my guy, I'm ready to leave," Cara told them in an authoritarian tone, one she had perfected from years of having underlings jump at her every command. Lexie knew that Cara didn't realize how extremely bossy she was, how often people misunderstood her aggressive personality, mistaking it for arrogance and rudeness.

The two agents shared a quick, hard glance, then Geoff Monday walked over to Cara, grinned and gestured toward the door. "Whenever you're ready, Ms. Bedell."

"Lexie, I'll be in touch first thing tomorrow. Hopefully, the police—" Cara cast Bain Desmond an imperious glare "—will have some information for us by then and we'll know how to proceed." She turned to Deke Bronson. "Take good care of Lexie. She's one of the few people I know who's actually worth her weight in gold."

Deke nodded. "Yes, ma'am."

As soon as Cara and Geoff left, Lexie smiled at the Dundee agent. "If you'll give me just a minute, I'll be ready to go."

He nodded.

"He'll be staying with you 24/7," Cara had told her, after she'd made the arrangements—without first consulting Lexie for an opinion—explaining that she had hired a couple of Dundee agents to act as bodyguards for the two of them. "I'd feel better if you moved in with me for the time being, but I know you won't do that. So do not argue with me about needing around-the-clock protection. Until we know who and what we're dealing with, we have to work under the assumption that your life is in danger."

Hours after the explosion, Lexie was still a bit shaky and unnerved. Leaning heavily on her cane, she walked over to Bain. As she placed her hand on his arm, she felt Deke Bronson's intense stare. In her peripheral vision, she noticed that he was watching her closely. *Don't assume anything,* she told herself. *It's nothing personal. It's his job to watch over you.*

"I'm sorry about tonight," Lexie told Bain. "I was looking forward to the burgers and our getting started on your Christmas shopping."

"Another time." Bain patted her hand affectionately, then glanced over at Deke. "Take good care of her. When it comes to Lexie, Ms. Bedell is right. Only I'd say Lexie is priceless."

"I'll protect Ms. Murrough with my life," Deke said.

Bain lifted an eyebrow. Lexie's breath caught in her throat.

She kissed Bain on the cheek. When she turned to Deke, she noted the scowl on his face and the tension in his jaw. Undoubtedly he was one of those people who didn't approve of showing affection in public. Well, too bad. She believed in it. She was a touchy-feely person. She hugged and kissed friends without giving her actions a second thought.

"My car or yours?" she asked as they walked out into the hallway, Deke two steps behind her.

"Yours. I drove over from Atlanta in a rental, which is supposed to be picked up later today. I believe someone on Ms. Bedell's staff will take care of that chore for us."

He paused just outside the door, picked up a black duffel bag and hoisted it over his shoulder, delaying their departure by half a minute.

When they arrived at the elevator, Deke reached around her and punched the down button. When the doors slid open, he grasped her arm, preventing her from entering. After he gave the interior a visual inspection, he urged her forward and into the car. Only then did he release her arm and hit the lobby-level button

"It'll take some getting used to, having a bodyguard," she told him.

"If you'll remember that everything I do is intended to keep you safe, we shouldn't have any problems."

"Hmm...I'll try to remember that."

She tried not to stare at him, but that didn't prevent her from being completely aware of him. He stood almost a foot taller than her own five-five, and he outweighed her by a good seventy-five or eighty pounds. His masculine presence filled the small elevator. Then there was the way he smelled. Clean and musky at the same time. Soap-and-water clean, a slight hint of some mild aftershave, and a male scent that was purely his own.

Neither of them spoke again until they reached the lobby, then he asked, "Where's your car?"

"In the employees-only parking lot in the back."

"Which door do we take to reach the parking lot?"

"Normally, we'd take the back." She glanced in that direction and noted the yellow police tape cordoning off the area.

He grasped her elbow. "Out the front, then."

Once outside on the street, she led and he followed, down the block and up the side street until they reached the alleyway behind the buildings. Sunset came fairly early in November. Shielded by the buildings on either side, the alley was dark and shadowed, even though it wasn't yet twilight. Deke made two quick, decisive moves. Subtle moves. He unbuttoned his jacket, then clamped his big hand around Lexie's upper arm. When he touched her, she instinctively glanced at him, but he wasn't looking at her. His attention was focused on their surroundings, his gaze scanning the alley, the back doors of the buildings and the four cars parked in the lot. Her eyes traveled from his lean, chiseled face down his thick neck to his broad shoulders and wide chest. As he moved, his open jacket shifted, and she caught a glimpse of his shoulder holster.

For half a second, Lexie couldn't breathe. She hated guns. It was the one thing she disliked about Bain Desmond—that his chosen profession dictated he carry a 9 mm handgun.

She should have realized that a professional body-guard would carry a gun. If she asked him to remove the weapon and not carry it, he would probably think she was crazy. And he would no doubt refuse.

"Which is yours?" he asked.

"Huh?"

"Which car is yours?"

"The white Subaru SUV."

She snapped open her purse, rummaged inside and pulled out the keys. He took them from her, marched her to the passenger's side, unlocked the vehicle and held open the door for her.

"Are you driving?" she asked. "Since I know where we're going, wouldn't it be simpler if I—"

"I'll drive." No discussion. No compromising.

She nodded.

"Do you need assistance?" He eyed her cane.

She shook her head, grasped the door, propped her

cane against the console, then heaved herself up and into the SUV. Once she was inside, he closed her door, walked to the back, opened the hatch and tossed his duffel bag inside.

After he opened the driver's-side door and got behind the wheel, he asked, "Where do you live?"

"If I were driving, I could take us directly there instead of navigating you through rush-hour traffic."

"And if you were driving and someone tried to force us off the road, would you know what to do?"

His question surprised her. The thought had never entered her head. "Oh. I'd never thought of that. Is that the reason…?"

"I told you, there will be a reason for everything I do." He started the engine. "It will make things easier if you simply accept that fact instead of questioning my actions."

"I'm sorry, but I find it difficult to not ask questions. I've always been very inquisitive. I want to know who, what, when, where and why." Her words held a glimmer of humor; her objective was to lighten the mood. "I used to be a reporter in my former life."

He didn't respond. Didn't smile. Instead his big hands tightened around the steering wheel. Apparently the man didn't have a sense of humor.

"I don't live far," she told him. "It'll take maybe ten minutes at most. I live in a loft apartment that Bedell, Inc. owned and Cara sold to me dirt cheap when I moved to Chattanooga a couple of years ago."

He pulled the SUV out of the parking lot to the side street. "Right or left?"

"Take a right." She gave him her address, then rattled off the directions to her home, assuming she would have to remind him when and where to turn, which streets to take and exactly which building was hers. But without her repeating anything, he drove them directly to her apartment, never having said a word the entire way.

"Where do you park?" he asked as he pulled up in front of the address she'd given him.

"In back," she replied. "See that narrow street?" She pointed at the just-wide-enough-for-one-vehicle road. "It's one-way. I drive in there and the lot's halfway along. It goes straight through to the street on the other side, and I have to go out that way."

"Is there a back entrance?" he asked.

"To the building? Yes."

"What type of security does the building have?"

"The tenants have to have a key to enter either the front or the back door."

"What about your apartment? Do you have a security system?"

"Yes, actually, I do."

"Good. What's your code?"

"I beg your pardon?"

"What's your code?" he asked again. "We'll want to change it. And you won't give the new code to anyone. Only you and I will know it."

"Is that necessary?"

"You're questioning me again."

She heaved a deep, slightly aggravated sigh. "Sorry."

He parked the car, got out, retrieved his duffel bag and was at the passenger's door before the tip of her cane hit the pavement.

When he reached out to help her, she jerked away and gave him a negative glare. He put his hands up, palms out, in the universal hands-off signal, apparently understanding that she didn't want or need his assistance.

He stepped back and allowed her to maneuver herself out of the vehicle and onto both feet. "There's a service elevator that I use," she told him as she headed toward the back door.

He followed her, and when they reached the back door, he held up her keys. "It's that one." She reached out and touched the correct key.

He inserted it in the lock and opened the back door. Once inside the dimly lit back hall, he grunted. "A good hard shove and that back door would come open, locked or unlocked."

"In the two years I've lived here, there's never been a break-in."

"You're lucky."

"Are you always so negative?" She punched the up button on the old service elevator. It was the only operable elevator in the building. The other tenants used the staircase most of the time; only she and Mr. Rafferty, the elderly gentleman who lived on the fourth floor of the five-story building, used the elevator on a regular basis.

Deke didn't respond to her question and remained silent as they ascended to the top floor of the 1920s structure. The fifth level of the building was a loft that had been used for storage in years gone by. Before she moved to Chattanooga, Bedell, Inc. had purchased the building and renovated it, turning it into a small condo complex, with one condo on each level. When she'd moved in two years ago, the loft had been a wide-open space, a blank canvas for her to decorate as she wished.

"The door key is the shiny brass one next to the

back-door key," Lexie told him. "The security keypad is on the right-hand side as you enter. My code is thirty-four, thirty-four."

He frowned.

"Before you tell me that it's stupid to repeat numbers in a code—don't. I change my code every year on my birthday. I'm thirty-four years old, so—"

"I'll change it tonight," he said, then unlocked the door, entered the apartment and disarmed the security system.

Feeling slightly disoriented because she was unaccustomed to having anyone else in control of her life in any way, Lexie crossed the threshold. Since she had ended her physical therapy sessions five years ago, she had prided herself on taking care of all her own needs and being dependent on no one. How could she explain to this man—this high-priced security agent—that his presence in her life disturbed her more than one level? First and foremost, she hated that she needed him to protect her. Second, she didn't like being sexually attracted to a man she didn't even know.

DEKE WASN'T SURE what he'd been expecting. He'd been in numerous loft apartments over the years, and although each had been different, the basic style had been the same. Modern and minimalist. But there was nothing modern or bare bones about the sight that met him upon entering the vast expanse of Lexie's place. He dropped his duffel bag on the wooden floor, which had mellowed with age to a dark patina and glistened with the sheen of fresh polish. The huge open room encompassed the kitchen—bright, white and airy, with stainless-steel appliances; a living room in varying shades of beige, brown and taupe and boasting a black baby grand piano near one of three sets of French doors; and last but not least, a formal dining room with a crystal chandelier and a mahogany table that seated six.

"Impressive," Deke said. "It must have cost a fortune to decorate."

"Most of the furniture was my grandmother's. I was her only grandchild, and she left an entire houseful of furniture to me," Lexie told him. "As for the cost of fixing this place up—I have a small fortune. Nothing to compare to Cara Bedell's, but more than I'll ever need."

He knew how she had acquired her small fortune, but unless he wanted to explain to her how he knew, he figured he'd better at least act as if he were curious. "What did you do, win the lottery?"

She shook her head. "I was involved in a work-related accident—" she tapped her cane on the floor "—and my mother and stepfather sued my employer. We settled out of court to the tune of three million dollars."

Deke faked a surprised expression, then walked farther into the loft and looked around. "How many bedrooms?"

She followed him toward the living room. "Two bedrooms, and two and a half baths."

He studied the layout of the apartment. "The bedrooms are side by side, there on the left."

"That's right. I didn't want the bedrooms or baths open, so when we closed them off, my contractor and I thought it best to partition off one side of the loft for them."

"No connecting door between the bedrooms." It was a statement, not a question.

"No, there isn't. Why?"

"How many windows in your bedroom?"

"Two."

"Does either open up onto a balcony?"

"No."

"Good."

"You're thinking about security, aren't you?"

"Yes, ma'am, that's my job."

"The fire escape connects to the balcony, which is accessible only through those three sets of French doors there." She indicated the doors in the living room. "The only way someone could reach the windows in the bedrooms would be if they could climb walls or had a five-story ladder."

He nodded but didn't speak. As he walked through one room and into another, studying the layout and grunting now and then, Lexie watched him with those big blue eyes of hers. He tried his best not to look directly at her unless it was absolutely necessary. Logically, he understood that she had no idea who he was, but on a primal gut level, he feared she might somehow know him, know what he'd done to her.

Stop worrying. She doesn't know who you are, he told himself.

She had no idea that the Dundee agent assigned to protect her was the man whose bullet had crippled her ten years ago.

Not long after the assassination of Babu Tum, Deke had resigned from the army, leaving the Delta Force and his career behind him. Less than three months later, Geoff Monday had parted company with the SAS, and joined Deke and several other former Special-Ops warriors to form their own team of mercenaries. During those renegade years, he'd kept track of Lexie Murrough's slow, painful recovery. The bullet she'd taken in the back had not been fatal, and the paralysis it had caused hadn't been permanent. But because of the delay in getting her to a hospital and starting her on steroids to control the swelling in her spinal cord, the injury had worsened. It had taken over a year before she could walk again, and then four more years of physical and psychiatric therapy had followed.

Once she'd resumed a normal life, he had lost track of her—over five years ago.

"This is my bedroom," Lexie said.

She swung open the door to reveal a pristine blue-and-cream room. A king-size bed with a blue-and-white checkered cloth headboard and matching stool at the foot dominated the large space. A photograph of the sky—blue and white and pale gray—hung over the fireplace mantel. Floor-to-ceiling blue-gray silk curtains hung from the two windows, and two blue-and-white print chairs flanked a small decorative table. Although the room was not excessively feminine, the bouquet of blue violets on the nightstand and the crystal candy dish on the table, as well as the blue-and-white floral room-size rug, indicated that this was a lady's bedroom.

"You should be comfortable in the guest room. It's not as large as this one, but there's a queen bed, and I believe it'll be long enough for you."

She led him to the next door, opened it and gestured for him to enter first. The walls were cream, the windows bare except for dark-brown wooden blinds. Two dark-walnut bedside tables flanked the bronze metal bed, and a Craftsman-style walnut bench rested at the foot. A quilt in a rusty-red and beige color scheme had been folded across the back of the bench. Clean lines. Not fussy. Pretty much unisex in decoration.

The lone sepia-toned photograph hanging over the bed caught Deke's attention. The bronze frame held a landscape that he recognized immediately. A serene pool surrounded by towering trees. An oasis in the desert a few miles outside Gadi's capital city.

A tight knot formed in the pit of his stomach.

"Do you like the photograph?" she asked.

He swallowed hard.

"Who took the photo?"

"A man named Marty Bearn." Her voice lowered to a mere whisper, the tone reverent and slightly melancholy. "He was a cameraman for UBC. He died in Gadi ten years ago."

"And he was a friend of yours?" God, how could he act as if he had no idea who Marty Bearn was or what his connection to Lexie was? With every breath Deke took, every moment he was with her, he was lying to her.

"Yes, he was. I'm godmother to his daughter." Lexie sucked in a deep breath. "She was born six months after Marty was killed."

What could he say? Nothing. Absolutely nothing.

He shouldn't be here. When Geoff had given him the chance to escape from this hell he was now in, he should have taken it. He should have gone with Cara Bedell and let Geoff guard Lexie. But instead of doing the sensible thing, he had demanded this assignment. And why? Because something deep inside him had given him no choice.

For ten years he had lived with the guilt and remorse, although after Lexie had resumed a normal life, he had tried to stop punishing himself. He and Geoff, both of them heading into middle age, had gotten out of the mercenary business. Geoff first, and after he'd gotten a job with Dundee, he'd talked Deke into joining him.

"We're overqualified," Geoff had said. "But it's the

perfect job for a couple of old warriors. And the pay is damn good."

Standing here, alone with Lexie Murrough, Deke felt as if his life had come full circle. Maybe fate had thrown him and Lexie together again so that this time he could take care of her instead of nearly kill her.

"Are you all right?" she asked.

"Huh?"

"I've asked you twice if you'd prefer soup and sandwiches or soup and salad for supper."

"Sorry," he replied. "I was thinking about something."

"Why don't you get your bag and settle in?" Lexie suggested. "I want to freshen up, change into my jeans, and then I'll get supper started. Sandwich or salad?"

"You don't have to fix anything," he said. "We could order in."

"I don't mind at all."

"You're sure?"

She nodded.

"Sandwich. And I like a lot of meat. More meat than bread."

"Why am I not surprised?"

When she smiled at him, so pretty and feminine and sweet, he wanted to grab her and kiss her. Hell, who was he kidding? He wanted to drag her over to the bed, strip off her clothes and screw her.

"Ham or roast beef?" she asked. "Or both?"

"Both."

When she left the bedroom, he heaved a deep breath in and out, glad she had gone before noticing his hard-on. Damn it, he had to take control of his body. He hadn't been this easily aroused since he'd been a teenager, when just about any female had turned him on.

It wasn't as if he had insisted on guarding Lexie so he could take advantage of her. But he'd noticed a certain look in her eyes, one that told him she could be persuaded. It wasn't unusual for a woman to become attracted to her bodyguard. In fact, it happened quite a lot. And sometimes an agent would have a brief affair with a client. But he couldn't let that happen this time. Not with Lexie.

Hadn't he hurt her more than enough ten years ago? Hadn't she suffered far too much because of him? He couldn't deny that the sexual attraction was there between them. But because of their past history, she was the last woman on earth he would ever seduce.

CHAPTER THREE

AFTER GIVING the place a thorough inspection, Geoff Monday decided that the Bedell mansion on Lookout Mountain was almost as secure as Fort Knox. That didn't mean some brilliant criminal couldn't figure out a way to penetrate the fortress, but the odds of that were slim to none. Unless a plane dropped a bomb directly on the old house, Cara Bedell was safer here than anywhere else.

Upon arriving two hours ago, they had gone through electronic gates that required a code to open, and once inside the massive antebellum house, she had given him a quick tour, showed him the security system, which included camera surveillance, and then assigned him a room.

"I'm sorry, Ms. Bedell, but this room won't work," he'd told her.

"I beg your pardon?" Cara Bedell looked sweet and wholesome, not glamorous or sophisticated the way one would expect the heiress to billions to look. The lady was a tall, rawboned, freckled redhead and, although not nearly as pretty as Lucie Evans, reminded Geoff of the lone female Dundee agent.

"I need a bedroom as close to yours as possible," he'd explained.

"Oh. Yes, of course. I wasn't thinking."

She had quickly taken him to another wing in the huge house, showed him her bedroom and pointed to the one directly across the hall. "Will that one do?"

"Yes, ma'am. Thank you."

Despite not being a great beauty, there was something downright appealing about Ms. Filthy-Rich Bedell. Within minutes of meeting her, he'd been aware of the fact that she was a take-charge, used-to-being-obeyed woman who didn't waste time with pleasantries. But whenever he'd pointed out the obvious to her, she hadn't argued with him and had so far acquiesced to his expertise. He figured she was smart enough to know that was why she was paying Dundee Security the big bucks—to get the best. And that was exactly what he and Deke Bronson were: the very best. Dundee's security and investigation team had no equal in the business. They were the cream of the crop.

Just as he started unpacking his bag and putting his clean underwear and socks in an antique dresser, his cell phone rang. After checking caller ID, he dumped his stuff into the drawer, closed it and answered the call.

"Hello, Dimples. You're calling rather late, aren't you?"

Geoff had been told by friends that he was a flirt, which he supposed he was, but he loved the ladies—all ladies, young and old, rich and poor, fat and skinny, pretty and plain. And one of his favorite ladies was Dundee's Ms. Efficiency. She always had a warm smile and a friendly greeting for him. He had given her the nickname because she had a set of gorgeous dimples.

"I finished putting together the preliminary reports on Ms. Bedell, Ms. Murrough and the Helping Hands organization," Daisy told him. "I've sent both as e-mail attachments to you and to Deke."

"Anything unusual? Something that warranted a phone call?" He placed the phone between his shoulder and ear, then removed his two sets of clothes, still on hangers, and searched for the closet.

"Nothing really. Just one of my odd feelings."

"Hmm... So tell me." He couldn't find a closet. The only door, other than the one that led into the hallway, opened up into the adjoining bathroom.

"Helping Hands is a charity organization," Daisy said. "Their reach is worldwide, with about a third of their efforts centered on poverty-stricken areas in the U.S. But two-thirds of HH's money goes overseas to third-world nations. One of the chief beneficiaries is a little African country called Gadi."

The word *Gadi* struck a nerve, but he didn't react, other than to say, "Yeah, and...?" He found an empty armoire lined with padded clothes hangers and realized this was the only closet space in the room. He shoved aside the fancy hangers to make room for his clothes, which were on the metal hangers from the dry cleaners.

"Ten years ago, Lexie Murrough was a reporter for UBC. She was in Gadi, at the capital, covering Babu Tum's inauguration the day he was assassinated. She took a bullet in the back when she got caught in the crossfire between Tum's guards and the assassination squad. Because of that, she was left partially paralyzed, and had to undergo several surgeries and years of physical therapy."

"And this is important to our case because...?

To this day, no one outside of top-secret British and U.S. intelligence knew that an elite squad of UK and U.S. special-ops soldiers had assassinated President Tum. After all, both countries claimed they no longer assassinated undesirables. And only two people knew that Deke Bronson had shot Lexie Murrough—Geoff and Deke.

"I'm not sure, but my gut tells me that there might be a connection between Gadi, Ms. Murrough and the bomb. After all, we know for a fact that some of the rebel factions in Gadi now belong to the Majeed, and they hate the U.S. What if they don't like Helping Hands being such a strong force in Gadi?"

"You know what, Dimples? Your talents are wasted as office manager. You should be an agent. You think like one."

Daisy laughed. "No, thanks. I prefer staying behind the scenes."

"We need to find out if—"

"There are three citizens of Gadi working there in Chattanooga at Helping Hands," Daisy told him. "Robert Lufti, Vega Sharif and Malik Abdel."

"Run a check on each of them."

"It's being done as we speak."

"You're always one step ahead of us, aren't you? You're one in a million. I hope you know that."

Silence.

"Dimples?"

"Hmm…?"

"You got terribly quiet there for a bit."

She laughed again. "I was just taking a minute to appreciate the compliment without letting it go to my head. I had to remind myself that you're free and easy with your praise."

"Ah, Dimples, you wound me." He chuckled. "I might exaggerate when I use my debonair British charm on other ladies, but never with you. Any compliment I've ever given you came straight from the heart."

"Yeah, sure." She quickly changed the subject. "I'll phone when I get preliminary workups on Lufti, Sharif and Abdel. It could take a couple of days to compile a full report."

"Thanks, love. I'll be in touch from this end once we get more info from the Chattanooga PD."

DEKE HELPED LEXIE clean up after supper, and although he did his best to contribute to the conversation she tried to maintain, he failed miserably. He wasn't good at idle chitchat. And he was even worse at sharing anything personal with another person. Finally they fell into a silence that filled the massive loft until Lexie turned on the CD player and Andrea Bocelli's voice, blended with Spanish guitars, vanquished the utter quiet.

Deke sat in the overstuffed tan leather chair aligned at a right angle to the plush, brown chenille sofa. When Lexie didn't sit, he watched her roam restlessly about the room. With each slow, deliberate step she took, aided by her cane, he experienced a stabbing twinge. She would never be free of that limp or the cane she relied on for support. And he would never be free of his guilt and the memory of the day he had shot her.

She walked toward the middle of the three sets of French doors. Before he could speak and tell her it wasn't smart to stand in front of anything glass and make herself an easy target, she opened them.

"Close them," he ordered.

She glanced over her shoulder. "What?"

"Close the doors and move away from them."

Obeying him instantly, she moved toward him. "I simply wanted to get a breath of fresh air. I wouldn't have stayed on the balcony more than a few minutes because it's chilly tonight and—"

"A long-range rifle could take you out like that." Deke snapped his fingers. "If someone wants to kill you, we have no way of knowing to what lengths they might go."

All color drained from her face. He realized she was remembering another time, another place. And another rifle shot.

"Yes, of course. It was stupid of me not to think about that, especially considering the fact that… You'd have no way of knowing, but once, years ago, I was shot in the back. That's why I have a limp, why I use a cane."

The muscles in his throat constricted, his chest ached and his pulse thundered in his head. Damn it, why was he here with Lexie? Why hadn't he taken Geoff up on his offer to guard her? This was only day one. He'd only been with her a few hours, and already he wanted to bare his soul and confess his sins.

"Mr. Bronson?"

"Yes?"

"Did I say something wrong?"

"No, why would you think that?"

"Oh, no reason, really. It's just when I mentioned having been shot, you got a rather odd expression on your face." She sat down on the sofa catty-corner from his chair.

People usually accused him of being stoic, of showing little or no emotion, telling him that his facial expressions gave away nothing. So why had she picked up what couldn't have been more than a momentary flicker caused by a memory that plagued him?

"Sorry. I wasn't aware that my expression changed."

"Actually, I'm not sure it did." She looked directly

at him. "It was more something I saw in your eyes. A flash of sadness."

Every muscle in his body tensed.

"I apologize," she said. "I can see you'd rather not talk about it."

"There is no *it*." He stood and turned his back on her. "I'll check the doors and windows now, then again after I take my shower." After he finished his inspection, he walked toward the guest bedroom. "If you'll excuse me?"

"Certainly."

With his hand on the door handle, he paused and said, "I'll check on you, too, before I go to bed. Do not answer the door, no matter who it is. Not unless I'm with you. And if you need me, don't hesitate to call out to me. Scream, if necessary."

"Yes, I will."

He escaped into the bedroom, closing the door, shutting out the sight and sound of Lexie Murrough. He didn't like the way she seemed to be able to read him so clearly, to see beyond the obvious.

This wasn't going to work. He'd been a fool to think it would.

Tomorrow he would call Geoff and let him know he'd been right—they needed to exchange clients.

THE LITTLE BOMB had been simple to construct and very easy to hide away in the storage closet at Helping Hands. Even if someone had caught him there, no one would have questioned him or suspected him of doing anything wrong, because everyone knew him. Luckily, he'd been able to enter and exit the closet without detection. If he was very careful, his next menacing act could be carried out as easily.

Although he was in the United States on a far greater mission, one that would soon come to fruition just in time for the Jewish and Christian holidays that were approaching, he had been given permission to claim the personal revenge that was his due. As long as his personal issues did not interfere with the job the Majeed had sent him here to do, he could threaten and torment Lexie Murrough, and even kill her when the time came.

Did she honestly think that a few good deeds would absolve her of guilt? She was just like all the other Americans who thought handing out food and medicine to the people of a suffering nation was enough penance for their nation's gluttony and greed. The United States and its closest ally, Great Britain, possessed a condescending attitude toward the African and Middle Eastern countries whose beliefs and lifestyles differed greatly from their vast majority. They felt they were right and all others were wrong. They plotted and executed horrendous crimes in secret, then presented themselves on the world stage as benevolent and fair.

He did not know the names of the men who had killed Babu Tum, nor would he recognize their faces. But he remembered one face, a face that, to him, had come to symbolize the United States. She had been there that day, covering the inauguration for her television network. She had been welcomed into Gadi, had taken advantage of the new government's desire to be publicized in a positive light, all the while knowing that a team of highly trained soldiers from her country and the U.K. would kill the newly elected president.

It was partial justice that she had been shot and almost died. But until she paid the ultimate price...

He could have killed her today. He could have placed

the bomb in her office. But that would have been too easy. Lexie Murrough deserved to suffer. He intended to see that she and the woman whose money allowed her to play the benevolent benefactor to Gadi both knew the true meaning of torment. And on the day when he and other members of the Majeed issued the United States a dire warning, Lexie Murrough would become just one more casualty in the great war of good versus evil.

CARA PROPPED the large, overstuffed down pillows behind her back and nestled into a comfortable position so that she could read. Since taking over as the CEO of her father's worldwide conglomerate, she had little time for reading, so she usually read at night for an hour or so before falling asleep. But tonight her mind wouldn't settle down enough for her to concentrate, and as she gazed at the open page of the latest Kay Hooper novel, the words seemed to run together.

This had been one hell of a day. It wasn't as if she hadn't become accustomed to handling crises on a weekly, if not daily, basis, but the bomb at Helping Hands had been totally unexpected. Why would anyone bomb the headquarters of a charity organization? And why would that same someone issue a threat to a woman such as Lexie Murrough?

Don't forget that he extended that threat to you, too, she reminded herself.

Being the primary heir to a sizeable fortune made her vulnerable to fortune hunters and crazies, and she seldom went out in public without a member of the corporate security force. Both the downtown Chatta-nooga headquarters and the family home here on Lookout Mountain had the best security money could buy. She believed in covering all her bases, in being overly cautious when it came to her life. That was why she had called in Dundee's. They would not only provide private bodyguards 24/7 for her and Lexie, but they would do their own independent investigation.

Lieutenant Desmond would cooperate with Dundee's, up to a point. Two years ago, when her half sister had come up missing, her father had hired Dundee Security, and Daddy dearest—may his soul rest in peace instead of rotting in hell, where he probably deserved to be—hired only the best. In that, she was her father's daughter.

Who was she kidding? She was Edward Bedell's daughter in more ways than she wanted to be. She not only resembled him—with her freckles, bright-red hair and tall, rawboned build—but she possessed an innate business sense that astounded her father's associates, especially those who had been leery of a twenty-four-year-old taking control.

When her cell phone rang, Cara hesitated before she checked the caller ID. Her former brother-in-law had been pursuing her, begging her to marry him, for two years now. Although she had discouraged him as much as possible without being unkind, he was the type who refused to take no for an answer. He made a point of phoning her several times a week, usually around this time of night, reminding her of how much he adored her.

Hogwash. Grayson Perkins loved Grayson Perkins. But to give the devil his due, Gray *had* actually loved her sister, Audrey; it was just that he'd loved her money even more. And that was what he loved about Cara—the Bedell billions. She might have been foolish enough to believe his lies when she was a teenager, but after having a crush on Gray all her life, she'd finally wised up.

When she noted the caller's number, Cara tensed. But not because it was Gray. She lifted the phone from the nightstand, flipped it open and said, "Hello, Lieutenant Desmond."

"Good evening, Ms. Bedell."

"Do you have something to report about today's bombing at Helping Hands?" she asked.

"No, ma'am, not yet. This is a courtesy call. I wanted to make sure you're following your bodyguard's orders and not giving him any trouble."

"Have you already called Lexie to make sure she's toeing the line?"

"I don't need to do that with Lexie. She's not as headstrong and impulsive as you are."

"I'd think you might drop by in person to make sure that big, hunky bodyguard of hers doesn't sweep her off her feet. After all, you don't want some other guy trespassing on your territory, do you?"

Bain Desmond chuckled. "You know that Lexie and I are just friends."

"And what are we, Bain? Certainly not friends."

"I guess we're just acquaintances, Ms. Bedell. I mean, what else could we be? You're who you are—the CEO of Bedell, Inc., who's worth billions—and I'm a CPD detective with less than fifty grand in the bank."

"East and West and never the twain shall meet, huh?"

"Something like that."

"I'm going to get married one of these days," she told him.

"Yeah, you probably will. Just don't marry Grayson Perkins."

"No chance of that."

"When you find yourself a husband, whoever he is, I'm not going to like him."

Emotion lodged in Cara's throat. She'd been slowly but surely falling in love with Bain Desmond since the first time she'd met him, when he'd been the detective assigned to locate her missing half sister, and now she loved him so much it hurt. She suspected that he felt the same way. But an old-fashioned macho guy like Bain could never get serious about a woman like her. They lived in two different worlds, and neither could exist in the other's.

"Someday there will be a woman who's more than just your friend," Cara said. "And I'll hate her."

Bain didn't say anything for a long moment; then he cleared his throat. "If I could, I'd be there with you to take care of you."

"I know."

She flipped the cell phone closed, laid it on the nightstand and swallowed her unshed tears.

HE LIFTED her into his strong arms, holding her close, protecting her from all harm. The clatter of battle, of gunfire and retaliation, of shouts and screams and the cries of the injured and dying, faded into nothing more than background noise as he carried her to safety. Barely able to endure the pain, she drifted in and out of consciousness, her thoughts a wild jumble of questions and blurred memories. The only constants in her world were the feel of his powerful, protective arms, the scent of his musky perspiration and a foggy glimpse of his smoky-gray eyes.

Reality blurred with fantasy, taking her away from the past where she'd been wounded and he had saved her.

He held out his open arms, inviting her into his embrace. She went happily, willingly, no other place on earth she would rather be. He slipped his arm around her waist and took her right hand into his left, and led her onto the ballroom floor. He waltzed her around the room, faster and faster, their bodies moving in perfect unison to the music and the beating of their hearts.

Suddenly her legs froze and she couldn't move. No, please, no. I want to dance and dance and dance.

He released her, moved away from her and slowly disappeared.

She cried out for him, begging him to come back, pleading with him not to leave her.

"Ms. Murrough!" The concerned voice broke through the haze and awakened her from a dream that had turned into a nightmare.

"Hmm…?" Her eyelids fluttered.

A heavy weight dropped down on the side of her bed. "Ms. Murrough? I heard you crying out. Are you all right?"

She opened her eyes. There in the semidarkness of her bedroom, with only the moonlight streaming in through the tall windows, she saw the hulking figure of a man sitting on her bed, hovering over her.

"Oh…oh, Mr. Bronson. I'm so sorry I woke you." When she pushed herself into a sitting position, she suddenly realized just how close he was. Eye to eye close. She gasped silently, and they both pulled back far enough that there was little danger of their bodies touching. "I was dreaming."

"From the way you were crying out, it sounded more like you were having a nightmare."

She nodded. "I suppose, in a way, my dream did turn into a nightmare."

"Are you plagued by nightmares very often?" he asked.

"I—I used to be," she admitted. "But I don't have them as often now."

He eased off the bed and stood. "Would you like a glass of water? Or I could make you some hot chocolate or—"

"Hot chocolate sounds good." She tossed back the covers and stood, then realized she was standing there in her silk pajamas, the ones that hugged every curve. "I'll make the hot chocolate, if you'll share a cup with me." She felt around at the foot of the bed for where she'd tossed her robe earlier that evening.

"I wouldn't mind a cup." He backed away from the bed and toward the open door. "I'll just go put on my pants first and meet you in the kitchen."

As he exited the room, she caught a glimpse of him in the moonlight. Wearing nothing but a pair of cotton boxers, his big, hard body glistened like a bronze sculpture. Just that one glimpse took her breath away. *My God, he's got a gorgeous body!*

Ten minutes later, with her in her robe and him in his slightly wrinkled tan slacks, they sat at the kitchen bar and sipped the hot cocoa she had prepared.

Lexie tried her darnedest not to keep looking at his bare chest, but how could a woman not stare? His hairy chest was broad, lean, muscular and apparently naturally tanned. His arms were large, every muscle well defined.

What's the matter with you? she asked herself. Was she transposing images of her dream man onto Deke

Bronson? Was her pulse racing and her stomach fluttering because of Deke, or because she had him confused with the memories of her long-ago rescuer?

"Ten years ago, after I was shot and learned I was partially paralyzed, I had a lot of nightmares." Lexie cupped the mug in her hands and stared down into the creamy brown liquid.

"That's understandable," he said.

She hazarded a glance his way and caught him staring at her. Their gazes met and locked for an instant. What was it that she saw in his eyes? Sympathy? Concern? Lust?

Lexie swallowed. "I don't remember much about what happened to me after I was shot. But I do remember one thing. It's a good memory, and it's always a part of my dream before it turns into a nightmare."

He didn't say a word, just kept staring at her, almost as if he were holding his breath waiting for her to tell him about that one good memory.

"There was a man who saved my life. A soldier. He lifted me up in his arms and carried me to safety. I don't know who he was. I never saw him again, and no one could or would tell me his name."

Deke clenched his jaw tightly. "He was probably just a guy doing his job."

She shook her head. "No, I distinctly remember hearing someone say, 'You can't take her with us.'" She sighed heavily. "I think he went against orders when he took me with him and saved my life."

Deke lifted his mug to his lips and sipped the cocoa.

The silence between them returned and lingered. They drank the rest of their hot chocolate without talking. Oddly enough, Lexie realized that they didn't need to talk. Just sitting there together quietly felt right, as if they were old friends who didn't need words.

Or old lovers…

CHAPTER FOUR

LEXIE WOKE suddenly, instantly knowing she had overslept. With eyes wide open and a nagging thought that she had forgotten something flitting through her mind, she turned her head so she could see the digital bedside clock.

Six fifty-seven.

Why hadn't her alarm gone off? She kept it set at six, and even on weekends, when she could sleep late, she usually woke no later than six-thirty.

After crawling out of bed, she grasped her cane, which had been propped against the nightstand, and padded barefoot toward the bathroom.

As she turned on the faucets and stared groggily into the mirror above the sink, she remembered that she hadn't set her alarm last night. She wouldn't be going in to work today. Just as she splashed cold water on her face, she remembered something else. She wasn't alone in her apartment. Deke Bronson had slept in her guest room.

After patting her face dry with a hand towel, she inspected her appearance more closely. The puffiness under her eyes would disappear within an hour or less, but there was nothing she could do to those unflattering bags right now. She could put on makeup and fix her hair, but if she did, Deke would know she'd done it solely for his benefit.

So don't do anything special to yourself. Maybe she should at least change out of her pajamas and run a comb through her hair. *No, don't do anything you wouldn't normally do.* She raked her fingers through her thick, wavy hair, rinsed her mouth out and grabbed her velvet robe off the hanger on the back of the door. Her silk robe lay at the foot of her bed, but feeling chilled this morning, she preferred something heavier. Besides, the velvet robe offered her more protection from Deke Bronson's subtle appraisal. It wasn't that he'd blatantly stared at her, or that his glances over her body had been offensive. Quite the opposite. The way he'd casually raked his gaze over her—more than once—had aroused her.

Just go out there and follow your usual morning routine.

What she would do was put on coffee and prepare breakfast. There was a box of frozen sausage biscuits in the freezer. And it wouldn't take ten minutes to make the coffee, heat the biscuits in the microwave and scramble eggs. Once she had set the bar with placemats and silverware, and poured their orange juice, she would knock on the guest room door and announce that breakfast was served.

As she crossed her bedroom, she managed to slip into her robe and knot the tie belt before opening the door.

Morning sunlight flooded the huge three-room expanse. She loved the triple set of French doors that led onto the balcony, because they afforded her a magnificent view. Late autumn in eastern Tennessee was always a lovely time of year, but especially this year, when the first frost had come late and the vibrant colors of the fall foliage were still at their peak. A week from now, closer to Thanksgiving, the colors would have faded, harkening the approach of winter. From almost every window in her home, she had a fabulous view of the Tennessee River. Real estate along the river was at a premium, and she knew that if Bedell, Inc. hadn't owned this building and sold her the loft at a bargain price, she wouldn't be living here now. Despite the sizable settlement she had received from UBC, she didn't squander her money, using it for necessities and donating most of the interest she drew from her money market account to Helping Hands. Her contribution was only a drop in the bucket compared to what Bedell, Inc. donated, but no gift of either time or money was insignificant.

"Good morning," a deep male voice said.

Gasping, Lexie jerked her head around and stared at the man standing in her kitchen. He was clean-shaven, and his short black hair was slightly damp. He wore jeans, a plaid shirt and a tan corduroy jacket. No tie. He lifted one of her orange UT mugs in a salute.

"Good morning," she replied. She eyed the coffee-maker. "You've made coffee?"

"It's fresh," he told her. "I'm finishing off the first pot."

"How long have you been up?"

"Since five-thirty." He glanced at the bar area, where he'd plugged in a small laptop computer. "I had some reports to go over."

"Did you get any sleep at all?" she asked.

"About four hours. I don't need a lot of sleep. Four or five hours are good for me."

She sighed. "Must be nice. I'm a seven-hour-a-night person. Less than six and I'm worthless." Her cane tapped softly on the wooden floor as she walked over to the coffeemaker. She reached into the cabinet overhead and removed another cup, this one bearing the University of Georgia bulldog mascot, then filled it to the brim.

"I just got off the phone with my colleague, Geoff Monday, who's guarding Ms. Bedell," Deke said. "They had an uneventful night, too."

Lexie sipped the coffee. Mmm…delicious. In reality, her night had been uneventful, though her dreams had been anything but. "That's good. No more threats. Maybe yesterday's bomb and threatening phone call were all there'll be, and that's the end of it."

"Maybe, but doubtful."

Lexie set her mug down, then hoisted herself onto one of the two stools and hung her cane's bronze handle on the edge of the bar. "You think it was just the beginning, don't you?"

"Probably." He joined her at the bar. After closing his laptop, he swiveled his stool around and faced her.

Her heartbeat did a stupid little rat-a-tat-tat when his dark gaze settled on her. Without thinking about what she was doing, she pulled the lapels of her robe together, all too aware that her nipples had peaked, and momentarily forgetting that she was wearing her velvet robe and not the one made of delicate silk.

His gaze drifted to where her hand rested in the center of her chest. He cleared his throat. "Is there any reason why Lieutenant Desmond should remove himself from this case?"

Taken totally off-guard by his question, she almost choked on her coffee. After coughing a couple of times, she stared at him quizzically. "Why would you ask such a question? I have no idea why you'd—"

"In the same way doctors aren't supposed to treat loved ones, it's a bad idea for a police officer to be directly involved in a case when he has a personal relationship with—"

"Bain and I are friends, nothing more," she said defensively. "And he and Cara are acquaintances." *Acquaintances who just happen to be in love with each other, but that's nobody's business except theirs.* "Being a Dundee agent, you're probably aware of the fact that Bain was the lead detective on Cara's half sister's murder case."

He nodded. "Yeah, I know." He paused for half a second. "So you're dating the lieutenant, but you're not sleeping with him?"

Surprised by his comment, Lexie glared at her bodyguard. His gaze met hers head-on. "That question was highly inappropriate," she told him.

"Maybe I should have put the question less bluntly, but—"

"Maybe you shouldn't have asked the question at all."

"I didn't ask out of idle curiosity," he told her. "I've been hired to protect you, to do whatever is necessary to keep you safe. In order to do that, I need to know as much about you and your life as possible. Someone set off a bomb at the headquarters of the organization you're in charge of, and then that someone telephoned you to threaten your life. I need your full cooperation in order to do my job and stop him before he does anything else."

Lexie saw no connection between the threat on her life and her personal relationship with Bain. But she wasn't about to be stubborn and difficult, not when it served no purpose.

"Bain and I are friends. We go out occasionally. We enjoy each other's company. But we are not lovers."

Only when Deke's facial muscles relaxed did Lexie realize how tight his jaw had been. Had he been angry with her for not answering his question immediately, so once she acquiesced to his wishes, his anger had subsided? Odd. Very odd.

Brushing aside any lingering tension between them, Lexie slipped off the bar stool, grabbed her cane and took a few steps toward the refrigerator. "I have frozen sausage biscuits that I can pop into the microwave. And if you'd like I can scramble—"

A cell phone rang, but the sound was muffled, as if coming from another room. As they listened, Lexie recognized the ring tone as hers. "It's mine," she told him.

"Where's your phone?"

"In my bedroom."

When she took a couple of tentative steps in that direction, he waved her back. "Stay. I'll get it for you."

Unaccustomed to being ordered about as if she were a helpless child—not since she had completed her physical therapy and begun a new life on her own— Lexie stopped dead still and glowered at Deke Bronson's broad back as he disappeared into her bedroom. She might have a slight physical handicap, but she despised being treated as if she were less capable than anyone else.

Don't get bent out of shape about it. After all, he didn't know that she hated being waited on and catered to. *Just fix breakfast.*

Before she had time to open the freezer compartment and remove the box of biscuits, Deke came out of her room with her cell phone to his ear.

He had answered her phone. How dare he!

"Yeah, yeah. Sure. We'll meet you there in about—how long will it take us to get to the Bedell house? Okay. Twenty minutes. Okay. We'll see you in forty-five." He walked over to Lexie, held out her phone and said, "It's Lieutenant Desmond."

She gave Deke a condemning glower as she grabbed the phone out of his hand. He lifted his eyebrows in a what-did-I-do? expression.

"Bain?"

"Morning, beautiful."

"Want to fill me in on what you told Mr. Bronson?"

"Mr. Bronson? Not on a first-name basis with your bodyguard?"

"No."

"I take it that there's a problem?"

"No, not really. I'm simply not used to having someone underfoot."

Deke came up beside her, reached into the freezer, removed the sealed box of sausage biscuits and took it over to the counter nearest the microwave.

Bain chuckled. "I have a very preliminary report on the bombing, and since Ms. Bedell has given the Chattanooga PD orders to share all info with her, I'm heading to the big mansion on the mountain as we speak."

"Any excuse to—"

"If you're implying that I don't have any real info and I'm using this as excuse to see her, then don't go there."

"*Is* that what you're doing?"

Quiet hesitation, then an admission. "Maybe. Am I that obvious?"

"Only to me, because I know how you feel."

"If I hadn't gotten sloppy drunk one night and cried in my beer…"

"It's our little secret. I promise. So, see you in thirty minutes." She ended their conversation, clutched the phone in her hand and walked out of the kitchen area.

"Breakfast will be ready in about two minutes," Deke called to her.

"It takes twenty minutes to drive from here to Cara's home, and you told Bain we'd be there in forty-five, which means I've only got twenty-five minutes to shower, do my hair and makeup and dress. I won't have time for breakfast." She made her way carefully into her bedroom, all the while expecting him to try to stop her.

Once inside her room, she closed the door and released a deep breath. *Don't think about him. Just get ready.*

Twenty minutes later, with her hair in a ponytail, a five-minute makeup job coloring her pale face, and wearing stone-washed jeans, her favorite lavender cotton button-down and her lightweight quilted purple satin jacket, she was ready.

Deke was standing in the middle of the living room—waiting.

"Let's go," she said.

He surveyed her from head to toe, then went over the same territory a second time, as if he thought he might have missed something the first go-round. He reached into his pocket and pulled out her key ring. "I commandeered your keys, since you won't need them and I will."

"Why won't—"

"Because you won't be going anywhere without me."

"Oh, yes, of course." Lexie wasn't sure how their arrangement was going to work out. This big, bad tough guy had been guarding her for less than twenty-four hours, and having someone shadow her every move was already getting on her nerves.

When they passed the bar, he picked up a brown paper bag and handed it to her. Not giving her time to question him, he said, "Travel mug with black coffee, and a sausage biscuit wrapped in a napkin. You can eat on the way."

She accepted what he no doubt thought of as a gift. *Be nice,* she told herself. "Thank you."

"You're welcome."

If she had expected him to smile, she would have been disappointed. Something told her that this man seldom smiled.

I wonder why.

When he opened the front door of the loft, she exited first and headed for the old freight elevator.

She figured Cara was having as big a problem adjusting to having a bossy Dundee agent running her life as she was. Actually, Cara was probably having a bigger one. Since taking on the enormous responsibility of running Bedell, Inc., having it thrust upon her at the age of twenty-four, Cara had been forced to get tough fast and not allow any weaknesses to show. That was something they had in common—both of them had been forced to mature quickly and grow a thick hide, but deep down inside, they were lonely, soft-hearted women.

AFTER GEOFF MONDAY told her that Lieutenant Desmond would arrive shortly to personally deliver a preliminary report about the bombing at Helping Hands, Cara had excused herself and rushed upstairs to her bedroom suite. Geoff had followed and now kept guard outside the door. When she'd dressed before breakfast, she'd put on her green sweats, intending to take her usual morning walk, never imagining that Bain would have anything to report this soon.

Cara knew she was no great beauty. She was too tall, too big, with broad hips and heavy thighs. And a body covered in freckles. Makeup hid most of the freckles on her face, and she paid a hairstylist a small fortune to tone down her Bozo-orange-red hair to a slightly less fiery shade. Having always been the Ugly Duckling to her older half sister's Raving Beauty, Cara had settled for looking wholesome and healthy. God, how she hated those two adjectives. She suspected any woman would, at least when they were used to describe herself.

Geoff probably wondered why she'd raced upstairs in such a hurry, but he was too much of a gentleman to question her actions. As long as he had no idea she'd panicked at the thought of Bain Desmond seeing her without makeup and wearing a pair of less-than-flattering sweats, she didn't much care what her bodyguard thought.

All right, so the rich-bitch side of her personality had dismissed Geoff the way she often did servants and Bedell, Inc. employees. It wasn't that she meant to act in a superior way—and God knew she didn't think of herself that way—but she had been raised by Edward Bedell with all the rights and privileges his billions afforded her. If not for having lived most of her life in her sister's bedazzling shadow, she would probably be a spoiled, worthless brat. Instead, she had worked diligently to learn about the conglomerate with its wide-reaching tentacles that spread around the world. She had earned her MBA at UT when she was twenty-two. And all things considered, at her current ripe old age of twenty-seven, she had decided that maybe it was better to have been blessed with brains rather than with beauty.

But right this minute, as she rummaged through her walk-in closet, she would have settled for just a tad more beauty. After trying on three different outfits and tossing each aside, she finally settled on a rusty-brown wool-blend suit, with a calf-length skirt and a jacket that hit her just below the waist. She chose a dark-turquoise silk blouse and deliberately left the top three buttons open. Her high, full breasts were definitely an asset, and she needed all the help she could get to impress Bain.

Dressed fit-to-kill, her makeup perfect, her short hair swept away from her face to expose her turquoise and silver earrings, she faced herself in the oversized cheval mirror.

How did she look?

She looked…rich.

What was the point of trying to impress Bain, of hoping he would notice how attractive she'd tried to make herself for him? It wasn't as if she had a prayer of even getting to first base with him. And it wasn't because he didn't find her attractive. He actually did, and had made no secret of that fact. No, he kept a wide distance between them solely because she was a billionaire.

Of all the men in the world for her to fall for, why did it have to be an old-fashioned, macho guy who would rather die than live off a woman's money? He'd made it perfectly clear that the two of them mixed like oil and water, that they lived in two different universes, and that there was no common ground where they could meet, fall in love, marry and live happily ever after.

Cara opened the door and walked into the hall. Geoff looked her over, then let out a wolf whistle. She smiled.

"Keep that up and I'll make sure you get a bonus," she told him.

He laughed. Geoff was not really handsome, but he was thoroughly masculine. Mr. Rough and Rugged. During their long conversation last evening, she'd learned he was half English and half Scot, and although he maintained a distinct UK accent, he had picked up some Southern words and phrases that seemed strange coming out of his mouth.

When she'd kept referring to him as Mr. Monday, he'd told her to just call him Geoff, to which she had replied, "Then you should call me Cara. After all, we're going to be together for Lord knows how many days, or even weeks."

Cara preened for Geoff, feeling totally relaxed around the big, brawny blond, understanding that his teasing was good-natured fun and not serious flirting.

"Dressing to impress the Chattanooga PD, huh?" Geoff made the comment in a joking manner.

Cara's smile wavered. "I have to dress to impress everyone. After all, I *am* Cara Bedell, and certain things are expected of me. Whatever would Lieutenant Desmond think if I greeted him in my old sweats?"

THE BEDELL BUTLER, a middle-aged man named Aldridge, escorted Bain into the living room. Bain had hated this damn mausoleum the first time he'd walked through the doors nearly two and a half years ago. Recently, Cara had done some redecorating, and at least the place seemed less austere and formidable, but for his tastes, the house was too big to be a home. A small hotel or a bed and breakfast, yeah, but a home where he would ever feel comfortable? No way in hell.

What difference did it make whether he liked this place or not, that he'd never feel comfortable here? It wasn't as if he would ever be living in the Bedell mansion.

"Please have a seat," Aldridge instructed. "Ms. Bedell and Mr. Monday will join you shortly."

"Yeah, thanks." Bain didn't sit; instead he wandered about the huge room. The furnishings probably cost more than he would earn in a lifetime. Why would anybody need such expensive stuff?

But it wasn't as if Cara had gone out and bought everything new. The furniture had been in her family for generations. Priceless antiques. Bain grunted. The only thing he owned that could be even halfway considered an antique was his great-granddad's old pocket watch, which he kept in a safe deposit box. He had come from people who had nothing material to show for backbreaking physical labor. His great-grandparents on all four sides had been dirt-poor farmers, his maternal grandfather had been a truck driver, and his paternal grandfather a Chattanooga policeman. His dad had followed in his own father's footsteps, and when Bain joined the force, the third-generation Desmond to become a blue knight, he'd made it a family tradition.

Bain studied a sculpture on the mantel, a nude male figure in bronze.

"Good morning, Lieutenant," Cara said from behind him.

He took a deep breath and turned to face her, then glanced past her at the Dundee agent guarding her back. He couldn't say he liked the fact that another man was spending twenty-four hours a day with Cara, but he was glad she had hired the best to protect her and Lexie. Since she'd taken over Bedell, Inc., after her father's suicide, he'd mentioned to her on more than one occasion that a person in her position should have a bodyguard. She had pointed out that the security at her home and downtown headquarters was first-rate, and that whenever she traveled, she took one of the company's security staff with her.

"Lexie and Mr. Bronson are meeting us here," Bain said. "I didn't see any point in going over the same information twice."

When his gaze connected with Cara's, he saw a flicker of yearning in her eyes. Could she see the same need in his? Probably. Although they'd never shared more than a couple of spontaneous kisses and hadn't come anywhere close to admitting they wanted each other, the hunger between them was undeniable. But it was a hunger they could never appease. If they ever did, it could only end badly for both of them.

Following Edward Bedell's suicide, shortly after he had admitted accidentally killing his elder daughter, Bain had been tempted to confess his personal interest in Cara. But only because he'd been concerned that her worthless, pretty-boy brother-in-law would take advantage of the crush she'd had on him since she was a teenager. Grayson Perkins was a sycophantic leech who had thought he could sweet-talk his way into marriage with a second Bedell sister. Thankfully, Cara had come to her senses before succumbing to the man's immense charm. But the jerk was still in Cara's life, still a VP at Bedell, Inc., and still clinging to the illusion that one day he would persuade Cara to marry him.

At least Cara didn't have to endure her stepmother's presence. She'd paid Patrice a small fortune to get rid of her, and now the fourth Mrs. Bedell was living happily in Europe.

"Would you care for coffee?" Cara asked as she approached Bain.

He shook his head. "No, thanks."

She held out her hand. "I appreciate your coming here yourself to give us the report instead of simply telephoning."

He eyed her long, elegant fingers—void of rings, the short, tapered nails painted with clear polish—and momentarily hesitated, but finally he took her slender hand and gave it a sturdy shake. "Just doing my job." He reluctantly released her.

With a wave of her arm, she indicated that he should sit. When he settled on the brocade sofa, she sat beside him, leaving a good three feet between them. In his peripheral vision, Bain noticed Geoff Monday taking a stance behind and to the right of the sofa.

"Was traffic bad this morning?" Cara asked.

Bain shrugged. "About usual for this time of day."

"Hmm… It looks like it'll be a beautiful, sunny day. The high is supposed to be around sixty-eight."

"Yeah, that's what Channel Twelve was forecasting."

As they sat there making idle chitchat, Bain almost forgot that they weren't alone, because the Dundee agent, like any good bodyguard, although nearby, was unobtrusive.

The pocket doors opened, and Aldridge stepped over the threshold. "Excuse me, Ms. Bedell, but there's a phone call for you." He held the portable phone in his hand, his palm cupping the mouthpiece.

"Who is it?" she asked.

"The gentleman didn't say, but he insisted it was urgent," Aldridge said. "'A matter of life and death' were his exact words."

Bain's gaze, which Cara had been deliberately avoiding during their meaningless conversation, collided with hers.

"You don't think it's—"

"Take the call," Bain told her. "I'll listen in on the extension. Is there still one in here?"

She nodded and pointed to the decorative crystal phone on the antique mahogany table in the corner.

"Later this morning, I'll get some guys up here to install the proper equipment to monitor all your calls. And we'll do the same for your lines at Bedell, Inc." He would also make sure all the phones Lexie used were monitored, too.

Cara rose from the sofa and reached out to take the phone from Aldridge, but she waited until Bain reached the extension before she put the handset to her ear and said, "This is Cara Bedell. What seems to be the emergency?"

Bain lifted the extension without making a sound.

The man spoke in a muffled, disguised voice. "If you withdraw your support of Helping Hands and publicly denounce Lexie Murrough as a selfish, self-serving hypocrite, I will spare your life."

"Who are you, and why are you doing this?" Cara asked.

She kept her gaze locked with Bain's. Geoff Monday did not interfere.

"Who I am is unimportant. I will give you forty-eight hours to comply with my wishes. If you do not, you will remain my enemy and thus must pay the price for your loyalty to one so unworthy."

The dial tone rang in Bain's ear. He replaced the

receiver and walked straight to Cara, who was still tenaciously gripping the cordless phone. Bain took her hand in his, eased apart her clutched fingers, removed the phone and gave it to Aldridge.

"Are you all right?" Bain asked.

"I will be, once I stop shaking." She offered him a weak smile. "The guy is crazy. For some reason, he hates Lexie. Of all people—Lexie, who is one of the kindest, most caring and giving human beings I've ever known."

Bain exchanged concerned glances with the Dundee agent. "We're definitely dealing with a dangerous person." As he cupped Cara's elbow and guided her back to the sofa, he filled Geoff Monday in on the caller's end of the conversation.

When they reached the sofa, Cara balked and hurriedly turned to face Bain. "I'm fine." He looked at her skeptically. "Really, I'm all right." She glanced over her shoulder at her bodyguard, then turned back to Bain. "Lieutenant, you should go ahead and report the call I just received and do whatever you need to do. Geoff won't leave me alone."

Bain barely stopped himself from grabbing her and hauling her into his arms. There was something definitely wrong with the world when a guy couldn't comfort a woman he cared about the way he cared about Cara.

"Should I call Lexie and tell her?" Cara asked.

"I'll get in touch with Deke Bronson," Geoff said. "If that's all right with you, Lieutenant Desmond."

"Yeah, sure."

Bain went out into the hallway, contacted headquarters, made a brief report and issued orders to his partner, Mike Swain. He couldn't be with Cara 24/7 the way her highly trained bodyguard could, but he could and would do whatever it took to find out who was behind the threats. He would personally see to it that this nut-job was stopped before he could hurt either Cara or Lexie.

HE STOOD in the back-entrance alcove of a building half a block away from Lexie Murrough's apartment, a self-satisfied smile on his face as he slipped the prepaid cell phone into his pocket. He had enjoyed hearing the fear in Cara Bedell's voice. She had tried her best to hide it, but he understood the sound of fear as only a person who had been horribly afraid himself could truly understand. As a boy, witnessing his father's brutal murder, he had known unparalleled fear, a child's real-life nightmare. He'd been barely twelve when he and his mother had been forced to flee Gadi, outcasts who became unwanted refugees in country after country. Eventually his mother met and married a good man who treated them both well. But his mother and stepfather had been killed in a car accident when he was fourteen, forcing him onto the streets to fend for himself. He would have died of starvation if it had not been for the kindness of a neighbor, Kalil Ben Riyad. He not only owed Kalil his life but his undying loyalty for saving him and in-troducing him to the Majeed.

He lifted the small binoculars hanging around his neck and focused on the parking lot behind Lexie's apartment building. He had no idea when she and her bodyguard would emerge, but he could wait. After all, he had nothing else to do this morning, and he didn't want to miss the look of shock on her face or her screams when she saw the surprise he had waiting for her.

CHAPTER FIVE

DEKE SLOWED his pace to accommodate Lexie's hindered gait. She hated that anyone who walked with her was forced to regulate their normal speed to hers. Before a crossfire bullet had hit her spine and partially paralyzed her, she had been reasonably athletic: jogging, swimming, playing softball and dancing. Now, she was doing well to walk and swim. But she was one of the lucky ones whose spinal cord had not been severed, causing irreversible damage. If there hadn't been a delay in starting steroids shortly after her injury, she might have recovered more quickly. But what was done was done, and even though she could never forget what had happened to her, she tried not to dwell on it.

So why was she thinking about it now?

Because Deke Bronson's presence in her life made her feel helpless, and helplessness was something she had struggled with for the past ten years. She might have a handicap, but she was strong, independent and perfectly capable of taking care of herself.

Except when her life was in danger from an unknown assailant.

Deke stepped in front of Lexie and opened the back door, then held it for her as she emerged from the apartment building into the sunny warmth of a beautiful autumn day. The distant sounds of a small city's hustle and bustle on a Thursday morning greeted them, as did the bright sunshine and clear blue sky. They were the only ones in the parking lot, although Lexie noticed a couple of people in the adjacent lot used by the tenants of a neighboring building.

"Stay here, please," Deke said as he visually scanned the area, taking special note of the four vehicles parked alongside Lexie's. "I need to check your car."

"Check my car for what?" No sooner were the words out of her mouth than she realized what he'd meant. "For a bomb?"

He nodded. "Keep your back to the door and stay right here, no matter what happens. Understand?"

She nodded.

"I need a verbal acknowledgment from you," he told her.

"Yes, I understand."

Lexie pushed her back and hips up against the closed door and watched while Deke walked toward her Subaru. Suddenly, a loud explosion shook the ground. The Lincoln Navigator parked at the end of the row of four vehicles exploded, shooting fire and smoke, and scattering debris as if it were raining metal and plastic fragments. Deke spun around and ran from the blast, heading straight for Lexie. Reacting instantly, she dropped the sack containing her sausage biscuit and coffee. The bag hit the concrete walkway, but the splattering sound was masked by her startled, frightened scream.

Trembling, gasping, but no longer screaming, Lexie reached out to Deke, but before he could get to her, a second explosion rocked the parking lot. The sleek, red Mustang parked beside the Navigator went up in flames.

Oh, God! Why would someone destroy her neighbor's vehicles?

Deke barreled straight into Lexie, grabbing her and pushing her toward the back door. Just as Deke grabbed the door handle with one hand and wrapped his arm around Lexie's shoulders, another explosion erupted. They both glanced back and saw that Lexie's SUV had died the same violent death as the Navigator and the Mustang.

When Deke opened the door and shoved her inside, she stumbled and lost her grip on her cane, which caught in the door, holding it partially open. Deke slid his arm around her waist, yanked her to his side and swung her around so that his body protected her, as he simultaneously kicked her cane across the concrete floor of the back hallway. The door slammed shut with a resounding wham.

Looking through the row of shattered windows across the back wall, Lexie saw the fourth vehicle, a white Mercedes, explode. Scared out of her mind, she clung to Deke. Involuntarily shivering as if half frozen and gasping for air, she realized she was on the verge of hyperventilating.

Take some deep breaths. Calm down. You're safe. Deke's safe. No one was hurt. Cars can be replaced.

Deke hurried her away from the windows and toward the elevator, which opened to reveal several residents, some in their robes and house slippers.

Roy and Betsy Morrison, a middle-aged couple who owned the Mercedes, emerged first, followed by Susan McKelvey, whose red Mustang was now smoldering outside in the parking lot.

"What happened?" Roy Morrison asked. "We were eating breakfast and heard the most godawful explosions."

"I looked out the window and saw fire and smoke coming from the Wilsons' Navigator," Susan said.

"Y'all need to go back into the elevator and return to your apartments," Deke told them. "I'm calling the police." He leaned down, picked up Lexie's cane and handed it to her, then yanked his cell phone off his belt and flipped it open. "All four vehicles in the parking lot have exploded."

Susan and Betsy gasped.

"Somebody deliberately bombed our cars?" A perplexed expression flashed across Roy's round, ruddy face.

Deke herded everyone into the elevator, then made his call. He spoke quietly, and with the Morrisons and Susan jabbering nonstop, Lexie couldn't make out everything he said, but she heard enough to know he was talking to Geoff Monday and not the police. The Morrisons departed on the second floor, then Susan on the third. Deke remained on the phone as they ascended to her loft.

"Yeah, lieutenant, she's safe. We're almost back up to her apartment."

Undoubtedly Bain was already at the Bedell home, she realized, and after speaking to Geoff Monday, Deke was now talking to Bain.

The elevator doors slid open. Deke motioned for her to get out, which she did, as he continued his conversation with Bain, mostly listening and occasionally replying in succinct sentences.

Once inside the apartment, he flipped his phone closed and hung it back on its belt hook, then turned to her. "You might want to sit down. You look pretty shaky."

He didn't need to make the suggestion twice. She went directly into the living room and all but fell into her favorite chair, letting her cane slip from her hand and onto the floor.

Deke came over and sat down on the sofa, straight across from her. "Are you okay?"

"Other than being terrified?" she said. "Yeah, I'm okay. I just feel like I might throw up."

"You'll be all right. Your reaction is normal. If you need to throw up, do it. Whatever it takes to settle your nerves."

"The cars exploding…" She took a deep breath. "It's connected to what happened at Helping Hands yesterday, right? It's the same person, and I'm his target."

"Probably."

"But why harm innocent people? Why blow up all four cars instead of just mine?"

"My guess is that he's making a statement. He wants to put the fear of God into you, Lexie. And I'd say he's succeeding."

She glared at Deke as what he'd said sunk in and she realized he was right.

"I'd be a fool not to be frightened."

"Yes, you would. It's how you handle your fear that matters. You have to protect yourself without giving in to fear."

"Who would do this? As far as I know, I don't have any real enemies, no one who wants to hurt me."

"He may be someone you don't know," Deke said. "A stalker or a secret admirer, or someone who, for whatever reason, doesn't approve of you and your work at Helping Hands. Or he could be someone from your past, someone who, for his own sick reasons, focused his hatred on you."

The salty bile that had risen into her throat traveled back down her esophagus, leaving a burning trail that went all the way to her stomach. "I need some water." She started to get up.

Deke motioned her back down. "I'll get it for you."

"I keep bottled water in the refrigerator."

As he walked toward the kitchen, he told her, "Lieutenant Desmond is on his way over here. He called in a report, and a couple of squad cars should arrive any minute." Deke opened the fridge and retrieved a bottle of water. "The bomb squad and CSI will be here soon to work the scene. It's possible there are more bombs."

Lexie's muscles tightened and her stomach churned. "Here in the building?"

Deke shook his head. "That's highly unlikely, but not impossible. If this guy had wanted to kill you yesterday, he would have placed the bomb in your office or a part of the building where he knew you would be. Same goes for the car bombs. If he'd wanted to kill you, he could have waited for you to get in your car before detonating the bomb."

Lexie heaved a sigh of relief.

Deke handed her the bottled water. "Ms. Bedell and Geoff are coming over, too."

Lexie twisted off the cap, lifted the bottle to her lips and took a hefty swig of the natural spring water. The moment the cool liquid hit her stomach, she moaned quietly. "The water was a bad idea." She reached down, picked up her cane and then stood.

"Need any help?" he asked.

She hurried as quickly as possible in the direction of the half bath that was located beside the dining room. "Oh, mercy. I'm not sure I can make it."

The words were no sooner out of her mouth than Deke rushed to her, swept her up into his arms and carried her into the powder room. He tossed back the commode lid and seat, situated Lexie in front of the bowl and propped her on her feet by keeping his arm firmly around her waist. She dropped her cane, which she'd been clutching against her side. When she bent over and heaved, Deke slipped in behind her, still supporting her securely.

After she threw up her morning coffee and some viscid stomach fluids, she lifted her head, wiped her mouth with the back of her hand and glanced over her shoulder at Deke. She hated for him to see her like this. After spending helpless months in hospitals and undergoing years of physical therapy that had required her to put her well-being in other people's hands, she had come to pride herself on being totally self-reliant over the past five years.

"Sorry." She whispered the one-word apology.

"Hey, I've seen grown men toss their cookies for less reason."

When she tried to stand up, she staggered. Thank goodness he hadn't released his hold. Standing perfectly still for a few minutes, she breathed deeply. Once the nausea and dizziness subsided, she pulled away from Deke.

"I'll be fine." She held on to the edge of the decorative, free-standing sink. "I need to wash my face and rinse out my mouth. You can leave me alone now." When he remained behind her, as if he were waiting to catch her if she wavered, she looked back at him and said, "Really. I'm all right."

He gave her a stern, concerned look, then walked out of the powder room and closed the door behind him.

Lexie gripped the sink's rim with white-knuckled strength. It wasn't like her to fall apart in a crisis, so why now? Maybe it was because in the past ten years, all her crises had been non-life-threatening. Not since that horrible day in Gadi all those years ago had she been faced with the possibility of dying or of her actually being the cause of someone else's death. She still blamed herself for Marty Bearn getting killed. No one else blamed her, not even Marty's widow or his daughter. But no matter how many people had exonerated her for the crime, she knew she was guilty. She'd been the overeager reporter who had told her young cameraman to keep filming when the assassination squad attacked and President's Tum's guard fired back.

If she and Marty had taken cover as soon as they'd realized what was happening, neither of them would have been shot. Marty would still be alive and she wouldn't—

"Lexie, are you sure you're all right?" Deke called through the closed door.

"I'm fine." Even to her own ears, she didn't sound convincing. "I just need a couple more minutes."

The first time she had been marked for death, it had been the result of being in the wrong place at the wrong time. To the man who had shot her, it had been nothing personal. He hadn't meant for his bullet to hit her; she had simply been caught in the crossfire. This time, danger had come to her, spoken her name and claimed her. To the man who had threatened her and Cara and Helping Hands, it *was* personal.

DEKE HAD LEFT LEXIE alone in the powder room for the past twenty minutes, checking on her twice and being told both times that she was fine. He knew better. She wasn't fine. Although she probably hadn't vomited again, she was sick. Sick with worry. And, no doubt, memories from a long-ago day, half a world away, were plaguing her. Was she reliving the moment her cameraman went down? Or the moment she took a bullet in the back? A bullet from his Colt M4A1 carbine. Was she asking herself why this was happening to her now, after she had finally put her life back together and was happy?

Or was she happy? Really happy?

Okay, so maybe it was chauvinistic of him, but he couldn't help what he was thinking, could he? Lexie Murrough was a beautiful, intelligent woman, and yet at thirty-four, she didn't have a man in her life. Unless you counted Bain Desmond, whom she said was only a friend. Yes, a woman could have a successful, satisfying life without being in a long-term relationship, but...

The doorbell rang, jerking Deke out of his thoughts. He trekked across the room, paused in front of the door and peered through the peephole, then unlocked the door and opened it to allow Lieutenant Desmond, Cara Bedell and Geoff Monday entrance.

"How's Lexie?" Desmond and Cara asked simultaneously.

"A little shaken up but okay."

"Where is she?" Cara charged into the loft, searching for her friend.

The powder-room door opened and Lexie emerged, her face pale, her makeup partially washed off and her shoulders bravely squared. "Y'all made it here in record time," she said.

Cara ran to Lexie and grabbed her by the arms, then looked her over from head to toe. "Thank God you're all in one piece." She glanced back at the detective. "Geoff and I followed Bain the whole way. People get out of the way for a policemen's flashing light."

Desmond came up behind Cara, reached around her and took Lexie's free hand. He gave it a squeeze. "I need to go downstairs and play ringleader to the circus out there. I'll get back to you as soon as possible, and I'll need you to answer a few questions."

"Go. Do what you need to do," Lexie told him. "Deke will take care of things here."

Desmond glanced at Deke. "Actually, I need Mr. Bronson to go with me and fill me in on what he saw. But Mr. Monday will stay here with you and Cara."

Cara pulled Lexie toward the sofa. The two women sat side by side and began talking softly, almost whispering.

When Desmond left the apartment, Deke went with him. As they waited at the elevator, Desmond asked, "Were there any people in those cars that blew up out back?"

"Not that I could see."

"Look, I haven't said anything to Cara, but she and Lexie will have to be told that another one of the employees who was injured in the bomb explosion yesterday died about three o'clock this morning."

"Crap," Deke mumbled under his breath.

"Whoever this guy is, he's killed two people already. If he wants Lexie dead, he's not going to stop trying until we catch him. Same things holds true for Cara."

"He knows where Lexie works and where she lives," Deke said. "And he has her cell phone number. My guess is that he's been planning this for a while, probably stalking Lexie, and maybe Ms. Bedell, too."

"Look, what I'm about to say has nothing to do with my doubting your abilities as a bodyguard, but Cara suggested—and I agree—that it would be best if Lexie moves into the Bedell mansion. The security system is top-notch, so it'll be far more difficult for anyone to get to either of them there."

"I have no problem with that suggestion," Deke said. "As a matter of fact, I agree. But I'm not the one you have to convince."

The elevator doors opened. Deke followed Desmond inside, and they rode down together, neither saying a word.

When they exited the elevator and walked outside, a group of Chattanooga PD employees swarmed about like worker bees, protecting the crime scene and gathering information.

"I need to speak to a few people, then I want you to go over every step you and Lexie took this morning after you left her apartment." Desmond lifted his hand and called to a stocky, redhaired guy in civilian clothes, but wearing a badge on a chain around his neck. As he came toward the detective, Deke noticed he was chewing gum ninety-to-nothing.

Suddenly Deke's cell phone rang. He removed it from his belt clip, noted the caller ID and answered.

"Yeah, Geoff, what is it?"

"Ms. Murrough just received another phone call from our mad bomber."

"Son of a bitch," Deke cursed. "What did he say?"

Silence.

"What is it?" Deke asked.

"The caller told her that she should have died in Gadi, and he was going to rectify that error very soon."

CHAPTER SIX

"IT'S ONLY temporary, just until Bain catches this guy." Cara sat on the bed while Lexie packed enough clothes for a week.

"I understand that I'll be safer at your place than here in my apartment, but I hate the very idea of being forced from my home by some psycho."

"I know. I'd feel the same way," Cara said. "And I promise that you'll be able to go back to work in a few days. As soon as the police department is finished with the crime scene, I'll have this place surrounded with security. If our mad bomber's goal is to scare us to death and somehow shut down Helping Hands, then we'll show him he can't do either."

"Yeah, we'll show him." Lexie forced a weak smile. "I'm sorry you're involved in this, and that Helping Hands is also a target. It's apparent that I'm the one this man has a grudge against."

Cara hopped up off the bed and, as Lexie closed her suitcase, put her hand on Lexie's shoulder. "Bain thinks that knowing there's a Gadi connection will help him find out who this guy is. He's either someone who's fixated on you and knows your life story, or he's someone from your past, or—"

"Or he has nothing to do with Gadi, and he said what he did to throw us off track."

Frowning, Cara squeezed Lexie's shoulder. "There is that possibility."

Geoff Monday peered into the bedroom. "You ladies need any help?"

"Would you get Lexie's bags, please?" Cara pointed to the midsize suitcase and small overnight bag lying at the foot of the bed.

"Yes, ma'am." He came into the room, picked up both bags and headed back into the living room.

"Where's Mr. Bronson?" Lexie asked.

"Deke's bringing the car around to the front of the building. He'll be waiting for us whenever we're ready."

Lexie nodded, then turned to Cara. "Thank you for providing me with a bodyguard. I know a Dundee agent is terribly expensive. I feel that I should be paying for—"

With a dismissive wave of her hand and a disapproving hiss, Cara stopped Lexie in midsentence. "Hell, I've got more money than God, don't I? At least that's what I've been told. What I'm paying our two Dundee agents is pocket change."

Cara's good-natured chuckle brought a wide smile to Lexie's lips.

"Ready?" Cara asked.

"Ready."

After Lexie armed her security system and locked her door, they rode the elevator downstairs and met Deke out front. He had parked Cara's Mercedes illegally directly in front of the apartment building and was standing, arms crossed over his chest, and hips resting against the hood in front of the car. The moment he saw them, he straightened to his six-four height and came forward to escort Lexie and Cara, while Geoff put the bags in the trunk.

Once settled inside, the two women in the backseat, with Deke driving and Geoff riding shotgun, Cara said, "Look, I'm going in to the office today. There are some things I simply can't handle from home. Geoff will be with me, and the security there is impeccable." She patted Lexie's hand. "Deke will take you to the house. I've already called ahead, and Aldridge has your rooms ready. Make yourself at home."

"Thank you." Lexie forced a smile.

Ten minutes later they dropped Cara and Geoff off at Bedell, Inc., where they were met by four security officers. As soon Lexie moved from the backseat to the front, Deke took off, straight down Broad Street. After a twenty-minute drive in silence, they arrived at their destination. The Bedell antebellum mansion had been built by one of Cara's ancestors, back when anyone with money and social standing in the Chattanooga area lived on Lookout Mountain. The security gates opened after Deke punched in the code Geoff had given him. He parked in the garage, as he'd been instructed, and then carried Lexie's bags to the front door, where Aldridge met them.

"Please come in, Ms. Murrough," the butler said. "I'll show you and Mr. Bronson to your rooms."

As they followed Aldridge, Lexie glanced around at all the opulence and wondered how anyone could be comfortable living in a house the size of a small hotel. She had been born into a middle-class family in Valdosta, Georgia. Her dad, who had died her freshman year of college, had been a high-school baseball coach and her mother a dietician at the local hospital. Their home had been a sprawling seventies ranch, with a swimming pool, which had made her the envy of the neighborhood kids. She had never been exposed to the genuinely rich until college, when one of her room-mates, a debutante from an old horse-breeding family from Kentucky, had invited her home for a weekend. Even Molly Louise Downs's Rolling Acres estate had been nothing to compare to the Bedell home. But then, the Downs had only been millionaires.

"If these accommodations aren't suitable, please let me know and I'll make other arrangements." Aldridge opened a door that led into a huge bedroom filled with antiques and decorated in various shades of green, blue and pink. A lady's bedroom.

"This is lovely." Lexie's gaze traveled around the room, taking in the four-poster bed, eight-foot armoire and the sitting area by the windows.

"Mr. Bronson, your room is next door," Aldridge said. "Each room has its own bath, but there is a con-necting door that locks." He glanced directly at Deke. "This used to be the nursery, and the connecting room was the nanny's."

"I'm sure it's fine," Deke replied.

Aldridge nodded. "I'll see that your luggage is brought up later." He looked from Deke to Lexie. "If that will be all?"

"Yes, thank you," Lexie said.

Deke nodded.

"Lunch is at one," Aldridge told them. "If you prefer it earlier or later, please let me know and I'll inform Mrs. Eddins, our cook."

"One o'clock will be fine," Lexie replied.

As soon as Aldridge disappeared down the hall, Deke walked over to the windows behind the sitting area, glanced outside and said, "This is quite a place, isn't it?"

"Yes," Lexie agreed. "It's rather formidable."

"Whoever said 'the rich aren't like you and me' sure knew what they were talking about."

Smiling, Lexie studied Deke Bronson, from his thick black hair, cut short and neat, to his big feet, clad in brown leather loafers. In his own super-masculine way, he was every bit as formidable as the Bedell mansion. She wondered if he was aware of that fact. Did he know he oozed sex appeal from every pore? Did he realize that she found him irresistibly attractive and yet, at the same time, everything feminine within her warned her that he was dangerous?

"Is there anything I can do to help you?" he asked.

"Uh…no, thank you. When Aldridge brings up our bags, I'll unpack and probably read for a while. I brought along a couple of paperbacks." She looked everywhere—over his shoulder, at the wall behind him—except directly at him.

"If you don't mind, I'll check out my quarters." He walked toward the partially open door that connected their rooms, then paused for a moment. "Don't lock this door. I'll respect your privacy and knock before coming in."

When her gaze met his, she saw something raw and primitive in the look he gave her. Or was she imagining things simply because of the way he made her feel? When she couldn't manage a verbal reply, she nodded her head. Accepting that response, he went into the adjoining room and quietly closed the door behind him.

With a fluttering rush tingling along her nerve endings, Lexie sucked in a deep breath as she slumped onto the pink-and-green striped sofa.

This is ridiculous! I'm acting like a teenager with a crush on a rock star.

Okay, so she hadn't had sex in quite some time, not since a very brief affair with an old colleague from UBC had ended rather unpleasantly three years ago. She had discovered that his real interest was in the three-million-dollar settlement she had received from UBC and not in her. Before that, she'd been celibate since she'd been shot and undergone several surgeries and years of rehab. Even before being crippled, she'd had a grand total of two relationships. She had lost her virginity her sophomore year in college, to the star pitcher of the baseball team. She'd been in love for the first time in her life. But when he was chosen for a major league team and knew he would be traveling all the time and constantly surrounded by adoring groupies, they had mutually agreed that he needed his freedom. The second time she'd fallen in love, she'd been twenty-four. She had actually been engaged to Wes Harris, an up-and-coming young Atlanta lawyer, when she went to Gadi ten years ago. Odd thing about Wes— he hadn't wanted to be tied down to a crippled wife. Why hadn't she realized before then that she'd been little more than arm-candy to him, someone he could show off and say, "This is mine. Isn't she gorgeous? Isn't she perfect?"

Having a sexual relationship with her bodyguard would be highly inappropriate. Surely the Dundee Agency had rules and regulations about such things. Besides that, she had just met Deke and knew nothing about him. She didn't have any idea how old he was, if he was married—oh, my God, what if he was married?

Lexie Murrough, you have lost your mind! There's a psycho out there threatening to kill you. You've had to move out of your home. You're being watched by a hired guard 24/7. And what's your greatest concern? Is Deke Bronson married or single?

DEKE LEANED his shoulders and the back of his head against the closed door and blew out an exasperated breath. He couldn't do this. He'd been nuts for thinking he could. This evening, when Geoff and Cara Bedell returned to the mansion, he would take Geoff aside and tell him that they needed to change clients. Between the two of them, they should be able to come up with a halfway legitimate-sounding reason for switching horses midstream.

Lexie Murrough had changed in the past ten years, since that long-ago day in Gadi when he had carried her bloody body in his arms. Against orders, he had taken her aboard the MH-60 Blackhawk that had rescued his four-man team of Special Ops agents who had been sent in to assassinate Babu Tum. Another four-man team had been sent with them, as backup, and all but one of the eight men made it back alive to the choppers.

Deke had waited outside her hospital room for hours, until he'd been forced to leave. He'd been told that his bullet had injured her spinal cord. She hadn't been the first innocent person caught in crossfire, and she wouldn't be the last. But he'd never shot a fellow American—a woman, for God's sake. For weeks afterward she had plagued his dreams, creating nightmares that nearly drove him crazy. Looking back, he knew that what had happened with Lexie had been the catalyst that prompted him to resign from the army and join Geoff Monday in the underbelly world of soldiers-for-hire. Working as mercenaries for over seven years, he and Geoff had formed a strong bond of male friendship. And when the nightmares about Lexie returned—and after every assignment, they had—Geoff was always there, helping him through those dark moments of the soul. On those occasions, they had gotten drunk and whored around as if there were no tomorrow.

He had kept track of Lexie for five years, during the surgeries and physical therapy that had given her back the use of her legs. Eventually he had admitted to himself that he was obsessed with her and that, for the sake of his sanity, he needed to cut her loose.

Fate had a way of playing cruel tricks on a guy.

Women came and went in his life, few lasting beyond two dates. Casual relationships, no strings attached. Here today and gone tomorrow. He'd been married once, when he was in his early twenties and a second lieutenant, fresh out of college and new to the army. Abby had been a blind date and a one-night stand he'd knocked up. She'd been an okay kid—only nineteen—and as unprepared for marriage and parenthood as he'd been. They'd given it their best shot, and for a while, he'd thought maybe they would make it, especially after their son was born. They had named him Andrew, after her grandfather, whom she had adored. Their little Andrew had lived ten weeks and three days. Crib death. Nobody's fault.

After they buried Andrew, they'd gotten a divorce and gone their separate ways. He hadn't seen or heard from Abby in years. The last he knew of her, she had remarried and had two kids, a boy and a girl.

Why am I thinking about Abby and Andrew? They have nothing to do with Lexie Murrough.

Having sex with Abby had been a youthfully foolish mistake. Despite hopping into the sack with him on their first date, she had actually been a good girl, just lonely and hungry for love and attention.

Lexie, too, was a good girl—a good woman. And she was the last woman on earth he should be thinking about having sex with, but there it was—the truth. He wanted Lexie. Just looking at her gave him a hard-on. Any man would want her. She was beautiful. She was loving and caring. And she was off limits to him.

It wasn't as if he was some green kid who thought with his dick instead of his head. He was forty-one damn years old. Old enough to know that whatever attraction he felt for Lexie was all mixed up with the old guilt and remorse he'd lived with ever since shooting her. Crazy as it sounded, Lexie was the only woman who had ever been in his life, been a part of him, for ten years. Yeah, so his relationship with her existed only in his mind and mostly in his nightmares. But the feel of her almost lifeless body in his arms had left an indelible mark on him, his mind and his soul.

Deke paced the floor, considering his options. He could ask Geoff to swap places with him, but that wouldn't take him completely away from Lexie. And that was where he needed to be—as far away from her as possible. He should call Daisy and tell her to find a replacement for him. But what reason could he give her? What could he say? Get me the hell away from Lexie Murrough before I toss her down on the nearest bed and fuck her until I can't see straight?

Pausing in the middle of the room, Deke rubbed the back of his neck and stretched his shoulders.

A light rap on the door that led into the hall gained his attention. "Yeah?"

"It's Aldridge, sir. I have your luggage."

"Be right there."

He opened the door and took his one duffel bag from the butler. "Thanks."

"Ms. Murrough asked me to inquire whether you'd like to join her for a walk around the grounds."

"I'll go over and talk to Ms. Murrough." Deke hitched his thumb toward the connecting door.

"Very good, sir."

As soon as Aldridge left, Deke tapped on the closed door between his room and Lexie's.

"Yes, please come in," she said.

When he entered her room, she turned from where she'd been standing near the windows, gazing out at the courtyard centered between the two main wings of the old house. She had removed her quilted jacket, revealing her simple button-down blouse tucked neatly into her jeans. A thin purple leather belt accented her small waist. He noted that despite her slender frame, she possessed a very appealing hour-glass shape. A womanly body. The kind of curvy body most men liked.

"Aldridge said you wanted to take a walk." Deke paused several feet away from her.

"I assume it's safe to take a walk, since the entire estate is fenced, and the fence and gates are monitored," Lexie said.

He glanced at her legs and then at the cane she held. "You don't want to overdo."

"Walking is good for me. It's the best exercise there is, and it's a great stress reliever."

"Does it cause you any pain—walking?"

"No, not any longer."

"But it did at one time?"

She nodded.

"I'm sorry." *God, you don't know how sorry I am. When I watch you limp as you walk, when I see you relying heavily on your cane, I wonder what you'd think of me if you knew I was the man who shot you.* When she looked at him questioningly, Deke cleared his throat. "I apologize for getting personal. It was none of my business."

"That's all right. I'm not overly sensitive about my handicap."

After clearing his throat again, Deke said, "Are you ready?"

"Let me get my jacket."

"Let me." He picked up the quilted purple jacket off the sofa arm and held it up so that she could simply walk into it.

Once she slipped it on, one arm at a time, changing her cane from one hand to the other in the process, Deke lightly ran his hands over her shoulders, then forced himself to stop touching her. He stepped away from her just as she turned and reached out to place her arm through his.

"I'll give you the grand tour," Lexie said. "There are several courtyards, outdoor and indoor swimming pools, tennis courts, a greenhouse, an old servants' cottage, a six-car garage—which you've seen—and several garden areas."

"How many acres?" Deke asked.

"I'm not sure. Probably five, at most, but every square foot has been utilized."

He led her out into the hall, moving as slowly as she needed him to. "And the entire estate is fenced?"

"That's right."

When she struggled slightly as they walked down the

large curving staircase, Deke wondered if this place didn't have an elevator. But he would be damned before he asked her. If there was one, apparently Lexie had chosen not to use it.

"How many entrances and exits are there to the estate?"

"I'm not sure, but I know there are both back and front entrances with electronic gates."

"Maybe we should confine our walk to areas near the house," he suggested. "At least until I've taken a look at the grounds and done a background check of all the servants."

"You can't possibly think that someone who works here in Cara's home could be—"

"Anything is possible. And at this point, everyone is suspect."

"How cynical."

"Yeah, well, a healthy dose of cynicism has saved my life on more than one occasion. In my business it pays not to trust anyone."

"I hope you don't have the same philosophy when it comes to your personal life." She gasped. "Oh, I'm so sorry, Mr. Bronson. That was highly inappropriate and none of my business."

Deke paused as they reached the marble-floored foyer. "We both seem to be asking questions that are none of our business, don't we? Spending so much time together, it was bound to happen and probably will again." *But you're going to get out of this assignment,* he reminded himself.

"With me, it probably will," she admitted. "I tend to be nosy. Some people politely call it inquisitive. When I was a reporter, all my friends said I was a natural."

Deke opened the front door and led Lexie outside,

out into the crisp autumn air and warm morning sun-shine.

"It's a glorious day, isn't it?" She looked up at the cloudless blue sky.

Deke followed her gaze. "Yeah, I guess it is."

Lexie smiled. "Only you'd probably never use the word *glorious,* would you?"

He grunted. "Probably not."

She tightened her hold on his arm. "There's a brick walkway all the way around to the back courtyard. We can see it from our bedroom windows. Did you notice all the chrysanthemums?"

"Those would be the yellow flowers in the big pots, right?"

She laughed. "Right."

Deke couldn't remember ever thinking a woman's laughter was beautiful. But Lexie's was. Almost as beautiful as the woman herself.

HE HAD A LITTLE over a month to torment Lexie Mur-rough before he would kill her. The day and time of her death had been decided by the Majeed's decree to strike at the heart of the Tennessee Valley and show the Americans how truly vulnerable they were. The Majeed had chosen this area of the country because no one would be expecting a series of attacks in small cities through-out the South. The purpose was not to kill the largest number of people possible but to show the citizens that they were not safe, and to remind this godless country that their days as a world power would soon come to an end.

His name—his true name—would be remembered. He would be counted among the faithful, a true hero of the cause. If only his father could see him now and know how brave, how strong and how fearless he had become.

"I will avenge your death."

Make the American whore pay dearly, his father's voice whispered inside his head, as it so often did. Sometimes they had entire conversations. *Set an example with her death. Show the world what happens to those who mock us.*

For ten years, Lexie Murrough's face had tortured him. That beautiful blond American reporter, the symbol of all that was evil in the Western world. He would forever associate her with his father's assassination.

He couldn't seek revenge against the soldiers who had stormed in during the inauguration and coldly, brutally murdered his father, because he had no idea who they were. But in the great holy war that was to come, all enemy soldiers would pay with their lives. In the meantime, he would punish Lexie Murrough. And if Cara Bedell did not withdraw her support from Helping Hands, she, too, would have to die.

CHAPTER SEVEN

"I HATE like blue blazes that I have to go on this damn business trip," Cara told Lexie. "Of all times for us to have a crisis in Mexico City. The managers and even the local VP have tried to resolve the problem, but it's becoming a lose-lose situation. I have no choice but to personally handle the negotiations and get things back on track."

"Stop stressing out about this," Lexie said. "You do what you have to do. I'll be fine. I'm living in this fortress you call a home, and I have an around-the-clock bodyguard."

"I know, but I feel as if I'm deserting you, going off and leaving you to face everything alone."

"I'm hardly alone. I have Mr. Bronson and Bain and a dozen Helping Hands employees, including Toni."

"Would you feel better if Toni came here and stayed with you?" Cara tossed her bottle of hairspray into her oversize cosmetics bag and dumped the bag into her Louis Vuitton suitcase.

"I don't need Toni here to hold my hand. Besides, I'll see her every day at work once we can get back into our building. Do you have any idea when…?"

"Whenever Bain gives us the green light," Cara said. "I have a security team in place, ready to go to work immediately, and for the time being, you'll have two personal bodyguards at your beck and call."

"I really think you should take Geoff Monday with you."

"He'll escort me to the airport, but I've arranged for my usual corporate security people—one man and one woman—to accompany me on this trip."

A soft rap on the door of Cara's bedroom suite alerted them before Geoff opened the door and peered inside. "Lieutenant Desmond is here."

Cara nodded. "We'll be right there." She turned to Lexie. "Ready?"

"I suppose so, although I almost dread whatever he's found out about the bombings."

"Knowledge is power."

"Yes, I know. But ignorance is bliss."

Cara and Lexie laughed, breaking the tension that fear and uncertainty had created.

When they entered the hallway, their bodyguards fell into step behind them, and followed them downstairs and into the living room. Lexie wondered if she would ever get used to having someone shadow her every move. Probably not.

Bain and his partner, Mike Swain, were standing on opposite sides of the huge room, and when the foursome entered, Sergeant Swain practically stood at attention.

Cara swept into the room with ease, immediately going into hostess mode, offering the detectives something nonalcoholic to drink and inviting everyone to take a seat. Bain sat on the sofa beside Lexie, while Cara took a seat opposite them. Sergeant Swain stood near the pocket doors, crossed his arms over his chest and scanned the room. Geoff and Deke took their positions at a discreet distance behind their charges.

"The CSI team finished up at Helping Hands today, so y'all can return whenever you'd like," Bain said. "But I suggest that you keep the area of the building where the bomb did the greatest damage closed off until it's cleaned up and repaired."

"A contractor is ready to go in immediately," Cara said. "Once he determines the building is safe, then Lexie can inform her employees that Helping Hands will be back in business at the downtown headquarters. But until then—be that tomorrow or next week—Lexie can conduct business from here. She can use my home office or the study, or whichever room suits her needs."

Bain looked at Lexie. "I suggest you limit the number of Helping Hands employees that you bring here to work with you."

Before she could reply, Deke added, "Make that no more than one or two. Only those you trust implicitly."

"I trust all my employees," Lexie said.

"Do you trust all of them with your life?" Deke asked.

When Lexie opened her mouth to reply, Bain spoke. "Why don't you have Toni help you, but no one else? Until we're certain that none of the Gadians who work at Helping Hands were involved—"

"You don't actually believe that Robert or Vega or Malik could be the bomber, do you?"

"Sorry, Lexie, but Toni is the only Helping Hands employee who we've ruled out so far." Bain pivoted slightly and glanced over his shoulder at Deke. "Ty Garrett phoned me right before I left to come here. He said that Dundee's is compiling a complete report on each employee and focusing on the Gadians. We're doing the same, but with Dundee's worldwide contacts and resources, I figure Garrett's report will be more in-depth than ours."

"I'm sure Ty told you that Dundee's will share all our information with the Chattanooga PD," Deke said.

Bain nodded. "At this point, we have two people dead as a result of Wednesday's bombing and one still in critical condition at Erlanger. That means we're dealing with a murder case. Luckily, there were no injuries related to this morning's car bombings."

"Thank goodness," Lexie whispered under her breath.

"Can you tell us something we don't know?" Cara asked impatiently.

Bain's gaze collided with hers. "We found the remote control our bomber used Wednesday in a Dumpster behind the building next door. The crime scene team was able to find pieces of the bombs from both yesterday and this morning." He glanced from Deke to Geoff. "As y'all know, bomb-scene searches can be hit-and-miss, but we recovered quite a bit of debris at both sites. Now the real work will begin with the lab analysis, which could take weeks."

"Is there anything we can do to expedite matters?" Cara inquired. "I can put all the corporation's resources behind—"

"This is a police matter," Bain told her, his voice even, but edged with aggravation. "If we're lucky, we might actually find the bomber's fingerprint on a fragment or use the parts to enable us to trace a source of one or more of the components."

"And just how can you do that?" Cara asked.

"I believe the FBI has a database of recovered bomb

parts that helps to determine if there might be a link between one blast and another," Deke said.

"That's right." Bain looked directly at Cara. "If our bomber has done this before, it's possible the FBI database can help us."

"Is that it? Is that all you can do?" Cara kept her gaze linked with Bain's.

"That's it," Bain said. "For now."

Cara rose to her feet. "Then if you'll excuse me, I have to leave for the airport as soon as possible." She glanced at Geoff. "Would you have my chauffeur bring the car around, please? I'll have Aldridge take my bags outside."

"Where are you going?" Bain asked as she stood.

"A business trip to Mexico City," Cara replied. "I'm taking the Bedell jet down there tonight, so I can be ready to roll up my sleeves and get to work on solving our problems first thing in the morning."

Bain eyed Geoff. "Is Mr. Monday going with you?"

"No, he's going with me to the airport, and then two Bedell, Inc. security guards will take over and accompany me to Mexico."

"While she's gone, I'll be relieving Deke whenever necessary, and also working with Ty on the investigative end of things when he arrives tomorrow," Geoff said.

Just as the meeting broke up, Aldridge appeared in the doorway.

"Yes, Aldridge, what is it?" Cara asked.

"A Ms. Wells and a Mr. Holston are here, and they say it's urgent that they speak to Ms. Murrough."

"Show them in," Cara said.

"Very well, madam."

Deke glanced at Lexie. "Ms. Wells is your assistant, right? Who is this Mr. Holston?"

"He's Toni's boyfriend," Lexie replied.

Deke nodded.

Within moments, Toni came rushing into the living room, Jafari following her. Toni, with her golden-tan skin, hazel eyes, slender body and cover-model face, and Jafari, with his aged-leather-brown skin, ebony eyes and stylishly-clad athletic body, were eyecatching singly, but together the two made a strikingly beautiful couple.

Toni's gaze darted around the room, but she quickly zeroed in on Lexie and made a beeline directly to her. "You are not going to believe this. I'm not sure I believe it myself. It's the craziest thing. And why someone sent it to me and not you, I can't imagine. At first I didn't understand what—"

"Calm yourself." Jafari placed his arm around Toni's shoulders. "Tell them what you're talking about."

"It came in today's mail, but I spent most of the afternoon with Jafari, so we didn't go back to my place until just a little while ago," Toni said. "And there it was in my mailbox."

"There what was?" Lexie asked.

"A manila envelope addressed to me, with no return address. And inside were newspaper clippings, or rather, copies of old newspaper clippings."

Toni had everyone's full attention at that point. "What kind of newspaper clippings?" Bain asked.

Toni pulled away from Jafari and reached out to take Lexie's hands in hers. "Articles from ten years ago, all about the assassination of Babu Tum in Gadi and about you, Lexie. About your cameraman being killed and you being shot, and about your mother and stepfather suing UBC and the huge settlement you received."

"Do you have the clippings with you?" Bain asked.

Releasing Lexie's hands, Toni slid her large leather purse off her shoulder, unzipped it and reached inside, then pulled out a manila envelope and held it out to Lexie.

Sergeant Swain moved quickly and grabbed the envelope by one corner. "There are already more than enough fingerprints on it as it is." He looked at Bain. "Should I get this to the lab right away?"

Bain shook his head. "If this package came from our bomber, I doubt he was stupid enough to leave any of his fingerprints on it, but we'll have the lab check it anyway. No telling how many postal workers handled it before Toni and Jafari did."

"Why send those clippings to me?" Toni stared at Lexie, a perplexed expression on her face.

"I don't know, but whatever his reason, it seems to be more proof that I'm his target," Lexie said.

"*If* the bomber sent the clippings," Geoff said.

"He did. I know, on some gut level—" Lexie laid her closed fist over her belly "—that the bomber mailed Toni the clippings, and that he's somehow connected to my past, to what happened to me in Gadi."

"That was ten years ago," Cara said. "Maybe his connection to Gadi is more recent. He could be someone who simply hates Americans and resents Helping Hands being involved in the rebuilding of Gadi since their civil war."

"There are too many possible scenarios for us to discuss them all tonight." Bain motioned to his partner, who was still holding the envelope pinched between his forefinger and thumb. "Sergeant Swain and I will keep in touch." He glanced at Cara. "Have a safe trip, Ms. Bedell."

"Thank you."

As soon as Bain and his partner exited the room, Cara excused herself, and Geoff followed her. After Toni hugged Lexie, they walked together over to the sofa and sat.

"This whole thing is just crazy," Toni said. "It doesn't make any sense. What's been happening these past two days is like something from a movie. We're just ordinary people living in Chattanooga, Tennessee. We should be safe to live our lives without fear."

"No one is safe now," Jafari said. "I believe 9/11 proved that to the world, but especially to America."

"Well, our bomber isn't part of some terrorist plot," Toni said. "He's just one crazy man who knows how to build bombs."

"He is a lone man with a specific agenda," Deke said.

"And what is his agenda?" Jafari asked.

"To torment Lexie before he kills her," Deke replied.

LONG AFTER everyone had left—the Chattanooga PD to do their job, Cara off to Mexico City to avert a business crisis, Geoff Monday to his bedroom for the night, and Toni and Jafari home to her apartment—Lexie found it impossible to relax, let alone sleep. She'd taken a shower and gone through her normal bedtime routine, even tried to read, but her mind kept drifting back to those newspaper clippings. Why send them to Toni? Did the bomber think Lexie's assistant didn't know anything about her past? Or did he send them to Toni to show Lexie that he could reach her closest friends, that they, too, weren't safe?

Why did the bomber hate her enough to want to kill her? What had she done to him?

You should have died in Gadi.

His words kept repeating themselves inside her head. Over and over again, a terrifying litany from which she couldn't escape.

I'm going to rectify that error very soon.

Did he really intend to kill her, or simply scare her to death?

Deke had pointed out that if he had wanted to kill her, he could have, either with the bomb at Helping Hands or with the car bombs. He was playing with her, tormenting her, like a cat with a captured mouse. But why?

There were factions in Gadi that resented any American presence in their country, even a benevolent organization like Helping Hands that was not involved in the country's politics. But why would they send someone to America to kill her? Why not wait until the next time she visited Gadi? And why torment her before killing her?

Because it's personal, an inner voice said.

He hates me. Not just America. Not just Helping Hands. But me, Lexie Murrough.

Apparently this man's hatred had been festering for quite some time. As far back as the day Babu Tum was assassinated? Was it possible that their mad bomber had been at the inauguration ceremonies that day? But why would he hate her? She had been a victim that day as surely as the newly elected president had been.

Giving up on getting any sleep, Lexie threw back the covers and got out of bed. It had been years since she'd needed medication to help her sleep on a regular basis, but she still kept a prescription updated for use on the odd night when one of the old nightmares returned to haunt her. After years of daily medications for pain, she hated to take any kind of medicine unless it was absolutely nec--essary. A mug of hot chocolate might do the trick. But she wasn't at home, where all she had to do was go into the kitchen and prepare something for herself. Here at the Bedell mansion, it would require a long trek to a kitchen with which she was unfamiliar. And she certainly wouldn't call one of the servants and wake someone up just to prepare a cup of hot chocolate for her.

Lexie paced around the room, looking out the windows, studying the artwork hanging on the walls, checking the contents of the antique bookcase and trying not to glance at the clock on the mantel.

After she had paced for a while, she sat down and tried to read again. Then, when she couldn't concentrate, she got up and walked toward the bathroom.

Just take a damn sleeping pill and go back to bed!

Hearing a bumping noise, she paused and listened, then realized someone was tapping on the connecting door between her room and Deke's. Apparently she had awakened him. She hadn't even thought about what a loud noise her cane made, thumping against the wooden floor.

Changing course, she moved to the closed but unlocked door and called his name. "Deke?"

"Are you all right?" he asked.

She opened the door just a crack. Peering up at him, she offered an apology for disturbing him. "I'm sorry if I woke you."

"I haven't been asleep."

"It's my fault. Living alone, I'm unaccustomed to having to think about anyone else, and I forget how noisy my cane can be. I'm just fortunate that Mr. Rafferty who lives in the apartment below me is hard of hearing." A fragile smile lifted the corners of her mouth. "I'll try to be quiet."

"You didn't keep me up," he told her. "As a matter of fact, Geoff and I have been discussing this case, and he just left to go to his room a few minutes ago."

Lexie eased open the door a little farther. "What in particular were y'all talking about?"

"Mind if I come in?" he asked.

"Uh…sure." Why hadn't she put on a robe before starting this conversation? Even her thin silk robe would have been better than nothing.

She gestured to the sitting alcove.

"Please, come in and sit down," she said.

Together they walked to the sofa, and after she sat and hung her cane over the narrow arm of the couch, Deke sat beside her. When standing, it was obvious just how tall he was, how broad-shouldered and muscular, but it wasn't until they were sitting side by side that she truly realized what a big man he was. He took up such a large portion of the small sofa that his left arm brushed against her right shoulder. Something purely feminine within her longed for him to lift his arm and put it around her.

"What do you know about your friend Toni's boy-friend?" Deke asked.

"Quite a bit, actually," Lexie replied. "Why do you ask?"

She looked at Deke, but he didn't look back. His gaze darted about the room, not settling on anything, as if he was deliberately trying to avoid making eye contact with her.

"He's not American," Deke said.

"No, he's not, but what has that got to do with—

My God, you don't suspect Jafari of being the bomber, do you?"

"I told you that everyone is a suspect."

"Jafari isn't Gadian. He was born in Ethiopia and grew up in London. His father was English and his mother Ethiopian."

"You don't mind if we run a check on him, do you?"

"I don't mind at all, but I'm sure you'll be wasting your time."

"You're too trusting, Ms. Murrough."

"And you're too suspicious, Mr. Bronson."

He finally looked at her then, and for half a second her heart caught in her throat. His intense gaze rattled her, because she saw yearning in his eyes. Or was she simply imagining it?

After swallowing, she breathed in softly, then said, "Considering the situation, don't you think it's ridiculous for us not to use our given names?"

"You're a Dundee client, I'm your bodyguard, your employee, and out of respect for our positions—"

"I'd feel more comfortable if you called me Lexie."

He nodded. "If that's what you want…Lexie."

Her name came from his lips slowly, softly. A verbal caress.

She shivered.

"Are you cold?" he asked.

"A bit chilly," she lied.

She felt his gaze drift over her, gliding smoothly down her throat, over her breasts, across her belly, then pausing at the apex between her thighs. After only a slight hesitation, he moved on and skimmed her legs, all the way to her satin house slippers; then he moved upward until he reached her chest. Her nipples pressed against the silk fabric of her pajama top, as if begging for his touch.

"Would you like me to get your robe for you?" he asked.

"Yes." She croaked the word. "Thank you. It's lying at the foot of the bed."

He got up, walked across the room, picked up her silk housecoat and brought it to her. When she grasped the sofa arm, intending to lift herself to her feet, he draped the robe over one arm, then placed his hands on either side of her waist and brought her up and onto her feet. Her body grazed his hard chest. At least he was still dressed, still wore his plaid shirt and tan slacks, and, thank God, he had removed his shoulder holster.

Holding her with one hand, he used the other to lift her robe and hang it around her shoulders. When she tried to slip her arms into the robe, she kept missing the sleeve openings, which made her feel like an idiot. Without saying a word, Deke assisted her, his movements swift and sure. Once her arms were in place, he pulled the lapels together and tied the sash.

Lexie could hardly breathe. He was so close, their bodies touching, his masculine heat warming her. Unable to resist the urge, she lifted one hand and laid it in the center of his chest.

He grabbed her hand in his and removed it, but he didn't release her. She looked up. He looked down. A sizzling current of lust ignited between them, both instantly recognizing the emotion for what it was.

"You don't want to do this," he told her.

She snatched her hand from his. "I'm sorry. I'm not usually so bold. It's just…" She shook her head. "I don't know exactly what it is."

"It happens all the time."

"What—your client coming on to you?" God, how embarrassing this was! She wished a hole would open up in the floor and swallow her.

"Female clients. Male bodyguards," Deke said. "I call it the somebody-to-watch-over-me syndrome."

"Oh, I see. This has happened to you so often that you've invented a special name for it, huh?"

"This is the first time it's happened to me," he admitted. "But I've seen it happen with other agents."

"Oh."

"If it makes you feel any better, I can tell you that the attraction works both ways." He lifted his big hand and brushed a strand of loose hair out of her face. When his knuckles brushed across her cheek, she shivered. "I've never been attracted to a client the way I am to you."

When she couldn't manage a reply, he said, "If you're uncomfortable with the situation, I can ask Geoff to—"

"I don't want Geoff. I want you." Realizing how her comment had sounded, she amended it by adding, "I prefer that you remain as my bodyguard. We're both adults. I believe we can deal with a little mutual attraction without acting on it."

"Yeah, sure we can." But the look in his eyes contradicted his words.

CHAPTER EIGHT

"IF YOU'RE determined to remain on this case, then swap assignments with Ty," Geoff suggested. "You need to get away from Lexie Murrough. The woman has you tied in knots. Every time you look at her, you remember that day in Gadi when she got caught in the crossfire."

Deke glared at his old friend. "Yeah, you're right." Partially right. Every time he looked at Lexie, he did remember that it had been his bullet that crippled her. Even though Geoff had tried to convince him that he could never be sure it had been his bullet that hit Lexie, he knew better. She had run directly into his line of vision just as he pulled the trigger. But he sure as hell wouldn't admit to anyone, not even Geoff, that for the past ten years Lexie had haunted him, that in a strange sort of way she was a part of him, of who he was and what he had become. He was a man whose soul was irrevocably damaged from years in the Delta Force and later as a mercenary. He might have escaped from his past and begun a new life when he'd hired on as a Dundee agent, but he had once been a trained killer. For those sins, there was no redemption.

"Why put yourself through this? What happened was an accident," Geoff said. "You know that as well as I do."

"If she knew the truth…"

"Don't do it. Don't tell her. Don't look to her for forgiveness. Just get on the phone, call Ty and—"

"No, you don't get it," Deke said. "This is my chance to do something for her, to take care of her, protect her. To make it up to her in some small way for having crippled her."

"You saved her life," Geoff reminded him. "Or have you forgotten that significant fact?"

"I haven't forgotten anything."

"I'm telling you—get away from her for her sake as well as yours. No matter what you do now, it won't change the past. Let it go. Let *her* go."

Deke glanced through the glass doors that opened into the indoor pool area where Lexie was finishing her laps and remembered what she had told him.

"Swimming is still one of the activities I can do as well as I did before…." When she had let her words trail off, he'd known she was thinking about that long-ago day in Gadi.

Lexie emerged from the pool, her body clad in a one-piece black suit that left nothing to the imagination. Although the suit was fairly modest by most standards, it clung to every curve, showing off her high, full breasts, small waist and curvy hips to their best advantage.

"She's beautiful, isn't she?" Geoff said.

Deke clenched his teeth. Yeah, she was beautiful, but he didn't need another man to tell him.

Geoff slapped Deke's back. "Do whatever you need to do to rid yourself of your Gadi demons. If that means staying on as Lexie's bodyguard and putting yourself through hell, then I suppose that's what you should do."

As Deke watched, Lexie eased down carefully and sat at the edge of the pool.

What if she slipped and fell when she tried to stand on the slippery tile surface surrounding the pool? He should have insisted on borrowing a pair of the dozen or more swim trunks kept for guests and gone swimming with her. That way he would be at her side, in case....

Damn, Bronson, she's gotten along for ten years without your help. You're acting as if she can't survive without you.

She picked up a large, colorful towel, and dried her face and hair. Deke swallowed hard and commanded his body not to react. Was being attracted to her, wanting her more than he'd wanted another woman in a long time, part of his punishment?

Once again in control of his body and his thoughts, he opened the glass door, walked into the pool area and left Geoff staring after him.

"Need some help?" Deke called to her.

She glanced over her shoulder and shook her head. "No thanks." Then she asked, "What time is it?"

"Two-twenty," he told her.

"That late, huh? Have Toni and the others shown up?"

"Not yet. But they're not due until two-thirty, are they?"

When she wrapped the towel around her neck and grabbed the bottom of a lounge chair to balance herself as she stood up, Deke held himself back. Every protective instinct he possessed urged him to help her, but he'd learned quickly that she hated being treated like someone with a physical handicap.

Once on her feet, she lifted her cane from where it hung on the back of the chair. "I need to grab a quick shower and get dressed. If they arrive before I'm ready, ask Geoff if he'll let them know I won't keep them waiting long. I was enjoying my swim so much that I forgot about the time."

"Geoff is going to stay here and wait for you," Deke told her. "I have some phone calls to make. I'll make the calls downstairs, so I can meet your employees if they arrive before you're ready."

Lexie frowned. "Please, don't interrogate them or frisk them or anything like that, okay?"

He studied her expression to see if she was joking.

She wasn't.

"Against my advice, you invited six Helping Hands employees here this afternoon," he said. "We do not have full background reports on these people. For all we know one of them could be—"

"They're not!" Lexie chopped her free hand through the air, expressing her exasperation. "But if you think one of them could be the bomber, then why not take this opportunity to study all of them while they're here? You can stand in a corner of the room and observe."

"I plan to do just that."

"Observe in silence. Understood?"

"Understood."

When she entered the dressing room connected to the pool area—which had only one way in and out—Deke stomped away across the tiled floor. Geoff opened the door for him as he exited.

"Keep an eye on her," Deke said.

"Are you actually taking my initial advice and leaving?"

"Drop it, will you?"

"Then you're not leaving?"

"I'm going to spy on her guests when they arrive. I've been given strict instructions not to frisk them or interrogate them or even speak to them, for that matter."

Geoff chuckled. "I take it that you implied one of her employees might be our mad bomber and she took offense."

"She's thinking with her heart and not her head."

"And what are you thinking with?"

Deke glowered at Geoff, then walked off before he said something he would later regret. After all, Geoff meant well. He was just trying to look out for a friend, whether that friend wanted him to or not.

Halfway down the hallway that led to the foyer, Deke ran into Aldridge, who nodded and spoke.

"Good afternoon, sir."

"Afternoon." Deke hitched his thumb in the direction of the foyer. "When Ms. Murrough's guests arrive, would you—"

"They just arrived, sir. I showed them into the study, as Ms. Murrough requested. I was on my way to let her know that they're here."

Deke waved his hand. "Don't bother. I'll tell her."

"Very well, sir."

Yeah, he'd let her know, only not right now. This was his opportunity to speak to her employees without her running interference.

The double pocket doors to the study had been left open, so when Deke approached, he not only saw all six people but heard them talking. Three were seated on the leather sofa, their backs to him. Toni and another woman stood together near the windows and were engaged in a quiet conversation, their backs also to the door. Another person paced the floor, and it wasn't until he paused, exposing his profile, that Deke knew for certain he was a man. Small, slender and, well, pretty, with his thick, wiry hair plaited in one long braid that hung down his back, he could easily be mistaken for a woman.

Deke slid up against the wall and inched closer to the door, then stood there and listened.

"I think the bomber mailed you those clippings because he wanted you to know that Lexie's reasons for her charity work in Gadi are directly tied to her past," one of the men seated on the sofa said. "Her motives for pouring so much money into Gadi could be seen as a salve to soothe her guilty conscience."

Toni snapped around and all but pounced on the man. "What do you think Lexie has to feel guilty about?"

"I did not say that she did," the man replied. "Only that perhaps it was what he wants you to think—that she wasn't always the generous and caring person she is now."

"Lexie was once a reporter, wasn't she?" another male voice, decidedly American, said. "She's made no secret of the fact that she was in Gadi covering the inauguration ceremonies the day the president was assassinated. We all know about her past. She has no secrets from us."

"If the police suspect the bomber is someone from Gadi, then, Robert, you and I will be questioned," the small man with the long braid said in a surprisingly deep voice as he glowered at the black man sitting on the sofa. "And perhaps you, too, Vega. Even though you are a woman, you are Gadian."

Deke continued listening to Lexie's employees, keeping out of sight while learning very little in the way of useful information. His conclusion was that each of them liked and respected Lexie, though if one of them hated her, he or she certainly wouldn't be stupid enough to admit it to the others.

He heard Lexie's cane striking lightly on the wooden floor several moments before she came up behind him and tapped him on the shoulder.

"What do you think you're doing?" she asked sotto voce.

He turned to face her. "Waiting for you," he answered just as softly.

"You were eavesdropping."

"I was gathering information."

"Why didn't you let me know my friends were here?"

"I was giving you time to shower and get dressed." He looked her up and down, noting she'd pulled her damp hair back into a ponytail and donned a pair of faded jeans and an oversized, long-sleeved cotton sweater. Fresh, clean, without a smidgen of makeup, she was one damn good-looking woman. No longer just another pretty girl, as she'd once been, but a woman in every sense of the word.

"Did you learn any deep, dark secrets while you were eavesdropping?" she asked, her voice rising.

Before he could reply, Toni Wells came to the door. "What are you two arguing about? Even if we couldn't make out what you're saying—"

"Deke was just playing detective." Lexie reached out and hugged Toni.

"Snooping, huh?" Toni smiled, showing a set of perfect white teeth.

"Something like that," Deke replied. "It's what I get

paid to do, along with using my body as a shield to protect Ms. Murrough."

Toni raised her eyebrows in a what's-going-on-here? expression. "Well, if I ever needed protection, I'd certainly want your body standing between me and danger."

"Really, Toni." Lexie's tone sounded as if she were scolding her friend, but her smile implied otherwise.

Toni slipped her arm through Deke's. "Come on in and join us. Our secrets are yours."

Deke liked Toni. He couldn't imagine anyone not appreciating how attractive she was or what a charming personality she had. He allowed her to escort him into the study, but once fully inside the room, he disengaged himself from her and moved quietly into a far corner, so he could survey the study and the people congregated there. A gold-framed portrait of a petite woman with red-gold hair dominated the room from its position over the mantel. Audrey Bedell, Cara's older sister, now deceased. His gaze traveled hurriedly over the antique furniture, the paneled walls and rows of floor-to-ceiling bookshelves before settling on the three people seated on the sofa: a young man, either African or African-American, a plump, middle-aged blonde and a guy in a business suit who kept squinting through his thick glasses. The effeminate man who'd been pacing had stopped and taken a seat. Deke noticed that he kept rubbing his hands together. Nervous? Or just an annoying habit? The sixth person, a young black woman with luminous dark eyes, remained by the windows, but she had turned and focused on Lexie as she entered the room.

"Thank y'all for coming here this afternoon." Lexie made the rounds of the room, squeezing hands and giving hugs. She was a touchy-feely woman who seemed to convey her thoughts and emotions through physical contact. "I have good news and bad news." She stood in front of the fireplace, all eyes on her.

When she glanced at Deke, everyone in the room followed her gaze, and suddenly they were all staring at him. "This is Deke Bronson, my bodyguard." She went through introductions quickly. "This is Vega Sharif." The doe-eyed black woman by the windows. "Malik Abdel." The pretty boy with the long, thick braided hair. "And Robert Lufti, Alice Kennedy and Farris Richardson." The other African man, the middle-aged blonde and the bespectacled businessman.

From the initial report on Helping Hands that Deke had studied, he knew that Robert, Vega and Malik were from Gadi, and that Vega and Malik had applied for U.S. citizenship. Alice was head of PR for the charity, and Farris Richardson was the accountant.

"The good news is that we're going back to work on Monday." A hum of unanimous approval vibrated throughout the room. "There will be a construction crew working to repair all the damage, and that should take several weeks. The bad news is that from now on, there will be heavy security in the building. One guard will patrol the exterior of the building, especially the back entrances and the parking lot. There will be two full-time guards on duty at the front entrance. They will check IDs, which will be issued to all of us when we arrive Monday morning, so try to get there about thirty minutes early."

"Are you coming in to work on Monday?" Farris Richardson asked.

"Yes, of course I am."

"Wouldn't it be wiser for you to stay here, where you know you'll be safe?" Vega moved farther into the room, a concerned frown etched on her face.

"Possibly," Lexie said. "But I refuse to allow some madman to dictate my actions and rule my life."

"Will more safety features, other than guards and employee IDs, be implemented?" Alice inquired. "And do you want me to issue some type of press release concerning the new safeguards?"

"I'll work with you on that press release," Lexie said. "And yes, there will be other safety features. Beginning Monday, the two back entrances to our building will no longer be accessible from the outside. They will be emergency exits and accessible only from the inside. And all visitors will be required to wear ID badges, and they must have an appointment beforehand."

"Do the police know anything more about who the bomber might be?" Malik asked, and Deke was once again taken aback by the pretty boy's baritone voice.

"No, not yet." Lexie glanced at Deke, as if requesting that he add something to her simple reply.

Deke cleared his throat, and once again everyone looked at him. "Dundee Security and Investigation agency is doing an independent investigation, and you should know that we're running background checks on every Helping Hands employee, including all of you. We're paying close attention to anyone with a connection to Gadi simply because, when the bomber called Ms. Murrough, he made a personal reference to Gadi."

"None of us would do anything to hurt Lexie," Vega Sharif told him, a slight quiver in her voice and a mist of tears glazing her black eyes.

"No one here is being accused of anything," Deke said.

"Certainly not," Lexie assured them. "Once Dundee finishes your background checks, they'll know what I already know—that each of you is a friend of mine and completely trustworthy."

Deke groaned inwardly. How could anyone her age, who knew the ugly side of the world the way she did, still be so damn trusting and caring?

For the next hour, Lexie discussed Helping Hands business with her "trusted" employees. Then they took a break, long enough for Aldridge to bring in a serving cart laden with tea and coffee, soft drinks and a variety of finger sandwiches. Afterward they worked for another hour and a half before finishing for the day. Deke had observed Lexie, studying the way she talked, her gestures, the way she smiled often and laughed easily. He had noted genuine affection coming from her and being returned to her, a symbiotic relationship in which others fed off Lexie's kindness and caring, and in return she absorbed their devotion and respect in a positive way. She possessed a genuine charm, as natural to her as breathing. She was a person who truly liked other people.

He and Lexie were as different as night and day. If he was ever charming, it was faked and used to his benefit. He didn't like people in general and usually saw the negative side of human nature instead of the positive. And he trusted no one.

At the end of the day, all but two of the Helping Hands employees had left, all except Toni and Farris Richardson. They huddled with Lexie behind the massive, ornate antique desk, deep in conversation. Deke remained merely an observer, a silent sentinel.

Aldridge appeared in the doorway. "Mr. Holston is here to pick up Ms. Wells."

"Please, ask Jafari to come in," Lexie said.

"No, no." Toni gestured with her hands. "I've got to run. We have a very special date tonight." She winked at Lexie. "I think he may pop the question."

Both women giggled, then exchanged another hug before Toni left.

When Richardson made no move to leave, continuing to chitchat and gaze at Lexie like a lovesick puppy, Deke wondered if he should step in and rescue her.

"Do you have dinner plans, Farris?" Lexie asked.

Damn! Why had she done that? Out of the goodness of her heart, no doubt. It had been apparent to anyone with eyes that Richardson had been waiting for an invitation.

"No, as a matter of fact, I don't."

"Then you should stay and have dinner with us."

"That's very nice of you to invite me, and if you're sure it won't be an inconvenience, I'd love to stay for dinner."

"It's simply a matter of asking Aldridge to see that another place is set." Lexie reached out and took Richardson's hand in hers, then said, "You've never been inside Cara's home before, have you? Would you like the grand tour?"

As excited as a kid who'd been asked if he wanted a free trip to Disney World, Richardson grinned from ear to ear.

Just what I want to do, follow Lexie and Mr. Dork around for the next hour while she shows him every room in this mausoleum.

As if she'd read his mind, Lexie told Deke, "If you'd prefer not to accompany us, I'm sure we'll be quite safe without you."

"You two can pretend I'm not here," Deke said. "I'll be so quiet you won't even know I'm following you."

Lexie offered Deke a sweet smile, one that wasn't reflected in her eyes, as she slipped her arm through Richardson's and led him out of the study.

AFTER SHOWERING and preparing for bed that evening, Lexie checked the clock on the nightstand. She'd been thinking about Toni for the past few hours, wondering if Jafari had indeed proposed to her tonight. Although Jafari was in America on a student visa while he attended UTC, that didn't necessarily mean that if he and Toni married, he would whisk her back to England with him someday. Selfishly, Lexie didn't want one of her dearest friends to live thousands of miles away. Maybe Jafari would decide to stay in America, right here in Chattanooga.

"I'm crazy about him," Toni had told Lexie. "He's the one, even if he is a couple of years younger than I am. It's not like I'm old enough to be his mother or anything."

Lexie wanted her friend to be happy, and Jafari clearly made her happy. He was a quiet, serious young man. A bit shy. Always courteous. Why Deke would consider such a sweet guy a possible suspect, along with Malik and Robert, was beyond her. But Deke was the suspicious sort, which she supposed made him good at his job.

How sad it must be not to trust anyone.

What sort of life had Deke lived to make him see the cup as half-empty instead of half-full? Then again, perhaps he'd simply been born with a negative personality.

A man like Deke needed to be surrounded by positive people, and when he married, he needed a wife who was his exact opposite.

When he married? How did she know he wasn't already married? He might have a wife and kiddies tucked away somewhere in an Atlanta suburb. Just because there had been a few sexual sparks between them didn't mean he was single. Some men flirted without realizing it, just as some women did. She'd been accused of being a flirt more than once in her life, but she really wasn't. She had a friendly, outgoing nature. Being friendly wasn't being flirty.

He's not married. I'd know if he was. I'd sense it.

When she heard the knock on the connecting door, she jumped and gasped.

"Yes?" she said.

Deke opened the door and stood there between their two rooms. "I wanted to check on you before I go to bed."

He was wearing a pair of pajama bottoms and no top, and was barefoot. Lexie tingled all over, the sensation radiating from her feminine core and spreading through her body with alarming speed.

"I'm fine," she managed to say.

He nodded. "Then I'll say good-night."

"Good night."

He stared at her, his gaze gliding over her like a lover's caress, then he turned, but before he closed the door, Lexie called to him.

"Are you married?"

His broad shoulders tensed. He kept his back to her. "No, I'm not married."

"Have you ever been married or engaged or—"

He turned around and faced her. "I was married briefly when I was in my early twenties. No other marriages, engagements or long-term relationships."

"I've never been married," she told him. "But I suppose you know that. I'm sure Dundee's worked up a report on me."

"They did." He crossed the threshold and entered her bedroom.

The ancient fight-or-flight instinct kicked in, and Lexie considered backing away from him as he approached her. She saw a dangerous hunger in Deke's eyes.

"Then you know I was engaged before I went to Gadi the first time."

Nodding, Deke continued walking toward her.

She held her breath.

"When I was wounded in Gadi and returned to the U.S. crippled, he walked out on me."

"He was a damn fool." Deke paused directly in front of her.

Her breath caught in her throat.

"You shouldn't have spent the evening flirting outrageously with Richardson. You have to know the guy's got a thing for you, and by fawning all over him the way you did, you only encouraged his fantasies."

Lexie gasped. "I was not flirting with Farris. I was being nice. He's a sweet man with very little self-confidence and not many friends."

"You were flirting."

"I was being friendly."

"You shouldn't have invited him to dinner."

"He's lonely."

"He's horny."

Lexie gasped again.

"You honestly don't know the kind of effect you have on a man, do you?"

She stared at Deke, genuinely puzzled by his question.

"Don't you know that when you smile at a guy, he wants to kiss you? And when you laugh, he wants to wrap you in his arms? And when you look at him as if he's the only man in the world, he wants to make love to you until you're both too exhausted to move?"

"No...I—I didn't know."

"Well, now you do."

He reached out, ran his hand under her hair and grasped the back of her neck. She stared up at him and knew he was going to kiss her. She had never wanted anything more in her life.

Pressing herself against him, loving the feel of his rock-solid chest and his blatant arousal against her belly, she gave herself over to the moment.

Deke released her so suddenly that she staggered on weak legs. Without saying a word, he turned and stormed out of her bedroom, slamming the connecting door behind him.

CHAPTER NINE

SATURDAY passed by uneventfully, as Friday had done. No bombings. No threatening phone calls. Except for the fact that she was not at home, where she longed to be, and there was a tough-guy bodyguard watching her every move, Lexie's day went by as usual. After their steamy encounter in her bedroom Friday night, Deke had pretty much handed her over to Geoff all day Saturday, without any explanation from either Dundee agent.

Why had Deke run from her? They had shared an intimate moment that should have ended in a kiss but hadn't. Yes, they were virtually strangers, and rushing into a physical relationship so quickly was crazy. But it wasn't as if they had been on the verge of having sex. It would have been a kiss. Just a kiss. Did the fact that she was handicapped turn him off, as it had her ex-fiancé? No, she didn't think that had been the problem. He'd been turned on. She had felt his erection, had seen the desire in his eyes. So what had happened? Professionalism? It was undoubtedly against Dundee's rules and regulations for an agent to become personally involved with a client. That must be it.

Lexie hadn't seen Deke since lunch yesterday. When he hadn't put in an appearance at dinner, Geoff had said that he was meeting with Ty Garrett, the Dundee agent in charge of the investigation.

"We checked with Ms. Bedell about using one of her cars instead of a rental," Geoff had explained. "She told us to take our pick."

As Lexie entered the breakfast room, she didn't expect to see Deke lifting the silver coffeepot and pouring himself a cup.

He glanced her way for half a second. "Good morning."

"Good morning." She stared at him, hoping he would look back at her so that she could try to gauge his mood. He didn't.

"Something sure smells good." Geoff, who had escorted her downstairs, walked past her and headed straight for the buffet-style setup on the sideboard. "I love your big American breakfasts. I'm a real fan of those Cracker Barrel restaurants. They serve a breakfast fit for a king."

Deke set his china cup and saucer down on the table, then returned to the buffet and filled his plate with eggs, sausage, potatoes and biscuits. Lexie walked over to the buffet and picked up a Royal Doulton plate.

"How did your meeting with Mr. Garrett go?" she asked.

Without even glancing at her, he replied, "It went okay. Ty has settled in down at the Sheraton Read House, and he'll stop by your office tomorrow to meet you and give you a report."

"Is there something I should know?"

"Not really. Nothing new," Deke said. "Not yet." He walked over to the table and put his plate down but didn't sit.

With his plate overflowing, Geoff headed for the

table. Lexie laid two slices of toast on her plate, and then dished up a bowl of fresh fruit. When she joined them at the table, Deke pulled out her chair.

She smiled at him.

He didn't return her smile. "Sit down," he said. "I'll get your coffee."

"Thank you." Why did she feel so awkward around him? It wasn't as if they'd had sex. For goodness sakes, they hadn't even kissed.

No one talked much during the meal. Deke responded when spoken to, and once he finished off his huge breakfast, Geoff started a conversation about what it must be like to be as rich as Cara Bedell. While they sat around drinking final cups of coffee, Lexie decided now was the right time to make her announcement.

"I'm going to church this morning."

"What?" Deke looked at her then, a no-way-in-hell scowl on his face.

"I'm not sure you should do that," Geoff said.

"You're not going," Deke told her.

"Why not? I don't intend to stay cooped up in this gilded cage for weeks on end. I'm going to church this morning and back to work tomorrow."

"I don't think I have the proper clothes for church," Geoff said.

"There really is no dress code," Lexie told him. "Khaki pants, with a shirt and tie will be just fine."

"If you're damned and determined to go, I'll take you," Deke said.

She and Geoff both stared at him.

Geoff didn't say anything. She said, "Thank you. I'll be ready in an hour. The church I attend is a twenty-five-minute drive from here."

"I'll be ready."

When she stood, both Deke and Geoff rose, too, but only Deke left the room with her. She walked ahead of him, taking her time. She surprised him by stopping at a well-camouflaged elevator at the end of the long hallway, just past the kitchen. Deke came up beside her.

"I can't imagine growing up in a house so big that you need an elevator," he said.

"I actually prefer using the stairs, but to save time, I thought I'd use the elevator this morning."

"Do you choose to use the stairs simply to prove a point?"

When the elevator door opened, Lexie stepped in, and Deke followed. The interior was small, about the size of the average powder room, and would hold no more than three or four people.

"Is that what you think—that I use the stairs just to prove to myself that I can?"

"Maybe. Or it could be to prove to everyone else that you aren't helpless, that you don't need any special treatment just because you use a cane."

Deke reached around her and hit the up button. His arm accidentally brushed against hers. A tingle of awareness jangled along her nerve endings. She had never been as sexually aware of another man as she was of Deke.

Think of something else, she told herself. *Don't let him see that you're flustered. Damn it, think of something, anything. Hmm...* The Bedell house. The elevator. Although the house was three stories—the third had once been the servants' quarters—the elevator went up only to the second floor and down to the basement, where the wine cellar and the laundry room were.

When they reached the second floor, Deke held the door open until she got off; then he followed her along the corridor that led to their connecting rooms.

She paused before entering her bedroom. "Thank you for agreeing to escort me to church this morning. It's important to me."

"I assumed it was. Otherwise, I wouldn't have agreed."

"But you don't approve? You'd rather I not go?"

"I'd rather you not go in to work tomorrow, too," he said. "If I had my way, I'd keep you here under lock and key."

A dancing-butterflies sensation warmed her stomach and sent internal quivers through her body. He had spoken as her bodyguard, but she had heard the underlying possessiveness beneath his words.

"I couldn't live that way," she told him.

"Yeah, I know."

He turned and walked away.

DEKE HADN'T BEEN inside a church since his grandfather's funeral twelve years ago. He supposed that if he'd ever truly loved anybody in his whole life, it had been that taciturn old man. Jim Mason, a machinist who had worked with his hands all his life, hadn't known how to communicate with his nine-year-old grandson any more than he'd ever been able to communicate with his wife or only child, Deke's mother. Big Jim, as he'd been known in Mineral Springs, Texas, had taken Deke in after his mother died and his good-for-nothing father skipped town. Deke and his grandfather had coexisted in the same silent house until Deke left for college. Although Granddad had never told him how he felt about him, he had shown him in a hundred small ways. Fixing him a hot breakfast every morning before he went to school. Encouraging him to play sports but at the same time to excel in academics. Helping him buy his first vehicle—a beat-up old truck—when he turned sixteen. Writing him once a week when he'd been away at college and then after he joined the army.

When Deke and Lexie arrived, the church was more than half full, and within fifteen minutes it was filled to capacity. He figured the sanctuary, including the balcony area, probably held at least five hundred, which was small in comparison to many of today's church buildings. As large as the congregation was, it appeared that Lexie knew more than two-thirds on a first-name basis. She had the kind of personality that had made her a good reporter and now a top-notch fund-raiser. People were instantly drawn to her, not only because she was beautiful, but because she projected warmth and caring. Everyone instinctively knew that Lexie liked people.

Every time she shook someone's hand or gave a fellow church member a hug, Deke's instinct was to pull her away, to cocoon her from any type of physical contact. He saw every person as a potential threat. If he didn't know someone, he didn't trust them. And God help them, Lexie seemed to trust everyone she knew. How could a woman who had nearly died in the crossfire of a battle between enemy soldiers maintain such a positive outlook on life?

"There's Farris." Lexie made her way through the throng of worshippers still milling around in the aisles, enjoying some preworship-service fellowship.

Deke groaned inwardly when he spotted the Helping Hands accountant. Farris Richardson was standing one aisle over, a big, goofy grin on his face, as he waved at Lexie.

People kept smiling at Deke, saying "Hello" and "Welcome" and "Good to see you here today," forcing him to be polite. Smiling wasn't an option. He was lousy at faked smiles, so he just nodded pleasantly and tried not to shove anyone while he kept in step directly behind Lexie.

Any place like this, where a huge crowd surrounded the client, was a bodyguard's worst nightmare. Especially a place that he'd been unable to inspect thoroughly before the event. He had to think of every person here as a possible threat to Lexie, even though the odds were that no one actually was. This was a house of worship, filled with husbands, wives, children, parents and grandparents, aunts, uncles and cousins, as well as neighbors and friends. People were laughing and smiling; babies were cooing and crying.

He'd spent too many years in uncivilized countries, in war-torn nations where he had been exposed to the dregs of society, and to the pitiful used and abused who would sell their souls for a loaf of bread.

As soon as Lexie reached Richardson, she gave him a quick hug and a peck on the cheek.

He grasped her hand and held it. "I wasn't sure you'd make it this morning. I'm happy to see that you did."

"Well, of course I did."

Completely ignoring Deke, Richardson asked, "Would you like to sit with me?" He nodded toward the pew directly beside him, where there was room left only for two.

Lexie squeezed Richardson's hand, then pulled free from his tight hold. "Oh, there's not enough room for all three of us, and I'm afraid Mr. Bronson will insist on sitting with me."

Damn right about that! And why had she referred to him as Mr. Bronson? Weren't they still on a first-name basis?

"Yes, yes, I see the problem." When Richardson glanced at Deke, his stupid smile vanished. He blinked a couple of times, then swallowed. "I—I don't suppose you'd consider taking the seat behind us, would you?"

Lexie turned to Deke, laid her hand on his chest and smiled. "Please."

Deke gritted his teeth, then said quietly, "If you insist."

For the next hour, Deke sat through the church service counting the minutes until it ended. He definitely felt like a fish out of water. And he didn't like having a heavy wooden bench between him and his client, although if necessary, he could and would leap over the pew to reach Lexie.

Finally, with the last song sung and the last prayer uttered, Deke managed to make his way past several congregants and reach Lexie before the dispersing crowd swallowed her up. When he grabbed her arm, she looked over her shoulder and smiled at him.

Did she have any idea how lethal that smile was?

He leaned down and whispered to her, "Let's get out of here."

She nodded, then patted Richardson's arm and said something to him that Deke couldn't hear. By the forlorn expression on the man's face, Deke assumed she had said goodbye.

Fifteen minutes and dozens of brief conversations with her fellow churchgoers later, Lexie and Deke emerged from the church and made their way out into the parking lot, where Cara Bedell's chauffeur waited with the Rolls. It hadn't surprised Deke this morning when Lexie had called the chauffeur by his first name—Eddie—and asked how his wife, whom she'd also called by name—April—was doing. Apparently anyone who came into Lexie's life mattered to her. How could he fault her for being who she was, even if it made his job of protecting her a lot harder?

Once in the backseat of the Rolls, Lexie asked, "How long has it been since you've gone to church?"

"A long time."

"Well, thank you very much for taking me today."

Keeping his gaze focused straight ahead at the chauffeur's back, Deke asked, "What's with you and Richardson? You may think you're just being nice to him, but he sees things differently. That guy's got a thing for you, and you're encouraging him."

"I most certainly am not," Lexie said, her voice a loud whisper.

"You hug him, you kiss him and you sit with him in church. You talk to him in a sweet, sexy voice that would give a saint wicked thoughts."

Lexie's eyes widened and her mouth gaped open as she stared at Deke in utter confusion. "I—I do not. I hug everybody. And I kissed Farris on the cheek. And I spoke to him in my normal voice, the way I speak to everyone."

"If you say so."

Lexie snorted. "I say so!"

As they sat together in silence from the church to the Bedell mansion, Deke realized that Lexie was stewing the entire trip. She patted her fingers on her purse and tapped one foot repeatedly. She clenched and unclenched her teeth several times, huffed loudly more than once, and finally crossed her arms over her chest.

Eddie pulled the Rolls up to the front of the mansion, hopped out and opened the car door. Deke got out, then turned to assist Lexie. He took her cane, hooked it over the top of the door, then grasped her hand and hoisted her up and onto her feet. She snatched the cane, hammering it against the pavement as she walked away from him. Not a word. Not a glance. Not even a hint of a smile.

"An apology is probably your best course of action at this point," Eddie said. "If you want my opinion."

Deke nodded. "Good advice. Thanks."

"Any time, sir."

Deke caught up with Lexie on the front veranda.

Bang, bang, bang, bang!

The sound came from behind them, near the front gates. Screeching tires. A speeding car.

Deke barreled into Lexie, tossing her onto the porch, coming down over her to protect her with his own body while he yanked his Glock from his shoulder holster.

"Deke?"

"Shh…"

Silence.

Deke replayed the popping sounds in his mind. Not gunshots, even though that had been his initial reaction.

"Are you all right?" he asked as he lifted himself up and off Lexie.

She nodded. "Uh-huh. Just scared half to death."

He reached down, grabbed her arm and dragged her to her feet. She clung to her cane as she rose from where she'd been lying on top of it.

The front door flew open. Geoff Monday, weapon drawn, scanned the scene, then emerged from inside the house. "What the hell was that noise?"

"I don't know," Deke replied. "Take Lexie inside while I have a look around."

She clutched Deke's arm. "Be careful."

"Yeah." He looked at Geoff. "Get her in the house. Now."

FIFTEEN MINUTES LATER, Deke walked into the living room where Geoff had taken Lexie. She had paced the floor, then sat for several minutes before getting up and pacing some more. Geoff had tried to reassure her, but she barely heard him over the thumping of her heartbeat drumming in her ears. Neither she nor Deke had been hurt, but she couldn't seem to relax. Had someone shot at them? Had that horrible noise been rifle fire?

Geoff had asked her more than once if she wanted a drink, something alcoholic to soothe her nerves. She had declined each time, but was beginning to think maybe she should take him up on the offer.

Lexie had just sat down again when Deke appeared in the doorway. She jumped up and hurried to him, but paused before throwing her arms around him.

"I called Lieutenant Desmond," Deke said. "He's on his way."

"Did you find anything?" Geoff asked.

Deke looked Lexie right in the eye. "I found fire-crackers. Apparently someone drove up, tossed them through the bars of the front gate and zoomed off."

"There are surveillance cameras at both gates," Geoff said. "Our culprit might have been caught on tape."

"Do you think whoever did this is the same person—the bomber?" Lexie asked.

"Possibly," Deke said. "Probably."

As if on cue, Lexie's cell phone rang.

"Where's your phone?" Deke asked.

"In my purse, over there on the—"

"I'll get it." Geoff rushed over to the sofa, opened the bag, pulled out her cell phone and looked at the caller ID. "Unknown."

When Lexie reached for the phone, Deke grabbed it, flipped it open and said, "Ms. Murrough can't come to the phone, so give me the message."

Lexie watched for any change in Deke's expression, but there was none. What was the caller saying? Making another threat? Or perhaps it was a wrong number. After all, they couldn't be certain that the firecracker incident was related to the bombings.

Deke flipped Lexie's phone closed and clasped it tightly in his big hand.

"Who was it? What did they say?" Lexie held her breath, afraid to hear his response.

Deke hesitated, then replied, "He said, 'No matter what you do, you can't keep her safe. The time for her to die is near.'" He paused. "Then the sick son of a bitch laughed."

Lexie didn't know if she made the first move or if he did, but suddenly she was enveloped in Deke's embrace. She wrapped her arms around his waist and laid her head on his chest.

"I'll check with Aldridge about the surveillance camera," Geoff said. "If he doesn't know anything about it, I'll contact the head of Bedell security."

"Let me know as soon as Lieutenant Desmond arrives," Deke said as he tenderly stroked Lexie's back.

"Sure thing," Geoff replied on his way out.

Deke cupped the back of Lexie's head and urged

her to look up at him. "He's wrong, you know. I *will* keep you safe."

"I know you'll try."

"I won't let him hurt you. I promise that I'll take care of you, no matter what I have to do."

She met his gaze, and for a split second she thought she recognized his eyes. Smoky-gray eyes looking at her with such concern, such compassion. Shaking her head, she pulled away from him.

"What's wrong?" he asked.

She stared right at him and saw Deke Bronson, not a ghost from her past. "I'm sorry. Just for a moment… It's nothing. My nerves are rattled. The firecrackers sounded like gunfire and—"

"And suddenly you were back in Gadi, ten years ago," he said.

She nodded.

"It's all right," he told her. "Certain things trigger flashbacks. It's happened to all of us."

"I almost died that day. If it hadn't been for a soldier— one of the assassins—I would have bled to death. I owe that man my life. When I looked into your eyes a minute ago, I saw his eyes. I suppose it's because he was my protector that day, and now, *you're* my protector."

CHAPTER TEN

LARRY NESMITH, the burly, silver-haired head of Bedell, Inc. security, oversaw the removal of the surveillance tape at the front gate. Lieutenant Desmond and Sergeant Swain supervised the gruff-voiced Vietnam veteran, who'd retired from the Chattanooga PD five years ago. It was obvious from their good-natured banter that the three men were old friends.

Ty Garrett had arrived practically at the same time Bain and Mike had, so apparently Geoff had phoned him either immediately before or after calling the police. A couple of crime-scene techs had shown up ten minutes behind the detectives and were still outside gathering evidence.

"Take a seat right here," Bain told Lexie as she entered the media room. When he put his arm around her shoulders and led her toward the front row of plush chairs, she thought she heard Deke growl. But the sound had been so faint that it could have been her imagination.

"The tape's set," Nesmith told them. "Ready when you are."

"Ready?" Bain asked her.

She nodded. Just as Bain sat down on her right, she sensed someone take the seat to her left and knew without looking that it was Deke. As much as she liked

Bain, trusted him, knew him to be a good man who could protect her, she felt safer with Deke nearby. The feeling was not something she could explain, because it was something she didn't completely understand. But she sensed that Deke would, indeed, lay his life on the line for her. Without any thought for his own safety. Without hesitation.

Nesmith fast-forwarded the tape until the timeline showed approximately five minutes before the fire-cracker incident. She watched carefully, hoping the tape had captured the face of the assailant. In a flash, a small, late-model red car pulled up, the driver's door even with the front gate. The window came down, a sleeved arm and gloved hand shot out and tossed something through the decorative wrought-iron bars. Then, lightning-fast, the vehicle sped away.

"Freeze it right there," Bain called out at the exact second that Nesmith paused the surveillance tape.

"Son of a bitch," Nesmith said. "The car tag is as plain as day."

"I'm already on it." Mike Swain jumped up, yanked his cell phone from his pocket and walked out of the room.

"I'd say that's enough for now." Bain stood. "We'll want to take the tape with us and have our own team go over it."

Nodding in agreement, Nesmith grinned. "I contacted Ms. Bedell, and she instructed me to cooperate fully with the Chattanooga PD."

Bain glanced down at Lexie, his eyes drifting from her face to her left hand, which she only at that moment realized was gripped protectively in Deke's right hand. When she stretched her fingers wide open, Deke released her. And when she started to stand, he got up first and helped her to her feet.

"You realize that we can't be certain this firecracker incident is connected to the bombings," Bain told her. "It could be nothing more than a coincidence. This might have been some kid playing a prank."

"Is that what you think?" Deke asked.

"Nope. I think whoever was driving that Ford Focus is our bomber." Bain patted Lexie on the shoulder. "I'm going to step outside and see if Mike's gotten any info yet."

Lexie hazarded a quick glance at Deke. His stoic expression told her nothing. "What do you think? Why would he toss firecrackers through the front gate? Why do something so harmless after setting off bombs for two days straight? Did he do it just to unnerve me?"

"You were more than unnerved. You were terrified. That harmless prank sent your mind and emotions straight back to Gadi on the day you were shot. And my guess is that our guy knew that was what would happen, or at least he hoped it would."

A distinctively Southern baritone said, "By tomorrow I should have full reports on the three Gadians working for Helping Hands, and within the week we'll have information on anyone with a connection to both Gadi and Ms. Murrough."

Lexie glanced over her shoulder just as Ty Garrett walked up to them, his gaze traveling over her slowly, appreciatively. Men seemed to find her attractive. Still. Even with a physical handicap. But enjoying looking at an attractive woman and becoming personally involved with someone who was physically challenged were two different things entirely. And even realizing that she judged all other men by her former fiancé's desertion didn't stop her from doing it. If a man who had professed to love her, who had asked her to marry him and spend the rest of their lives together, had been unable to accept her when she became less than perfect—"slightly flawed" had been the way he'd put it—then how could she believe any other man could see past her imperfections?

Illogical thinking? Yes, of course. But perfectly reasonable to an emotionally scarred woman who no longer based her decisions on pure logic.

"I have every faith in my employees, Mr. Garrett," Lexie said. "I'm sure that when all is said and done, you'll find that you agree with me."

"Yes, ma'am, I'm sure you do. It's easier to accept that a stranger would try to kill you than a friend or trusted employee."

Before Lexie could reply, Bain shot through the door, his partner right behind him. "The car was reported stolen this morning. The owner left it unlocked, with the keys in it, while he ran into a convenience store to pay for gas and pick up a few items. When he came back out, the car was gone."

"Anybody see the guy who took the car?" Ty asked.

"Not a soul," Bain replied.

"Then we have nothing," Geoff Monday said.

"Probably not," Bain admitted. "But we'll check things out more thoroughly, find out where the convenience store is located, talk to the clerk who was working there this morning and interview the guy who owns the car."

"Thank you." Lexie smiled gratefully at Bain.

Bain shrugged, then glanced past her at Larry Nesmith, who had just removed the surveillance tape from the player.

"Wait up and I'll walk out with y'all." When Nesmith passed Lexie, he said, "Sorry the tape didn't help us ID the guy." He looked at Deke. "If you Dundee boys need anything from Bedell, Inc. security, just let me know." He pulled a business card from his inside coat pocket and handed it to Deke.

Deke took the card, stuck it in the breast pocket of his jacket and said, "Sure thing."

Once the room cleared, with only Lexie and Deke remaining, he asked, "How about a late lunch?" He glanced at his wristwatch. "It's after three, and you haven't eaten anything since breakfast."

"I really don't think I could eat a bite. But if I were at home, in my own place, I'd go into the kitchen and fix myself a cup of tea and—" She cleared her throat. "I hate this so much. Being forced from my home, being scared out of my mind by firecrackers, needing twenty-four-hour-a-day protection."

"I wish I could take you home, but you're safer here."

"I may be safer, but I'm not sure I can stay here indefinitely without losing my mind."

"We'll take it one day at a time."

She sighed. "You're right. There's not much else we can do, is there?"

ALICE KENNEDY had been widowed for six years. Her twenty-year-old twin daughters were away at college. Her parents were dead. And her only sibling lived in California, an older brother she hadn't seen since their mother's funeral three years ago. For all intents and purposes, she was alone in the world except for a handful of girlfriends with whom she went shopping, shared lunches and occasionally attended a play or the symphony. If not for her PR job at Helping Hands the past couple of years, her life would have been unbearable.

Alice was lonely.

Her friends didn't approve of her relationship with Robert Lufti. He was not only fifteen years her junior, but he was a different race, a different religion and was a citizen of another country.

"What could you possibly have in common with this man?" her friends had asked.

She hadn't known what to say. How do you explain to old friends that the young man who was so completely unsuitable for you made you inexplicably happy? Robert was quiet and easygoing, with a shy smile and a brilliant mind. He had introduced her to a world she'd never known. Different music, different foods, different views on many subjects. And he had re-introduced her to passion, the kind she hadn't known since she was in her twenties. Now, at forty-three, she found herself madly in love with a man who would someday break her heart.

"You are very quiet," Robert said as he walked up behind her where she sat at her dressing table staring at herself in the mirror.

When he put his hands on her shoulders, she laid her cheek against his left hand and sighed contentedly. "I was wondering how long this can possibly last—you and me."

He lowered his head and kissed her neck on either side, then reached around to pull her robe apart. When his hands cupped her breasts, her feminine core tightened. She wanted him again, although they had just made love.

"It will last as long as it is supposed to last," he whispered against her ear.

That hadn't been what she wanted to hear. Foolishly,

she wanted him to declare his undying love and tell her that their affair would last forever, would continue as long as they lived.

"Nothing lasts forever, does it?" She sighed.

"Are you still upset that I did not stay the night last night?" he asked. "You think I have another woman? I do not."

"You tell me there's no one else, but when you leave me the way you did last night and then are two hours late for our afternoon together today…"

He kissed her neck. She shivered.

"There is only you," he told her.

She clasped one of his hands and ran his open palm down over her belly until she reached the apex between her thighs. Without more prompting, he slipped his fingers between her moist feminine lips and found the sensitive nub hidden there.

When he fondled her with expert ease, she leaned her head back against his naked body and gave herself over to the moment, putting all her hopes and dreams and concerns from her mind.

VEGA SHARIF completed the letter she had written to her sister but did not seal the envelope. Tomorrow, during lunchtime, she would go to the post office, buy a money order and place it in the letter before airmailing it back home to Gadi. She lived modestly here in America, in a small apartment that she shared with a college student, Casey Prescott, who attended UTC. Vega and Casey had met as teenagers in Gadi when, as a member of a missionary group from her church, Casey had visited Vega's village. It had been in part due to their friendship that Vega had converted to Christianity, a move that had upset her family. Only her one sister Nahid, a nurse who ran a clinic in their village, would even speak to her. From time to time Vega sent Nahid a little money to help buy supplies. Even with the generosity of Helping Hands, the clinic was forever running short of funds. There were too many villagers sick with AIDS, too many young mothers dying in childbirth, too many children in need.

Despite the kindness and friendship of so many at her church and at Helping Hands, Vega often felt like an outsider. As much as she loved America and longed to become a citizen, she had often wondered if she should return to Gadi and work with her sister in the clinic. But everything changed when she met Hamal Gazsi, an intern at Erlanger Hospital. He, too, was a foreigner who had been raised Muslim and was now a Christian. He, too, longed to be a citizen. He, too, was torn between his desire for a new and better life in the United States and guilt that he was not returning home to help his countrymen in Bahram, another African nation no bigger than Gadi.

Hamal had phoned her early this morning to tell her that he couldn't meet her at church and go out for lunch afterward, because he had to cover for another intern who was sick.

"I'll see you tomorrow," he had said. "I'll stop by Helping Hands at noon and take you to lunch."

She was not in love with Hamal, not yet. She liked him very much. And he liked her. But she truly did not know him. He seldom talked about his life in Bahram or his family there. He preferred listening to her talk, often telling her that she fascinated him. Even so, Vega suspected that Hamal would one day ask her to marry him. And she would probably say yes.

AT FOUR O'CLOCK, a sales rep from the local Mercedes dealership showed up at the front gate of the Bedell mansion, followed in a second car by an associate. After Geoff Monday made a quick phone call to Cara at her hotel in Mexico City, the salesman was allowed to drive the new black Mercedes C240 up to the front steps and present the keys to Lexie.

Lexie took the keys reluctantly when the salesman said, "Here's your new car, Ms. Murrough. A gift from Ms. Bedell. This baby is fully loaded. However, I have been authorized to exchange it for another, so if you don't like the color or would prefer another model, simply let us know."

Momentarily stunned, Lexie was speechless.

"I'm sure this car suits Ms. Murrough," Deke said.

Finding her voice, Lexie clutched the keys in her hand and smiled at the salesman. "Thank you for bringing the car all the way out here on a Sunday afternoon."

"You're quite welcome." The salesman bowed, as well he should have, considering his commission from the sale. The man was no fool. He knew that pleasing Lexie meant pleasing Cara Bedell, and pleasing Cara could be worth a great deal of money to him and his employer.

While Geoff escorted the Mercedes salesman to the front gate, where his associate waited outside, Lexie inspected her new car.

"You can always send it back tomorrow," Deke said.

"No, I can't. It wouldn't do any good. Cara wouldn't understand, and she'd just send me something else. A Jaguar or a BMW. She has no idea what an extravagant gift this is. To her, the price of a new Mercedes is peanuts."

"I'm not sure I'd want to be that rich."

"Cara is generous with her money. She knew I'd need another car, so her first impulse was to buy me one. It never entered her mind that I could afford to buy my own, or that I might prefer to choose the car myself."

Deke ran his hand across the roof of the sleek hardtop. "There was a time when I thought driving a car like this meant you were somebody. I'd have done just about anything to own one."

Lexie heard a hint of self-chastisement in his voice. "I take it that somewhere along the way, you changed your mind."

"Yeah. After I bought one."

"And when you owed a Mercedes, that didn't make you feel like somebody?" she asked.

"Nah. But by that time, I'd already figured out it isn't what a man owns that defines him. It's what he does."

She laid her hand on his arm, but when she heard Geoff approaching, she eased her hand away.

"If you'd like, I'll park this beauty in front of the garage," Geoff said.

Lexie tossed him the keys. "Yes, thanks, that would be great."

"Old Bronson here had a black Mercedes a few years back," Geoff told her. "But he didn't keep it long."

Deke cast his friend a shut-the-hell-up glare.

Geoff gave Deke an apologetic glance, then climbed into the car, started the engine and drove it toward the back of the house.

"Did you sell your Mercedes?" Lexie asked.

"No." Deke cupped her elbow. "It's getting chilly out here now that the sun is setting."

She allowed him to escort her up on the veranda.

Curious at the way he'd avoided answering her question, she asked, "If you didn't sell your Mercedes, what happened to it?"

Deke opened the front door and held it for her. Once they entered the foyer, he replied, "I totaled it."

"You had a wreck?"

"Yeah."

"Were you hurt?"

"Not nearly as bad as the car."

"What happened?"

"I was driving too fast and lost control."

"Oh." She realized that if she wanted more details, she wasn't going to get them from him. "I think I'll go upstairs to my room, but there's no need for you to go with me. I believe I'll be safe alone for a little while, don't you?"

"Tired of having someone shadowing your every move, huh?"

"Something like that."

"I'll walk you to the elevator."

When she nodded, he fell into step alongside her. At the elevator, he waited until the door opened and she entered, then he told her, "I'll check on you in about thirty minutes."

"Okay, thank you."

There had been a time in her life when she'd hated being alone. That had been the old Lexie, the girl who had liked to party, to travel the world, to rub elbows with important people. Now she preferred quiet times with no one around. But perhaps she had been spending too much time alone. Alone was good. Lonely wasn't. And recently she had realized that she was lonely, that she needed more in her life, that she needed someone special.

Well, it isn't going to be Deke Bronson. He's your

temporary bodyguard, not your boyfriend, not your lover, not the answer to your prayers. As soon as the mad bomber was found and stopped, Deke would leave, and she would never see him again.

IF THERE WAS one thing Toni Wells didn't like, it was being stood up. And lately, Jafari had been making a habit of either breaking a date at the last minute, showing up late, or not showing up and not even bothering to call. If she weren't so hog-wild, crazy in love with the guy, she would never put up with the roller-coaster ride their relationship had become during the past couple of weeks. In the beginning, when they'd first met five months ago, he'd been the perfect gentleman in every way. Thoughtful, considerate, catering to her every whim. Then, about ten days ago, he had changed. He seemed distracted, as if she wasn't as important to him as something—or someone— else. When she had confronted him about his thoughtlessness, he had apologized and begged her forgiveness.

"I am concerned about my classes," he had told her. "I must spend more time devoting myself to studying."

She had accepted his explanation, especially because afterward he had been especially attentive and loving, so much so that she'd been certain he was planning to ask her to marry him. But so far, he hadn't brought up the subject of marriage. And today's little faux pas was the last straw. Her mother had come to Chattanooga for the day to have lunch with her and to meet Jafari. Only Jafari had shown up late and offered a flimsy excuse.

"I am so sorry, but when I went outside to leave my home, I saw that my car had a flat tire."

Just how long did it take to change a flat tire? Toni

and her mother had been eating dessert when Jafari finally arrived.

For the rest of the afternoon, Jafari had done his best to impress Toni's mother, but he would have to do more than be charming to gain Toni's forgiveness this time. After her mother had left to go home to Atlanta, Toni had asked Jafari to leave.

"Please, do not be angry with me," he had said.

"I'm not angry. I'm hurt and disappointed."

"Forgive me."

"I need time to think about it," she had told him. "I love you, Jafari, but I will not put up with the kind of behavior you've shown lately."

"I will go. For now. I will give you time to forgive me. And then—"

She had all but shoved him out the door. "I'll call you when I'm ready to talk."

He had left without putting up a fight.

Ever since then, she had been sitting alone, brooding and polishing off a bottle of her favorite chardonnay.

Men! Damn 'em all.

DEKE WENT into the kitchen, where he encountered Mrs. Eddins, the Bedell cook. When she inquired if she could help him, he thanked her and told her what he wanted.

"It won't take more than ten minutes," she said. "You can wait, or I'll let Aldridge know when it's ready."

"I'll just come back in ten minutes."

Deke made his way to the mudroom that led onto a small, enclosed patio used mostly by the household staff. He could use a stiff drink right about now, but in the mood he was in, one drink could easily lead to another. When on duty, he never got drunk. As a matter of fact, it had been nearly a year since he'd tied one on. Not since...

Seven years ago, he had forgone getting rip-roaring drunk on the anniversary of Andrew's death. Instead, he had gotten in his shiny new Mercedes, driven up Interstate 55 from Biloxi, where he'd spent the weekend with a lady friend, and had, as the saying goes, "put the pedal to the metal." A Mississippi highway patrolman had clocked Deke going a hundred just a few minutes before he lost control of the car and careened off the road. He had plowed down a barbwire fence, some thick shrubbery, a couple of saplings and finally smashed into the side of a ramshackle old barn. If he hadn't been wearing his seat belt, he probably wouldn't have survived. As it was, he wound up spending two weeks in the hospital and another two months recuperating.

Andrew had been dead nearly eighteen years, and most of the time Deke managed not to think about his son, who would now be a young man if he'd lived. But two days out of every year, he could think of little else. On Andrew's birthday—January twenty-first—and the day he died, two and a half months later, on April fourth.

Odd, how deeply he mourned a kid he hadn't wanted in the first place. If he'd had his way, Abby would have aborted their child. He hadn't loved her, hadn't loved their baby-to-be, but he'd done the right thing and married her. And after Andrew was born, Deke had grown to love his child. When his son died, Deke hadn't known how to react, hadn't known what to do or how he should feel. It had taken him a long time to admit that he felt guilty for not wanting Andrew in the first place, and he wondered if God had punished him for not being a better father.

If he had it to do over again...

No second chances, Bronson. You learned that lesson the hard way.

He would never get a second chance to be a good father to his son, to right all the wrongs. And he could never change what had happened to Lexie Murrough, what he'd done to her. But he could take care of her now. He owed her that much.

AFTER SAYING his last prayer of the day, he rose to his feet and stretched. If it had not turned so cool late in the day, he would have gone out for a long walk. To think. To figure out a way of showing her how important she was to him. He needed her, at least for a while longer. She was in love with him, or gave every indication of being devoted to him, but he had disappointed her more than once lately, had not given her all that she needed from him. He could not afford to antagonize her again. Tomorrow he would buy her flowers. Women seemed to love flowers, especially when they believed them to be a token of love or a plea for forgiveness.

He sat down on the barstool in front of his laptop computer, which he had placed on the counter that separated his efficiency kitchen from his living room. He eased it open and turned it on.

He was expecting a message from Kalil, a man he honored above all others. He had, as many had before and after him, become a Muslim because it pleased Kalil. And because it made him a true brother to all others in the Majeed. He was not as good a Muslim as he should be, but no one questioned his loyalty and devotion to the Majeed and the organization's second in command, his father figure, the great Kalil Ben Riyad. He was prepared to make the ultimate sacrifice for Kalil, who had handpicked him as one of four for the important events soon to come. The honor of dying for a cause far greater than one individual was his destiny, as it had been his father's. The only difference was that he had chosen the sacrificial death awaiting him, while his father had died a martyr, slain by evil men, his greatness publicly mocked, ridiculed for the whole world to see by that American whore, Lexie Murrough,

His gaze fixed on the computer screen. His hand quivered as he touched the keyboard. As he checked his e-mail, he sighed deeply when he saw that he had received a message from Kalil. He had been waiting impatiently for nearly two weeks, hoping for word from his master, longing to know the chosen day when the Majeed would strike at the very heart of America. His vision momentarily blurred as his excitement built. He opened the e-mail. After blinking his eyes several times, his vision focused, enabling him to read the brief message.

My dear son, your Christmas present is to be delivered on December twenty-first. You will be notified of the exact time. Father.

His heartbeat accelerated. His hands trembled. Perspiration dotted his upper lip. He had less than six weeks to prepare. Less than six weeks to punish Lexie Murrough before taking her with him on his final journey. Only their destinations differed. She would rot in hell, and he would ascend to heaven to receive his reward for serving Allah.

LEXIE HAD LEARNED meditation from one of her physical therapists, a woman who practiced it herself and believed in the healing benefits of quiet reflection. At one time, a few years ago, she had meditated twice every day, but the busier her work schedule became—just when she needed meditation the most—she had actually meditated less. But this evening seemed like the perfect time to focus on a method of relaxation and control that had helped her in the past. She could not change what was happening to her, only the way in which she reacted. She could give in to the fear and uncertainty, or she could find ways of dealing with it.

Just as she closed her eyes and allowed her mind to focus only on her breathing, a soft rap at her door interrupted her. Sighing heavily, she rose from the sofa, grabbed her cane and walked to the door.

"Lexie?" Deke called quietly.

She opened the door and found him standing there holding a silver tray in his hand.

"I've brought you some tea and a snack."

She stepped back to allow him entrance. He walked over to the sitting area, placed the covered tray on the table between the two armchairs and motioned for her to come and sit down.

Although she really wasn't hungry, she could certainly drink some hot tea. "Thank you. This is very nice." When she sat, he whipped off the linen cloth to reveal a teapot covered with a floral cozy, a single china cup and saucer, and a plate of assorted delights: cheese and crackers, apple slices, raisins and oatmeal cookies.

Her stomach rumbled. "I guess I am a little hungry." She smiled at him.

"Mrs. Eddins and I weren't sure how you take your tea, so she included lemon, sugar and cream," Deke said.

"I take it plain."

He filled the cup to the brim, then lifted the china saucer and handed it to her. The first sip was delicious, and she told him so.

"Enjoy," he told her. "If you need me for anything…"

"Please don't go. Stay."

"Are you sure you wouldn't rather be alone?"

"I'm sure."

He took the seat opposite her but didn't continue the conversation. He watched her while she savored every sip of that first cup of tea. The silence between them lingered, but it wasn't unpleasant in the least. Somehow it seemed natural, as if they were old friends simply enjoying the time alone together.

After a second cup of tea, which she poured, and while nibbling on a cookie, Lexie turned to Deke and asked, "Have you always been good at taking care of other people?"

Narrowing his gaze, he stared at her, apparently puzzled by her question.

"As my bodyguard, you've been exceptionally kind and caring. You went out of your way to be considerate by bringing me tea this evening. I was wondering if your being so nice to me was more than just doing your job."

He didn't reply immediately, and she could tell that he was giving his response due consideration. "I've never been good at things like this." He gestured to the silver tray. "No one has ever referred to my actions as being nice, and they'd be right, so don't assume my serving you tea is anything more than my taking good care of a client."

She felt as if he'd slapped her. But it was her own fault. She had put him on the spot by implying that he had done something extraspecial for her, something personal, something he didn't ordinarily do for a client.

He corrected you on that misconception pretty damn fast, didn't he?

A barrier of uneasy silence arose between them. She felt uncomfortable now and could tell by the tension vibrating all around them that he felt the same way.

Deke said nothing when she reached over and poured herself a third cup of tea. She drank it slowly, not enjoying it the way she had the first two.

"I served ten years in the U.S. Army before becoming a soldier of fortune for six years and then hiring on at Dundee's a couple of years ago," he told her, finally breaking the awkward silence. "I've always taken care of myself and my men…and now my clients."

"I'm certain you're the very best at what you do, otherwise you wouldn't be working for a firm that Cara Bedell employed. She hires the best money can buy," Lexie said. "It's my good fortune that you take such good care of your clients."

Deke rose to his feet. Standing there, towering over her, he said, "I'll take good care of you. I'll stand between you and any danger that comes your way. But that's as far as it goes, as far as I'll allow it to go."

Warmth flushed her cheeks. "I'm sorry if I embarrassed you. It wasn't my intention. Believe me, we won't need to have this discussion again. Just chalk it up to my suffering from…what did you call it? The someone-to-watch-over-me syndrome?"

He nodded.

"I'll see you in the morning, then." She tried her best to fake a smile, but her lips would not cooperate.

"Good night, Ms. Murrough."

She sat there until Deke disappeared behind the connecting door, then she planted her cane on the floor and stood. Tears pooled in her eyes, and restrained emotion burned in her throat. If she wept aloud, he would hear her. Clenching her teeth as tears trickled down her face, she hurried to the bathroom. Once inside, she closed the door, leaned her head back and opened her mouth to draw in a deep breath. She pressed her clenched fist across her mouth to block the sound, then cried her heart out.

CHAPTER ELEVEN

THERE WAS only one word to describe Monday morning at Helping Hands. Chaos. Utter chaos. Geoff worked with the Bedell, Inc. security personnel that Larry Nesmith had handpicked for the positions, but the charity's nearly two dozen employees were unaccustomed to going through a metal detector, or having their briefcases and handbags searched. Checking IDs for all twenty-two, plus providing them with badges they would have to wear whenever entering or exiting the building, had taken several hours. Adding to the chaos was the fact that local florists had made countless deliveries, and both flowers and fruit baskets now graced more than one employee's desk. It seemed as if at least half the female employees had received flowers from boyfriends, husbands, friends and well-wishers. At this very moment, Lexie's office looked like a flower shop. She alone had received seven arrangements, everything from red roses from Farris to a potted plant from the mayor.

Then there was the eight-man construction crew working to repair the damage done by the bomb. Beating, banging, sawing and hammering only added to the tension permeating the entire building.

For the past hour, Lexie had dealt with agitated co-workers milling in and out of her office with complaints and recommendations, as well as handling endless phone calls. The current call was from Cara.

"Looks like I'll be stuck here in Mexico City for a while," Cara said. "Negotiations are not going well. It could be the end of the week before I'm back in Chattanooga."

Lexie assured Cara that she had everything under control at Helping Hands, that with Bedell, Inc. security and the three Dundee agents, she and the other employees felt perfectly safe.

Just as Lexie finished her conversation and took a free breath, her phone rang again. Toni grabbed it before Lexie could, pointed her finger at Lexie and shook her head.

"I'm sorry, but Ms. Murrough has gone to lunch," Toni told the caller. "I'll be happy to give her a message." She listened patiently, cordially ended the conversation and replaced the receiver. "It's one-thirty, and you need a break, somewhere quiet and peaceful." She tapped her wristwatch, and then looked at Deke, who was standing in the corner, his arms crossed over his chest. "Get her out of here. Quiet and peaceful, remember?"

"I can't go out for lunch," Lexie said. "There's too much that needs to be done."

"And it *will* get done. Just not right now. And not all of it by you." Toni picked up Lexie's purse off her desk and handed it to her. "Take a couple of hours for lunch, relax, and then come back and face this madhouse. I'll hold down the fort until you return."

"But don't you have lunch plans with Jafari?" She already knew there was no engagement, so she refrained from bringing up that potentially sore subject.

Toni huffed. "Not today. We had a disagreement yesterday, and I'm not speaking to him until he pays penance."

"What on earth did he do?"

"Don't change the subject. I'll fill you in on the woes of my love life later. Go to lunch. Now."

"Okay. I'm going." Lexie stood, adjusted her cane and turned to Deke. "I can't think of anyplace close where it's quiet and peaceful. Maybe we should just pick up—"

"I know a place," he said, his gaze not quite meeting hers.

"You do?"

"Toni told me where to take you," Deke said. "The reservations are already made."

Lexie looked at him questioningly but didn't say anything. After the wild and crazy morning she'd had, she wasn't going to argue. She could use a few minutes away from all the bedlam.

When they emerged from the elevator at the lobby level, they saw Jafari speaking with the security guards at the front desk. Although he kept his voice low and was being exceedingly polite, Lexie could tell that he was unhappy about being delayed.

Lexie walked over to the guards and said, "Mr. Holston is my assistant Toni's boyfriend. Please issue him a visitor's pass."

"Yes, ma'am," the security guard, whose badge read Blount, replied. "We've checked his ID and were just going to call Ms. Wells to verify he is who he says he is."

"No need," Lexie said. "I can vouch for Mr. Holston."

"Thank you very much, Ms. Murrough." Jafari lowered his head politely, his movements a semibow.

Lexie laid her hand on his arm and nodded toward

the elevator. "Go on up there and take your punishment like a man."

When Jafari stared at her, a confused expression on his face, she said, "Whatever you did, tell her you're sorry and that you'll do whatever is necessary to make it up to her."

"Ah, yes, yes." Jafari smiled. "I will do that. Thank you."

As soon as Jafari entered the elevator, Deke grasped Lexie's elbow and asked, "If you've finished giving advice to the lovelorn…"

She yanked her arm from his grasp and glowered at him, then walked toward the front door. He followed her outside onto the sidewalk, where they ran into Hamal Gazsi, the young intern from Erlanger who was dating Vega. Hamal was clutching a bouquet of flowers in his hands. He nodded and spoke, but didn't stop.

"And that was?" Deke asked.

"Dr. Gazsi. He's Vega's boyfriend."

"What are you running here, a dating service or a charity organization?"

Lexie smiled, but didn't pause and didn't glance Deke's way. "I'm running a charity organization with employees who have personal lives. You do know what those are, don't you?"

The moment she'd snapped out the last comment, she wished it back.

They rounded the corner and headed toward the alley where Deke had parked Lexie's new Mercedes. A Bedell, Inc. security guard strolled past them, nodded and said, "Good afternoon, Ms. Murrough."

Deke opened the car door for her, but stood back and didn't offer her his assistance. By the time she was seated, he had rounded the hood and had the driver's door open.

Once inside, his seat belt on and the key in the ignition, he glanced briefly in her direction before starting the engine and maneuvering the car out of its spot.

"You didn't need to check the car for a bomb?" Lexie asked.

"No, that's why there's an outside security guard, to provide extra surveillance for the parking lot and the back entrances."

Deke eased the Mercedes into midday traffic and within minutes turned down Broad Street. A few minutes later, he pulled into the valet parking area of the Sheraton Read House. The renovated hotel possessed the elegance of historical charm and Georgian architecture.

When Deke parked and got out, Lexie assumed he was taking her to Porter's Steak House for lunch. But instead, he led her into the hotel, picked up a key at the front desk and escorted her into an elevator.

"Where are we going?" she asked.

"Everything has been arranged," Deke said. "I commandeered Ty Garrett's room for a couple of hours, and Toni ordered us lunch."

"We're borrowing Mr. Garrett's room here at the hotel?"

"Yep."

The elevator door opened. Deke stepped out and waited for her. When she emerged, she allowed him to take her arm and escort her down the hall.

"This is rather extravagant," Lexie said. "You and Toni shouldn't have gone to so much trouble just so I could get away from the office for a little while."

"Forget 'a little while.' My instructions were to keep you away for a couple of hours." Deke opened the door to the hotel room and waited for her to enter.

The room was designed to reflect the hotel's elegant past, and the furniture was antique reproductions and the style classically traditional. The curtains were open to allow afternoon sunlight in and to give the occupants a view of downtown's Broad Street.

A dining table had been set for two.

Lexie made her way over to it and found an appetizing lunch ready for them. Shrimp cocktails. Caesar salads. Turkey club sandwiches. Fresh fruit. And large glasses of iced tea.

Deke pulled out a chair for her. As she sat, she glanced over her shoulder and up at him. "This looks delicious, doesn't it?"

He nodded.

When he sat across from her and placed his napkin in his lap, Lexie lifted her glass and took a sip of the refreshing iced tea.

Apparently Deke wasn't in a talkative mood, but then, what had she expected? On short acquaintance, she had learned he was a man of few words, so expecting to while away a few hours in idle chitchat with him was probably out of the question.

They ate in silence until finally, as she finished her salad, Lexie said, "This was a really nice gesture, but totally unnecessary. We'll be finished eating soon and can go back to the office."

"I'm not taking you back to the office for at least two hours," he told her, then bit into his club sandwich.

"What I am supposed to do—sit around and twiddle my thumbs?"

Deke swallowed, took a hefty swig of iced tea and replied, "Watch TV, take a nap—"

"I have no intention of doing either. If I have to stay here, I'd rather talk." She nibbled on her sandwich.

"Talk?"

"You know—conversation. You say something and I reply. I say something and you reply."

He looked downright uncomfortable. "Talk to each other about what?"

"Nothing. Everything. The story of my life. The story of yours. Details about marriages, engagements, college, high school, kindergarten. Parents, siblings. All that getting-to-know-you stuff that people talk about."

"I'm your bodyguard," he told her. "Not your new boyfriend."

Why did he insist on saying things that made her feel as if he was warning her off, putting up a defensive barrier between them by being rude?

"You're being an ass, you know," she told him, her voice edged with anger. There was no need for him to keep reminding her that as far as he was concerned, she was off limits.

He narrowed his gaze as he looked at her. "I'm sorry."

"If you're really sorry, then humor me and just pretend you're talking to another guy."

"My imagination isn't that good."

Her anger subsided, its survival impossible in the face of such honesty, and without a moment's hesitation, she plunged ahead. "I was an only child who had doting parents. I was a spoiled kid who had fun in high school, was homecoming queen in college and dated a star athlete. My dad died while I was in college, and two years later my mom remarried. My stepfather's a nice guy. He has a son who's married and has two daughters. What about you?"

"What about me?" He finished off the last drop of iced tea.

"Parents? Siblings?"

"My parents are dead. No siblings."

"College?"

"University of Texas at San Antonio. I went into the army straight out of college."

"Are you originally from Texas?" She pierced a pineapple tidbit with her fork.

"Yep."

Lexie studied Deke for a long moment. "You're not making this easy."

"I'm doing my best," he told her. "I'm answering your questions."

"With as few words as possible." She set her fork on the edge of the fruit cup and laid her napkin on the table.

"I'm not a big talker."

"So I've noticed."

Lexie scooted back her chair, lifted her cane and stood. When she walked across the room, she half expected him to follow her.

He didn't.

She stood by the windows overlooking Broad Street and waited for him to come to her.

He didn't.

"How long were you married?" she asked.

"A year."

"Did you break her heart, or did she break yours?"

Silence.

Lexie glanced over her shoulder. He wasn't looking at her, and she turned back to the window.

"Nobody's heart got broken," he finally said.

"I find that hard to believe."

"Why?"

"Because when two people are in love and—"

"We weren't in love."

"Oh."

Silence.

Even with her back to him and his movement undetectable, Lexie sensed him approaching and knew the moment he stood behind her. She was aware of him on every level, felt his heat and masculine power, and reacted as instinctively to his presence as if an invisible link bound them.

"I've been in love twice," she said, but didn't turn to face him. "Once when I was in college, and then later with my fiancé. Well, actually, maybe it wasn't real love the first time. I was young, and as much in love with love as I was with Jamie Fowler. I was a little brokenhearted when we split, but nothing like when Wes Harris dumped me." She took a couple of deep, gulping breaths. "It was my own fault for falling in love with such a jerk. I should have known he wasn't the kind of man who could love deeply and completely. He was far too self-centered. When Wes turned his back on me because he didn't want a wife who was flawed, I thought I'd die."

Standing behind her, Deke gently clamped his big hands down on her shoulders. Without realizing what she was doing, she swayed backward against him. And when she did, he engulfed her completely, skimming his open palms over her arms and downward until he circled her waist. She rested the back of her head against his chest and closed her eyes. Sighing. Loving the feel of him. Knowing she was safe in his arms.

"Please don't feel sorry for me," she said.

With his body so closely aligned to hers, she felt his muscles tense. He leaned his head down and pressed his jaw against the side of her temple as he tightened his embrace. He didn't say a word. He simply held her.

They stood there in front of the windows with her wrapped in his strong, protective arms, and everything else faded away, leaving them the only two people in the world. No pasts. No futures. Only that moment in time.

When she turned slowly in his arms and looked up into his storm-cloud-gray eyes, she saw what he was feeling. Such raw hunger startled her.

"Deke…?"

Without any preamble whatsoever, he swooped down and took her mouth in a ravaging yet tender kiss. Something savagely beautiful exploded inside her, a sensation unlike any she had ever experienced. Passion, longing and a hunger to match his, and yet a unique sense of knowing that what was happening between them was meant to be.

When she responded with equal fervor, he deepened the kiss, taking full advantage of her invitation. After letting her cane drop to the carpeted floor, Lexie lifted her arms and draped them over his broad shoulders. He eased one hand down to cup her hip and pulled her against his arousal. Every nerve in her body tingled. His other hand slipped under the hem of her cotton sweater and splayed across her back, his fingertips rubbing across the hooks on her bra.

Lost in a sexual fog of pure pleasure, Lexie didn't object when he undid her bra and dipped his head downward to kiss the side of her neck. She sighed heavily when he kissed her throat as he slid one hand between their bodies and inched it upward from her waist. He inserted a couple of fingers under the edge of her loose bra and lifted the cup away from her breast. When he ran his thumb over her nipple, she whimpered softly and gave herself over completely to her own desire.

She wanted him to make love to her, needed him as she had never needed anything or anyone.

He tenderly squeezed one breast and then the other, then toyed with each nipple until Lexie thought she would scream. She wanted his mouth on her, wanted his tongue to replace his fingers.

Suddenly a distinct ringing sound managed to break through the roaring beat of her heart. Damn his cell phone. And damn whoever was calling.

Slowly and obviously reluctantly, Deke slipped his hand from underneath her sweater, then grasped her shoulders and pressed his forehead against hers. His voice a deep growl, he told her, "I have to get that."

She blew out a deep breath. "I know."

He released her, yanked his phone from the belt clip and said, "Bronson here."

While he took the call, Lexie somehow managed to refasten her bra, her hands trembling so badly that it took her several tries.

Deke's conversation was one-sided, with the caller apparently doing most of the talking. Deke replied with single words—damn, yeah, sure, immediately—and then ended with, "We're on our way."

"What is it? What's wrong?" Lexie asked.

He reached out and gripped her shoulders firmly. "There's been an accident."

"What kind of accident?" Her heartbeat accelerated. Fear tightened her stomach muscles.

"Malik Abdel has been shot."

"Is he dead?"

"Don't know," Deke said. "Lieutenant Desmond called your office, and Toni handed the phone over to Geoff. All he told Geoff was that Malik is being rushed to Erlanger, so I assume he's still alive."

"But who'd shoot Malik? And why?"

"I don't know, honey. But we'll find out."

CHAPTER TWELVE

WHEN THEY ARRIVED at the ER, Geoff Monday met them outside the entrance. "No word on his condition. They just rushed him up to surgery."

"What happened?" Lexie asked. "Do you know any details?"

"Not really," Geoff said. "Lieutenant Desmond is still at the scene, but he said to tell you that he'll speak to you as soon as he can."

"Is anyone else here?" Lexie glanced at the automatic doors to the ER.

"Toni and Vega and that Richardson guy," Geoff replied. "Alice Kennedy and Robert Lufti stayed behind to keep things running at the office."

The ER doors swung open. Toni came rushing out and straight to Lexie. After a couple of tearful hugs, Toni stepped back and wiped her damp cheeks with her fingertips.

"He's such a good guy, you know," Toni said. "He had big plans for the future. Becoming a U.S. citizen was so important to him. How could something like this happen to him?"

"Bad things happen to good people," Lexie said. "You know that as well as I do."

"He'd gone out for lunch." Toni shook her head

sadly. "You know how he likes to do that, how he loves trying out different restaurants."

"He was on his way back from lunch when it happened," Geoff said. "Apparently someone shot him while he was driving, and he wrecked his car. At first the incident was considered an accident, until the paramedics discovered he'd been shot."

Toni grasped Lexie's hand. "Come on inside. I left poor Vega with Farris, and he's absolutely worthless in a crisis. He needs more coddling than a five-year-old."

As soon as they entered the waiting area, Farris hurried over to Lexie. With tears in his eyes and his hands quivering, he reached out and hugged her. "It's horrible. Simply horrible." He clung to her. "God only knows which one of us will be next."

Lexie's stomach muscles clenched. Had Malik been shot by the mad bomber? She had thought perhaps he'd been the victim of a carjacking gone wrong, or that maybe the shooter had something personal against Malik, although he was so charismatic that she couldn't imagine anyone not liking him.

Deke clamped one big hand down on Farris's shoulder, and the smaller man jerked his head back and stared wide-eyed at Deke. When Deke gave his shoulder a persuasive yank, Farris took the non-too-subtle hint and quickly released Lexie.

"Poor, poor Malik." Farris bowed his head and closed his eyes. His thin lips moved silently, but Lexie knew he was praying. What she didn't know was whether his prayer was completely sincere or if it was partly for show. Farris had a tendency to want others to be aware of just how pious he was.

Deke gave Geoff a "handle him" signal, then cupped

Lexie's elbow and encouraged her toward a row of empty chairs. When Deke helped her into a seat, then took her cane from her and hung it over the back of the adjoining chair, she didn't protest. In fact, she was grateful. Right now, she could use all the support she could get—both physical and emotional.

She moved her small shoulder bag into her lap and grasped it with both hands. Although she wasn't trembling, she felt jittery and desperately needed an anchor.

"Farris is an idiot," Toni whispered as she sat beside Lexie. "An educated idiot, but an idiot all the same. Of all the things for him to say…"

"It's all right," Lexie told her. "Really. Farris is just Farris. He's frightened. And with good reason."

"We're all unnerved," Toni admitted. "But until all the facts are in, he should keep his mouth shut."

Lexie's cell phone rang. She clutched her purse tightly. "I should have turned it off before we came in here." By the time she unzipped her leather bag and reached inside for the phone, Deke was standing in front of her with his hand outstretched. Without hesitation, she turned the phone over to him.

As he moved toward the exterior doors, he motioned to Geoff, who left his post keeping Farris at bay and took up Deke's position guarding Lexie. She watched Deke walk outside and disappear.

Toni reached over and patted Lexie's hands, which were still clutching the sides of her open purse. "Don't jump to conclusions. It might not be *him.* It could be Alice or Robert calling from the office. Or your mom or Cara or—"

"No, it's him. He's calling to tell me that he shot Malik."

"You can't know that for sure."

Lexie ran her tongue over the tips of her teeth and breathed deeply in an effort not to cry. If the mad bomber was now targeting her friends and employees... Dear God, what had she ever done to this man to make him hate her so vehemently?

Her gaze never left the ER exit as she waited for Deke to return. If only she were wrong about the caller. Maybe Toni was right. It could be someone else. But her mother wouldn't call her cell number unless it was an emergency. And Robert or Alice would probably call Toni.

It could be Cara.

Deke returned through the electronic doors, his expression telling her nothing. Nervous tension tightened her muscles and accelerated her heartbeat. He came over to her, squatted down in front of her and took her hands in his. That wasn't a good sign. It had to be bad news.

Toni draped her arm around Lexie's shoulders.

Lexie looked Deke square in the eyes.

"You want it straight or sugarcoated?" he asked.

Oh, God! Oh, God!

"Straight," she told him.

He squeezed her hands. "He said to ask you how it feels to know you're responsible for a friend's death."

Emotion lodged in her throat, momentarily cutting off her air. Shutting her eyes and clamping her jaws tightly, Lexie absorbed the emotional pain, and then she released a long, cleansing breath before looking at Deke again.

"Damn." Toni's eyes widened.

Lexie couldn't speak. What could she possibly say in response to such a question? Was the caller referring to Marty Bearn, who had died half a world away ten years ago, or did the man believe that he had killed Malik today?

Deke gave her hands another squeeze, then rose to his feet. He hadn't returned her cell phone. Did he think the man would call again?

Lexie wasn't sure how long they stayed in the ER waiting area. Although it seemed like hours, in reality, it probably wasn't more than thirty minutes. Farris had excused himself to go to the chapel, and Geoff had mentioned going for coffee. But before Geoff had a chance to leave, one of the ER nurses came out and asked to speak to a member of Malik Abdel's family.

While Lexie struggled to stand, dropping her purse on the floor as she reached for her cane, Deke responded to the nurse's summons. By the time Toni picked up Lexie's purse and she managed to get on her feet, the nurse was gone and Deke had turned to face them.

This time, she could read his expression. Even the stoic Mr. Bronson couldn't hide the regret she saw in his eyes.

Lexie paused so abruptly that Toni actually bumped into her.

"He's dead," Lexie said.

"No, don't say that." Toni laced her arm through Lexie's.

As Deke walked toward them, Geoff approached from the opposite side of the room. When the four came together, Deke hesitated, and she could tell that he dreaded relaying the bad news.

"Is he dead?" Toni blurted out.

"Yeah," Deke said. "He died a few minutes ago."

Lexie felt as if a wall of bricks had collapsed on top of her. She swayed ever so slightly.

Deke reached out and grabbed her upper arm. "I'm taking you home. Now."

"I can't go home," she replied. "There are arrangements to be made. I'm sure he'd want his body sent home for burial, but we should have a memorial service of some kind here. And Alice will have to issue a press release and—"

"And those are all things that I can take care of," Toni told her.

"No, it's my job. I should be the one to—"

"Let Toni do it." Deke urged Lexie into motion, aiming her in the direction of the exit.

"What about Farris?" Lexie asked.

"You go with Deke," Geoff told her. "I'll go with Toni to inform Richardson, and then I'll take them back to Helping Hands."

Lexie nodded agreement and didn't put up any further protests when Deke escorted her outside, straight to her new Mercedes, and belted her securely into the passenger seat.

As he pulled out of the parking lot, she said, "I want to go to my apartment."

"That's not a good idea."

"I don't care. I want to go home." She sucked in huge gulps of air as tears pooled in her eyes. "I need to go home. Please."

Clenching his jaw, Deke maneuvered the luxury car out into the traffic. Then he said, "It wasn't your fault."

Tears streamed down her face. She swallowed several times. Overcome with emotion, she couldn't speak for several minutes.

"Your going home and making yourself more vulnerable to attack won't stop him from targeting someone else, if that's his intention," Deke said.

"There's no way to guard all my friends and all the

Helping Hands employees," Lexie finally managed to say. "If he wants to kill me, why target other people?"

"To make you suffer," Deke replied.

MALIK ABDEL was dead, a casualty of his own stupidity. By being Lexie Murrough's friend and employee, the Gadian traitor had chosen the wrong side. His death, although unfortunate, had been necessary.

He wanted Lexie to suffer, as he and his mother had suffered after his father's death. Before he killed her, he wanted her to experience the agony of knowing she was responsible for the deaths of others, people she cared about and would mourn, as he and his mother had mourned.

He would take another life. Soon. He would not give Lexie time to recover from this loss before he struck again. The next victims had been chosen with great care. And with each death, Lexie would suffer more and more.

Smiling to himself, he thought about December twenty-first, the day he would make the ultimate sacrifice. By dying for a cause worth far more than his own life, he would receive the greatest rewards in heaven.

But for now, he would have to pretend that he, too, mourned Malik Abdel. It would be expected. And he would have to be supportive and caring when his woman turned to him for comfort. Malik had been her friend, and his death would affect her greatly.

He should prepare himself to be questioned by the police. He was not certain that he would fall under suspicion, but he was a foreigner and had no alibi for the time Malik was shot, no witness to come forward and say they had seen him miles away from the scene.

He was always careful. His actions could not jeopardize the Majeed's plans. He was allowed this personal vendetta only if it did not conflict in any way with his duties connected with the upcoming strike against the United States.

DEKE MET Bain Desmond at the door, stepped out into the hallway and eased the door closed behind him.

Desmond frowned. "Why the hell did you bring her back here?"

"Because she needed to come home, at least for tonight."

"How's she doing?"

"How do you think?"

Desmond nodded. "This shouldn't be happening, especially to someone like Lexie, who gives her all to help other people."

"Shit happens."

Desmond glared at Deke. "So how much have you told her?"

"Everything I know."

"Was that wise?"

"Yeah, I think it was. And I'd advise you not to lie to her or even sugarcoat anything. She deserves the unvarnished truth."

"You think she can handle it?"

Deke inclined his head toward the closed door. "That lady in there is one of the strongest women I've ever known."

Desmond eyed him speculatively. "You admire her, too, don't you?"

Did he admire her? Damn right he did. He admired Lexie, respected her, wanted her, and whether he liked it or not, he was crazy about her. Or maybe he was just crazy. If he thought for one minute that he could ever have her...

"Look, I just got her to lie down a few minutes ago. She's worn herself out making phone calls in between going to the bathroom to cry in private. Even though Toni said she'd handle all the arrangements, Lexie insisted on being the one to telephone Malik's family in Gadi."

"Dear God," Desmond grumbled.

"Yeah, tell me about it. She was a brave soldier until afterward, then she spent fifteen minutes in the powder room."

"So is this your subtle way of suggesting I come back later?"

Deke sensed her presence before he heard the door open.

"That won't be necessary," Lexie said. "Please, Bain, come on in."

Deke and Desmond turned to face the bleary-eyed woman standing in the apartment doorway.

When the lieutenant walked over to Lexie and kissed her cheek, Deke saw red. How stupid was that? He couldn't remember ever being so damn jealous, but then, he'd never felt so totally possessive before, either.

"Would you care for some coffee or tea?" Lexie asked, playing the good hostess as she led them inside.

"Nah, nothing for me." Bain put his arm around Lexie's waist and escorted her into the living room.

Deke wanted to shout *Get your damn hands off her!* Instead, he kept quiet as he closed and locked the door.

Once they were all seated, Desmond on the sofa with Lexie and Deke across from them, the lieutenant ran his hands up and down his thighs, as if trying to stall for time. Deke understood. The last thing either of them wanted to do was cause Lexie more pain.

Desmond turned to her. "Malik was shot in the head. After taking a look at his car and speaking to the doctors in the ER, my initial guess is that he saw his killer. He was shot at close range, less than a block from the restaurant. The parking lot exits onto a back street, and apparently Malik had just pulled out when it happened."

"Then someone else should have seen the killer, too, right?" Lexie looked at Desmond with hope in her eyes.

"You'd think so," Desmond replied. "But so far, we don't have a witness."

"And no one heard the shot?" she asked.

Desmond shook his head. "A couple of people thought they heard a car backfire."

"I assume you're running a check to see if any of the Gadian employees at Helping Hands owns a gun," Deke said.

Desmond glanced at Deke. "Yeah, we're running a check on all the employees, as well as friends and relatives."

"Does that include Vega's and Toni's boyfriends, too?"

"Sure does."

"Do you actually consider Jafari and Hamal or anyone associated with Helping Hands a suspect?" Lexie asked.

"Yes, unfortunately, I do," Desmond replied.

Unconsciously, Lexie wrung her hands together. "I can't believe that he's anyone I know personally. That would mean that someone who pretends to like me actually hates me enough to not only want to kill me, but to kill people I care about."

"Whoever he is, he's not rational," Desmond told her.

"We're dealing with a psycho, so don't expect logic from this guy."

"And don't think you can figure out why he hates you," Deke said. "In his own sick mind, he has a good reason. To anyone who's sane, his reason would seem ludicrous."

Desmond took Lexie's hand in his. "Do me a favor?"

"What?"

"Go back to the Bedell estate. You're safer there."

"I will," she said. "Just not tonight. I need to stay here in my own home, sleep in my own bed." She looked pleadingly into Desmond's eyes. "Try to understand."

Desmond cupped her chin gently. "I'll call you in the morning."

She offered the lieutenant a fragile smile.

When Desmond got up and headed for the door, Deke followed him out. They paused in the hallway, a few feet beyond the half-closed apartment door.

"Take care of her," Desmond said.

"That's my job," Deke told him.

Desmond grunted. "Yeah, I know, but something tells me that keeping Lexie safe is more than just a job to you."

"Meaning?"

"If you take advantage of her, you'll have to answer to me."

"She doesn't need you to protect her," Deke said, barely controlling his anger and his jealousy.

"Doesn't she? You might be able to protect her from everyone else, but who's going to protect her from you?"

Deke bristled. "Whatever does or does not happen between Lexie and me is none of your business."

"I'll make it my business if—"

"Let's not make this a pissing contest," Deke warned. "She doesn't belong to either one of us."

Desmond glowered at Deke but didn't reply. He just nodded, grunted and then walked away.

When Deke reentered the apartment, he found Lexie in the kitchen preparing tea.

"I fixed you a cup, too," she told him as he approached.

"Thanks."

She dropped the used tea bags into the garbage and turned around to face Deke.

"You and Bain didn't come to blows, did you?" she asked, the corners of her mouth curving into a half smile.

"Were you eavesdropping?"

"I didn't have to. I know Bain, and I'm getting to know you better every day. You're both big, strong, macho guys who want to keep me safe." She picked up one mug and held it out to him. "Even though I'm not actually involved with either of you, both of you have made some kind of claim on me, haven't you? Bain is a good friend. He cares. He's probably sensed some of the energy going on between you and me, and he's concerned. Right?"

Deke took the mug from her and sipped the hot tea but didn't respond to her question.

"And even though, as my bodyguard, you've tried to keep things professional between us, you can't deny that we're strongly attracted to each other. This afternoon, if—"

"I shouldn't have allowed things to get out of hand," Deke said. "It was my fault, and I'm sorry. It won't happen again."

Leaving her mug sitting on the counter, Lexie walked

over to Deke and looked up at him. "Then I don't suppose I can persuade you to hold me in your arms all night long, can I?"

CHAPTER THIRTEEN

"LADY, you shouldn't say something like that to man who's trying his level best to keep his hands off you." Deke clutched the mug of tea.

"Then my offer does tempt you?" she asked.

Her fragile smile broke his heart. She needed something from him, but he wasn't sure if even she knew exactly what that something was. A warm body lying beside her in the dark. Strong arms to hold her close. A shoulder to lean on. Or did she want a man who would be around for the long haul?

"I'm tempted," he told her. "But whether or not I can give you what you want depends on what you're offering."

"Right now, if you need it to be sex, then that's what I'm offering. But…I just need someone to hold me, to help me make it through tonight without falling apart. Can you understand?"

He set the mug on the counter and then held out one hand to her. She stared at his offered hand, hesitated, then accepted by placing her hand in his.

His fingers closed, securely gripping her.

They stood there staring at each other.

Deke wanted to sweep her up in his arms, carry her to bed and make love to her until morning. But that wasn't what she really needed.

Yanking gently on her hand, he pulled her to him. She gazed up at him, a silent plea in her eyes.

Such blue, blue eyes.

"I understand how it feels, wanting not to be alone," he said. "And you're not alone, Lexie. I'm here. I'll hold you all night long. No sex. Just comfort."

She wrapped her arms around him, laid her head on his chest and wept quietly, so quietly that it took him a couple of minutes to realize she was crying. He stroked her back tenderly, doing his best to soothe her. God, how he wanted her, wanted her so much he ached with the longing to be inside her. Holding her this way was sheer torture, but he would endure this and worse if it helped her.

He would do anything for Lexie.

She hugged him, then lifted her head and asked, "Would you please remove your gun?"

He nodded. She stepped away from him and watched while, without a moment's hesitation, he took off his jacket, tossed it on the bar, then removed his holster and laid it on top of his jacket.

She returned to his arms so eagerly that it was as if there was no other place on earth she'd rather be. "Will you really stay with me all night? I don't want to be alone."

Words were unnecessary. Deke lifted her up and into his arms. She went willingly, wrapping her arm around his neck and laying her head on his shoulder. He carried her to the sofa, sat down and held her in his lap.

"Thank you," she whispered.

"Anything for you," he replied.

They stayed there on the sofa, her soft, warm body curled against him, until she fell asleep. Her left hand rested between his back and the top of the sofa; her right hand lay nestled over his belly. Her breathing was slow and steady, her breath brushing like a feather across his neck. Deke rested his chin on the top of her head and savored the sweet scent of her clean hair.

"Lexie?" he called quietly.

She didn't stir.

"I'm going to carry you to bed," he whispered, as he stood with her cradled in his arms.

He made his way into her bedroom, deposited her on the bed, then eased the spread and covers down on one side, shifted her, and turned down the covers on the other side. Leaning over, he grasped one of her feet, removed her shoe and tossed it onto the floor, then lifted the other foot and repeated the process. She wore a pair of navy slacks, with a matching jacket and neat white blouse. He managed to remove the jacket, but he knew when to leave well enough alone. If he removed anything else, there was no way he would be able to keep his hands off her.

Deke unbuttoned his shirt, jerked the ends up and out of his slacks and removed his belt and shoes. He crawled into the bed beside Lexie, slid one arm under her and pulled up the covers to his waist. Immediately, she snuggled against him.

He draped his other arm around her protectively, then kissed her temple. She sighed. He kissed her cheek. She sighed again.

Deke groaned silently.

He had the hard-on from hell.

Lexie slept.

Deke lay awake for hours. Holding her. Wanting her. And yet thankful that he could offer her security and comfort.

Hours later, he finally dozed off for a while, and

when he woke shortly before dawn, it was to find Lexie all but lying on top of him. Her right leg was pressed against his hip, and her left leg, bent at the knee, rested on top of his left thigh. Her left arm draped across him, her index finger curled around a clump of chest hair. Every muscle in his body felt stiff from lying in one position for such a long time. When he stretched and then turned toward her, Lexie curved around him and buried her face against his neck.

God help him! A man could stand only so much.

Don't do it. Don't give in to temptation. She needs you to be strong.

If the past weren't standing between them, Deke wouldn't hesitate to make love to her. But he knew the unforgivable secret that lay between them, and she did not. If she knew that he was the man who had shot and crippled her…

He could hold her, comfort her, protect her and, if necessary, lay his life on the line for her, but he could never be her lover.

Deke didn't sleep again, and when morning came, he rose from the bed, drew the covers up and over her, and kissed her parted lips. Then he gathered his shoes and belt, went into the guest room's adjoining bath, stripped out of his clothes and stood under a cold shower.

ICE HUNG *from the trees. A shower of white surrounded her. She lay alone in the snowdrift. Naked. Abandoned. And freezing to death. Shivering from the cold, she tried to move but couldn't. She lay there helpless, knowing that, without him, she would die.*

Lexie's eyes flew open.

She'd been dreaming. Another nightmare.

But she was cold. So cold.

No wonder—she was lying atop the covers.

Deke! Where was he? The last thing she remembered was sitting on his lap on the sofa, with him holding her.

Lexie scooted to the edge of the bed and sat up, then looked around as her eyes adjusted to the morning sunlight streaming through the windows. She saw her cane propped against the nightstand. Deke must have brought it in here and left it for her.

But where was he? She glanced back at the bed and noticed a dent in the other pillow. Had he slept with her? Was that the reason she had rested so peacefully, without waking, without dreams, until only a few moments ago?

Last night she had practically begged him to hold her, to stay with her. She'd even offered to have sex with him.

Oh, God!

Well, you didn't have sex with him. You're still dressed, still have on your bra and panties, as well as your slacks and blouse.

She had to face him sooner or later, but not until she'd showered and changed clothes. Not until she'd had time to pull her thoughts together and decide how to go about thanking him for being such a gentleman.

Half an hour later, Lexie emerged from her bedroom, hair still damp and beginning to curl in long loose tendrils around her shoulders, dressed in black jeans and an oversize red sweater that hung to midthigh. And prepared to apologize to Deke for being so needy last night and to tell him how much she appreciated the way he'd taken care of her.

As she approached the kitchen area, Deke turned from the stovetop, where he was flipping pancakes, and smiled at her.

"Morning, sleepyhead. I'd begun to wonder if you were going to snooze the day away."

Deke Bronson smiled at her. Would wonders never cease?

"You're smiling." The words flew out of her mouth before she could stop them.

He chuckled. "I don't smile much, do I?" He motioned to her. "Come on over, sit down and have some breakfast. I've got the pancakes almost ready and that's—" he nodded to the coffeemaker "—a fresh pot of coffee."

"How long have you been up?"

"A couple of hours." He poured her a cup of coffee and set it on the bar that separated the kitchen from the open loft area.

She hoisted herself up on a bar stool and hooked her cane over the end of the bar. "You slept with me last night."

"You asked me to hold you in my arms all night long, and that's what I did."

"Thank you."

"It was my pleasure." He returned his attention to the pancakes, lifting them onto the waiting plates, stacking them atop the ones he'd already prepared.

"Deke…?"

He set a plate in front of her and another on the placemat alongside hers, then he came around the bar and sat. "It's okay, Lexie. Nothing happened. I just held you."

"I know. And I want to thank you for that, too."

"You should." He grinned. "Not many men have the willpower to hold a gorgeous woman all night long without jumping her bones."

Lexie smiled back at him. "I probably wouldn't have minded."

"You would have regretted it this morning." He shrugged. "Besides, I don't take advantage of women when they're vulnerable."

"You're an honorable man."

He glanced away. "I haven't always been."

"We've all made mistakes, done things we wish we could change." She reached over and caressed his arm. "I'm a good listener, if you ever want to—"

"Were you planning to stop by Helping Hands this morning before the funeral?" Deke asked, effectively changing the subject.

"Oh, mercy, I'd almost forgotten that Peter Adderly's service is at eleven."

She couldn't miss Peter's service. It was bad enough that she hadn't flown to Mississippi for Eugene Newberry's funeral. At the request of his siblings, Eugene's body had been shipped home to Harrisburg. On behalf of Helping Hands, Lexie had sent flowers. And she and Cara and a few others who had known Eugene well had sent smaller arrangements, too. The young man had been new to the organization, at the job less than two months before he'd died in the bombing.

"No worries. It's only eight forty-five," Deke told her.

"Peter was a grandfather," Lexie said. "Five grandchildren. He was always showing people new snapshots he'd taken of them. Three girls and two boys. He was such a proud papaw."

"It's no more your fault that those two men were killed than that Malik was shot. You are not responsible for the actions of a madman."

"I know, but—"

"No buts." Deke pointed to her plate. "Eat your pancakes before they get cold." He opened the syrup bottle, upended it and poured, then handed it to her.

"I suppose I have to go back to the Bedell estate this evening, don't I?" She covered her pancakes with syrup. To hell with counting calories today.

"You'll be safer there, and easier to protect."

"He's not going to try to kill me right away, is he? He plans to keep hurting me by killing the people I care about." She lifted the cup to her lips and took a sip of coffee.

"There's no way to know for sure what he'll do next, or when."

PETER ADDERLY'S funeral left Lexie with a headache caused by crying, one of those brain-foggy aches that aspirin wouldn't cure right away. Helping Hands was closed for the funeral, and only Lexie and Toni went to the office afterward, around three-thirty. With plans for Malik's memorial service finalized and arrangements made to send his body back to Gadi, they ended their day around six that evening. Jafari had attended the Adderly funeral with Toni and had come back to pick her up after work.

"He's on his best behavior," Toni had told Lexie before she left. "I haven't forgiven him yet, so he knows he's on probation."

Lexie knew it was only a matter of time before the two lovebirds kissed and made up. In the two years she had known Toni and met half a dozen of her boyfriends, she had never seen Toni so in love.

Ty Garrett had phoned twenty minutes ago and asked for a meeting with Lexie. The background reports on her employees had come in, and he'd thought she would want to go over them. They now sat around the oval table in the conference room at Helping Hands: Lexie, Deke, Geoff and Ty.

She couldn't help studying the three men. And comparing them. Deke and Geoff were the oldest, both probably close to forty, if not there already. Deke was the tallest and largest of the three. There weren't that many six-foot-four guys as big as he was, unless they were professional linebackers. His black hair and dark complexion made his gray eyes all the more extraordinary. With his military-short blond hair, darkly tanned skin and sky-blue eyes, Geoff was amazingly attractive considering the fact that he was far from handsome. Solidly built, with broad shoulders and muscular arms, and a respectable six feet tall, he exuded masculine power. A dark-haired, dark-eyed Southern boy from Arkansas, Ty Garrett was the youngest of the three Dundee agents, probably in his midthirties, and had the long, lean build and upper-body strength of a young Clint Eastwood.

Ty placed his briefcase on the table, opened it and removed several file folders off the top of a rather large stack. "I printed out all the info on the ones I thought y'all needed to take a look at."

He handed each of them a folder. "I discarded the one on Malik Abdel."

Lexie opened the folder and scanned the names. Robert Lufti. Alice Kennedy. Farris Richardson. Toni Wells. Jafari Holston. Vega Sharif. Hamal Gazsi.

"I don't understand why Alice and Toni are on this list," Lexie said. "They were both born and raised in the U.S. And I've known them both for more than two years. Besides that, they're both women, as is Vega."

Ty nodded. "Yes, ma'am. But they're three women who are involved with possible suspects."

"You consider Jafari, Hamal and Robert suspects?" She glared at Ty. "And Farris—you've got to be kidding."

"At this point, they're our top contenders," Ty said.

Deke, who had been reading the reports rapidly, commented. "Three of them being foreigners, born in Africa, and either directly or indirectly connected to Helping Hands, seem to be the chief reasons they're prime suspects, right?"

"Yes, that and a few discrepancies in their background checks," Ty said. "In each of their cases, something sent up a red flag."

Lexie's heart sank, and not simply because she knew and liked all four men, but because three of her friends were in love with three of these men. Dear God, if Jafari… No, it couldn't be him. Toni would be devastated. But it wasn't Robert. He was such a sweetheart. And he had made Alice so happy, even if everyone believed that their affair would be only temporary. Lexie knew the least about Hamal, but he had been in the U.S. for nearly six years, had graduated from medical school in this country and had applied for citizenship.

With silence prevailing in the large conference room, Lexie read and studied each file, as did Deke and Geoff. Although she noted the discrepancies in several of the men's background checks, she couldn't understand why the red flags had gone up at Dundee's. And apparently Geoff and Deke weren't entirely sure, either.

"Okay, Robert Lufti has an uncle and a cousin who belong to a militant group within Gadi," Geoff said. "I can understand why he wouldn't want to include that information on his résumé. But a large percentage of Gadians have relatives who at one time or another found themselves on the wrong side of their civil war, so why—"

"True, but both his uncle and his cousin are still active in the underground anti-American faction that has close ties to other African and Middle Eastern terrorist groups," Ty explained.

"Young Dr. Gazsi neglected to mention that he was adopted, and there is no record of who his biological parents were or where they came from." Deke tapped the open folder. "I suppose he could have been born in Gadi and lived there until he was adopted."

"We're digging deeper," Ty said. "But information from that part of the world is sketchy at best, and it's possible that even Gazsi doesn't know anything about his real parents."

"What about Jafari?" Lexie asked. "I didn't see anything in the file that would make you suspicious of him. He's a British citizen, and the information on his parents and his life before coming to the U.S. coincides precisely with what he's told Toni."

"True enough," Ty said. "But Jafari was not born in England, and the records of his existence before ten years ago are still incomplete."

"I'm sure there are perfectly reasonable explanations for all these red-flag issues." Lexie glanced around the room and noted the skeptical looks on the Dundee agents' faces. "Y'all do realize that it's quite possible that the killer is not associated with Helping Hands in any way and may not even know me personally?"

"Anything is possible," Geoff told her.

"You're allowed to let your personal feelings cloud your vision," Deke said. "But we have to look at each probable suspect with no preconceived opinions. We know that often the worst criminal appears to be gentle and kind and even charming."

"I still can't imagine why you included Farris. The man is as harmless as—"

"Your harmless accountant spent six months in a mental hospital after stalking and threatening his ex-wife," Deke pointed out to her.

"I know all about that. He was upfront about his past emotional problems when I hired him."

"But he didn't mention that he's still under psychiatric care, did he?" Ty looked at her point-blank. "He sees a therapist once a week, even now, seven years after his release from the hospital. Did you know that, too?"

"No," she admitted.

"Because of his past mental instability, we can't dismiss him as a suspect," Geoff said.

"I understand." She hated this, all of it, digging into people's private lives, uncovering secrets that should be kept hidden. Hadn't everyone past the age of consent done something they regretted, that they wished they could change, that they were ashamed of? And simply being foreign—a different nationality, different race, different religion—shouldn't make a person suspect. But on the other hand, she understood that it was the Dundee agents' job to err on the side of caution.

Several loud raps on the closed door announced the arrival of the Chattanooga PD. They had expected Bain to arrive earlier, but he'd phoned to say he was running late because he was waiting for a specific report that might shed a bit more light on the investigation.

When Bain entered the room, he looked directly at Lexie and smiled. The three Dundee agents stood, and the men all exchanged handshakes. Bain came to her, leaned down, put his hand on the back of her chair and asked, "How are you doing?"

"I'm all right." When he looked at her skeptically, she added, "Really, I'm doing fine. Deke's been taking good care of me."

Bain glanced at Deke, then said, "I'm glad to hear it."

"So what's the new information you have to share?" Ty Garrett asked.

"I have a complete report on which Helping Hands employees and their family members own guns." Bain walked over to the coffeemaker in the corner, poured himself a cup and took a seat beside Lexie. "And I have an initial firearms identification on the bullet the doctor removed from Malik."

"I assume your lab ran the bullet through the FBI's Drugfire system," Ty said.

"We did," Bain replied. "And we didn't get a hit."

"But you have a good idea of what type of weapon was used," Geoff said.

"The bullet's a 9 mm," Bain said. "Came from a semiautomatic pistol, probably a Smith and Wesson."

"And who, if anyone, on our suspects list owns a gun that fits that description?" Deke asked.

"Alice Kennedy owns a 910 DA Smith & Wesson she reported stolen a few months ago," Bain said. "And one of the secretaries at Helping Hands, Lynette Seales, owns one, too. A few others own guns, but not 9 mm semiautomatics."

Lexie glanced around the room. "I know what y'all are thinking—that since Robert and Alice are involved, he stole her gun. I refuse to believe—"

"Lexie, sweetie, no one is accusing Robert of anything." Bain offered her a sympathetic pat on the arm. "More than likely whoever shot Malik wasn't stupid enough to use a gun that could be easily traced back to him."

"But you'll have to question Alice and Robert, won't you?" Lexie heaved a distressed sigh.

"Sorry, but yes," Bain said. "And we'll also ask Lynette Seales to give us her weapon for a ballistics comparison."

"Has the Chattanooga PD run a check on alibis?" Ty asked.

"We're still doing that, but if you're asking about Robert, Jafari and Hamal, then yes, we've spoken to each of them, but unfortunately—for us and for them— none of them has a convincing alibi for the approximate time Malik Abdel was shot."

Deke grunted. "Interesting. What were their alibis?"

"They were all alone. Jafari says he was at home studying for a test, but he can't prove that's where he was. Hamal said he had dropped Vega here at Helping Hands after lunch and was driving back to his apartment to get some sleep before his next shift at the hospital. And Robert had gone out to pick up a late lunch for Alice and himself, and it just so happens the restaurant was only a few blocks from where Malik was killed."

Lexie could not accept the possibility that one of these men hated her enough to kill her or that one of them was capable of murdering Malik in cold blood. "So they're all still suspects, aren't they?"

"Yeah, they are," Bain admitted. "But we aren't ruling out the possibility that they're all three completely innocent, and our killer is someone else."

Deke slid back his chair, stood and glanced around the room. "If y'all don't need us, it's after seven, and Lexie hasn't had dinner. I'd like to take her home—back to the Bedell estate—so she can eat and get some rest. It's been a long day for her."

Bain patted her arm again. She smiled at him. "Go," he told her. "There's nothing you can do here. I'll get copies of our ballistics reports and share what I've got with Monday and Garrett. Anything you need to know, they'll pass on to Bronson."

Bain and Deke flanked her chair, the expressions on their faces telling her that both men wanted to assist her but neither dared. She rose to her feet, retrieved her cane and laced her arm through Deke's. "I'm ready."

Deke led her out of the conference room, down the hall and to the elevator. On the ground floor, one security guard remained stationed in the lobby. He spoke to them on their way out. The moment they stepped onto the sidewalk, she felt Deke tense and knew his senses were on high alert, preparing in case of an attack.

The starry night sky appeared little more than a complementary canopy over the cityscape of downtown Chattanooga, alive with lights and the sounds of late-evening traffic. As they strolled around the end of the block and headed toward the back alley parking area, a carload of rowdy teens drove by. They shouted and whistled, and one hung out a back window and blew kisses at Lexie.

Deke stopped instantly and all but picked her up, in order to put her behind him, and flung back his jacket to reveal his holster. The teens raced off at lightning speed.

Deke turned to her. She was trembling from head to toe.

He grasped her by the upper arms. "Are you okay?"

"I'm fine. Just unnerved. I'm not sure what scared me the most—those crazy kids or your quick move to protect me."

He ran his hands up and down her arms. "Come on. Let's get out of here."

She took his arm once again, and he kept in step with her as they entered the parking lot. The security lights cast a mild cream-white glow to illuminate the area. Her Mercedes was one of only four vehicles still there, and it was parked closest to the street. As they approached her car, Deke paused, then whipped back his jacket and removed his gun from its holster.

"What's wrong?"

"I don't see the guard anywhere, so just stay close, okay?" He inched toward the Mercedes.

Lexie did as he had ordered and stayed right with him. Suddenly she realized that there was something all over her windshield, something dark red. And whatever it was, it had been smeared across every window.

"What is it?"

"Come with me—now. No arguments." He moved them back hurriedly, farther and farther away from her car, stopping only after he had her up against the building and was shielding her with his body.

"Take my cell phone and call Geoff," Deke told her. "Tell him to get down here pronto, and bring Ty and Lieutenant Desmond with him. And tell him to use one of the back doors."

Without question, she did as he had instructed, while he kept watch, though for who or what, she didn't know.

Within minutes, Geoff, Ty and Bain, weapons drawn, came storming into the parking lot.

"What's going on?" Bain asked as the threesome surrounded Deke and Lexie.

"Lexie's car is covered with what I'm pretty sure is blood," Deke said.

"Where's the night guard?" Ty asked.

Bain pulled his weapon, carefully rushed toward the Mercedes and inspected the windows. With guns in hand, the other two Dundee agents made a quick inspection of the parking lot.

Bain called, "It's blood, all right, but I'm not sure if it's human or animal."

"It's human," Ty hollered. "I just found the night guard."

"The poor bastard is a bloody mess," Geoff said.

CHAPTER FOURTEEN

BAIN SHARED a table with Geoff Monday and Bedell, Inc.'s head of security, Larry Nesmith. Each man was nursing a beer. They had spent the past hour at downtown Chattanooga's version of an English pub—Hair of the Dog pub, to be exact, a relatively new bar and grill that was fast becoming a favorite of Bain's, since the place stayed open until three in the morning.

The first time he'd stopped by, he'd run into Cara Bedell and that worthless brother-in-law of hers, Grayson Perkins. After that, he had dropped by occasionally on the off chance she might be having lunch or dinner here, but their paths had crossed only one other time. One night, when Cara had dropped by alone, they'd wound up sharing burgers and playing darts upstairs while listening to the jukebox.

He had kissed her that night.

"Where's the loo?" Geoff asked.

Bain pointed Geoff in the right direction just as the waitress delivered his second pint of Guinness. He lifted the mug to his lips and took a hefty swig.

"Blake Ritchey was only twenty-seven," Larry said. "His wife is expecting around Valentine's Day. Their first child."

"How long had he worked for Bedell?" Bain asked.

"Two years. Fine young man. Ex-military."

"We'll find this guy," Bain said. "He's no amateur. Even though the bombs weren't sophisticated, they weren't run-of-the-mill, either. And shooting a man in a moving car the way he killed Malik Abdel took skill. But the dead giveaway was the sneak attack on Ritchey and the way he butchered that boy."

"He's been trained." Larry downed the last of his third beer. "One of those terrorist organizations would be my guess."

"Dundee's hasn't unearthed any proof that any of the Africans associated with Helping Hands has ever belonged to a terrorist organization."

"Maybe they need to dig a little deeper."

"Or maybe someone needs to contact somebody in D.C.," Bain said.

"Homeland Security?"

"Yeah. You got any connections? Know anybody?"

"Everybody I know is either dead or retired. But have Monday get in touch with Sawyer McNamara. He used to be FBI. And if he can't get the info, my guess is Sam Dundee can."

"Do you know Dundee?" Bain asked.

"Yeah, I met him years ago when I was working a case and he was guarding the chief suspect. My guess is that if anybody can find out classified information, it'll be the Dundee Agency, probably Dundee himself."

Bain's cell phone vibrated against his hip. He removed it from the belt clip, checked the caller ID and said, "I need to take this call." After sliding back his chair, he stood. "I can't hear myself think in here."

"You're calling kind of late, aren't you?" Bain said as he made his way toward the men's room.

"You weren't asleep, were you?" Cara Bedell laughed. "Don't bother to answer. I can hear music. Where are you? Hair of the Dog?"

"You know me too well."

"I spoke to Lexie earlier, and she told me what happened tonight."

"Yeah, she's had a rough couple of days. Hell, she's had a rough week."

"She's blaming herself for everything."

"I know."

Halfway to the men's room, Bain met Geoff returning to their table. He nodded to him but kept walking. Once inside the empty restroom, he continued his conversation.

"How are things going in sunny Mexico?" he asked.

"Better than they were, but things are still a mess, and some of the people I'm dealing with are royal pains in the ass."

"When are you coming home?"

"Do you miss me?"

He wanted to shout, "Hell, yes." He missed her every day, wanted her every day, even when she was only a few miles away at her office or up on Lookout Mountain in that big old family mansion.

"You're safer in Mexico than you'll be here," he told her. "Why don't you just stay down there until we catch this guy?"

"You know I can't do that. I have a business to run, and the only reason I left Lexie to face this guy alone is because I had no choice but to come down here and get things back on track. If I hadn't, we'd have lost millions of dollars, and hundreds of people would have lost their jobs."

"So when are you coming home?"

"Probably this weekend. Want me to call you when I know for sure?"

"I could meet you at the airport and give you a police escort to Lookout Mountain."

"I'd like that."

God, he was skating on some mighty thin ice. He knew better than to plan time alone with Cara, but heaven help him, sometimes a guy just couldn't do what he knew was good for him. Changing the subject before he started going all mushy and making a fool of himself, Bain asked, "How'd Lexie sound to you?"

"Not good, but doing her best to fake it. You know our Lexie, always trying to be an independent, tough little cookie."

"Her bodyguard's got a thing for her," Bain said.

"And that's bad?" Cara chuckled. "Remember, I've seen Deke Bronson. Believe me, no woman would mind having him take a personal interest in her."

"I've warned him. She's vulnerable right now. I don't want to see him take advantage of her."

"Bain Desmond, you stay out of Lexie's love life. Stop playing big brother. She has a right to fool around with anybody she wants to, and that includes Deke Bronson."

Before he could stop himself, he asked, "Are you fooling around with somebody down there in Mexico?" Shit! Even though he'd asked in a joking manner, Cara was no dummy.

Silence.

"Hmm… Got yourself a Latin lover, huh?" That's it, *Desmond, dig yourself in deeper.*

"No Latin lovers," she told him. "No lovers here or there or…or anywhere."

"Yeah. Me neither."

"Pick me up at the airport when I come home?"

"Just call me and let me know when."

"Bain?"

"Yeah?"

"Take care of yourself, okay? Don't get shot or anything stupid like that."

"Sure thing."

"Bye."

"Bye."

After clipping his phone back on his belt, Bain walked out of the restroom, went back to the table to join Larry and Geoff, and downed his pint of Guinness.

ALICE WOKE from an unpleasant dream, glanced at the bedside clock and groaned. Two-twenty. She looked at the other side of the bed. Empty. Where was Robert? Had he gone home? Surely he wouldn't leave her in the middle of the night. Not again. She had no idea what kind of demons plagued him, what horrible memories from his childhood in Gadi tormented him so much that he seldom slept through the night. Occasionally she would find him wandering around outside in her backyard or sitting in the living room staring off into space. And a couple of times since they had become lovers, he had left her in the middle of the night and gone back to his apartment.

After getting out of bed, she put on her housecoat to cover her nakedness. She hadn't slept nude—ever—until Robert became her lover. He always slept nude and thought it strange she would wear anything at night.

After checking the bathroom and the other upstairs bedroom, Alice made her way downstairs. She searched the house but found it empty. After turning on the overhead kitchen light, she stopped at the sliding glass doors leading to her patio. Cupping her hands on either side of her temples, she peered outside. Robert was standing on the patio, as naked as the day he was born, his arms crossed over his chest and his gaze riveted to the dark sky.

Thank God a privacy fence surrounded her back-yard, otherwise she might have some startled night-owl neighbors.

Alice eased open the sliding doors and stepped outside. The predawn chill hit her immediately.

"Robert?" she called softly.

He didn't respond.

"You must be cold," she told him. "Please, come back inside."

When she reached out and touched his arm, he shiv-ered, then he turned and looked at her. She took his hand in hers, and he followed her back inside the house as meekly as a small child. Obedient and trusting.

She took both of his hands in hers. "Are you all right?"

He nodded.

"Can't you talk to me, tell me what's bothering you?" She brought his large, strong hands to her lips and kissed each one.

He clenched his jaw, then grabbed her, pulled her into his arms and held her fiercely. With his mouth against her temple, he murmured, "I will miss you when I return to Gadi."

Alice's pulse leaped. Already she felt a profound sense of loss. She had allowed Robert to become far too important to her, knowing all along that one day he would leave her.

"I'll miss you, too," she barely managed to say.

"I must go home. My people need me. I would not be happy here in America for the rest of my life."

"I—I understand."

He clasped her face with his hands and looked deeply into her eyes. "You would hate Gadi. It is still, in many ways, a primitive country. You belong here."

"Robert?" *What was he trying to say to her?*

He kissed her. Tenderly.

"I wish to make love to you, Alice." He took her hand in his. "Come back to bed with me."

She followed him up the stairs to their bedroom. No, not their room. *Her* room. Silly of her to think of them as a couple when she knew in her heart of hearts that they had no future together.

WAKING in a semidark room, it took Lexie a couple of minutes to realize where she was and why she wasn't in her own bed at home. Deke had brought her back to Cara's mansion on Lookout Mountain last night, after— Oh, God, that poor man! Deke had shielded her from the horrific scene as best he could, but overhearing the others talking about how the guard had been butchered, she'd envisioned his bloody body all too clearly.

Blake Ritchey. That was his name.

She hadn't fallen apart, hadn't lost it there in the parking lot behind Helping Hands. By sheer willpower, she'd held herself together. And when Deke had suggested taking her home, Bain had sent them on their way.

"I can come by in the morning and take your statements," he had said, then ordered Deke, "Get her out of here."

Lexie pushed back the covers, rose into a sitting

position and glanced around the room, seeking and finding Deke Bronson. He was resting on the sofa in the sitting area, halfway reclining, a couple of decorative pillows stuffed behind his head. He rose and looked at her. Their gazes locked.

"Lexie?" He said her name so quietly that she barely heard him.

"What time is it?" Before he could reply, she glanced at the lighted digital clock on the nightstand. "Oh, it's nearly five. I thought it was earlier."

"Go back to sleep if you can. It was close to midnight before you finally drifted off."

"Did you get any sleep at all?"

"Some."

"I didn't think I would be able to sleep." She slid to the edge of the bed and placed her bare feet on the floor. "Did you put something in that cup of hot chocolate you insisted I drink last night?"

"Guilty," he said. "Nothing strong. Just a mild over-the-counter sleeping pill so you could get a little rest. I keep a pack in my shave kit. I know I should have asked your permission, but—"

"It's all right. Really. I trust you." She glanced around, looking for her cane. "But next time, ask first, okay?"

"Okay." He got up, removed her cane from where he'd hung it over the back of a chair and brought it to her.

Lexie wasn't sure why she trusted Deke so implicitly, why she knew that he would never hurt her, that anything he did, he did to protect her, to care for her. Despite what had happened to her in Gadi ten years ago, she still had a positive outlook on life, still believed that most people were basically good. But after the way

Wes had treated her, she had never again trusted herself—her life or her heart—to another man.

Lexie looked up at Deke, then held out her hands. He propped the cane against the nightstand, took her hands in his and lifted her to her feet. Standing there, their bodies touching, their breaths mingling, she tilted her head and stared right at him.

"Thank you for taking such good care of me."

"It's—"

"Please don't say it's your job."

"What do you want me to say?"

She pulled her hands from his and reached for her cane. He stepped aside to give her the space to maneuver on her own.

"I don't know what I want you to say," she told him as she made her way across the room to the windows. The distant glimmer of security lights and the faint glow of a half moon illuminated the outside world and shadowed the bedroom with soft, dim radiance.

Deke came up behind her but didn't touch her. Didn't speak.

"Tell me about your wife," Lexie said. "Why did you marry her if you didn't love her?"

He didn't reply immediately, and Lexie knew she'd had no right to ask him such a personal question. But she wanted to know more about this man who was willing to risk his own life to protect her. What past experiences had made him who he was today?

"Abby was a sweet kid. A bit on the wild side, but she had a good heart," Deke said. "I got her pregnant. I did the honorable thing and married her. We were both miserable, stayed married less than a year, and got a divorce."

"You have a child?" The thought of a former wife

didn't really matter, especially if Deke hadn't loved her. But a child… She instinctively knew that Deke would never walk away from a son or daughter.

"I *had* a child. My son died when he was only a couple of months old."

Lexie whirled around to face Deke and found him staring down at the floor. When she reached out to touch him, to offer him sympathy and comfort, he moved back, away from her.

"Deke… I'm so sorry. I—I had no idea."

"It doesn't matter," he mumbled. "It was a long time ago. Nearly twenty years."

"Even so, to lose a child… That's not something you could ever—"

"Don't project your feelings onto me," he told her, looking her in the eyes. "You asked why I married a woman I didn't love. I told you. It's all in the past. Abby. And Andrew."

"I didn't mean to pry."

"Yeah, you did. You're curious about me. You wonder what makes me tick." He grabbed her upper arms tightly, his gaze boring into her. "Believe me, honey, you do not want to know the real Deke Bronson. I'm not the man you think I am. I've done some unforgivable things, things you could never understand."

Her breath caught in her throat. She saw the pain in his eyes, and sensed his bitter regret and hunger for absolution.

"What if I told you that I don't care what you've done in the past? What if I told you that all that matters is now, the person you are today, the man I see before me? Strong and brave, intelligent and kind. A man capable of putting others before himself, of—"

"Damn it, Lexie, you don't understand." He tightened his grip on her arms, his big fingers biting into her flesh. Realizing what he'd done, he relaxed his hold immediately, but he didn't release her.

She pulled one arm free and lifted it so that she could caress his cheek. He reached up, grabbed her hand and held it between them. With his jaw clenched and his eyes closed, he lowered his forehead until it rested against hers.

"I've done some bad things, too," she said. "In a way, it's my fault that my UBC cameraman, Marty Bearn, was killed in Gadi. I—I told him to keep filming after the attack on President Tum. If I hadn't done that…"

Deke brought her hand to his lips, opened it and kissed the center of her palm. "Nothing that happened in Gadi was your fault. You were in the wrong place at the wrong time. So was your cameraman. And the men who killed Tum and his advisors and guards—they were just doing their job, following orders. The man who shot you…"

"Didn't mean to shoot me," she said.

Deke swallowed hard. "Could you ever forgive him for what he did to you?"

"I have no idea who he was, if he was one of the soldiers sent to assassinate President Tum or if he was one of Tum's guards. And it really doesn't matter. Everything that happened from the time I was shot until I woke up in the hospital is a blur. The only thing I remember is that one of the soldiers saved my life."

Deke cleared his throat. "I…uh, think I'll go shower and change clothes. If you won't need me for a while."

I need you. I need you to hold me and kiss me and make slow, sweet love to me. I want you to tell me that you're falling in love with me, just like I'm falling in love with you.

"Go," she told him. "Take a shower. I'm fine. I'll probably do the same."

"If you call down to the kitchen and ask for coffee, make it a pot for two," he said as he headed toward the connecting door between their rooms.

"I believe Mrs. Eddins arrives in the kitchen at five-thirty. I'll call down and order coffee then."

Lexie stood and watched as Deke disappeared behind the closed door.

What had he done in his past that he thought was so unforgivable? And why did he think she wouldn't understand, that she wouldn't be able to accept the truth about the man he had once been?

CHAPTER FIFTEEN

THE NEXT FEW DAYS passed by uneventfully. No more threats. No bombs. No shootings. No slaughter. Lexie wondered if the man who had wreaked so much havoc in her life was simply tormenting her by making her wait and wonder. When would he strike next? What would he do? Who would be his next victim? But today was not about her, not about being frightened or worried, not about finding a killer and putting him behind bars. Today—this beautiful, unseasonably warm November Friday, with a promise of rain in the humid air—had been chosen for Malik's memorial service. A simple, dignified goodbye to a young man who had died all too soon and without cause. On Monday, Malik's body would be shipped home to Gadi, where his family would bury him in his native soil. The promise of a future in America for Malik had ended with his death, but not his dream of someday bringing his younger brother and sister to the United States. Lexie was determined to find a way to fulfill his promise to his siblings.

"Ready to go in?" Deke cupped her elbow.

"I want to wait for Toni." Lexie checked her wristwatch. "She's running late, but I'll give her a few more minutes."

"Why don't we go inside and wait?"

"I'd rather wait here, if you don't mind."

"Sure. We'll stay out here as long as you like." He held up a large, closed, black umbrella he carried. "If it rains, I'm prepared."

"You're always prepared, and I'm grateful. Thank you."

A sporty dark blue Monte Carlo whipped into the funeral-home parking lot.

"There's Toni," Lexie said.

Wearing a stylish taupe silk suit, Toni emerged from the driver's side of the car just as the passenger door opened and Jafari jumped out.

"They must have kissed and made up," Deke said. "This is the first time I've seen them together all week."

"I believe he's spent a great deal of time groveling in order to get back in her good graces. Toni loves him, but she has her standards. She demands to be treated well."

"Smart woman," Deke said.

Toni rushed toward the funeral-home entrance where Lexie and Deke waited. Jafari kept pace with her, but whenever he tried to take her arm, she pulled away from him.

"I think he has a bit more groveling to do," Deke whispered to Lexie.

"I think you're right."

Slightly winded, Toni walked up the steps, gave Lexie a hug and said, "Sorry I'm late." She gave Jafari a condemning stare. "I didn't know Jafari would be coming with me."

"Good afternoon, Miss Murrough." Jafari nodded courteously. "Mr. Bronson."

Deke tapped his watch. "We have less than five minutes before the service starts."

"Sit with me." Lexie grabbed Toni's hand.

"Oh, God, Lex, I dread this."

"Yeah, me too."

TWO HOURS later, with the memorial service behind them, the mourners congregated at Helping Hands, filling the second-floor conference room and spilling out into the hallway. A local string quartet played a variety of Gadian folk music especially chosen for the occasion by Vega. Alice had arranged for the caterer to prepare a few Gadian specialties to mix in with the finger foods and drinks being served. Security for this shindig was tight, with a dozen Bedell, Inc. uniformed guards manning the lobby, the parking lot and each floor of the building. If Deke had had his way, Lexie would have skipped this affair altogether. But since she was hosting the post-memorial gathering, she felt compelled to attend.

Actually, she had insisted on being here.

And despite the huge turnout—both at the memorial service and here at Helping Hands—Deke felt relatively certain Lexie was safe. After all, it would take an idiot to try something today, with not only a dozen Bedell guards and three Dundee agents but half a dozen of Chattanooga PD's finest in attendance.

Glued to Lexie's side, Deke watched her as she worked the crowd. And that was exactly what she did, only in a positive, unselfish way. She provided comfort and sympathy, her obvious affection for Malik shared with the other mourners, his friends and coworkers. From time to time Deke made eye contact with Geoff and Ty, who mixed and mingled with the crowd, ever vigilant, prepared to act at a moment's notice.

As the afternoon wore on, he began to notice Lexie's fatigue and the valiant way she fought against it. Only he knew that she hadn't slept well for the past couple of nights and that she had refused to take any medication, not even an over-the-counter sleep aid.

"I don't like to take medication unless it's absolutely necessary," she had told him. "I took more than enough painkillers and other meds during my years of recovery to last me a lifetime."

Deke tried to persuade her to leave Helping Hands before she passed out from sheer exhaustion, but she refused. Not even Bain Desmond was able to convince her. So they stayed, hour after hour, until the throng slowly dispersed. Then, one by one, Lexie's friends said goodbye to her before leaving. Toni and Jafari. Alice and Robert. Vega, who was alone, having explained that Hamal had been unable to change shifts with another intern and sent his regrets. Farris Richardson was one of the last to leave, and he made a big show of mourning, tears streaming down his cheeks, trembling hands and a need for several hugs from Lexie.

"Before we go, I'd like to check a few things in my office," Lexie told Deke at last.

"Can't that wait? You're dead on your feet." He glanced down at her slender size-seven, chunky-heel pumps. Gray leather, a shade darker than the simple gray dress she wore.

"It'll take only a few minutes. I promise."

Deke motioned to Geoff and Ty, who were standing across the room, waiting. They would canvass the building, checking for any stragglers, as would the

Chattanooga PD, before leaving the nighttime security to the Bedell guards.

When they reached her office, Deke opened the door, switched on an overhead light and scanned the interior. Just checking things out.

The sun had set and twilight had descended, creating a colorful display in the early-evening sky, which made for a spectacular view from Lexie's office windows. The promise of rain had not been fulfilled. Not yet. But the humid air still hinted of a storm brewing.

Lexie sat behind her desk, and opened a bottom drawer that held a row of hanging file folders neatly arranged and each identified with a colorful label. Deke walked over behind her to stand in front of the windows, so that he could keep an eye on the door and also shield her. She pulled out a file, laid it atop the blotter on her desk and opened the manila folder. She took a notepad from the center desk drawer and a pen from a decorative glass holder, then copied down what appeared to be a couple of names. Zada Abdel, age eighteen, unmarried. Musa Abdel, age twenty, unmarried. She added other basic information about the two, then tore the sheet from the notepad, folded it in two, opened her gray leather purse and slipped the sheet of paper inside. After she closed her purse, she turned around and looked up at Deke where he stood behind her chair.

"I'm ready now," she said.

"Want to tell me what that's all about?" He inclined his head toward her purse.

"I wanted to make sure the information on Malik's younger brother and sister was correct. He spoke of them often, and of his dreams for them. He planned to bring both of them to America, and I intend to do all I can to make that dream come true."

"After losing Malik, do you think his parents will want their other children to leave Gadi?"

"Malik's parents are dead, so if I can arrange for his brother and sister to come here as employees of Helping Hands, it will be their decision whether or not to accept my offer."

Lexie's cell phone rang. She opened her purse, removed the phone, checked the caller I.D. and smiled. "It's Cara."

Deke nodded.

Lexie flipped open the phone and put it to her ear. "Hello, Cara."

Deke waited patiently while Lexie carried on a brief conversation with her friend, ending it by saying, "See you in the morning."

"I take it that Ms. Bedell is coming home tomorrow," Deke said.

"Actually, she's flying in tonight, but she said not to wait up, that it will probably be really late, possibly after midnight."

"Has she contacted Geoff?"

"Yes, she mentioned that she had informed him that she would have a police escort home."

Deke lifted his brows. "Desmond?"

Lexie smiled. "That would be my guess."

"Hmm…"

"Why don't you ask?"

"Ask what?"

"Ask what's up with Cara and Bain."

"It's none of my business," Deke said.

Lexie shoved back her swivel chair, used her cane for balance and support as she stood, then grasped her purse from the desk and slipped the slender strap over her shoulder.

When they exited her office, Deke turned off the lights. In the hallway, they encountered a Bedell, Inc. security guard, who nodded, spoke and continued his surveillance rounds.

Once inside the elevator, Lexie asked, "If you loved a woman and she loved you, but she was a billionaire and you lived on a cop's salary, what would you do?"

"You're determined to tell me all about Ms. Bedell and Lieutenant Desmond, aren't you?"

Lexie smiled. "You're avoiding answering my question."

"Sometimes, no matter how much two people want each other, even love each other, they can't overcome a major issue that stands between them. No matter what the romantics say, love does not conquer all."

"It should."

"It doesn't."

The elevator doors opened; Deke stepped out first, scanned the lobby area and nodded to Lexie. As they passed the security guard's desk, he called her name.

"Ms. Murrough, one of the guards found this—" pinching the upper edge, he held up a plain white business envelope "—in the ladies' restroom on the second floor. It was lying on the sink counter, and it's addressed to you."

Deke glanced from the envelope in the guard's hand to Lexie's pale face, and cursed under his breath when he noticed her stricken expression.

"I'll take it." Deke held out his hand.

The guard gave him the envelope. "Should I tell Detective Desmond?"

"I'll tell him," Deke said.

Lexie gazed at the envelope, now pinched between Deke's thumb and forefinger. "Are you going to open it?"

Deke examined the envelope carefully. The letters that formed her name were simple block printing.

"Call Desmond. Tell him to get down here. I doubt there's any evidence—fingerprints, DNA or anything like that—on the envelope, but just to be sure, he'll want the crime lab to check it out."

After Lexie called Bain, he showed up in no time flat, took the envelope, dropped it in a plastic bag and said, "Let me deal with this."

"I want to know—" Lexie said.

"No, you don't," Bain told her. "Unless there's something in the message that might help Dundee's keep you safer than you are now, you don't need to be bothered with some nut-job's rambling threats."

"I suppose you're right."

Bain looked to Deke. "When I know something, you'll know something."

Deke nodded, then cupped Lexie's elbow and led her outside to where Eddie was waiting with the company limo. As the Rolls glided through the Friday evening traffic, Lexie leaned her head back and closed her eyes.

"He was there today, wasn't he?" She sighed. "Right there at Helping Hands, pretending to mourn Malik's death." She opened her eyes and turned to Deke. "He probably went to Malik's funeral, too."

"Possibly."

"There must have been at least a hundred people at Helping Hands this afternoon, and any one of them could have—" She gasped. "But why leave it in the ladies' room? I mean, if someone saw a man leaving the ladies' room, wouldn't they have mentioned it?"

"Try to stop thinking about that damn envelope," Deke said. "Desmond will question the guards, and have the lab go over the envelope and whatever is inside with a fine-tooth comb. Let *him* figure out how it got in the ladies' room and who might have put it there."

TONI ALLOWED Jafari to walk her to her door, but when he started to come in, she stopped, turned and held up both hands. "Not so fast."

He stared at her, a puzzled expression on his handsome face.

"I didn't tell you that you could come in."

"How long do you intend to punish me?" he asked.

"I'm not sure. As long as I want to. Until I feel certain that you understand how hurt and angry I am."

"I understand." He held up his palms pleadingly. "I will do anything you ask to obtain your forgiveness."

Toni smiled. That was just what she wanted—a truly repentant lover, one who would think twice before he ever disappointed her again.

"I think you know what I want." She lifted her arms up and around his neck. "If you really love me and want to share your life with me, then—"

"I do, but I am a poor man, only a student with a very small income from my part-time job. I cannot afford to buy you a ring or offer you—"

She kissed him, effectively silencing his excuses.

ALICE AND Robert sat quietly in the den, the television tuned to a local channel delivering the evening newscast. But neither of them paid much attention to the TV as they rested on the sofa, Alice cuddled close to Robert, his arm around her shoulders.

"When are you leaving?" she asked, knowing that he would return to Gadi soon. Malik's death had triggered something elemental inside Robert, something that called him home—to his people and the land of his birth.

"I have not spoken to Lexie about it," he said. "I did not think it was the proper time."

"She'll hate to lose you." Alice swallowed her tears.

Robert took Alice's hand in his. "Please, do not cry. I cannot bear to see you unhappy."

"Then don't leave. Stay here. Stay with me."

"I cannot stay. I have a duty to… A man's life is not always his own. He has obligations."

"Stay through Christmas, at least. Please."

"Christmas is your Christian holiday. It means nothing to me."

"We won't celebrate it as a religious holiday," she told him.

"Your daughters will come home for the holidays," he said. "What would they think of me? Of us?"

"I honestly don't know." Alice squeezed his hand. "I suppose I should have already told them about us, but at first I thought…well, I didn't realize our relationship would turn into a full-fledged affair or that I'd fall in love with you."

"You shouldn't love me," he told her. "I have nothing permanent to give you in return. I cannot marry you. I cannot build a life with you."

"I know." She lifted her lips to his and kissed him.

"Just give me what you can while you can. It'll have to be enough for both of us."

IN HER SMALL KITCHEN, Vega set the table for two, then checked on the casserole warming in the oven. Hamal had come to Helping Hands to pick her up shortly before the post-memorial reception ended. During their drive to her apartment, he had been unusually quiet. And now he waited silently and patiently for her to serve him dinner. When—if—she married him, he would expect her to be a dutiful, obedient wife, but because they were now Christians and living in America, he would not expect her to be completely subservient. They had discussed their futures, and even though Hamal had not asked her to marry him, he had implied that they would share their lives and build a future together.

As she removed the casserole from the oven, he walked into the kitchen. After she set the dish on a potholder in the center of the table, he pulled out her chair.

"Thank you."

He placed his hand on Vega's shoulder. "I will complete my internship in the spring. I am not certain where I will be offered a residency. Perhaps not here in Chattanooga. If—if I must leave, would you go with me?"

Vega's heart skipped a beat. She turned slowly and faced Hamal. "If I were your wife, I would go with you wherever you go."

Blushing, he bowed his head and looked down at the floor. "I would not ask you to go with me unless you were my wife."

"Then are you asking me to marry you?"

He lifted his head and looked at her, a shy smile curving his lips. "Not tonight. I do not have a ring. And I wish to propose in the proper way. But I…that is, we could have a June wedding. I believe that is customary in this country."

"A June wedding would be nice."

Vega cupped Hamal's face between her open palms and kissed him.

BAIN READ the message again.

"Their blood is on your hands."

Succinct and to the point. Each letter of each word had been individually cut and pasted onto the sheet of paper to form the damning sentence.

An initial inspection of the envelope and the plain white sheet of paper tucked inside had offered very little evidence, except for the smudged prints on the edge of the envelope. Although the lab would do a complete workup on the envelope and sheet of paper, Bain figured they would wind up with nothing. Their guy was too smart to leave any real evidence behind.

If they could find a witness, someone who might have seen a man slipping in or out of the women's rest-room, they would at least have some kind of lead. But questioning over a hundred guests would take time. And it could wind up being a wasted effort, since there had been so many people crowded into a small space, with guests coming and going.

And it didn't help that the entrance to the women's restrooms on the second floor was two-sided, leading to the men's room as well.

Bain checked his watch. Cara's plane would be

landing shortly. If he intended to be at the airport to meet her, he needed to leave now.

It would be good to see her. Home. Safe and sound. And as crazy as the thought was, he felt as though she was coming home to him.

CHAPTER SIXTEEN

CARA DISEMBARKED at 11:38 p.m. The two Bedell, Inc. guards—Jason Little and Wanda Marcum—who had accompanied her on her business trip to Mexico City exited the private jet with her, Jason in front and Wanda behind. When her feet touched the rain-slick tarmac, she noticed a shadowy figure standing near the gate. Her heart did a crazy rat-a-tat-tat the moment she recognized the lone man as Bain Desmond. She lifted her hand and waved. He stepped beneath a security light and waved back at her, a lopsided semigrin on his face. She'd never been so glad to see anyone. Ever.

A few minutes later, with all the mundane matters handled by Jason and Wanda, Cara turned to the man who was patiently waiting for her. She walked over to him and smiled.

"Ready to go?" he asked.

"Ready." *I wish you'd grab me, kiss me, tell me how much you've missed me, and then take me home with you and make love to me for days on end.*

"It's good to have you back in Chattanooga," he said.

"It's good to be back. How's Lexie?"

"She's doing okay."

"Thanks for picking me up tonight." *Can't you see how much I want you to hug me?*

"I'm in the 'Vette," he told her.

"Then it's a good thing Wanda is going to see that my luggage gets home." Cara smiled. "I don't think all four suitcases would fit in your car."

"Probably not."

Can't you just pat me on the back or shake my hand? Just touch me, damn it!

"Are you hungry?" he asked. "We could stop by—"

"I ate on the plane."

"Yeah, of course you did." He shrugged. "I forgot that you have all the comforts of home on that thing. I'm surprised you don't have a world-class chef on board."

"That might be perceived as slightly decadent by our shareholders." Cara smiled.

Bain smiled back at her, then cocked his head to one side and nodded, indicating that he was ready for them to leave. Now.

"Maybe we could stop somewhere for a drink," she suggested as she followed alongside him.

"Hair of the Dog pub?" he asked as they left the terminal.

"Or we could stop by your place." *There, Bain Desmond, I've all but asked you to take me home with you tonight.*

"All I've got is a bottle of Jack Daniel's and a six-pack. If you want a decent drink, I'm sure you have better stuff at your house."

"Then, when we get to my house, why don't you come in for a while and—"

"I might. We'll see."

The wet sidewalk and pavement glistened beneath the glow of the security lights, and puddles of rainwater shimmered in low-lying areas as they walked to his car.

"It didn't rain all day, did it?" she asked.

"Nope. Not a drop until a few hours ago, then the bottom fell out. Didn't y'all run into the storm coming in?"

"No, we didn't. It must have come in from the west and not the south."

"Yeah, probably did."

When they reached the Corvette, Bain opened the passenger door for her and stood there until she crawled inside the low-slung sports car. Within moments, he revved the motor and drove away from the airport.

"Want me to turn on the radio?" he asked.

"No. I'd rather talk."

"Sure."

"Geoff Monday has kept me up-to-date on the situation with our killer," she said. "I hate it that I missed Malik's funeral, but I couldn't manage to get all the loose ends tied up until late this afternoon."

"It's the price you pay for being the big boss."

"Yes, I suppose it is. But sometimes the price seems a little too high."

"Who are you kidding, sugar? You love what you do. You were born for it. Literally."

"Do you think so?"

"Yeah, and so do the board and all the stockholders. They thought you weren't up to the job when your old man died, but you've proven them wrong."

She shifted in the seat until she managed to turn sideways. "Yes, I guess I have shown them, haven't I?"

"And you loved doing it."

"I love knowing I'm capable of filling my father's rather large shoes and of possibly, given time and cooperation from the board, being able to expand Bedell,

Inc.'s philanthropic endeavors while at the same time keeping profits steady."

"And you need to keep those profits steady, don't you? You not only have tens of thousands of workers worldwide depending on them, but what would Step-Mommy Dearest and darling Grayson do without the Bedell millions to maintain them in the lifestyle to which they're accustomed?"

"If I'm lucky, I'll never see Patrice again as long as I live, and I'm sure I won't have to as long as I keep signing those settlement checks every January first." Cara had despised her father's fourth wife from the day he'd brought the bitch home. And her sister Audrey had hated the woman even more, if that was possible. In time, even their father had come to see Patrice for the money-grubbing whore she was.

"And what about Grayson Perkins?"

Cara cringed at the thought of how madly in love she had once been with her former brother-in-law. Actually, considering the fact that she'd had a crush on the man since she was thirteen, she supposed her feelings for him had been more of an insane infatuation than real love. It had taken falling—falling hard—for a real man to make her realize the difference. What she had felt for Gray paled in comparison to what she now felt for Bain.

"Gray is a valuable asset to the company. He learned a great deal about the business under Daddy's tutelage. And he was Audrey's husband. He's family."

"When's the last time he asked you to marry him?"

"Actually, not since this past summer." Cara frowned, thinking about Gray's promise to keep asking her to marry him until she finally said yes. "I'm afraid he thinks that sooner or later he'll wear me down."

"Will he?" Bain gave her a quick, sidelong glance.

"What do you think?"

"I think you could do a hell of a lot better than Pretty Boy Perkins."

"I agree." She gazed at Bain longingly, unable to stop herself. If he looked at her now, he would see the yearning in her eyes.

They continued talking about this and that. The weather. Politics. Bedell, Inc. The Chattanooga PD. Thanksgiving coming up next week. She invited him to join her for the holiday. He declined, saying he was spending the day with his sister and her family in Mc-Minnville.

When Bain drove through the gates of the Bedell estate, Cara wondered if he really would come in for a drink, or if he'd walk her to the door, turn her over to Geoff Monday and say good-night. If he didn't join her for a drink, it would be a typical Bain Desmond way of dealing with their relationship.

Good God, Cara, you and Bain don't even have *a relationship.*

Bain parked his 'Vette in the drive, got out, rushed around the car and opened the door for Cara.

"Are you coming in?" she asked.

"Maybe I'd better not."

"Coward."

"Damn it, Cara, you know as well as I do that—"

She reached out and laid her index finger across his lips. "One drink. And I promise I'll be on my best behavior."

"Let's not tempt fate," he told her.

She huffed loudly, then headed for the veranda. Bain hurried along behind her, keeping in step as she all but ran to the front door. By the time she managed to find her house key, the door opened and there stood Geoff Monday.

"Oh." Cara gasped. "Good evening. No, I suppose I should say good morning, since it's past midnight. You must have been watching for us."

"Yes, ma'am." Geoff eyed Bain, then asked, "If you don't need me right now, I'll—"

"Stay," Bain told Geoff.

"No, please, go to bed," she said. "Bain's coming in for a drink, and after he leaves, I think I can manage to find my way safely to my bedroom."

"Whatever you say." Geoff saluted her. "You're the boss."

As Geoff headed down the hallway, Bain hung in the open doorway, neither leaving nor entering.

"Please, come in," Cara said.

He stepped over the threshold and into the foyer, then paused. "It's been a long day. I'm tired. You're tired. You should go to bed, and I should go home."

"I offered to go home with you. By now, we could both be in your bed and—"

He grabbed her by the shoulders. Finally he was touching her. But none too gently. Anger glimmered in his dark eyes. He was spitting mad. And aroused. They glared at each other, intense passion radiating between them. Searing hot. Vibrantly stimulating. A hunger that only sex could appease.

"Cara." Her name came from his throat in an agonized moan.

Her lips parted as she sighed softly.

Bain jerked her to him, lowered his head and took her mouth in a savage, demanding kiss. Her heartbeat went wild. Her body clenched tightly, then unclenched as a tingling sensation radiated from her feminine core and set her nerve endings on fire. She returned the kiss, claiming him as surely as he claimed her.

She slid her left arm around his waist, laid her right hand on his chest and pressed herself against him. He was rock-hard, as aroused as she was.

When he ended the kiss and they came up for air, he clasped the back of her head with his open palm and buried his face against her neck. She clung to him, wanting him desperately.

"We can't do this." He growled the words, then lifted his head, released her and took a step back and away from her.

"Bain?" She held out her arms. "Stay with me."

"Do you think I want to go? Damn it, Cara!" He looked at her as if he could devour her, then turned and headed for the door.

When he went outside onto the veranda, she ran after him, calling his name, but he walked straight to his car and got in, without looking back. His name died on her lips.

She stood there on the porch, the cool November wind chilling her, and watched while he drove down the driveway and through the wrought-iron gates. When the taillights on his Corvette dimmed to red dots and finally disappeared, she turned and went back into her house. Her mansion. Part of her birthright. She was a Bedell, with all the rights and privileges that entailed. She was worth billions. She could buy anything her heart desired. Anything and everything—except the one thing she wanted most. Bain Desmond. A man who could not be bought.

Cara closed and locked the front doors, then walked to the end of the hallway and armed the security system.

On her way to the central staircase, she paused and glanced into the study. Dying embers glowed in the massive fireplace, casting a shadowy shimmer over the room. She walked inside, crossed the room and flipped on the banker's lamp atop the massive mahogany desk. She stood there and stared at Audrey's portrait hanging in a place of honor over the mantel.

"You'd know what to do, wouldn't you? If you wanted Bain, you'd find a way to have him."

Her older half sister had been a seductress.

Unfortunately, she wasn't.

CHAPTER SEVENTEEN

THANKSGIVING this year bore no resemblance to any of Lexie's previous Thanksgivings, the main reasons being that she wouldn't see her mom, that she would be having dinner at the Bedell mansion, and that she had a bodyguard dogging her every move. At least her mother and stepfather weren't upset that she wasn't coming home for the weekend. Since her stepbrother's wife had insisted on flying to California for Thanksgiving with her folks—and taking the beloved grandchildren with them—Lexie's mother had decided that she and her husband should treat themselves to a seven-day Caribbean cruise for the holiday.

The Bedell cook, Mrs. Eddins, had prepared a feast fit for a king and queen, from roast turkey and honey-baked ham to candied sweet potatoes and half a dozen pies and a couple of cakes. There was enough food to feed an army, which they could have seated at the dining-room table. There were only five of them, however: Cara, her brother-in-law Grayson Perkins, Geoff Monday, Deke and Lexie. Ty Garrett and Bain Desmond had been invited, but both had declined. Bain had, as he'd told Cara, gone to McMinnville for the day to see his sister and her family. Ty had flown home to Arkansas for a big Garrett family get-together and would return on Saturday.

No sooner had Grayson arrived, around twelve-thirty, than Lexie picked up Deke's and Geoff's immediate disdain for the man. She wasn't sure if they had instantly disliked him on sight or if Bain had filled in one or both of them on Grayson's background. Whatever the reason, the two testosterone-driven males merely tolerated their insipid, strutting-peacock counterpart.

If she was completely honest, Lexie would have to admit that she didn't like Cara's brother-in-law, either, despite the fact that he was handsome and charming. Maybe a little too handsome and definitely much too charming. He had the kind of old-movie-star good looks that set female hearts aflutter. Cara had confessed to her that she'd had a secret crush on Grayson for years—until she'd eventually seen through that perfect pretty-boy veneer into the man's weak, needy core.

During most of the meal—from appetizers to the entrée—Grayson and Geoff had kept the conversation going, with Cara and Lexie injecting comments from time to time. Deke had been his usual taciturn self, speaking when spoken to, but for the most part simply listening and observing.

Geoff declined dessert. "No, thank you, ma'am. I couldn't eat another bite." He slid back his chair and stood. "But I think I'll have another cup of coffee."

"I'll ring for—" Cara said.

"No need." Geoff held up his hand in a don't-bother gesture. "I can get it myself."

"I've become so accustomed to servants that I can hardly get along without them," Gray said, in a condescending tone.

Cara frowned at him, then got up and followed Geoff

to where the coffee service sat on a small sideboard. "I think I'd rather postpone dessert until later, too. But coffee sounds great."

Geoff grinned at her, and Lexie glanced at Deke, noticing his lips twitch, as if he were trying not to smile. She thought she knew what Deke was thinking.

Grayson's a prissy, snobbish little prick.

"Cara, I'd really love some of Cook's marvelous coconut cream pie," Grayson said. "She did make one this year, didn't she?"

"Actually, I don't believe she did," Cara replied. "I think she decided to make lemon meringue instead."

Grayson wrinkled his nose. "I detest lemon meringue."

"There's plenty to choose from," Cara told him. "Come over and take your pick."

"Well, I suppose if everyone else is serving themselves, I will, too."

When Lexie stood, Deke rose and came around to her side of the table. She smiled at him and said, loudly enough for everyone to hear, "I think I'll walk off that big dinner I just ate." She turned to Deke. "Would you mind going for a stroll outside in the fresh air?"

"It's unseasonably cold today," Grayson said as he studied the array of desserts, which included chocolate pie, caramel pie, lemon meringue, pecan, apple and pumpkin, along with the cakes. "You wouldn't catch me wandering around outside getting my face chapped by that terrible wind."

"I'll get our coats," Deke whispered. "You stay here with Geoff. I won't be gone long."

Lexie nodded to Deke as he left.

"Don't forget that we need to go over the final plans for the Black and White Ball sometime this evening,"

Cara said. "We have three weeks to make sure every *i* is dotted and every *t* is crossed."

"I promise that we'll make time to hole up in the study later," Lexie told her. "Most of the work has already been done. It's just a matter of double-checking everything."

"Oh, I do so love elegant parties," Grayson said. "I'm truly looking forward to the ball. All the best people will be there, of course." He smiled broadly at Cara. "You're inviting the governor, aren't you? And Senator and Mrs.—"

"We're inviting everyone we think will donate generously to Helping Hands," Cara told him. "The invitations go out tomorrow, and that's one of the reasons Lexie and I need to double-check everything tonight."

"Oh, yes, I'd almost forgotten that you'll be asking for donations to help fund Lexie's little African charity."

Geoff Monday coughed several times, apparently doing his best not to laugh out loud.

Cara groaned. "Gray, Helping Hands is not 'Lexie's little African charity.' It's an international organization to help the underprivileged around the world, including here in the United States."

"I think I'll meet Deke in the foyer." Lexie looked sympathetically at Cara, her glance telling her friend that she understood there was nothing Cara could do about Grayson's ignorance. He was, unfortunately, family, and Cara was the type of person who took care of her own. "We'll get together later and iron out any problems concerning the ball. I promise."

Cara offered Lexie a thanks-for-not-calling-Grayson-an-idiot smile.

By the time Lexie entered the grand foyer, Deke was

waiting for her. As he helped Lexie on with her dark-purple all-weather coat, he mumbled, "I'd rather freeze my ass off in twenty-below weather than spend another minute with that jerk."

"I don't think it's cold enough outside for us to freeze," Lexie told him. "But I share your sentiments. A little bit of Grayson Perkins goes a long way." As she spoke, she removed her knit gloves and matching cap from her pockets.

Deke put on his tan trench coat, then opened the front door and held it until Lexie walked onto the veranda. She positioned her cap on her head and slipped on her gloves. After he closed the door and took her arm, they walked down the steps and onto the front driveway.

The sun was warm; the wind was cold. Since it was past three in the afternoon, there would be only another hour or so of sunlight, and once the sun set, the fifty-something-degree temperatures would drop rapidly.

"We won't stay out long," Lexie said.

"I'll be fine as long as you are," he told her. "We'll stay out as long as you'd like. I know how important a good walk every day is to you."

"I need the exercise, especially after that huge dinner I just ate."

"Worried about your figure?" Deke asked, a humorous twinkle in his eye.

"As a matter of fact, I am. I gained thirty pounds years ago, after my surgeries, because I was so inactive. Anyway, I lost twenty of it, but I've never been able to shed those final ten pounds."

"You don't need to lose them. You're perfect just the way you are."

"I'm far from perfect."

"That's a matter of opinion."

Lexie laughed, loving him for telling her such sweet lies.

She tightened her hold on his arm as they took the walkway that led around the outer edges of the estate. They strolled peacefully, not talking for a while, enjoying the crisp fresh air and each other's company.

"I've got fifty-nine acres on a lake in Alabama," Deke said, ending their silent interlude. "I'm going to retire down there in another ten years or so. Maybe get a few head of cattle and a couple of old hunting dogs."

Surprised by his uncharacteristic personal confession, Lexie stopped dead still and stared at him. "Why, Deke Bronson, did you just start an honest-to-goodness meaningful conversation?"

His lips twitched. "Yeah, I guess I did. Taking a walk like this, everything so quiet and private, it got me to thinking about my place in Alabama. The house is old and probably needs tearing down, but it's good enough for me and Geoff and Ty and some other fishing buddies."

"I used to go fishing with my dad," Lexie said. "Gee, I hadn't thought about that in years." She sighed. "I miss my dad. He was a great guy."

"You still have your mother, right? And you like your stepdad, don't you?"

"Yes to both questions. And I'm fond of my stepbrother, his wife and their children, so I guess I'm lucky when it comes to family. It's just that sometimes, I wish…" *Don't go there. You've already shared too much of yourself with Deke.*

"What do you wish?"

"Nothing. It's silly."

"Hey, remember that this conversation stuff works both ways."

Lexie laughed. "So it does."

"So, tell me, what do you wish for?"

"Woman stuff, I suppose. I want a husband and children and a life outside my job. Don't get me wrong, I love the work I do at Helping Hands, and I'd never want to give that up, but I want more."

"That's not a silly wish."

"Yes, it is." She laced her arm through his, and they started walking again. "Do you know how difficult it would be for me to trust a man again after the way Wes treated me? I actually got involved with a guy a few years ago, only to find out that his interest in me was the three-million-dollar settlement I received from UBC. Thankfully, I wasn't in love with him and I'd never fully trusted him, so our relationship hadn't gone much past casual dating."

"Someday you'll find a man you can trust completely."

"Don't take this the wrong way or think I expect anything from you, but…well, I trust you, Deke. I don't know why, but I do. I've trusted you almost from the moment we met."

"Damn." Deke uttered the single curse word under his breath.

"When I'm with you, I feel safe," she told him. "And it's more than just your being my bodyguard, so don't give me that someone-to-watch-over-me-syndrome talk."

"You know that when we catch this guy—the mad bomber, the shooter, whatever you want to call him—my job will be done, and I'll leave and go on to the next assignment."

"I sort of hoped you'd want to stay in touch, maybe

even take me down to Alabama sometime to see your fifty-nine acres on the lake."

"It wouldn't work for us, Lexie."

Although his comment made her feel like crying, she didn't. She kept walking, slowly, carefully, with Deke holding her arm securely.

"We can't be friends? We can't stay in touch and visit each other?" She was grasping at straws, and they both knew it.

He paused, slid his arm around her waist and turned her to face him. When she didn't look up, he reached down, cradled her chin between his forefinger and thumb and lifted her chin.

"I'd want a lot more than friendship from you," he said. "But I'm the wrong guy for you. I'm not the man you need, not the man who can make you happy."

"Don't you think I should be the one to make that decision?"

He released her chin, ran his fingertips down her throat and slipped his cool hand beneath the collar of her coat. His thumb pressed against the pulse in her neck. "I told you before that you don't really know me. There are things in my past that you could never forgive. I've done things that you'd never understand."

"Try me," she told him.

"What?" He stared at her, a perplexed expression on his face.

"Tell me about one of those unforgivable things you've done."

"No."

She laid her glove-covered hand on his chest. "I trust you with my life every day. The least you can do is trust me with one—"

"I was a Delta Force commando," Deke said. "And later I was a mercenary, a hired killer. For most of my adult life, I made my living killing."

Lexie's mouth opened in shock. "Oh, Deke, how horrible."

He pulled away from her and turned half around, so that she couldn't see his face.

"Deke?"

"Yeah?"

She walked up behind him, laid her open palm on his back and then rested her head against his shoulder. "That's in your past. You aren't that man now."

She felt him take a deep breath, then exhale, but he didn't turn and didn't respond to her touch.

"Please, do not tell me that you don't hold my past against me," he said. "Don't say you forgive me. You don't know everything. If you did, you'd hate me."

"I could never hate you." She eased her arm around his waist. "You must know that I'm falling in love with you."

"Oh, God, Lexie…no, don't."

He turned quickly, his eyes narrowed, his jaw tense, and yanked her into his arms. When his mouth covered hers, she responded immediately, giving herself without reservation, the passion of her kiss asking for more. He deepened and intensified the kiss, his tongue exploring her mouth as his hands explored her body, caressing her shoulders, her back and her hips.

When they were both breathless, Deke lifted his head and pressed his cheek against hers. "Don't love me, Lexie. I don't deserve your love."

She held on to him for a little while longer, then released him and said, "I'm sorry, but I can't help it. I *am* falling in love with you, and I think maybe you're falling in love with me, too."

"No, I can't—"

She placed her hand over his mouth. "I know, I know. You're my bodyguard. I'm your client. You've done unforgivable things and don't deserve my love. You're the wrong guy for me. You can't give me what I need. I got it. I heard you the first time. But it seems my heart doesn't care what you say."

Suddenly a woman's voice screamed their names.

"Is that Cara?" Lexie asked.

"Lexie! Deke!" Cara came running around the house, not wearing a coat, her eyes wide and filled with tears. She waved her arms frantically.

Geoff Monday caught up with her just as she neared Lexie.

"What is it?" Lexie asked. "What's wrong?"

"It's Vega," Cara said. "She's—she's been—" Cara gulped.

"Vega has been rushed to the hospital," Geoff said. "She was involved in a hit-and-run accident."

"How badly is she hurt?" Lexie grasped Cara's trembling hands.

"I don't know," Cara replied.

"The police officer who telephoned here was looking for you, Lexie. He said that all he could tell me was that Ms. Sharif had been rushed to Erlanger."

"I need to go to the hospital now," Lexie told Deke.

"I'll have Eddie bring the car around," Cara said. "We'll all go."

Lexie looked at Deke and asked, "Do you think…? Would he…?"

"I don't know," Deke replied. "But I doubt that Vega being run down is nothing more than a coincidence."

CHAPTER EIGHTEEN

WHEN THEY arrived at the hospital, Sergeant Mike Swain met them at the emergency entrance, which surprised Lexie, though she realized immediately that it shouldn't have. Since Bain was out of town for Thanksgiving, it made sense that his partner would handle things in his absence. And anything potentially connected with the Helping Hands murders would fall under their jurisdiction.

"Vega's in surgery," Swain said. "I was told there's some internal bleeding, along with a collapsed lung and several broken bones. At this point, they don't think her injuries are life-threatening, but they won't know for sure what they're dealing with until they get inside and see the extent of things."

"Exactly what happened to her?" Cara asked.

"Let's get out of here," Swain said, glancing around at the other people entering and exiting the ER. "There's a surgery waiting area where we can go. I'll explain what I know on the way."

He gave Lexie and Cara sympathetic glances, then, side by side, he and Cara led the parade out of the ER and toward the elevator. Geoff Monday stepped back, allowing the detective to lead, but he stayed directly behind Cara. Lexie and Deke followed.

"From the report the first officers on the scene gave me, here's what we think happened," Swain said. "A guy lost control of his car and apparently careened off the road and up on the sidewalk, where he hit Vega. Then he pulled the car back onto the street and drove off. But he crashed into another car about three blocks away, and his car flipped and landed against a nearby building."

"Are you saying that what happened to Vega was an accident?" Lexie asked. "It really was a hit-and-run?"

"As far as we know, yes," Swain replied. "The guy driving the car had a passenger with him. Neither was wearing a seat belt. Both of them were seriously injured in the wreck, and they're both here in this hospital, too. The driver isn't expected to live, and the passenger is critical."

"So there's no way you can question either of them," Geoff said.

"Not at this time, but if they do survive, they'll both have a lot of questions to answer. I wouldn't be surprised if we discover the driver was either drunk or high. The hospital will do a tox screen to determine what, if any, drugs were in their systems."

When Lexie and the others arrived at the surgery waiting area, they found Hamal Gazsi pacing the floor, his shoulders slumped, his head bowed. He strode back and forth across the room as if the only thing that prevented him from screaming was keeping his body in constant motion.

Sergeant Swain and Cara entered the room first, then Geoff, and finally Lexie and Deke. Lexie walked toward Hamal and called his name. He halted his frenzied pacing, looked up at her with wild eyes, and slowly shook his head back and forth.

"She cannot die." His voice trembled, and tears dampened his round, cherubic face. "She is going to be my wife. We have decided to marry in June, the proper month for an American wedding, yes?"

Lexie approached Hamal, but she suspected if she tried to touch him in a comforting manner, he would fall apart completely, so she restrained herself. "Vega is going to live. We'll pray for her and—"

"She had eaten dinner with me here in the hospital cafeteria," Hamal said. "We wanted to share our Thanksgiving together. How is it possible that only a few hours later…?" His voice cracked. He turned from Lexie and began frantically pacing again.

Cara came up beside Lexie. "Shouldn't we do something to help him?"

"I can't think of anything that will help him other than good news about Vega."

"Or a strong sedative," Deke said.

Lexie's heart broke for Hamal. His actions spoke volumes about his feelings for Vega. It was obvious that he truly loved her.

Deke placed his hand in the center of Lexie's back and nodded toward the completely empty seating area. "You should sit down." Since only emergency surgeries were performed on holidays, the six of them were alone in the waiting room tonight.

During the next four hours, nurses came and went, as did other hospital employees who knew Hamal and were working the evening shift. Each one came over and spoke to Lexie. It seemed everyone knew Vega, who had told them all about Helping Hands and about Lexie. Eventually, one of Hamal's fellow interns slipped him a mild sedative, nothing strong enough to knock him out, but enough to calm him so that he finally sat down and sobbed quietly.

The young intern, a cuddly-cute man who had the face of a fifteen-year-old but the build of a huge teddy bear, had come over to Lexie first and introduced himself. "I'm Jimmy Hodiak. Dr. Hodiak. I'm another intern here at Erlanger. We're concerned about Hamal, so we decided one of us should do something to help him." He'd opened his hand to show her the tablet. "It's just a mild sedative, but the guy needs something to bring him down a notch or two before he explodes."

"I agree. Thank you." Lexie had squeezed the young doctor's hand. "You don't have an update on Vega, do you?"

"No, ma'am, I'm afraid I don't. She's still in surgery, but the last we heard, everything's going okay."

A few more staffers came by to check on Hamal, each one seeming genuinely concerned about him. Finally, after four and a half hours of waiting, a man in green scrubs showed up in the doorway, a weary expression on his deeply lined face. The moment Hamal saw the doctor, he jumped to his feet.

"Dr. Noles!" Hamal rushed toward the door.

When Lexie struggled to stand, Deke assisted her.

"Vega came through the surgery just fine," Dr. Noles said. He went on to explain in detail the extent of Vega's injuries, using medical terminology that Hamal obviously understood. But despite all her years dealing with doctors and her time in hospitals, most of what the doctor said was pretty much Greek to Lexie.

"She is in the intensive care unit now, where she will probably remain for a few days." Dr. Noles finally said something everyone understood. "But barring any complications, we should be able to move her into a private room by Monday." He clamped his hand down on Hamal's shoulder. "Your fiancée is a lucky young lady. I believe she's going to be all right."

The surgeon glanced around the room. "There is nothing any of you can do for Vega tonight. I suggest you all go home and get a good night's rest. You can come back to see her tomorrow. But only one or two at a time can go in during ICU visitation, so why don't you wait until afternoon and allow Hamal the morning visits alone?"

Once Dr. Noles left, Hamal slumped over so that his head almost touched his knees. He keened softly for half a second, then righted himself and turned to Lexie and the others waiting nearby.

"Our prayers have been answered," he said.

"Indeed they have." Lexie walked over to him and patted him on the back. "You should get some rest, too."

"I shall. I shall. I will sleep there." He pointed to a small sofa in the waiting room.

"If there's any change, call me immediately," Lexie told him. "And if there's anything I can do, anything Vega needs…"

"You are a good friend," Hamal said. "When I am allowed to see Vega in the morning, I will tell her that you were here, that you and Ms. Bedell stayed with me during her surgery."

Lexie barely made it out of the waiting room before she started crying. She couldn't hold back her tears any longer, crying as much from relief as anything else.

Cara put her arm around Lexie. "Go ahead and cry. Cry for both of us."

Lexie managed one nod, then swallowed her tears

and dabbed at her eyes and damp cheeks, brushing away the moisture. She understood what Cara meant. In recent years, Cara had been forced to exert great control over her emotions, which now made it more difficult for her to cry. Having lost her sister and her father within months of each other, then facing the daunting task of becoming CEO of a multi-billion-dollar conglomerate at such a young age, she'd had only one real choice. She'd had to get tough fast in order to survive.

Deke whipped a handkerchief from his inside coat pocket and handed it to Lexie. Smiling weakly, she accepted it and wiped it over her cheeks and eyes.

Once they reached the ground-floor lobby, Cara used her cell phone to instruct Eddie to bring the Rolls around to the front entrance.

Sergeant Swain escorted them outside. "We'll keep y'all posted on things with the hit-and-run driver."

"When will Bain be back from McMinnville?" Cara asked.

"Tomorrow sometime," Swain replied. "He's staying over at his sister's tonight."

WHEN THEY ARRIVED at the Bedell estate, neither Cara nor Lexie wanted to be alone, so the four of them went into the kitchen, and together they prepared ham and turkey sandwiches, found potato chips in the walk-in-pantry, poured glasses of tea and cola, and sliced off chunks of pie. Although both women insisted they couldn't eat a bite, once their late-night snack was on the table, they changed their minds.

Deke wanted to comfort Lexie, to reassure her that what had happened to Vega truly was an accident, nothing more than a horrible coincidence. But his gut instincts cautioned him. Although he and Geoff hadn't gotten a chance to be alone and discuss the matter, he felt certain that his old friend agreed with his assessment: there was more to Vega's accident than met the eye. For now, Dundee's would leave the investigation to the Chattanooga PD, but once they rendered a verdict, the agency would go in behind them and see if any minor detail had been missed.

"Some Thanksgiving Day, huh?" Cara said.

"At least at the end of the day, we still have something to be thankful for," Lexie reminded her. "Vega survived, and her surgeon believes she's going to be fine."

Cara stretched, lifting her arms over her head. "Why is it that emotional stress can make you feel as if you've been hit by an eighteen-wheeler?"

"We're all tired and stressed." Lexie glanced at the food on their plates. "I guess we should eat a bite, then try to get some sleep."

Cara nodded as she brought her sandwich to her mouth. She took a small bite and then another. Looking over at Geoff, she smiled and said, "You make a mean ham sandwich, Mr. Monday."

"Thank you, ma'am. We aim to please."

"I hate to think how many calories are in this thing, with all the cheese and mayonnaise." Cara eyed the chips. "I love these things." She picked up one. "I could eat a whole bag all by myself." She laughed.

Geoff chuckled. "Exercise is the key to eating what you want without adding extra pounds. Since I hit forty, I've had to increase my time in the gym."

"My idea of exercise is walking," Cara told him. "I try to make time to circle the estate at least once a day."

"Walking is great exercise, but you should take advantage of the gym you have in the basement," Geoff said.

"That was Daddy's gym." Cara's smile vanished. "I haven't been down there since he died."

"Why don't you have it redone to your specifications?" Geoff suggested. "Change it from a man's workout room to one that meets your needs."

"I just might do that." Cara popped the potato chip into her mouth, then followed it with another and another.

Deke studied Lexie as she sipped on her cola and picked at her food. For the most part, she nibbled while listening to Geoff and Cara's conversation. Deke sensed that it was only a matter of time before Lexie would need another good cry. She was a highly emotional woman, comfortable in her own skin and not ashamed to express her feelings.

"How about a piece of pie?" Deke asked her.

"No, thanks."

"Cake?"

"Hmm… Maybe."

"What'll it be? Just tell me and I'll get it for you."

"A tiny slice of the German chocolate."

"Would you believe that's my favorite?" Deke said. "How about I get a big piece and we share it?"

Lexie nodded.

"Hey, would you mind getting me a piece of pumpkin pie while you're up?" Cara asked.

"Glad to." He looked at Geoff. "Want anything?"

"I'll get something when I finish my second sandwich."

Deke played host, cutting slices of the requested desserts and setting the plates on the table. After sliding his chair over next to Lexie's, he sat, picked up his fork and said, "Dig in."

Lexie sliced off a bite of the deliciously rich cake, put it in her mouth and sighed.

"Good?" Deke asked.

"Heaven."

Deke smiled.

While Geoff and Cara shifted their conversation to, of all things, the benefits of dark chocolate over milk chocolate, Deke encouraged Lexie to eat more cake. But after three bites, she set her fork down and scooted back her chair.

"Please, finish eating," she told him. "I think I'll go up to my room now."

Deke dropped his fork, swallowed his last bite of cake and stood up. "I'll go with you."

They said good-night to Cara and Geoff, then headed for the elevator. Deke had noticed that Lexie's limp was decidedly worse when she became overly tired, as she was tonight. When they left the elevator on the second floor, he walked her down the hall to her room, then opened the door and reached inside to flip on the light switch.

"Want some company for a while, or would you rather—"

"Please, stay with me," she asked him, her blue eyes misted with tears.

He walked in behind her and closed the door, then reached out and did what he'd wanted to do all evening—he pulled her into his arms. Without a moment's hesitation, she wrapped her arms around his waist and laid her head on his chest. He stroked her back as he pressed his cheek against the top of her head.

"Go ahead and let it out," he said. "Don't hold it in. If you do, it'll make you sick."

"Oh, Deke… I was so afraid that Vega would die, and that the man who had run her down was…"

The emotional dam within Lexie burst, allowing her to weep until she was spent. And all the while, Deke held her, comforted her, and whispered consoling comments.

"It's all right, honey."

She gulped softly.

"Stop blaming yourself," he told her.

She lifted her head and gazed at him through a veil of tears. "Deke?"

"What do you need, Lexie?"

"I need for life to make sense again." She exhaled a deep sigh. "I need to stop feeling so afraid of what will happen next. I need to escape from reality, even if it's only for a few hours."

Deke recognized the look in her eyes, the silent plea for him to take her away from the fear and anger and remorse. God only knew how much he wanted to give her those few hours of escape, how desperately he needed to be the man she thought he was. But how could he make love to her with such a dark secret standing between them?

An inner voice urged him to forget about the past and take what he wanted, what Lexie wanted. She didn't know the truth, might never know. *She wants you, needs you. Making love to her wouldn't be selfish. You would be doing it as much for her as for yourself.* On the flip side, his conscience kicked in. *You can't do that to her. You cannot make love to Lexie. It wouldn't be fair to her.*

Yeah, sure, there was an off chance that it hadn't been his bullet that struck Lexie that day in Gadi. But Deke knew the odds were that he had shot her, nearly paralyzed her, put her through years of painful recovery. As much as he wished he could believe otherwise, he was ninety-nine-percent certain he had shot her.

Before she gave herself to him, she had a right to know the truth, didn't she? *And once she knows, do you think she'll ever look at you the same way? She'll have every right to despise you.*

"Deke?" Standing on tiptoe, she lifted her arms up and around his neck, offering her mouth to him, begging for his kiss.

Desire overrode common sense. Just one kiss, he told himself. But one kiss wasn't enough. Would never be enough. He grasped her hips and all but lifted her off her feet as he captured her mouth. She clung to him while their tongues mated in imitation of an even more intimate act. The rational part of his brain ordered him to stop, to put an end to this before it went any farther. But lust rode him hard, annihilating the warnings and urging him to take what he wanted.

He swept Lexie up and into his arms, then carried her across the room and deposited her on the bed. He yanked off his jacket, removed his holster and laid his weapon atop the jacket, which he'd tossed onto the foot of the bed. Lexie reached for him the moment he came down over her, straddling her by placing his knees on either side of her hips. When he buried his face against her neck, she wrapped her arms around him.

With deliberate intent, Deke undid the buttons on her beige silk blouse, taking his time, savoring each new inch that he revealed. She lay beneath him, watching him, her gaze switching back and forth from his hands to his face. When he reached the waistband of her brown slacks, he yanked the blouse free and finished unbuttoning it, then spread the edges apart to expose her lace bra. While he slipped his hand beneath her shoulder blades to unhook her bra, Lexie began unbuttoning his shirt. The moment her hands grazed his chest, his sex hardened painfully. As he eased his fingers up inside the loose cups of her bra and covered her breasts gently, she gasped, then reached up and caressed his bare chest.

Deke thought he would lose it right then and there. The mere touch of her fingertips drove him wild.

She rose up just enough for him to glide her blouse over her arms and off. Her bra followed, leaving her naked from the waist up. Before Deke could take what he wanted, she kissed a trail from his throat to the center of his chest, and then she flicked each of his nipples with her tongue. He groaned deep in his throat and lowered his head to her breast. He couldn't stand much more of this.

While he suckled greedily on one nipple, he stroked the other one with his thumb and forefinger. He had to take her soon or he would die.

Lexie moaned, reveling in the arousing sensations spiraling through her body. When Deke unzipped her slacks and delved his hand inside her panties, she struggled to undo his belt. He helped her unbuckle it, then quickly lowered his head and kissed her belly. She shivered when he inserted his tongue into her navel as his fingertips caressed her breasts.

She cupped her hand around his erection, only the barrier of his briefs separating her palm from his flesh. "Make love to me, Deke."

He was dying, and only burying himself deep inside her could save him.

He had never wanted anything more than he wanted Lexie. But he had no right to claim this woman, to make her his in the most basic, elemental way a man can possess a woman. And yet, God help him, he didn't think he could deny himself. Or her...

When he grasped the waistband of her slacks, she lifted her hips to enable him to remove both her slacks and her panties. He rose up and off her, tossed her clothing onto the floor, and then hovered over her, devouring her with his gaze.

She was as beautiful as he had imagined she would be. Skin like rich cream satin. Full, round breasts. Tight pink nipples. A thatch of golden hair between her slender thighs.

"You're beautiful," he told her.

"But not perfect," she said very softly.

"You're wrong. You *are* perfect."

"Oh, Deke."

He kissed each breast. She sighed. He licked a moist path from between her breasts to her navel, then paused before moving south and nuzzling her blonde curls.

She clutched his shoulders, urging him to move back up her body. He licked a trail upward until he stopped at her lips and kissed her. She sighed against his mouth as she ran her hands beneath his slacks and briefs to cup his taut buttocks.

"I love you, Deke. I love you so much."

Her declaration of love hit him like a dash of cold water, dousing the flames, forcing him out of the sexual haze that had consumed him. He froze instantly, realizing how close he had come to hurting Lexie again. And this time it would have been deliberate.

When he rose up and off the bed, Lexie sat up and stared at him. "What's wrong?"

He balled his hands into tight fists and cursed himself for a fool.

"Deke?"

He barely managed to zip his pants over his rock-solid erection.

Lexie yanked a satin throw off the foot of the bed, wrapped it around herself and slid to the edge of the bed. When she held open her arms to him, he shook his head.

"God, Lexie, I'm sorry."

"Sorry about what? I—I don't understand."

He knelt down in front of her and took her hands in his. "I can't make love to you."

"Why? Is it because I said I love you? I'm not asking for a commitment or anything. I'm not demanding you say you love me or—"

"I don't have the right to make love to you," he said. "No matter how much I want to. It's killing me. Ripping me apart. I want you so much."

"Then why did you stop?"

"I don't know if I have the guts to tell you why."

She squeezed his hands. "Tell me. Please."

"I can't bear the thought of you hating me."

"I could never hate you."

"If only that were true."

"I love you. Whatever it is, just tell me. I'll understand."

Deke shut his eyes, leaned his forehead against hers and took a deep, steadying breath. When he tried to pull away from her, she held fast, but he yanked free and stood. She stared up at him, a thousand questions in her big blue eyes.

"You know that I was once a Delta Force soldier," he said.

She nodded.

"I was part of an elite two-nation squadron that was sent on secret assignments. Assignments authorized by our governments." He swallowed hard. "One of my assignments…ten years ago…"

How could he tell her?"

God, help me!

"I was a member of an elite force sent into Gadi ten years ago to assassinate Babu Tum."

"Then you were…?"

"I was in Gadi, at the inauguration, the day you were caught in the crossfire, the day you were shot."

"Oh. Oh, Deke. It all makes sense now," she said, teardrops trickling down her cheeks. "From the moment we met, I felt a connection to you. I felt as if I knew you." She smiled. "Your eyes…I thought I remembered your gray eyes, but then I thought my mind was playing tricks on me, confusing you with the man who— Oh, my God, Deke, you saved my life that day, didn't you!"

Pain cut through him like a thousand knife blades ripping the flesh from his bones. If only he could accept the adulation and love he saw in her eyes. Knowing that her love would soon turn to hate, that the adulation would be replaced with revulsion, tortured him in a way nothing, except Andrew's death, ever had.

"You don't understand," he told her, barely managing to speak. "I—I'm the man who shot you."

CHAPTER NINETEEN

As DEKE'S confession replayed inside her head, Lexie tightened her hold on the satin throw she held together securely just above her breasts.

I'm the man who shot you.

No, she wouldn't believe it. She couldn't.

I'm the man who shot you.

No, no, no... Lexie keened mournfully as she rocked back and forth.

"Lexie?" Deke looked at her, deep concern in his expression.

As tears blurred her vision, making Deke nothing more than a dark, hulking image at her bedside, Lexie shook her head. "No, no... Please, no."

"I'm sorry. I am so very sorry."

"Go away."

"Lexie, please..."

"Leave me alone!" she screamed.

Hugging herself, whimpering, dying inside, Lexie rocked back and forth. When she heard the door close, she knew Deke had gone, that she was now alone. All alone.

She flung herself across the bed and cried. And cried. And cried some more. Until her whole body wept, until every fiber of her being mourned the loss of a dream.

As she wrapped her mind around the truth, she had to accept the fact that not only had Deke Bronson been one of Babu Tum's assassins, he was the man who had shot her. The man she had fallen in love with was the man whose bullet had almost severed her spine ten years ago.

Please, God, no. This is all wrong. Make it right again.

She lay curled in a fetal position, weeping quietly, feeling as if her whole world had suddenly exploded in her face, leaving her bare to her bones.

"Lexie?" Cara called from the doorway. "May I come in?"

Lexie couldn't speak, couldn't move. The awful pain in her chest immobilized her.

She felt someone sit down on the side of the bed and knew it must be Cara. She tried to lift her head, tried again to speak, but couldn't. Cara inched backward into the bed until she came up alongside Lexie, then she lay down beside her and wrapped one arm across Lexie's waist.

"I'm sorry, Lex," Cara said.

Lexie tried her best to stop crying, but without success.

Cara brushed Lexie's hair out of her damp face and patted her head. "Go ahead and cry. Damn Deke Bronson, whatever he did. Damn all men. They're not good for anything except to break your heart."

Lexie lay in agony, her only comfort the kindness of her friend. Cara stayed with her, consoling her as best she could.

WITH HIS BELT unbuckled and his shirt unbuttoned, Deke paced the floor in Geoff's bedroom. Never in his entire life—not even the day he shot Lexie—had he hated himself more than he did right now.

"Why the bloody hell did you tell her?" Geoff demanded.

"I had no choice." As nausea churned inside him, Deke clenched his fist and crossed his arm over his belly.

"What do you mean, you had no choice?"

"She told me she loved me." Her sweet confession tormented him.

"A beautiful woman that you have a major thing for tells you that she loves you, and your first thought is confessing what you consider your most grievous sin? Are you fucking crazy, Bronson?"

As a rush of salty bile burned up and into his throat, Deke snorted in self-contempt. "Yeah. I'm crazy. Crazy for not listening to you in the first place. Crazy for not running like hell as soon as I realized my client was Lexie Murrough."

"When she told you that she loved you, you could have said thank you very much, I'm fond of you, too, and left it at that."

Deke glowered at Geoff. "You don't get it. I was on the verge of making love to her. If she hadn't... I'd have taken her with no thought of the consequences. But when she said, 'I love you,' I knew the only way to stop myself was to tell her the truth."

"So you did it to save her from the horrible man who's spent the past ten years torturing himself because there's a possibility his bullet was the one that hit her during an exchange of crossfire no one could keep track of."

"We both know that it's more than just a possibility," Deke said. "It's a probability."

Geoff reached up and clamped his hand down on Deke's shoulder. "Give her time to get over the shock and then—"

"Call Ty and tell him I need to swap jobs with him. He can do guard duty, and I'll head up our investigation."

"Yeah, yeah, sure. But in a few days, when the dust settles, you need to tell Lexie that even though you might be the man who shot her, you're also the man who risked everything to save her."

"She knows."

"She knows what?"

"She knows I'm the man who picked her up and carried her to safety that day. She said she remembered me…remembered my eyes."

"She can't remember much," Geoff said. "She was in and out of consciousness most of the time, and when we boarded the helicopter, she was completely out it."

"The past can't be changed. All that matters now is keeping her safe. Since I can't stay on as her bodyguard, I really wish you would take over, and when Ty returns from Arkansas Saturday, he can take over guarding Cara."

"Does Lexie know that I was there that day, too? You know, you could have told her I was the one who shot her."

"I wouldn't lie to her. We both know it couldn't have been you."

Geoff squeezed Deke's shoulder. "I'll call Ty in the morning. In the meantime, I can handle looking after Lexie and Cara until he returns. You can arrange for a rental car in the morning and take over Ty's room at the Read House."

"Thanks."

"I'll make sure you know everything that's going on with Lexie. And I'll speak to Cara to see if she's okay with me taking over as Lexie's bodyguard while Ty guards her."

"Take good care of Lexie," Deke said.

"You know I will."

CARA STAYED with Lexie through the night, listening as her friend sobbed out the story of Deke's role in her near-death, until Lexie finally cried herself to sleep sometime after three. Cara wondered just how much more her friend could endure. It wasn't bad enough that some crazed madman was striking out at Lexie through the people she cared about and had promised to kill her, but her bodyguard turned out to be a ghost from her nightmare past. If Deke Bronson hadn't already left, Cara would have personally kicked his ass out the front door. And she would have sicced the dogs on him, too. *If* she'd had guard dogs, which she didn't.

Later, as she put the finishing touches on her makeup, Cara heard a rap at her bedroom door. "Be there in a minute," she called.

She hurriedly applied a peachy lip gloss, then shoved back the vanity stool and exited her dressing room. When she opened the bedroom door, Geoff Monday nodded and said, "Morning."

"I'm glad you had the decency not to say *good* morning."

"Everyone had a difficult night last night," Geoff said.

"Why are all men such bastards?"

Geoff looked at her wide-eyed but said nothing.

"No answer?" she asked.

"I assumed that was a rhetorical question."

"I suppose it was."

"I need to ask you something," Geoff said.

She eyed him questioningly. "Ask."

"Would you have a problem if I took over as Lexie's bodyguard and Ty became yours?"

"Why?"

"Lexie knows me. She's comfortable with me. I thought it might make things easier for her."

Cara studied him for a full minute, then said, "There's more to it than that."

"Deke and I go way back. If he can't keep watch over Lexie, he wants me to do it, because he believes I'm the next best thing to him."

"Just how far back do you two go?"

"All the way back to Gadi."

Cara drew in a deep breath, then exhaled on a soft whoosh. "You've known all along, haven't you?"

"That Deke thinks his bullet is the one that hit Lexie and nearly paralyzed her for life? Yeah, I've known all along."

"Why did he do it? Why did he keep this assignment after he realized who he'd be guarding? Didn't he know how she'd react when she learned the truth?"

"If he hadn't told her himself, she still wouldn't know. Give Deke a little credit."

"She's in love with him, you know," Cara said.

"I need to talk to her, to tell her what happened that day." Geoff looked at Cara, a plea for understanding in his eyes. "What Lexie's feeling isn't one-sided. Deke's had a thing for her all these years."

"I believe what he's felt is called guilt."

"Yeah, there's that, but it's more. Haven't you noticed the way he looks at her? A guy doesn't look at a woman that way unless she's eating him up inside."

"Are you saying that he's in love with her, too?"

"Maybe. I don't know for sure. All I do know is that

Deke's punished himself enough for the past ten years. He doesn't need Lexie to—"

"Don't say anything to her about that today. Wait until tomorrow to talk to her," Cara said. "Give her time to recover a little before you hit her with more truths."

"You're right. I'll wait." Geoff looked straight at her. "And what about my taking over as Lexie's body-guard?"

"Ask Lexie. If she's okay with the switch, so am I."

LEXIE HAD LEFT the Bedell estate only once on Friday, long enough for Geoff to drive Cara and her to the hospital so that they could see Vega. She had forced herself not to cry in front of the other woman, who had looked up from her ICU bed and smiled.

"I will be fine," Vega had reassured her. "I am getting the very best care."

Lexie and Cara stayed for ten minutes, then left so that Hamal could visit. Seeing his devotion to Vega pleased Lexie, but at the same time, it reminded her of what she'd hope to find with Deke. An impossible dream? She had been so sure he cared deeply for her. But all along, his concern for her had been the result of his guilt and not of love.

When Geoff had requested that he take over as her bodyguard, she had agreed, really not caring who took Deke's place.

"As long as I don't have to see Deke Bronson," she'd told Geoff, "it doesn't matter. You're fine. Ty Garrett is fine. Any Dundee agent willing to take over will do. It doesn't matter to me."

After her visit with Vega, she had returned to Cara's home and gone straight upstairs to her room and stayed there until this morning. Aldridge had brought her supper on a tray around six-thirty yesterday evening, and Cara had stopped in an hour later to check on her.

"You barely touched your dinner," Cara had scolded.

"I don't have much appetite."

"If you want to talk some more, I'm available."

"Thanks, but not tonight," she'd said.

She had slept fitfully, tossing and turning, checking the clock every couple of hours. And when she had finally managed to sleep for a while, she had dreamed. In her dream, Deke made passionate love to her, bringing her to a mind-blowing climax. Then suddenly, as she was in the throes of passion, she looked up to see a gun in his hand—and the gun was pointed directly at her. She screamed, begging him not to shoot her. When she awakened, she was trembling, and tears dampened her pillow.

Feeling sleep-deprived and emotionally numb, Lexie forced herself to go down for a late breakfast. Geoff escorted her to the dining room, where Cara and Ty were drinking coffee and talking to Bain Desmond. Apparently, when Geoff had summoned him back to Chattanooga, Ty had flown in early. The moment Lexie entered the room, they stopped talking. Bain stood, came over to her and kissed her cheek.

"How was your Thanksgiving with your sister?" she asked.

"It was good," he said. "But a real madhouse, with four kids of their own and her husband's whole family there, too. There are fifteen grandkids altogether, ranging in age from six months to sixteen years."

"It must be nice to be part of such a big, close-knit family."

"Yeah, I guess it is."

"This isn't a social visit, is it?" Lexie asked.

"Partly. I wanted to see how you're doing." When Cara cleared her throat, Bain added, "After what happened with Vega and all."

Lexie knew that Cara had told him about Deke Bronson. "Do you have any news for us about the accident?"

"Come on in and eat your breakfast. We can talk later. I'm here unofficially."

"Why don't you sit down?" Cara said. "Let me get you something. What do you want?"

"I can serve myself. Really."

"Indulge me. Let me do something for you."

"Coffee would be nice," Lexie said. "Thank you."

Geoff rushed over and pulled out a chair for her. She sat, hooked her cane on the back of the chair to the left of her and patted the seat of the chair on her right. "Bain, come sit by me. I'd rather hear your news now. I can eat later."

Bain sat beside her just as Cara placed a cup of hot black coffee on the table in front of her. "Thank you," she told Cara, then turned to Bain. "Please, if you know something about Vega's accident, tell me."

Bain hesitated. "There's bad news and more bad news."

"That's the only kind of news there seems to be lately." Lexie's hand trembled. She opened and closed it several times before attempting to lift the china cup to her lips. After taking a sip of coffee, she looked directly at Bain.

"The driver of the car that ran Vega down died about three this morning," Bain said. "He never did regain consciousness."

Lexie nodded, and then took another sip of coffee. When Cara set a plate filled with French toast and fresh fruit in front of her, Lexie mouthed the words *thank you*.

"The passenger is going to live," Bain said. "He tested positive for crack cocaine and if he makes it, he knows he's looking at jail time." When Bain hesitated, Lexie knew there was more, and that she wasn't going to like what she heard.

"Just tell me."

Bain glanced from Lexie to Cara to Geoff Monday, and then back at Lexie. "The passenger, a guy named Dustin Casey, confessed that his buddy had told him he had a job to do that would earn him enough money to keep them in crack for a week."

"And that job was?"

"To kill Vega Sharif," Bain said.

"No, please tell me that someone didn't hire that man to…" Lexie rubbed her forehead. Her worst fears had just been confirmed. Vega was another victim of the madman's obsession.

"Casey never met the person who hired his buddy, and he can't tell us anything about the guy, only that his friend, Josh Bassett, had never killed anybody before, and he offered to give Casey forty percent of the payoff if he'd go with him."

"Do you have *any* information about the man who hired Josh Bassett?"

"Casey told us that his buddy said he didn't know the man's name, but he wasn't American, and that he was a black man and had a wad of cash big enough to choke a horse."

"Vega's accident wasn't an accident after all. Deke was right." Lexie hesitated, not wanting even to think about Deke Bronson. "He said he didn't believe it was a coincidence."

Bain nodded but avoided making direct eye contact with her. "Unless Casey is lying to us, the odds are that the man who hired Bassett is the same one behind everything else."

"I've suddenly lost my appetite." Lexie stared down at the plate of food and thought she was going to be sick.

When she shoved back her chair, Bain reached over and gripped the armrests with both hands, effectively trapping her.

"Don't do this to yourself," he told her. "You know damn well that none of this is your fault."

Deke's voice echoed inside her head, telling her the same thing that Bain had just told her. She longed for Deke, wanted him here to hold her, comfort her and tell her everything would be all right. That he would make it all right. But Deke wasn't here. And he wasn't the man she'd thought he was.

"Lexie, are you all right?" Bain asked.

"Huh? Oh, yes, yes, I'm all right."

"We'll find him. I promise you. Between the Chattanooga PD and Dundee Security, you've got the best working on the case."

"Please, find him before he hurts someone else."

CARA SPENT most of Saturday trying to keep Lexie entertained. They shopped on-line for shoes and purses, for winter sweaters and handcrafted silver jewelry. They went swimming in the morning, and then Cara had Mrs. Eddins prepare them sinfully delicious hamburgers and French fries for lunch. They strolled around the estate in the afternoon, needing only light jackets, since the temperature had risen into the high fifties again. Ty went with them, and Lexie suspected that Geoff was spending some time on the phone with Deke.

The more she tried not to think about Deke Bronson, the harder it was to put him out of her mind. And the images she had of him in her head were all mixed up. Good guy or bad guy? Saint or sinner? Who was he really? Her shooter or her rescuer? For the past ten years, she had suspected that one of Babu Tum's assassins had accidentally shot her when she'd gotten caught in the crossfire, but she had never dreamed that someday she would come face-to-face with that man. All her memories, from the moment the bullet entered her back until she woke in the hospital, were of a pair of smoky-gray eyes. She had dreamed of those eyes, had fantasized about the man who possessed those hypnotic eyes. And she had turned him into a larger-than-life hero, someone no other man could possibly live up to.

After eating an early supper of homemade vegetable soup and grilled cheese sandwiches, Lexie and Cara persuaded Ty and Geoff to play poker with them. They played for pennies, which Cara kept in a massive glass jar. Each player started with the same number of coins, and at the end of two hours, Cara had won back every cent.

"How did you learn to play poker like that?" Ty asked as he stood up and stretched.

"Actually, my father taught me. Edward Bedell was a man who never lost."

Cara's easy smile disappeared, and Lexie knew she was remembering that in the end, her father had lost not only his elder daughter but his own life.

"It's been a long day," Lexie said. "I think I'll say good-night."

Cara hugged Lexie, then walked over to Geoff and whispered something to him. Afterward, he escorted Lexie into her bedroom, but instead of going through the connecting door to the room that had been Deke's and was now his, he stayed with her. It was as if he were waiting for her to say something.

"What is it?" she asked.

"I'd like to talk to you."

"About the case? About your duties as my bodyguard? About—"

"About Deke."

Somehow she had known that was what he would say.

"I don't want to talk about him."

"I know you're hurt and angry and—"

"I'm not having this conversation with you."

"Lexie, Deke would do anything for you. The last thing he ever wanted to do was cause you more pain."

"How do you know so much about what Deke wants, how he feels, why he played me for a fool?"

"Lexie, he did *not* play you for a fool." Geoff came straight to her and stood there until she looked at him. "I was there that day in Gadi. I was a British SAS officer, part of the squad sent into Gadi to assassinate Babu Tum. I was with Deke through it all."

She stared at him, barely able to believe what he was saying. "Then you saw what happened. You saw him shoot me and—"

"No, I didn't see you get shot. But I know you were caught in the crossfire, and that whoever shot you didn't mean to."

"What do mean, whoever shot me? Deke told me that *he* shot me."

"Deke believes that, but there's no way he can be

one hundred percent certain. There was too much gun-fire all around us."

"But it's highly likely that he did shoot me, isn't it?"

Geoff took a deep breath. "Yes, it's possible, even probable, that he shot you. But it is, without a doubt, a certainty that he's the man who saved your life. He went against orders when he picked you up and took you with us all the way to the chopper that was waiting for us. He risked his life and the lives of his men—and that included me—to get you out of Gadi alive and see that you were taken to a hospital."

Lexie's throat tightened with emotion. "I remember his eyes. I thought I was dying, and then I felt his arms around me, and I looked up into those concerned gray eyes. I focused on his eyes, telling myself that he would take care of me, that he wouldn't let me die."

"If he had listened to me, he would have left you there and you'd be dead. If you want to hate someone, hate me, not Deke."

"I don't hate Deke."

"He needs to know that. He's spent the past ten years punishing himself for what happened that day. And it wasn't his fault. You were in the wrong place at the wrong time, and that's all there was to it."

"When he came to Chattanooga to be my bodyguard, did he know—?"

"Neither of us had any idea that you were the presi-dent of Helping Hands."

"Then why, when he realized who I was, didn't he swap positions with Ty Garrett, or why didn't he just go back to Atlanta and let Dundee send someone else to be my bodyguard?"

"Why do you think?"

"I don't know."

"He saw this as a second chance, as an opportunity to protect you, to somehow make up to you for what happened in Gadi." Geoff looked her in the eyes. "I don't think he realizes it, and he probably wouldn't admit it if he did, but Deke Bronson cares as much about you as you do about him."

"No, that's not possible. What he feels for me—*all* he feels for me—is guilt and maybe pity."

"You know it's more than that."

"I—I can't talk about this anymore. I won't." She glowered at Geoff. "Please, leave me alone. And tell Ty Garrett that I want him as my bodyguard from now on, starting first thing in the morning."

"Certainly, if that's what you want."

"It is."

Geoff nodded. "Good night, Ms. Murrough."

He went into the adjoining bedroom and closed the connecting door. Lexie stood trembling, her emotions all over the place. She had fantasized about the man who had rescued her that horrific day in Gadi. But she'd had nightmares about the man who had shot her. She loved Deke Bronson. But she couldn't love the man who had put a bullet in her spine.

Wrong place. Wrong time. An accident. He's punished himself for ten years. He cares about you as much as you do him.

Geoff Monday's words rumbled inside her head, tormenting her until she wanted to scream. Lexie walked into the bathroom, closed the door, stripped off her clothes, turned on the shower and stepped beneath the warm, peppering spray. And then she screamed. Long and loud and hard.

CHAPTER TWENTY

DEKE HADN'T been sure if Bain Desmond would even talk to him, let alone meet him. So when the detective agreed to share lunch with him and suggested the Hair of the Dog pub, Deke had been surprised. It had been a week since he'd seen Lexie, a week since he'd revealed himself as her shooter, but he had been able to keep close tabs on her, thanks to Geoff and Ty.

"She's holding it together," Ty had told him. "Better some days than others."

Although there hadn't been another attempt on the life of anyone Lexie knew and Vega Sharif was on the mend in a private room at Erlanger—guarded 24/7—little had improved in Lexie's life. Geoff had sent Deke copies of the three threatening messages Lexie had received this past week, each subsequent message more detailed than the one that came before it. All three letters had been delivered by the U.S. mail and had prophesied that there was an appointed time for her to die. And like the message left in the ladies' room during Malik Abdel's postmemorial reception, the three new notes used lettering cut from magazines and newspapers, then glued together to form sentences. Each note underwent a thorough inspection by the CPD lab, but they came up with very little. No DNA, no fingerprints, nothing distinguishable in any way. And the type on the envelopes had been created by a laser printer, the kind used by hundreds of local businesses. The guy threatening Lexie knew what he was doing, which further proved that he was no amateur.

When Deke entered the pub, he caught sight of Desmond immediately. The detective half rose from his seat and waved, motioning for Deke to join him. The dark wood interior, along with wrought-iron railings and warm lighting, gave the place a casual, relaxed feel. But right at the moment, Deke wasn't feeling very relaxed.

When he neared the table, Desmond stood and offered his hand.

Deke shook hands with him, and then the two men sat opposite each other. "Thanks for meeting me," Deke said.

"I figured, why not?" Desmond grunted. "Look, we're on the same side. You want to keep Lexie and everyone she cares about safe. So do I. So does the Chattanooga PD."

Deke nodded. "I wasn't sure what you'd think about me once you knew—you *do* know, don't you? If Lexie didn't tell you, then I'm sure Cara Bedell did."

"Cara told me that you confessed to Lexie that you were the soldier who accidentally shot her back in Gadi ten years ago." Desmond scrutinized Deke as if he were trying to somehow gauge his worth as a man. "It took guts to tell her the truth. I admire that about you, Bronson."

A waiter paused by the table and asked to take their drink orders.

"Coffee for me," Desmond said.

Deke ordered iced tea.

When the waiter was out of earshot, Deke said, "This Black and White Ball they've planned is a bad idea."

"Tell me about it. I've tried my best to convince Cara to cancel the damn thing."

"She won't listen to you, huh?"

"She and Lexie agree that canceling the ball would mean they're allowing a madman to dictate their lives," Desmond told him. "We're dealing with a couple of strong, independent women who'll do what they damn well please."

"Ms. Bedell is paying Dundee a small fortune, not only to guard her and Lexie, but for our investigative and advisory services. But on this issue she refuses to take our advice."

"Cara can be hardheaded. Once she makes up her mind about something, she relentlessly pursues it."

"Providing the proper security for an event that large will be almost impossible. The guest list numbers over two hundred. And just dealing with the extra staff coming and going that day and night will be a nightmare. There will be the catering staff, the florist and his staff, members of the band and numerous delivery people, not to mention the extra household staff. And what about the valet service?"

"Monday and Garrett have agreed that Dundee's will help us run background checks on everyone who's been invited and anyone hired to work the ball, no matter how lowly their position."

"This guy is someone—"

"Coffee for you." The waiter placed the steaming mug in front of Desmond, then removed a glass from his tray and set it in front of Deke. "And iced tea for you." He glanced from Deke to Desmond. "Are you guys ready to order?"

"I want the Tramstopper," Desmond said, then

looked at Deke. "Best meat loaf sandwich I've ever tasted."

Deke glanced hurriedly at the menu. "I'll take the Boar." He'd never eaten a BLT he didn't like.

"You were saying?" Desmond asked as soon as the waiter left to put in their order.

"This guy is someone who slips in and out of Helping Hands. He's either an employee, or he's a close friend or family member of an employee."

"Has Dundee's been able to get hold of more detailed information about Robert Lufti and Jafari Holston?"

"We're working on it," Deke said. "Sawyer Mc-Namara is using some of his government contacts. And we're looking deeper not only into Lufti's and Holston's past histories, but into Hamal Gazsi's, too."

"Why Hamal? You don't think the guy would hire someone to kill his fiancée, do you?"

"What better way to throw us off his scent and make him look innocent?"

"He'd have to be a cold-blooded son of a bitch, and an Academy Award-winning actor to boot."

"I imagine you've run into a few of those over the years in your line of work."

"A few," Desmond said, as he lifted his coffee mug. "But probably not nearly as many as you encountered when you were a mercenary. No doubt you even worked for a few guys like that."

Deke nodded, then peeled the paper from his straw and stuck it down in the glass of tea. "Geoff has spoken to Larry Nesmith, and he'll bring two dozen Bedell security guards with him the night of the ball. Geoff will be at Cara's side all evening, and Ty will stay with Lexie. I'll be there, too, trying to be as inconspicuous as possible."

"I don't intend to be far from Cara," Desmond told him. "Mike will be there, too, and I'm working on commandeering a dozen of the CPD's finest."

"Sounds like we've got the security situation under control, but you and I know that this guy can still slip in under our radar and strike without warning."

"I did suggest to Lexie and Cara that maybe they should ask our three primary suspects not to attend the ball."

Deke snorted. "Let me guess. They refused to believe that any one of them—Lufti, Holston or Gazsi—could possibly have committed such heinous acts."

"As badly as I hate to admit it, they could be right. Our guy might not be foreign. He could be someone local simply pretending to be foreign just to throw us off."

"I suppose you've already checked out this theory of yours, haven't you?"

Desmond grinned. "Yeah. And so has Dundee's—right?"

"We came up with two possibilities," Deke said.

"Rufus Estes and Lou Franklin."

"One is an ex-con with a background in explosives who's married to Helping Hands employee Renee Estes," Deke said.

"And Lou Franklin, a Vietnam vet and former sniper who's been very vocal in his opposition to the U.S. giving aid to foreign countries. His daughter, Monique, works at Helping Hands, but supposedly father and daughter do not get along."

"At least neither man has been invited to the ball," Deke said. "We've gone over the invitation list backward and forward."

"But Robert Lufti will be there, since he's an employee. And Toni Wells will bring Holston as her guest, and if Vega is able to attend, she'll bring Gazsi. I've asked Larry Nesmith to make sure his guards keep close tabs on all three men."

"Estes and Franklin are long shots, but we need to keep tabs on them. Better safe than—" Deke stopped in mid-sentence when the waiter approached with their food.

Deke and Desmond ate, enjoying the meal, pausing to discuss strategy for the charity ball and what their guts were telling them about the man intent on killing Lexie.

Halfway through lunch, Desmond glanced toward the door, got a peculiar look on his face and said, "Uh-oh."

"Huh?"

"Did you arrange for Garrett to bring Lexie and Cara here for lunch?" Desmond asked.

Deke spun around in his seat and followed Desmond's gaze to the entrance. Every muscle in his body tensed when he saw Lexie.

"No, I did not arrange this," Deke said. "I wouldn't put Lexie in such an awkward position."

"Then I must be to blame."

"How's that?" Deke couldn't take his eyes off Lexie. She was wearing her purple all-weather coat, but without the cap, leaving her blond curls loose and slightly wind-blown.

"I mentioned to Cara that I was meeting you here for lunch, so this harebrained scheme must be hers."

LEXIE WOULD have been content eating at her desk today, as she often did, but Cara had come by Helping Hands and insisted Lexie go out with her.

"We'll just run over to the Hair of the Dog for chili,"

Cara had said. "We won't stay long. I can't take more than an hour away from the office."

Sensing that for some reason it was important to Cara that they share lunch, Lexie had gone along, albeit somewhat reluctantly. Ty escorted them into the pub, while Geoff gave Cara's chauffeur instructions as to when to pick them up, cautioning him to stay with the Rolls at all times. While Cara spoke to one of the waitresses, Lexie glanced around. As she scanned the lunch crowd, her gaze halted on Bain Desmond. Smiling, she lifted her hand to wave—and then she saw the man sitting across from Bain.

Her gaze met Deke's and locked instantly.

She had spent the past week trying not to think about him, yet thinking of little else. He plagued her thoughts day and night. Daydreams. Nightmares.

Lexie grabbed Cara's arm. "Deke's here with Bain."

Cara followed Lexie's line of vision. "Hmm…so he is."

"Did you and Bain set this up?"

"Don't blame Bain," Cara said. "This was entirely my idea."

"I don't understand. How could you do this to me? You know how I feel about seeing Deke."

Cara lowered her voice to a whisper. "I know how you feel about him. You're in love with him. And regardless of what you say, you really want to see him again. Admit it."

Lexie turned around and headed for the door. Cara caught up with her, clutched her arm and said, "Come back. Please."

Lexie hesitated.

"At least go by his table and say hello." Cara looked pleadingly at Lexie. "That's all I ask. It's just one tiny baby step for both of you."

"I can't!" Lexie jerked loose of Cara's light hold and marched out the door, Ty Garrett right behind her.

When Ty and Geoff passed each other, as Ty followed Lexie onto the sidewalk, Geoff asked, "What's wrong?"

"Apparently, we're leaving," Ty said. "At least Ms. Murrough and I are."

"Eddie won't be back with the car until two," Geoff said.

Lexie paused and glared at Geoff. "I suppose you were in on it, too, weren't you?"

"Huh? In on what?"

"Deke's in there." Ty hitched his thumb toward the pub. "He's eating lunch with Lieutenant Desmond."

"Go back inside and look after Cara," Geoff said. "Ms. Murrough and I need to talk."

Ty nodded, then reentered the pub. Lexie clutched her cane with one hand while she clenched her other hand into a tense fist. She stood there on the sidewalk, her gaze darting about nervously. The last thing she wanted to do was listen to Geoff defend his old elite forces comrade.

"I had no idea Deke would be here," Geoff told her. "If I'd known… Look, I understand that you're hurt and confused and angry. But don't you think maybe you owe it to Deke—and maybe to yourself—to give him a chance?"

"Why would I owe Deke anything?"

"Oh, perhaps because he saved your life."

"After he almost killed me."

"What's bothering you more, knowing Deke could have been the soldier who shot you, or being plagued by doubts about his true feelings for you?"

Lexie closed her eyes, hating Geoff for being brutally honest with her.

He grasped her arm. "I'm not trying to hurt you. I'm trying to make you see the truth for what it is. If you think you're in pain, think about how Deke feels. Or don't you care how he feels?"

She didn't want to care, but she did. She cared far too much. "I don't hate him. Please tell him that, will you? And tell him that I know it wasn't his fault, that I know he didn't mean to shoot me."

"Why don't you tell him yourself?" Geoff looked over Lexie's shoulder.

She turned slowly, balancing herself with her cane. Deke Bronson was coming out of the pub, but he stopped abruptly when he saw Lexie and Geoff. She and Deke stared at each other, neither of them moving, each of them barely breathing. Her body ached with wanting him. Just the sight of him made her want to cry for what might have been.

Deke broke eye contact first, then turned and walked away.

"Deke," Lexie called to him.

He stopped, stood there on the sidewalk a good ten feet away from her, then cautiously turned to face her.

"Could we take a walk around the block and talk?" she asked.

"I don't think that's a good idea," he replied. "It's not safe for you to be out in the open like this for very long."

"Oh, yes, of course, you're right."

"Let me call Eddie," Geoff suggested. "He can have the limo here in a couple of minutes, and you two can drive around the block a few times."

"What do you say, Lexie?" Deke asked.

"All right."

"Take her back inside for now," Deke told Geoff. "I'll wait out here for Eddie."

Five of the longest minutes of Lexie's life passed before Deke came inside the pub and got her. Eddie had the Rolls waiting at the curb, and once she and Deke slid into the backseat, he eased out into midday traffic and drove up Market Street. The two of them didn't speak to or look at each other for several minutes.

"I don't hate you," Lexie said.

Deke breathed in and out deeply, then looked at her. "I wouldn't blame you if you did."

"I know that you didn't mean to shoot me, that what happened was no one's fault. It was just an accident. I really *was* in the wrong place at the wrong time."

"I don't know what to say. I didn't expect you to… Lexie, are you sure about this?"

"Am I sure that I don't hate you? Yes, I'm sure. Geoff told me that you've punished yourself more than enough for something that wasn't your fault."

"It *was* my fault."

She shook her head. "We were both in Gadi on assignment. My network sent me there to cover a story they thought had little significance. Our government sent you there to kill a man who, had he lived, would have continued using his power for immense evil. I was doing my job. You were doing yours. If I had gotten out of the way when the first shots were fired, I would have been safe. And Marty Bearn would still be alive. He wouldn't have been shot by one of Tum's guards."

"When are you going to stop blaming yourself for your cameraman's death?" Deke asked, his gaze moving over her face.

"When you stop blaming yourself for what happened to me," she replied.

"Lexie?" He looked at her longingly.

"Tell Eddie to take me back to the pub," she said. "I need to grab a quick lunch before I return to work."

"Thank you for talking to me, for telling me—"

"I can't deal with anything else," she told him. "Not now. Let's give it some time and see how we both feel."

"Whatever you want."

He tapped on the privacy window separating the driver from the passengers and told Eddie to take them back to the pub.

DEKE RETURNED to the Read House at two-fifteen. When he entered the foyer, he found three men waiting for him. Two he knew—Sawyer McNamara and Sam Dundee. One he didn't know.

"You should have called to let me know y'all were coming and I'd've been here when you arrived," Deke said.

"We just got here," Sawyer replied. "We picked up Rob Copeland at the Chattanooga airport and came straight here."

Deke studied the five-ten, lean and fit stranger. Graying, neatly cut brown hair. Clean-shaven, except for a narrow mustache. A conservative dark blue suit and a nondescript tie. Deke pegged Rob Copeland for a government agent.

"Let's go up to your room, so we can talk in private," Sam Dundee said.

Deke had met Sam years ago, when they'd both been much younger. Sam must be nearly fifty by now, but he was as muscular and trim as he'd ever been. His blond hair was streaked with silver, and there were a few lines fanning out from the corners of his eyes, but other than that, he hadn't changed much. At six-four, the owner of Dundee Security was one of the few men with whom Deke literally stood eye to eye.

No one spoke on the ride up in the elevator. Once they entered Deke's room, Sawyer and Rob Copeland inspected it thoroughly.

"It's clean," Sawyer said.

"You think someone might have bugged my room while I was out for lunch?"

"Probably not, but we need to be careful," Copeland said.

"Just what's going on?" Deke asked.

"Rob's with Homeland Security," Sam explained. "It seems Dundee's has inadvertently brought undue attention to three men who have come under the government's scrutiny recently."

Deke's brow wrinkled. "Meaning?"

"We've been digging around trying to get information on three men who are possible suspects in the threats against Lexie Murrough," Sawyer said. "We had no idea that all three men are of interest to our government."

"And just why would they be of interest?" Deke asked.

"What I'm about to tell you is top secret information," Rob Copeland said. "Sam and Sawyer have vouched for you and your service record—"

"Just spit it out," Deke told the agent.

"A few months ago, we came upon some interesting information, and even now we're continuing to gather intel," Copeland said. "There is a terrorist cell, part of the group that calls themselves the Majeed, operating somewhere in the South. They're plotting an attack on a number of government sites sometime soon, possibly on Christmas Day."

"And how does this plot connect to Lufti, Holston and Gazsi? Do you suspect them of being part of the terrorist cell?" Deke asked.

"We obtained information about each man that remains privileged at this time. I'm sorry we can't share it with Dundee Security, but we're asking that you stop digging into these men's pasts, at least for the time being. They're three of over a hundred men that we're interested in."

"And you're interested in them because…?" Deke asked.

"Each of those three men has a family connection to a terrorist group. At this time, we have no evidence directly linking any one of them to the Majeed, but we're receiving updated information on a regular basis, so it's only a matter of time before we narrow down our suspects."

"And you have no idea which government sites have been targeted?"

"No, not at this time," Copeland replied.

"So, you're telling me that Lexie Murrough's life—"

"Stop right there." Sam Dundee held up his hand as a signal to Deke.

Deke glared at Sam.

"Rob is going to share information with us, as much as he can, as soon as he can," Sam said. "Until then, if Dundee's does its job, we'll keep Ms. Murrough and Ms. Bedell safe."

Deke looked Rob Copeland square in the eyes. "Do you know if one of your suspects has a reason to kill Lexie Murrough?"

"My information doesn't single out any one of them as having a reason to want Ms. Murrough dead," Copeland told him. "But I can tell you this, and it's all I can tell you—all three men have a connection to Gadi. Holston and Gazsi, as well as Lufti."

CHAPTER TWENTY-ONE

WITH THE gala Black and White Ball under way, the Bedell Estate hummed with excitement. Lights shone from every window, limousines and luxury cars circled the drive, and music drifted out of the house and onto the cold December wind. People said that snow was in the air and thought how wonderful it would be to have a real white Christmas, something seldom seen in Chattanooga. Although he'd had to wear a tuxedo on a couple of previous occasions in his job as a bodyguard, Deke felt like a fish out of water at a ritzy shindig like this. Only the Bedell, Inc. security force wore uniforms tonight. The half dozen CPD officers in attendance had on formal attire, as did the three Dundee agents.

With Ty guarding Lexie and Geoff guarding Cara, Deke was free to move around inside and out, check in with the Bedell guards and the police officers, and keep on top of everything. Lexie and Cara were scheduled to make their grand entrance in fifteen minutes, so he had taken the opportunity to escape from the bedlam inside, but he definitely wasn't about to lose track of the time. He intended to return to the foyer at precisely seven-thirty. While he stood at the end of the veranda, as far from the front door as he could get without going into the yard, he watched while the elite of Chattanooga and southeast Tennessee entered the mansion. Movers and shakers. Old money and new. Politicians and business executives. If they were likely to write out a five-figure check, they had been invited.

As the blustery north wind whipped around the side of the house, Deke wished he'd put on his overcoat. Even if he stayed out here only ten minutes, he would be cold as ice by the time he went back inside. After cupping his hands together, he lifted them to his mouth and blew his warm breath into the hollow space in between.

He sensed the man's presence before he caught a glimpse of him in his peripheral vision. Lieutenant Desmond looked as if he felt every bit as uncomfortable in his tux as Deke did in his. Basically, Deke was an old country boy whose idea of dressing up was having to wear a tie, and he suspected Desmond's background wasn't all that different.

"I don't know about you, but my gut is tied in knots," Desmond said as he approached. "There are just too many things that could go wrong tonight."

"What I don't want to see is one of your men or one of the Bedell guards getting jumpy and doing something stupid."

"My guys will be okay," Desmond told him. "And Larry Nesmith's people are well-trained, but they're all nervous. Larry has cautioned them not to overreact to anything that happens."

"I won't be far from Lexie all evening," Deke said. "I trust Ty to protect her, but—"

"Like I trust Monday to protect Cara."

They looked at each other, a silent understanding passing between them. When all was said and done, each man intended to be there to protect his woman.

"I'm going to walk around the house and take a last-minute look before the ladies make their grand entrance," Desmond said. "I want to check in with the guards at every entrance."

"See you inside."

Desmond nodded, then stepped off the veranda and headed around the side of the house.

Deke rubbed his hands up and down his arms, and walked toward the front door. He dreaded this night, dreaded going back inside, dreaded the moment Lexie would enter the ball and make herself a target. He hadn't seen her in the past two weeks, and he was hungry for the sight of her. After their private talk in the back of Cara's limousine, he had hoped Lexie would contact him, but she hadn't. Apparently she wasn't ready for another conversation about their relationship. Maybe she never would be.

LEXIE CHECKED her appearance in the floor-to-ceiling wall of mirrors in the small dressing-room alcove. Amethyst and diamond dewdrops dangled from her earlobes. A matching bracelet circled her wrist, and a matching necklace graced her throat. She owned a few pieces of nice jewelry, including one strand of expensive pearls, but the million-dollar baubles she wore tonight belonged to Cara, part of the extensive jewelry collection accumulated by generations of wealthy Bedell women. The Black and White Ball had been Cara's idea, and Lexie had gone along with it because she was willing to do almost anything to acquire donations for Helping Hands. While Cara had been born into a circle of socialites to whom this was just one more event on their year-end calendar, Lexie came from a more modest background. To people like Lexie's family, a dance at the small country club where her parents had been members was a big deal.

Lexie checked her watch. Seven twenty-five. Almost showtime. She opened her bedroom door and found Ty Garrett, looking quite handsome in his tuxedo, waiting for her. When they arrived at the head of the central staircase, Cara and Geoff approached from the opposite wing of the house. She and Cara exchanged nervous smiles, then took their escorts' arms and waited together at the top of the stairs. Seconds ticked by, then a minute, then another.

The band stopped playing. A second later, a repetitive drumroll served its purpose and caught everyone's attention. All eyes lifted to the top of the staircase.

Lexie took a deep breath. She knew Deke would be here tonight, was probably already here. The nervousness tapping along her nerves was due in part to concern for her own safety and that of her friends. But it was also partly due to knowing she would see Deke after a gap of two weeks. She had picked up the phone to call him at least once a day, but she had stopped herself each time. No matter what had occurred in the past, Lexie knew one thing for certain—she was in love with Deke Bronson, in love with the gray-eyed man who had rescued her that day in Gadi, in love with the Dundee bodyguard who was willing to die to protect her.

"Ready?" Cara asked.

"Ready," Lexie replied.

THEY WERE expecting him to strike tonight at the Black and White Ball. Security was tight. And knowing he was a suspect because of his alien status, he realized he would be watched closely this evening.

He smiled.

Let them watch me.

They would see him with his woman. A man in love. Nothing more. When he made his move, it would be so subtle that no one would even notice.

Dundee Security was digging into his past. They would run into a dead end. His true identity was buried so deeply that no one could find it. His mother's family had seen to that, to protect them both from the people who had killed his father. He didn't know why his father's assassins hadn't murdered his mother and himself the day they gunned down his father, along with his loyal guards and cabinet ministers. He had lived his life bearing the name of a man who had not been his father. He had been forced to live a lie, to pretend to be someone he was not.

Because of the American and British infidels!

Before he died, before he killed Lexie Murrough, he would tell her who he was and force her to beg him for forgiveness.

For three weeks he had lulled Lexie and her entourage of protectors into a false calm by doing nothing except send warning messages. If they were wise, they would understand that those twenty-one days had simply been the calm before the storm. And what better time to create a deadly storm than in a sea of American millionaires?

He would show Lexie Murrough that no one could protect her or her friends, that they were as vulnerable to attack and death as his father had been.

WITH A ROUND of applause from the guests, Lexie and Cara descended the staircase, their bodyguards acting as their escorts. Cara looked lovely in black satin, but Deke focused on Lexie. She was a vision in a white silk gown that draped each curve, caressing her breasts, her waist and her hips as he longed to do. Diamond-and-amethyst jewelry shimmered around her neck, on her left wrist and dripped from her earlobes. She had swept her curly blond hair up into a thick French twist, leaving wispy tendrils framing her face.

He should be the man standing beside her, not Ty Garrett. He should be the man protecting her, guarding her from all harm. And not because it was his job and she was his client. But because she was his. She had belonged to him since that day in Gadi when he had carried her in his arms, willing to sacrifice everything and everyone to save her.

If their paths had never crossed again, if she had never come back into his life, he might eventually have found someone else. But even if he had, his passion for Lexie Murrough would have haunted him to his dying day. Now that she was a part of his life, however briefly, now that he had come so close to truly possessing her, there could never be anyone else for him. If that was love, then he loved Lexie.

Deke blended in with the crowd, moving farther and farther away from Lexie as she and Cara entered the fray. For the next two hours, he monitored the event, keeping tabs on every Bedell guard and every police officer. He made the rounds inside and outside, even checking on the caterers in the kitchen twice. Holston, Lufti and Gazsi had arrived with their dates, Toni, Alice and Vega. The three couples appeared inseparable, probably because each man was aware he was being closely watched.

Deke had passed through the ballroom earlier and hadn't seen Lexie, although he'd caught a glimpse of Ty Garrett's back, which told him that Lexie was sitting down in front of him. Sitting out the dance.

As he walked around the room, staying close to the wall and away from the dance floor covered with men in black tuxedoes and women in black or white evening gowns, he studied the crowd. He didn't think he'd ever seen so much bling all in one place. The combined worth of all the jewelry adorning the ladies here tonight probably exceeded twenty million. And that could be a low estimate.

Now Deke caught sight of Lexie in a far corner. She was standing staring at the dancers, and even if no one else noted the wistful look in her eyes, he did. Lexie wished she could dance. She longed to be in a man's arms, out there with the other couples.

He had sworn he would stay away from her. He'd had good intentions. But the best-laid plans... When Deke walked up beside Ty, Lexie forced a smile.

"Good evening," she said.

"Good evening," he replied. "You look beautiful."

Before she could reply, he leaned over and whispered to Ty, "Ask her to dance."

Keeping his voice low so that only Deke could hear his response, Ty said, "I have asked. She said no."

Without giving his actions any thought, Deke held out his hand to Lexie. "Would you like to dance?"

Her eyes sparkled for half a second, and then the light in her baby blues died suddenly. "I don't dance anymore." She glanced at the cane in her hand.

"It's a slow dance," he told her. "Leave your cane with Ty and hold on to me for balance."

"I—I don't know."

He grasped her hand in his and pulled her toward him. She drew in a quick, surprised breath when he took the cane from her and handed it to Ty. Then he all but lifted her off her feet as he led her cautiously onto the dance floor, careful to keep a firm hold around her waist. Standing perfectly still, she stared up at him, her eyes wide with uncertainty.

"I can't do this. I—I can't dance."

"Yes, you can." He eased her toward him with the gentlest force possible. Staggering slightly, she clung to him. "Slow and easy. Tiny steps. Don't think about dancing, just move with me while I hold you in my arms."

She tried, her steps hesitant and faltering.

When she looked down at her feet, he said, "Look up, at me."

She lifted her gaze to meet his and offered him a fragile smile.

He swayed her tenderly back and forth, side to side, to the rhythm of the bluesy jazz tune, something featuring piano, cornet and bass. With each passing moment, she relaxed more and more, trusting him completely. She even loosened her hold about his neck and eased the tight grip she had on his hand.

"You're the most beautiful woman here tonight," he told her.

"It's the diamonds." Smiling, she shook her head so that the dewdrop earrings shimmied. "They've bedazzled you."

"*You've* bedazzled me."

"I've missed you."

Her confession hit his chest like a ton of bricks,

knocking the air out of him. He pressed his jaw against her temple and drew her closer, all but swallowing her slender body in his embrace.

"Does that mean you're ready for me to come back as your bodyguard?"

"No." She gazed up at him.

"No?" He searched her face, hoping to understand her response.

"If you come back, it has to be as more than my bodyguard."

Deke's chest constricted with suppressed emotion. "If that's what you want." He exhaled, releasing the tension inside him. "I'll come back on your terms, whatever they are."

"What do *you* want, Deke?"

"You." He pressed his lips against her forehead, then leaned down and whispered, "I want you, Lexie, any way I can get you."

The music ended abruptly, followed quickly by a drumroll and then Cara Bedell's voice. "Ladies and gentlemen, the night is young, and we have a fabulous buffet set up in the dining room. Eat, drink, dance, but don't forget to write out a check to Helping Hands International and give it to our accountant, Mr. Farris Richardson."

Decked out in a tuxedo with tails and a ruffled shirt, Richardson beamed from ear to ear as he stood beside Cara alongside the podium that had been set up next to the band.

"Dig deep, my friends, and give generously," Cara said. When she stepped away from the podium, she went straight into Bain Desmond's arms, and he led her onto the dance floor.

The band played another tune suitable for slow dancing, but Lexie squeezed Deke's hand and said, "Thank you for the dance."

"Am I being dismissed?"

"Only temporarily," she told him. "You have your duties tonight, and I have mine. I'm supposed to be schmoozing the contributors."

"What about later tonight, when the ball ends?"

"We'll both be tired," she said. "And thankful that everything ended on a peaceful note." She squeezed his hand again. "Tomorrow is Sunday. Why don't you come by after lunch and we'll talk about us, about what you want and what I want, and how we'll deal with the past and what we'll do about the future."

"I meant what I said, Lexie. I want you on your terms. Whatever you want or need from me, I'll give you."

"What you want and what you need are just as important as what *I* want and need." She stood on tiptoe and kissed his cheek. "Think about it, decide what it is you truly want, and tell me tomorrow."

Ty met them as they came off the dance floor, handed Lexie her cane, and escorted her out of the ballroom and toward the dining room.

Deke watched them until they disappeared, all the while replaying Lexie's last comments over in his mind.

What do I want? What do I need?

He wanted Lexie. He needed her. But did he love her? Was he even capable of love?

CARA WAS EXACTLY where she wanted to be, where she wished she could stay forever. In Bain Desmond's arms. But this dance would end all too soon, and he would leave her. He exposed her to minute glimpses of happiness, but that was all he could offer her. They could not change who they were, she the heir to the Bedell fortune and he a Chattanooga police detective. In another world, where they were equals, they could be lovers. They could even marry and have children and live happily ever after—if there was such a thing as forever happiness. But in the real world, be it his world or hers, they could not coexist. She could not live in a four-bedroom, two-and-half bath house in the suburbs, drive an SUV and join the PTA. And that was the type of wife Bain wanted. The type of wife he needed. He couldn't move into the Bedell mansion and live off his wealthy wife's billions. He was the old-fashioned kind of man who had to be the breadwinner, the one who wore the pants in the family.

"You're smiling," Bain said as he danced her around the room, keeping their bodies close.

"I was thinking about you," she admitted.

"Was I naked?" He chuckled.

Cara rested her head on his shoulder. "Why can't we just have an affair?"

His muscles tensed. His arm around her waist tightened, and he threaded his fingers through hers, then brought her hand to his lips and kissed her knuckles. "Because if I ever make love to you, even once, I'm not going to be able to let you go."

She nuzzled his neck.

He shuddered.

"It's not fair," she murmured against his throat.

"I don't suppose you'd ever give all of this up, would you?"

She lifted her head, looked directly into his eyes and

said, "If no one else would be affected by my actions, I'd seriously consider it."

Bain snorted. "I wouldn't be worth your giving up billions, sugar. Besides, you have way too many people depending on you to keep the Bedell, Inc. ship afloat."

"Sometimes, I want to sink the damn Bedell, Inc. ship."

"No you don't. You love being top dog and running the show. It's what you were born to do." He ran the back of his hand across her cheek. "I think this is where I say something like 'in this crazy mixed-up world, the problems of two little people—'"

She slapped her hand over his mouth. "Don't joke about us."

He gripped her wrist and lifted her hand from his mouth, then planted a kiss in the center of her palm. "Save the last dance for me." He released her and walked away, leaving her on the dance floor.

Before she had a chance to recover from his abrupt departure, Grayson popped up, seemingly out of nowhere, and slipped his arm around her waist.

"You look ravishing, sweetheart," Gray said. "Those emeralds—" he ogled the earrings and necklace "—bring out the green in your eyes."

"I need a drink," Cara said.

"Come with me and I'll get us some champagne."

Reluctantly, she followed Gray off the dance floor and toward the nearest waiter carrying flutes of champagne on a silver tray.

She would drink champagne with Gray, even dance with him, and she would sweet-talk and arm-twist donations from as many of her guests as possible, but at the end of the evening, she intended to be back in Bain Desmond's arms.

I will *save the last dance for you.*
Tonight. And for the rest of my life.

WITH A BEDELL, INC. guard standing behind him, Farris Richardson sat behind the desk, smiling happily as people came by, some giving him cash donations, while most wrote out checks or signed pledges. A few simply placed envelopes on the desk and walked away, no doubt expecting Farris to mail them a receipt. As eleven o'clock drew near, the entire desk was covered with stacks of checks and cash and several yet-to-be-opened envelopes. Lexie and Cara beamed happily as they thought of how much good Helping Hands could provide to the underprivileged thanks to the generosity of so many Tennesseans.

"Are you close to having a grand total for us to announce?" Cara asked Farris.

"No, not yet." He tapped the adding machine, hitting the subtotal button. "But as of right this minute, it looks like we've collected close to two hundred thousand."

"Oh, that's wonderful," Lexie said.

Cara glanced at the stack of unopened envelopes. "Most of those will be hundreds and fifties, so they're not apt to change the total by much."

"Every dollar counts," Lexie reminded her enormously wealthy friend, to whom a hundred dollars was mere peanuts. "You need to remember that not all our guests tonight are millionaires."

Cara put her arm around Lexie's shoulders. "Thanks for reminding me. I need you around all the time to keep me connected to the real world."

"I'm pretty good at giving you a reality check, aren't I?"

A reporter who had been buzzing around all evening taking snapshots of the guests, but mostly worrying Cara half to death, asked that she and Lexie pose with the stacks of donations.

"I'll make sure it's in tomorrow's edition," he said. "And I'll guarantee we'll run an address where folks can send their own contributions."

Cara gritted her teeth, but Lexie only laughed. "Come on. Force yourself to smile at the camera. It's for a good cause."

"Hey, buddy," the reporter said to Farris. "How about you open up one of those envelopes, take out the money, and once Ms. Bedell and Ms. Murrough are in place on either side of you, hold up the cash. That'll make a great shot."

"I need to touch up my lipstick," Cara said, pulling Lexie aside. "We'll be ready in just a sec, okay?"

Cara snapped the catch on her purse, delved inside the tiny evening bag and brought out a tube of peach-tinted gloss.

Lexie's gaze moved back and forth, from Cara putting on fresh lip gloss to Farris, who had picked up a half-inch-thick envelope. Either someone had donated a large amount of cash or the envelope was filled with one dollar bills.

"Okay, I'm as beautiful as I'm ever going to be." Cara snapped her purse closed.

Lexie glanced from Farris, who was in the process of opening the envelope, to Cara who was running her fingers through her short, exquisitely styled hair.

Boom!

The sound and flash of a nearby explosion created panic.

People screamed and ran. Lexie gasped. Cara cried out.

Before either of them knew what was happening, four men charged toward them. Bain and Geoff reached Cara simultaneously, and together lifted her off her feet and sandwiched her between them. Deke shoved past Ty Garrett and barreled into Lexie, taking her down to the floor and covering her with his body.

CHAPTER TWENTY-TWO

ALL HELL BROKE LOOSE. People ran over one another trying to escape, only a few paying any attention to the Bedell guards, who were doing their best to usher people to safety outside. Chaos reigned supreme as the crowd ran, screaming hysterically, out into the freezing December night. Frightened men and women knocked one another down in their frantic flight.

Deke lifted himself off Lexie, then stood, grabbed her hands and yanked her to her feet. "Are you all right?"

"Yes." She squeaked the one-word reply.

Nearby, Desmond shoved Cara into Geoff Monday's arms, looked her dead in the eye and said, "Stay with Monday. Do what he tells you. Understand?"

She nodded, then asked, "What the hell happened?"

Desmond glanced around the rapidly emptying room, his gaze stopping at the desk where Farris Richardson had been sitting. "Holy shit!"

"What?" Cara turned to follow Desmond's gaze. He whirled her around to face in the opposite direction. "Don't look. You don't want to see it."

"Deke?" Lexie called out. "What is it? Is Farris all right? Has he been hurt?"

Deke swallowed hard. What could he say? Farris

Richardson was far from all right. And he was more than hurt. Deke suspected that the Helping Hands accountant was dead. Apparently he had taken the full force of what Deke suspected had been a letter bomb. Richardson's face was burned beyond recognition, his hands mangled and seared, and fragments of the desk—shards of wood—had penetrated his body. The security guard, slivers of debris embedded in his bloody face and piercing his uniform, was hunkered several feet behind Richardson's body, his eyes glazed over in shock.

"You and Cara go with Ty and Geoff," Deke said. "Outside." He looked over at Geoff. "Take them out through the kitchen and go straight to the servants' cottage. Keep them there until Desmond or I contact you and tell you it's safe to bring them back to the house."

Lexie reached for Deke. "Is Farris…?"

"He's probably dead," Deke told her. "There's nothing you can do for him. Just go with Ty. Now!"

Deke cast a glance toward Desmond, who was already on his cell phone calling for assistance: police backup, paramedics, firefighters, the whole nine yards, then went straight toward Richardson and the wounded guard. By the time Desmond completed his call, two of the six CPD officers attending the party had made their way to join him.

"The others are working on crowd control," one young officer told Desmond. "People out there are going nuts."

Desmond looked from one officer to the other. "Yarbrough, help Bronson with the wounded guard. Burrell, I want you to secure the scene immediately."

Desmond called out to Deke, "What's the situation?"

"Richardson's dead," Deke said. "The guard's in shock, but his wounds seem to be superficial." He helped the stunned guard to the nearest chair. "Sit here. Help is on the way. Do you understand?"

The guard didn't move or speak, simply stared off into space.

"What do you need me to do?" Deke asked Desmond.

"Come with me. We need to make sure no one leaves the estate until we've questioned everyone. We've got a long night ahead of us."

Deke nodded, then followed Desmond outside, to where a terrified crowd of rich, powerful people awaited them.

HE STAYED with his woman, pretending to be as dazed by events as everyone else. When the others questioned exactly what had happened, he acted as puzzled as they were. And when they were told that Farris Richardson was dead, he faked shock and remorse. He had become very adept at acting the part of both a devoted lover and a friend to everyone at Helping Hands.

Lexie Murrough, are you agonizing over the loss of yet another friend? Do you blame yourself for another person's death?

The thought of Lexie suffering pleased him, and knowing she would suffer even more in the days ahead brought solace to his heavy heart. Only by taking Lexie Murrough's life could he ever hope to avenge his father's murder.

The police and the Dundee agents had thought they were so smart, thought they had thoroughly screened everyone entering the Bedell Estate today and tonight. But who would suspect that a guest would be able to

bring a bomb to the Black and White Ball and slip it un-
detected past the guards? Preparing the letter bomb had
been simple enough. Three and a half ounces of explosives. A "mouse-trap" mechanism, cocked when he
inserted the device into the envelope. Then he had
placed the envelope in his inside coat pocket and removed it, unobserved, as he passed by the table where
the Helping Hands accountant was collecting donations. Then all he'd had to do was make sure he and his
woman were in another room for the remainder of the
evening, so that when Farris Richardson tore open the
envelope and released the striker, they would not be
directly caught up in the panic after the bomb exploded.

"I REALLY WANTED to see Lexie before we left," Toni Wells
complained as Jafari drove her car out through the gates
of the Bedell mansion at one-fifteen Sunday morning.

"The police would not allow you to see her," Jafari
said. "She and Ms. Bedell are safe. Mr. Bronson told
you so himself. You can call her later today."

"Can you believe what happened?" Toni burrowed
deeper into the bucket seat and crossed her arms over
her chest. She was chilled to the bone from standing
outside in the freezing cold for over an hour, until the
fire and police departments had inspected enough of the
Bedell mansion to allow people back inside one downstairs wing. "Poor Farris."

"It is unfortunate that Mr. Richardson died in such a
terrible way."

"Why can't they catch that madman?" Toni choked
back her tears, determined not to cry.

"It appears that he is always one step ahead of them."
Toni reached across the console and grasped Jafari's

arm. "I'm sorry that they consider you a suspect. The idea is ludicrous. If they knew you the way I do…"

He smiled at her. "What you think of me is all that matters. The police and the Dundee agents are only doing their jobs. Because I am not an American citizen, because I was raised as a Muslim and—"

"It's not just you, you know. They've been investigating Robert and Hamal, too."

"I do not take it personally, and neither should Robert and Hamal."

"I'm just glad you were with me all evening long," Toni said. "That should convince them that they need to broaden their search and stop concentrating on you."

ALICE WAS CONCERNED about Robert. He had been unnaturally quiet ever since they left the Bedell estate. In fact, he had barely spoken a dozen words to her, even before the police allowed them to leave. Realizing how deeply affected he'd been by the bombing, she had insisted on driving.

"Please, drop me at my apartment," Robert told her.

"No, you shouldn't be alone. Not after what happened. We need each other, tonight of all nights."

"They suspect me. You know that, don't you?"

"Is that what's bothering you?" She hazarded a quick glance in his direction. He was sitting stiff as a poker, his gaze straight ahead. "Jafari and Hamal are suspects, too. And I know for a fact that they've been investigating everyone who works at Helping Hands, and any suspicious members of their families."

"I am a suspicious person because I am from Gadi. They know that my uncle and my cousin are members of a—"

"And they know you did not plant the letter bomb that killed Farris tonight. You were with me the whole evening. You have an alibi."

"They will think that perhaps either you are lying to protect me or that I could have somehow slipped the letter on the desk without your noticing what I was doing."

"Then they would be wrong on both counts, wouldn't they?"

"Yes, they would be wrong."

VEGA WEPT QUIETLY. She wished she could stop crying, but she couldn't. Hamal had been very understanding, very kind.

He would make her a good husband.

"Try not to think about what happened," Hamal told her.

"I've tried." She sucked in a deep breath and wiped her face with her fingers. "But I keep wondering, when will he stop? How many of Lexie's friends will he try to kill? Will he try to kill me again?"

Keeping one hand on the steering wheel of his Chevy Cobalt, Hamal reached over and tenderly squeezed Vega's hand. "I wish I could be with you all the time, day and night, to keep you safe."

She held on to his hand. "He is an evil man. He is capable of murdering innocent people without cause."

"I am sure he believes he has just cause to do what he is doing."

Vega jerked her hand away. "Hamal!"

"I am not defending him. I only said that he must believe he has just cause to do the horrible things he has done. People can always find a way to justify their actions."

"You must not say such things. The police could misunderstand you, and that would be very bad."

"The police will not arrest me for something I did not do, but they must do their job and look at every possible suspect."

"I hate your being a suspect. How can they think you would pay someone to kill me? If they knew you as I know you…"

"You must not worry, my dear Vega. Everything will be all right."

LEXIE'S GAZE followed Cara, who had spent the past few hours alternating between pacing the floor in the living room of the small servants' cottage and sitting beside Lexie. For the most part, Ty and Geoff stayed out of their way, speaking when spoken to and otherwise simply keeping watch. Deke had called twice, the first time to check on how they were doing, and to inform them that the police had completed a partial inspection of the mansion and were beginning to allow people to go back inside the house to get out of the cold. His second call had been to tell her that the police were allowing the guests to leave after they finished questioning them, and that he would be coming to the cottage to talk to her soon.

Lexie wasn't sure what she had expected to find in the servants' cottage, but the partially furnished but otherwise empty house had surprised her. She supposed she had thought that someone still lived there.

"Aldridge and Mrs. Eddins are the only servants who live in," Cara had explained. "Aldridge has his own quarters on the third floor, and Mrs. Eddins's rooms are off the kitchen. The other servants live off the estate and come in daily. No one has lived in this cottage since before I was born."

Apparently the small house had been kept up outside but mostly neglected inside, except for an occasional cleaning. Even though what little furniture remained was dusty, the living room was actually in decent condition.

"Didn't Deke say that he'd come get us?" Cara asked. "If the house is clear, what's taking him so long?"

"I'm sure he'll be here as soon as he can get away." Lexie suspected that part of Cara's irritation came from the fact that Bain hadn't called her. "And he didn't say he'd come get us, only that he would talk to us. I'm sure he and Bain still have their hands full."

"Who said anything about Bain Desmond?" Cara came to a standstill, whirled around and glared at Geoff. "Why can't you and Ty take us back to the house? Why do we have to wait on Deke?"

Geoff shrugged. "I don't know, but I'm sure Deke has his reasons for asking us to wait for him."

"Why don't you call him and see what's keeping him?" Cara planted her hands on her hips. "Or give me your cell phone and *I'll* call him."

Lexie patted the sofa cushion beside her. "Cara, come sit down. Please."

Cara glared at Lexie, then shook her head and clicked her tongue in self-disgust. "Oh, Lex, I'm sorry. I'm being a real pain in the ass, aren't I? And here you are staying so calm."

"I'm not all that calm," Lexie admitted. "I think I'm just numb. I'm having a difficult time believing that Farris is dead. I don't understand how someone got a bomb into your house past all the guards."

Cara sat beside Lexie, hunched her shoulders as she leaned forward and stared down at the wooden floor. "If it was a letter bomb like they think, then anyone could have brought it into the house inside their coat or jacket or even in a purse. It would have been a simple matter to leave the envelope on the donation table and walk away unobserved."

"He's very smart, whoever he is."

Cara grabbed Lexie's hand. "They're going to catch him and put him in jail. And we'll make sure that he's punished for what he's done."

"Poor Farris." Fresh tears pooled in Lexie's eyes. "Damn, I've got to stop crying."

A loud rap on the door gained everyone's attention. With gun drawn, Geoff moved toward the door.

"It's me, Bronson."

Geoff didn't holster his gun, but he did lower his hand to his side and open the door while Ty stayed in front of Lexie and Cara.

When Deke entered, he nodded to both Dundee agents, then went straight to Lexie. Bain Desmond entered behind Deke and closed the door. The moment she saw Bain, Cara jumped up and ran to him.

As Deke approached Lexie, his gaze traveled over her from head to toe. When she tried to stand, he laid his hand on her shoulder and gently urged her back down on the sofa.

"The police are only partially finished checking the house," Deke told her. "It's an enormous place, over twenty-five thousand square feet. It'll probably be morning before we can be sure the entire house and grounds are clean."

"How is the security guard?" Lexie asked.

"As far as I know, he's going to be fine. The last I saw of him, he was on his way to the hospital."

"Did you see Toni?"

"Just for a minute. She and Jafari have gone home. Just about everyone has been allowed to leave."

"Alice and Robert?"

"Yeah."

"Poor Vega. This was her first night out since she was released from the hospital. Did you talk to her?"

"I stayed with her while Bain questioned Hamal."

"Why did he do that? Hamal isn't—"

Deke cupped Lexie's chin with his thumb and forefinger. "The police questioned everybody, but Desmond took Hamal, Robert and Jafari aside and questioned them himself."

"And?"

"And nothing."

"Was anyone else hurt?"

"No. Just Richardson and the Bedell security guard."

Deke sat beside Lexie. "Geoff will be taking Cara up to the house. The wing of the mansion where her bedroom suite is located has been cleared. It could be another two or three hours before they finish going through the east wing, so you'll need to stay here for a while longer."

"Will you stay with me?"

"I'm taking over as your bodyguard as of right now," Deke said. "I'll send Ty out there to see what he can do to help Desmond."

BAIN WALKED with Cara and Geoff from the cottage to the kitchen entrance of the mansion.

"Maybe I should have waited with Lexie until the rest of the house is clear," Cara said.

"Deke will stay with her and take care of her."

"Yes, I know he will."

"You need to get some rest, if you can."

She looked at Bain, her eyes pleading with him for what she dared not ask.

When they went inside the kitchen, Geoff walked off, leaving Bain and Cara alone. Geoff paused by the exit that led into the back hallway. "I'll wait out here for you," he told Cara.

"Yeah, okay. Thanks." She turned to Bain. "You have to find the son of a bitch. He's already killed four people and tried to kill Vega. Lexie could be next."

"Or you," Bain said.

Cara crossed her arms over her waist and hugged herself. Bain grasped her wrists, eased her arms apart and held her hands on either side of her hips.

"You know that I'd stay with you if I could," he told her.

She leaned into him and stretched up just enough so she could rest her forehead against his. "You don't know how much I need you."

Bain groaned. "Damn, sugar."

She lifted her head and stared right at him. "You're not the only cop on the police force, you know. Let somebody else—"

He grabbed her face, cradling her cheeks with his open palms and kissed her. Hot. Forceful. Hungry. But he ended the kiss all too quickly, lifting his head and releasing her, and took a gulping breath.

"I've got to get back to work."

She nodded. "Yeah, I know."

He stared at her.

She gave him a gentle shove. "Go. Leave. I understand."

"If you need—"

"I'll be fine. I have my own personal bodyguard. Besides, I'm Cara Bedell, and if I need anything, I know how to get it. I'll just buy it."

DEKE WENT from room to room, checking out the old servants' cottage. He'd hoped to find a bed in one of the two bedrooms, but both were empty except for stacks of boxes and one bed frame. No mattress.

"Find what you're looking for?" Lexie asked as she came up behind him.

"I thought maybe I'd find a bed where you could sleep." He turned around in the narrow hallway and faced her. "You have to be exhausted."

"Why can't we go to my apartment? There are two perfectly good beds there. And after what happened here tonight, don't tell me that I'm safer here than I am in my own home."

"You'd have been perfectly safe here if you and Cara hadn't insisted on having that damn Black and White Ball." Deke barked the accusation at her.

"Thank you for reminding me that, once again, it's my fault a friend is dead!"

"Damn it, Lexie, I didn't mean it that way, and you know it."

"I haven't asked you how, with all the Bedell security guards, six police officers and three Dundee agents, someone was able to bring a bomb into Cara's home, have I?"

"If you're intent on playing the blame game, then, yeah, there's enough blame to go around. Everybody can take a helping. You, me, Cara, Desmond. The Bedell security guards, Dundee and the police officers. But when it comes right down to it, the one person to blame is the guy who put the letter bomb on Farris Richardson's desk."

Lexie glared at Deke. "He's dead because of me. Because he was my friend." She clenched her teeth together tightly, and keened with guilt and pain.

"Damn it!" Deke clutched his hands into fists, the anger inside him longing to hit something, anything, in order to release some of his rage. He was saying all the wrong things, making Lexie feel worse, when all he wanted to do was pull her into his arms and hold her.

"Why doesn't he stop tormenting me and just kill me?" Lexie looked at Deke, and the anguish he saw in her eyes ripped out his guts.

He grabbed her shoulders and shoved her back against the wall with such force that he knocked the cane out of her hand. When her back hit the wall, her eyes widened and her mouth opened on an inaudible gasp.

"Deke?"

He manacled her wrists in his hands, lifted them up and against the wall on either side of her head, then lowered his mouth to hers and kissed her. She moaned. He deepened the kiss, thrusting his tongue inside to pillage and plunder.

When they were both panting for breath, he released her wrists and brought his hands down over her shoulders. He shoved aside the white silk shawl, pushing it down her arms until it fell free and floated to the floor. While he kissed her throat, she threaded her fingers through his short, black hair and whispered his name.

He nuzzled her neck, raking his tongue across the diamond and amethyst necklace, and down to the silk bodice of her gown. As his tongue explored the space between her breasts, exposed by the plunging neckline, he slid his hands behind her and unzipped her evening gown. The moment he accomplished his goal, he yanked the bodice downward until it fell about her waist and exposed her breasts.

As he lowered his mouth to one breast, he clasped her buttocks, drew her up against him and ground his sex against her mound.

He intended to have Lexie Murrough. Here and now.

CHAPTER TWENTY-THREE

KEEPING LEXIE PRESSED against the wall, Deke practically ripped the silk gown from her body, leaving her in nothing but her lace panties, garter belt and hose. With shaky hands, she helped him shed his jacket. Then he removed his holster, bow tie and shirt. While he struggled with the zipper on his slacks, she clung to him, kissing his neck and shoulders. After he removed his slacks and kicked them aside, he knelt in front of her and buried his mouth against the triangle of blond curls covered by a wisp of white lace. She trembled when he lifted his head and inserted his tongue in her navel.

She held on to his shoulders to balance herself as he concentrated on unhooking her stockings from the garter belt. After he removed one stocking, he tossed it aside and went to work immediately taking off the other one. Then he removed her lace-and-satin garter belt.

They were both naked, except for her panties and his briefs. As he stood up straight, she lifted her gaze to meet his.

Neither spoke.

And then he touched her, his fingers gently skimming across her chest directly above her breasts. She held her breath as he moved his hand over her breasts, across her stomach and down between her thighs. Her legs parted, allowing him to inch his fingers inside her panties. He found her core and stroked it tenderly.

Lexie felt his touch through her whole body, a tingling vibration that radiated from her feminine center. Whimpering softly as he petted her, she leaned her head back against the wall and closed her eyes.

Deke lifted his fingers from between her moist, feminine lips just long enough to grasp the edge of her panties and pull them down over her legs. When they fell to her ankles, she lifted one foot and then the other. Deke kicked the panties aside and knelt down. When he parted her feminine folds and lowered his mouth, she gripped his shoulders with white-knuckled strength. His tongue replaced his fingers, delving, teasing, stroking, until Lexie's body tensed. With one final hard stroke, he carried her over the edge and into an earth-shattering climax.

While she shivered and moaned with release, Deke took off his briefs, allowing his sex to spring free, then lifted her up and pressed her buttocks against the wall. With her legs wrapped around his hips and her arms draped over his shoulders, he rammed into her with one powerful lunge. She cried out from the sheer pleasure of having him inside her and hungrily sought his mouth.

Deke kissed her deep and hard, then began moving in and out of her body. Slowly at first. Long, deep thrusts. Possessing her with deliberate ease.

As the tension inside her rebuilt, she moaned and urged him on. He increased the tempo, his lunges accelerating in speed until he was pumping into her, bouncing her butt against the wall.

He came first, shuddering, groaning, holding her so tightly that she could barely breathe. And then her climax hit. Wilder and more forceful than the first. She cried out, trembling with release.

Ragged breaths. Sweat-slick bodies. The musky scent of sex.

Lexie eased her legs down his hips and thighs, and touched her toes to the floor. Deke buried his face against her neck and held her pressed into him as closely as it was possible for two humans to be connected.

Sated, her body languid and content, she whispered, "I love you."

He lifted his head and gazed into her eyes. "You're mine," he murmured softly against her parted lips.

"And you're mine," she told him.

Deke lifted her up into his arms and carried her into the living room, leaving their discarded clothing behind. He deposited her on the sofa.

"I'll be right back," he said. "If we don't get back into our clothes, we're going to get awfully chilly in a little while."

When he returned a few minutes later, he was wearing his slacks and shirt. He tossed his tuxedo jacket on the sofa. After helping her to her feet, he pulled her dress over her head, turned her around and yanked up the zipper. Then he picked up his jacket and draped it around her shoulders. And when he swept her up into his arms and sat down with her on his lap, she simply curled herself around him and laid her head on his shoulder.

They sat there for several minutes, warm in the afterglow of lovemaking, as reality set in.

"I didn't use any protection," he said. "I should have. I'm sorry."

"It's all right," she told him. "I could have asked you to stop."

"How would you feel if it turns out you're pregnant?"

"I can't imagine anything more wonderful than having a child with the man I love."

"God, Lexie, how is it possible that you can love me?"

She caressed his face. "How would *you* feel if I'm pregnant?"

"I'd feel like the luckiest man in the world."

She smiled, then kissed him sweetly, a featherlight brush across his lips.

THE JANGLE of his cell phone lying on the lone end table woke Deke from a sound sleep. Something warm and soft and slightly heavy was pressing him down into the old sofa. When he opened his eyes and saw Lexie lying on top of him, he smiled.

She roused, lifted her head from his chest and said, "I think your phone's ringing."

He rose from the sofa, taking her with him into a sitting position, then stretched out his arm until he managed to reach his cell phone. He picked it up and answered, "Bronson here."

"How's Lexie this morning?" Bain Desmond asked.

Deke glanced at the closed blinds on the windows and noted morning sunlight peeking through the slats. "She's fine. In fact, she was still sleeping until your call woke her. What time is it?"

"Nearly eight o'clock," Desmond said. "I called because I thought you'd want to know that the house and grounds are clean as a whistle. I'm over here having breakfast with Mrs. Eddins, if you and Lexie would care to join me."

"Have you been here all night or…?"

"Yeah, I haven't been home for a shower and shave

yet. My hunger outweighed my need to look good this morning."

Lexie tugged on Deke's arm. "Who are you talking to?"

"Desmond," Deke told her. "He said the house and grounds are clear."

"Is he still here?"

Deke held out his cell phone to her. "Do you want to talk to him?"

She took the phone, put it to her ear, slid off Deke's lap and asked, "Bain, how is Cara this morning?"

A couple of questions later, she ended by saying, "Ask Mrs. Eddins to put on a pot of fresh coffee. We'll be up there in a few minutes." Then Desmond said something to which she replied with a delighted gasp. "You're kidding? How much? Three inches?" After she said goodbye, Lexie returned the phone to Deke. "Bain said it snowed early this morning and it only stopped coming down a couple of hours ago."

"I take it that we're joining him for coffee."

"As much as I'd like for the two of us to cocoon ourselves away from the world, we both know we can't. Not now."

"If I had my way, I'd take you as far away from Chattanooga as possible. I'd do anything to keep you safe."

"I can't leave Chattanooga. This is my home. My friends are here. My job is here."

"And a psycho who plans to kill you is here."

"I know. But—"

He tapped his index finger on her lips. "I'm not arguing with you. I'm not trying to persuade you to leave Chattanooga. I was simply stating the obvious."

She wrapped her arms around his neck and drew him close for a good-morning kiss.

"I need you," she said. "I'm not sure I can make it without you."

"I'm not going anywhere. You couldn't run me off with a stick."

Lexie did need him, at least for now, he admitted. Until the bomber was caught, until she was safe. She thought she loved him. Maybe she did. Hell, maybe he loved her, too. But how could either of them be sure of how they really felt when they were both carrying around so much baggage from the past? A part of him would feel guilty to his dying day for what had happened to her in Gadi. And even if she didn't blame him, would the day come when she would look at him and all she would see was the man whose bullet had crippled her?

He had never wanted a woman the way he wanted Lexie. And making love to her had only made him want her all the more. Once wasn't enough. A hundred times wouldn't be enough. Over the years, she had become an obsession, and now that they were lovers, she was a fever in his blood.

He could debate the wisdom of their being lovers, could berate himself for having taken her without using protection, but what it all boiled down to in the end was one simple fact. They wanted each other, and they both knew that it was only a matter of time before they would make love again.

Ten minutes later, Deke carried Lexie over the snow-covered walkway that led from the cottage to the driveway. Even though she had told him she was perfectly capable of walking, he'd simply lifted her into his arms anyway.

When they arrived at the kitchen door, Lexie reached down and, using the tip of her cane, knocked a couple of times. Deke had expected Desmond to open the door, but instead Mrs. Eddins did.

"Come on in out of the cold," the cook said.

Deke carried Lexie into the kitchen, then stopped abruptly when he saw Desmond on the far side of the room, deep in conversation on his cell phone.

"You can put me down," Lexie said.

Deke set her on her feet. "I'll get us some coffee."

"You don't have to wait on me."

"Go sit down, woman."

Lexie smiled at him, but her smile vanished when Desmond ended his conversation and walked toward them.

"What is it?" Lexie asked. "Is there more bad news?"

"No." He shook his head. "No more bad news. But I do need to speak to Bronson for a couple of minutes. Just a few things from last night we need to go over."

"Go right ahead. Pretend I'm not here."

Desmond spoke to the cook. "Mrs. Eddins, would you get Ms. Murrough some coffee while Mr. Bronson and I step out into the hall for a couple of minutes?"

Before Lexie had a chance to respond, Deke followed Desmond out of the kitchen and into the back hallway.

"What's going on?" Deke asked.

"Just how long has Dundee Security known that there's a terrorist cell plotting an attack on a government site somewhere in or near Chattanooga?"

AFTER A SHOWER and shave, a cup of coffee and a goodbye kiss from Lexie, Deke drove into town with Lieutenant Desmond for a meeting at the Read House with the police chief, Sawyer McNamara and Homeland Security agent Rob Copeland. He had hated lying to Lexie, telling her that he was going to police head-quarters to work with Desmond on a strategy to bring the killer out in the open. She'd had a skeptical look in her eyes, but she hadn't questioned him.

On the drive off the mountain, Deke and Desmond talked briefly, enough so that Desmond understood that whatever Deke knew, if anything, he wasn't at liberty to discuss.

"The chief is fit to be tied," Desmond said. "It seems a friend of a friend of one of these guys made an anony-mous phone call to the station late last night, after the news of the bomb at the Bedell estate was broadcast on every local TV station."

"And why would anyone take an anonymous phone call seriously?" Deke asked. "We both know that—"

"The caller said that a member of the Majeed had been assigned to Chattanooga and was waiting for orders to bomb a federal building."

"And what could this possibly have to do with the threats against Lexie?"

"Our caller said that the agent assigned to Chattanooga had been given permission to pursue a personal vendetta."

"What kind of vendetta?"

"A vendetta against the president of Helping Hands International."

"Son of a bitch," Deke said. "So that's why we're meeting with your chief, my boss and Homeland Secu-rity. You think Lexie's stalker and this terrorist are the same man."

"Apparently Homeland Security thinks so, too," Desmond said. "And I have a gut feeling that Dundee's already knew all about it."

AFTER AN HOUR of in-depth discussion among the interested parties, the Chattanooga police chief, Douglas Cleveland, and Detective Desmond knew everything that Dundee's knew. Desmond now understood why Deke was so adamant that either Robert Lufti, Hamal Gazsi or Jafari Holston was probably Lexie's stalker.

As the meeting came to an end, and after a warning that for the time being everything had to be kept under wraps, Rob Copeland added one last tidbit of information.

"It has come to our attention that former President Babu Tum's son, Esayas Tum, is still alive, that his mother's family arranged to keep the boy's identity hidden, and that they moved him and his mother out of Gadi years ago. We believe this young man is an active member of the Majeed and possibly belongs to the group that is working here in the southeast."

"Are you saying that Babu Tum's son could be the terrorist assigned to bomb a federal site in Chattanooga?" Deke cursed under his breath, then charged toward Rob Copeland. Before he could get his hands on the agent and shake more information out of him, Sawyer McNamara stepped between the two men.

"Let's talk a walk," Sawyer said to Deke. "You need to cool off."

Deke picked up his overcoat on the way out of the room. Sawyer was right. Attacking a federal agent wasn't the best way to help Lexie.

Once they went outside and walked up Broad Street, Sawyer said, "For what it's worth, I'm not sure Copeland knows the identity of Babu Tum's son."

"But if he did, he wouldn't tell us, because if the police

arrest the son of a bitch, then we'll alert the terrorist cell
that Homeland Security is on to them and their plot."

"Copeland isn't being an ass without a damn good
reason. They're on the verge of finding out what the
federal targets are and when the cell plans to attack."

"But in the meantime, one of the Majeed's nut-jobs
is running around killing Lexie Murrough's friends and
planning to kill her at *the chosen time*." Deke's gut
tightened. Realization dawned. "Damn it to hell! He's
planning to kill Lexie on whatever day they've chosen
to hit the federal targets. If Copeland knows—"

"If he knows, he'd tell you only on a need-to-know
basis."

"Well, I need to know."

"If you do something stupid, you'll wind up getting
your ass hauled off to D.C. Is that what you want?"

"No."

"Then keep a close watch on your client, and I swear
to you that as soon as the information you want is available, I'll get it to you."

DEKE AND LEXIE made love late that afternoon, and he used
protection. Later, just as the sun set, they shared dinner
with Cara and Geoff in the atrium, where the twilight
colors of the December sky enveloped them in the dying
rays of sunlight. Bain Desmond phoned to tell them that
the chief had ordered an immediate autopsy on Farris
Richardson and his body would be released for burial on
Tuesday. While Cara stayed with Lexie in the study when
she telephoned Richardson's family, Deke walked out
into the hall with Geoff and filled him in on his morning
meeting with Sawyer and Homeland Security.

"So you figure old Babu Tum's boy is the one after Lexie?"

"Yeah, but what I can't figure out is why he hates her so. She was as much an innocent bystander as Tum's wife and kid were that day."

"The son probably knows that American and British assassins killed his father, but he has no idea who we were. On the other hand, Lexie's name was in every newspaper and broadcast on every TV station after what happened. And the footage her cameraman shot that day was shown for weeks afterward."

"So he focused his hatred on Lexie? That's insane."

"Yes, it is, but our man *is* insane, isn't he? His reasoning is distorted."

Lexie came out of the study, and walked over to Deke and Geoff, effectively putting an end to their conversation. "I'm going up to my room now," she said.

"We'll talk more in the morning," Deke told Geoff, then joined Lexie, cupped her elbow and walked her down the hall. "Did you speak to Richardson's parents?"

"No, but I did talk to his sister. She said that Farris had wanted to be cremated, and that's what she and her parents intend to do. And since her parents are elderly and neither one is in good health, she thinks the sooner the funeral, the better. She'd like to have the service Tuesday afternoon."

"I'm sorry you have to go through this again."

Lexie paused and stared at him. "Are you going to tell me what's going on?"

"I don't know what you mean."

"You and Bain were whispering this morning, then you went off with him to police headquarters and stayed for hours. And just now, you and Geoff acted as if I had interrupted some top-secret meeting."

Deke led her into the elevator. "Can't you just let me handle it?"

"Handle what?"

The elevator opened on the second floor. Deke held the door for her.

"Desmond and I are privy to some information that may, in the long run, help us catch this guy," Deke told her. "But right now, we don't have all the facts, and until we do, I'd rather not go into it with you."

"Why not?"

He grasped her shoulders but stopped himself just short of shaking her. Why did she have to be so damn inquisitive? Why couldn't she just let him deal with all the bad stuff?

"If I promise to tell you everything, once all the facts are available, will you let me take care of you and do all the worrying for now?"

"You promise to tell me everything?"

"I promise." And he wasn't lying. He *would* share all the facts with her—when he actually knew them.

CHAPTER TWENTY-FOUR

THE NEXT few days passed by without incident, but considering the circumstances, the Christmas spirit bypassed the staff at Helping Hands. After consulting with Cara, Lexie had declared a two-week paid holiday for the employees, with regular hours resuming after New Year's. Cara arranged for one of the corporate accountants to handle Helping Hands' financial matters until Lexie could find a replacement for Farris. On Monday, Lexie had met with Toni and Alice to formulate a press release and organize a limited schedule for the remainder of the year. Christmas was one of the organization's busy times, with so many people in need of assistance during the holidays. Luckily, most of the work had been done well before the Black and White Ball, which left only a few loose ends to tie up. But preparations for the new year couldn't be delayed, so it had been decided that Lexie, Toni, Alice and Robert would work half days the rest of the week.

The next day they had all left the office at noon in order to drive to Cleveland, Farris's hometown, to attend his two o'clock funeral. Three funerals in one month were three funerals too many as far as Lexie was concerned. Five good people had died because of a madman's obsession with punishing her for a crime she hadn't committed. Although she blamed herself that so many people had been killed, she knew she was being irrational. Deke had made her realize that there was nothing she could have done to have prevented their deaths.

Deke. She didn't know how she would have gotten through today without him. In a very short period of time, he had become the center of her world. But then again, even though she had actually known him only a little over a month, she had been having a fantasy affair with him for ten years. Since the moment he had lifted her bloody body off the ground in Gadi that day and she had looked into his steel-gray eyes.

As Deke drove her Mercedes through the iron gates at the Bedell estate, Lexie felt a sense of panic, though she didn't know what had prompted it. As if instinctively knowing something was wrong, Deke glanced over at her.

"What is it?" he asked.

"Nothing, really," she told him. "I just had this moment of panic. I wanted to run as far from this place as possible." She paused and allowed her mind to focus on what she really wanted. "I want to go home, to my own place. And I want my life back. The one I had before… Oh, Deke, I don't know how much more of this I can stand. Farris's funeral was so… His parents were pitiful, weren't they?"

Deke pulled the car up in front of the house, killed the motor and, leaving the keys in the ignition, got out, rounded the hood and opened her door. When he held out his hand to her, she clasped it as if it were her lifeline. In a way, that was just what Deke had become: her lifeline.

"I'm not going to take you home," he said. "But what if I take you away from here, and the two of us escape to someplace private and yet safe?"

He helped her up and out of the Mercedes, pulling her against him and gazing down into her hopeful eyes.

"I'd say you're a miracle worker."

"I've been known to pull off the impossible a few times," he said.

"Then work your magic. If I've ever needed a little abracadabra to take me away from the real world, it's today."

"Come on inside and stay put in your room while I have a talk with Aldridge and Mrs. Eddins." Deke led her to the front door and into the house. "Give me an hour." He looked her over from head to toe. "Change out of that black suit. Put on something comfortable, and I'll be back to pick you up in just a little while."

During the next hour, which she spent alone in her suite upstairs, Lexie gladly changed out of the black suit and put on a pair of gray cotton yoga pants and an over-size, long-sleeved, magenta T-shirt. Then she made a few phone calls.

Cara had gone straight from the funeral back to work and probably wouldn't be home until late tonight.

"I'm a week behind on everything," Cara had told her. "I'll have to put in some long hours between now and Christmas if I want to have a prayer of catching up."

Lexie hated interrupting Cara at work, but she had promised she would phone her as soon as she and Deke arrived back at the mansion safe and sound. She kept the conversation brief, then immediately called Alice, who had attended the funeral alone and, when asked about Robert, had gotten misty-eyed.

"Hey, can you talk for a few minutes?" Lexie asked when Alice answered the phone on the fifth ring.

"I can always make time to talk to you."

"I don't mean to pry, but I'm concerned about both you and Robert. Why didn't he come to Farris's funeral this afternoon?"

Silence.

"Alice?"

"He told me that he just couldn't go to another funeral, that he had spent his life going to funerals, watching his family and neighbors in Gadi die. He said he was sick of death."

"Oh, poor Robert."

"He's going back to Gadi after the first of the year."

"What?"

Alice gulped, swallowing her tears. "We ended things last night. Our love affair is officially over."

"Oh, Alice, no. Why?"

"He said it was best this way. A clean break before my daughters arrive home for the holidays." Alice whimpered. "I never told the girls about Robert."

"Is there anything I can do, talk to Robert or—"

"No! Please, don't say anything to him. And I'm afraid there's nothing you can do for me."

After her disheartening talk with Alice, Lexie tried to call Vega, but there was no answer at her apartment, and Vega didn't own a cell phone. She figured that Vega had gone to the hospital to have dinner with Hamal, who had been unable to change shifts today and therefore hadn't been at the funeral.

Exactly fifty-five minutes after Deke had promised to provide Lexie with a safe getaway, he knocked on her bedroom door. When she opened the door to him, the first thing she noticed was his smile. A closed-mouth, self-satisfied smile. The second thing she noticed was that he, too, had changed clothes. He had changed into jeans and a faded navy-blue sweatshirt, partially covered by his overcoat.

"Are you ready?"

"Am I dressed appropriately?" she asked.

"Perfectly. Except you'll need a jacket."

"Give me a minute."

He waited in the doorway while she retrieved her purple all-weather coat, then helped her into it. She took his hand and followed where he led. Down the hall, into the elevator, through the kitchen and out the back door.

Within a few minutes, she realized they were heading toward the servants' cottage at the back of the estate. "Just what have you done?" she asked.

"You'll have to wait and see."

When they reached the cottage, Deke maneuvered her in front of him, eased open the door just a fraction, then reached up and covered her eyes with his hands.

"No peeking until we're inside," he told her.

He walked her into the living room, then removed his hands and waited for her reaction. *Startled* was the only way to describe what she felt, and then delight and happiness. And appreciation.

Deke eased her coat off her shoulders, then removed his own and tossed them both onto a ladder-back chair sitting against the back wall.

"You did all this for me," she said as her gaze traveled over a room she barely recognized. Flames sparkled and crackled brightly in the fireplace. Candles flickered softly across the mantel and on the white-cloth-covered table in front of the fireplace. A pair of large wingback chairs flanked the small square dining table. And where the seen-better-days sofa had once sat, an old iron bedstead decked out in white linens and huge down pillows now dominated the small space.

"I know it's not your apartment, and bringing you here isn't as good as taking you home, but I hope it meets with your approval."

She turned to him, tears in her eyes, and smiled. "Our own safe little getaway."

"Ah, honey, don't cry." He reached out and swiped the tears from her cheeks.

"They're tears of joy and gratitude," she said.

He grasped her shoulders. "Come on over here and sit down. Mrs. Eddins pulled together a quick spaghetti supper." He led her to the table, pulled out her chair and seated her. Then he picked up a bottle and showed it to her. "She even commandeered a bottle of wine from the Bedell wine cellar."

Lexie watched while Deke walked over to the double windows that overlooked a small herb garden, still used by Mrs. Eddins. He drew back the old curtains to expose the lovely view. In the distance, the sun hung low in the western sky, its final rays dappling through the branches of a huge oak tree near the brick wall at the back of the estate. Before returning to the table, he bent over and fiddled with something on the floor on the far side of the bed. Suddenly soft, sweet music filled the room. Lexie gasped. It appeared that Deke had thought of everything needed to create a perfect romantic hideaway. And he'd done it all for her.

When he sat across from her and poured wine into their crystal flutes, Lexie sighed heavily.

"What's wrong?" He studied her, his gaze narrowing as he tried to gauge her mood.

She reached across the table and took his hand in hers. "Nothing's wrong. Everything is perfect."

"But?"

"I'm sitting here with the man I love, surrounded by romantic perfection, and I'm happy. I don't have a right to be happy. Farris is dead." Deke squeezed her hand. "His funeral was only a few hours ago, and here I am, with you, feeling gloriously alive and… It's not right."

Deke caressed her trembling hand. "That's how you *should* feel, gloriously alive. If the death of someone we care about serves any purpose, it's to make us appreciate our own lives. There's nothing wrong with being glad you're alive."

She withdrew her hand from Deke's, placed it in her lap with her other hand and bowed her head. "You were right. Farris had a crush on me."

"Who could blame him?" Deke asked.

Lexie lifted her gaze to meet his. "I tried to kind to him."

"You were very kind."

"I wish he'd had a happier life."

"Maybe next time around, he will."

Lexie stared at Deke. "Are you talking about reincarnation?"

"Yeah. Who knows, huh?"

"It's a nice thought."

Deke lifted his glass. "Here's to living life to the fullest, whether we get one time around or a dozen."

Lexie lifted her glass, clinked it against Deke's, and then they each took a sip of the bold, red wine.

During the next hour, Lexie allowed herself the escape that Deke had lovingly provided, putting thoughts of death aside in order to celebrate life. They ate a delicious meal, drank half the bottle of wine, and then

Deke lifted her up and into his arms and danced in place, just barely moving to the whispery soft and romantic tunes on the jazz CD he'd brought. They kissed and caressed, but nothing more. Just a tender sharing.

Deke walked her over to the double windows and eased her down onto the window seat, then refilled their glasses. After giving Lexie hers, he situated himself behind her and with his free hand, he pulled her back against him and wrapped his arm around her waist. They sat there, sipping the wine, the back of Lexie's head resting on his chest and watched as twilight changed to night and dark clouds obscured the stars. Only a distant lone security light cast any illumination over the herb garden.

They didn't talk. Words were unnecessary.

Lexie allowed her mind to drift, to recall happy moments in her life. Her childhood with two loving parents. Her first prom. Being crowned Homecoming Queen at the University of Georgia. Being hired as reporter for UBC. Wes Harris asking her to marry him. Damn, why had she thought of Wes? Because in the beginning of their relationship, he had made her happy.

Her thoughts invariably turned to the moments that had changed her life forever. Even now, after ten years, she could almost feel the bullet as it entered her back.

As if sensing that Lexie needed comforting, Deke set his almost-empty wineglass on the floor and circled her comfortingly with his strong arms. She closed her eyes and absorbed his strength.

In her mind's eye, she saw a pair of smoky-gray eyes. His eyes. Her rescuer. The phantom lover from her dreams. But he was not a dream, not a phantom lover.

He was Deke Bronson, and he was here, in the flesh, holding her in his arms, offering her whatever her heart desired.

And her heart desired Deke.

TONI STEPPED out of the shower, dried off and slipped into her satin pajamas. She didn't own any cotton underwear or sleepwear. Her preference in intimate apparel was for dainty, feminine and sexy things, garments made of silk, satin or lace. If Jafari were spending the night, she would have chosen one of her sheer teddies, probably the red one, which was his favorite. He had wanted to stay with her, and she'd wanted him to stay, but a little abstinence was good for both of them. He needed to learn that when he upset her, she wasn't going to hop in the sack with him whenever his dick twitched. Of course, the opposite also applied. He knew that she would reward him for good behavior. She just didn't want him to become too sure of himself. He needed reminding on a regular basis that she held the keys to the kingdom.

Besides, he'd been acting odd all day, ever since they'd left Farris Richardson's funeral. It was almost as if he'd wanted to pick a fight with her for some reason. He had disagreed with almost everything she'd said, then quickly apologized, only to do it all over again. They had managed to make it through dinner here at her apartment—a meal she had lovingly prepared for them—before she'd blown her stack and told him to leave.

"I will come back later," he'd said.

"Don't bother."

"Then I will call you to say good-night."

"All right. You can call me." When he leaned down to kiss her, she turned so that his lips brushed her cheek.

As much as she loved Jafari, she was beginning to have second thoughts about marrying him. Not that they were officially engaged. What if their marriage turned out to be one fight-and-then-make-up event after another, as apparently their dating routine had become? Toni wasn't sure she wanted to spend the rest of her life that way. Passionate relationships had their pluses, especially in the sack, but when two people argued most of the time, wasn't their relationship doomed?

The moment Toni opened the bathroom door and walked into her bedroom, she smelled smoke. Crap! Had she left the oven on? If so, why hadn't her smoke alarm gone off? Groaning, she remembered that she hadn't changed the batteries in the alarm in well over a year.

The closer she moved toward the door leading into her living room, the stronger the smell, and when she opened the door, she saw a haze of gray smoke floating over the entire room.

What the hell?

Then she heard yelling and screaming and someone banging on her apartment door. A neighbor? A fireman?

Dear God, was her building on fire?

"Toni, open the door," Jafari hollered.

When she ran through the haze of smoke, she began coughing as the lethal gray vapor entered her lungs. By the time she grasped the warm doorknob, she could barely breathe. Jafari was still banging repeatedly on the door.

When Toni opened the door, she threw herself into Jafari's arms, but her relief at being rescued was short-lived. A wall of flames was dancing up the hallway, straight toward them.

CHAPTER TWENTY-FIVE

LEXIE STRADDLED Deke's lean hips and brought herself down over him, taking his sex into her body slowly, maddeningly, playing the temptress. When she withdrew and dangled her lush breasts over his face, he grasped her hips, bucked up and impaled her. Crying out with pleasure, she sank onto him, taking him fully inside her. He licked first one tight nipple and then the other before sucking greedily. She set the tempo. Slow and easy, up and down, riding him in a steady rhythm. While his mouth worked one breast and his right hand caressed the other, he slid his left hand over her hip and stroked her naked butt.

She increased the pace, riding him harder, creating more friction. He didn't know how much longer he could wait, but he would try his damnedest, because he wanted her to come first. As she took him in a heated frenzy, he fought the urge to let go, the feel of her hot, wet sweetness milking his sex almost more than he could endure.

And then suddenly her intimate muscles tensed, tightening around him, and a gush of moisture engulfed his penis. Taking charge of her orgasm, Lexie pounded herself against his rigid sex until she squeezed every ounce of satisfaction from the act. As she cried out, quivering and gasping, Deke clutched her hips, flipped her over and hammered into her. Seconds later, he came so hard that he felt as if the top of his head had blown off.

He slid his sex-damp body off her and onto the bed. She snuggled up to him and draped her arm across his naked belly. He was drunk on orgasm happiness, his body relaxed and ready for sleep. But the woman lying in his arms needed more, deserved more. He glided his hand over her naked hip and loved the way she quivered at his touch, her body overly sensitive as a result of her nerve-stimulating climax.

"Thank you," Lexie murmured, her lips against his chest.

He cupped the back of her head and urged her to look at him. She lifted herself up, propped her elbow on her pillow and stared down at him.

"Thank you," he repeated her words.

She smiled. "I dreamed about our making love."

"Did you?"

"Uh-huh. Well, it was sort of us making love. It was my gray-eyed rescuer making love to me."

"I wish—"

She captured his lips in a hush-don't-talk kiss.

He rolled over, half on top of her, and deepened the kiss. She draped her arms around his neck, and when he lifted his head, she sighed contentedly.

Suddenly his cell phone rang.

"Damn!" He pulled out of her embrace, then got out of bed and walked over to where his phone lay on the table, next to the remnants of their meal. Instantly recognizing Geoff's cell number on the caller ID, Deke answered, "Yeah, what's up?"

"We just got a call from Erlanger hospital," Geoff said. "The caller asked for Lexie, so Cara took the call herself."

"What's happened?"

"There was a fire at Toni Wells's apartment."

"Is Toni all right?"

Lexie slid across the bed and sat on the edge, instantly alert. "Who are you talking to? What happened to Toni?"

"All we know is that she suffered some pretty bad smoke inhalation," Geoff said.

"Damn!"

"There's more."

"What do you mean?"

"Alice Kennedy's house burned down."

Deke swallowed. "The son of a bitch set both fires."

"Yeah, that would be my guess," Geoff said.

"How's Alice?"

"Don't know. The paramedics brought her in to Erlanger, but the hospital rep Cara spoke to didn't have any word on her condition."

"Damn it, Deke, tell me what's happened!" Lexie cried out.

"We'll meet y'all up at the house in a few minutes," Deke said, then hung up the phone and turned to Lexie. God, he hated telling her that two more of her friends had been targeted by the Gadian madman.

ON THE DRIVE downtown, Deke stayed on the phone most of the way, contacting Ty Garrett and Bain Desmond, who was also on his way to the hospital. While Deke spoke to Bain, Geoff contacted the hospital, so by the time Eddie pulled the limousine up to the entrance, they knew that Toni was in the ER, and Jafari, who had also suffered smoke inhalation, was with her. And Alice was being treated for third-degree burns and severe smoke inhalation, but at least she was alive.

When they entered the ER—an all too familiar scene—the first person Lexie saw was Bain. He made his way to them, meeting them in the middle of the waiting area.

"Toni and Jafari are being released tonight," Bain said. "Luckily, they made it out of the building, but there were a couple of people who didn't."

"What about Alice?" Lexie asked. "How bad—"

"I don't know. All they'll tell me is that she's unconscious and received some third-degree burns. I do know that if it hadn't been for a couple of firefighters who dragged her out, she'd be dead."

"What about Robert? Did they rescue him, too?"

"Robert wasn't there," Bain said.

"Oh, yes. I'd forgotten," Lexie said, recalling her recent telephone conversation with Alice. "They're not together anymore."

Bain shook his head. "The firemen reported that they didn't find anyone else in the house, so I telephoned Lufti at his apartment after I got here about ten minutes ago to tell him what had happened. He seemed pretty shook up. He's on his way here now."

"I want to see Toni," Lexie said. "And then I want to talk to Alice's doctor." Her gaze locked with Bain's. "Do whatever you have to do to make it happen. Please."

Deke clamped his hand over her shoulder. She glanced up at him, and saw her fear and concern reflected in his eyes.

Five minutes later, Lexie and Deke were allowed

into the ER cubicle where Toni sat on an examining table, Jafari at her side, holding her hand. They were both covered in soot from head to toe, and fragments of what looked like ash clung to Toni's curly black hair.

"Oh, Lex!" Toni held open her arms.

Lexie hugged her friend, then cupped her face and looked her over. "Are you really all right?"

"They say I'll be fine." She gazed up adoringly at her boyfriend. "Thanks to Jafari. He saved my life."

Lexie looked at Jafari through a mist of grateful tears. "Thank you. And thank God you're both all right."

Toni grasped Lexie's hand. "Bain told Jafari about Alice's house burning down tonight, too. Have you seen her? Is she going to be all right?"

"I haven't seen her," Lexie said. "I've asked to speak to her doctor as soon as possible. The minute I find out anything, I'll let you know."

A nurse came into the room and shooed Lexie and Bain out, but before she turned her attention to Toni, she told them, "Dr. Harrelson is having Mrs. Kennedy moved upstairs to ICU. You can probably catch him right now, if you still want to speak to him."

"Go find him," Lexie told Bain. "I'll follow you."

Bain didn't have to go far. Dr. Harrelson had just stepped out of the room across the hall. While Bain delayed him, Lexie made her way over to him as quickly as possible.

"Ms. Murrough?" Dr. Harrelson nodded.

"How's Alice?"

"I have her sedated, and we'll be moving her up to ICU shortly. She's suffering from severe smoke inhalation and third-degree burns on her back."

"Is she going to—"

"Mrs. Kennedy's burns are confined to one area of her back. The paramedics informed us that a large piece of heavy debris had trapped her on the floor of her living room. I can't guarantee anything, but her prognosis is good. Barring complications, she should recover." The doctor turned to go. "If you'll excuse me…?"

"Yes, yes, thank you."

Bain draped his arm comfortingly around Lexie's shoulders.

ROBERT LUFTI swept into the ER waiting room like a manic whirlwind, his eyes wild, his hands trembling. "Where is Alice?" he yelled. "I must see Alice."

Deke caught Robert before he barged into the private area where patients were being attended to by the ER staff. Robert spun around and glared at Deke.

"Calm down," Deke told him. "Keep acting like a lunatic and they'll kick you out of here. You don't want that, do you?"

Robert shook his head. Tears pooled in his sable-brown eyes. "Please, let me see her."

Deke squeezed Robert's shoulder. "As soon as the doctor says it's all right. But for now, you're just going to have to wait with the rest of us."

"I should have been there with her tonight," Robert said. "If I had been with her, I could have—" He pulled away from Deke and closed his eyes.

Lexie and Desmond returned to the waiting area, and when Lexie saw Robert, she went directly to him. Bain came over and spoke to Deke. "When did he get here?"

"Just now. He came roaring in like a wounded lion."

"Is his concern for Alice real, or is it all an act?"

"Don't know."

"Well, he now heads my list of suspects," Desmond said. "Hamal Gazsi was on duty here at the hospital when both fires started. And Jafari was with Toni. According to her, he saved her life. So that leaves Robert Lufti."

"Can you take him in and question him?" Deke asked.

"Nope. Not enough reason to, and we have absolutely no evidence against him." Desmond lowered his voice so that only Deke could hear him. "Sure would help us if Homeland Security would be a little more forthcoming with their information."

ON WEDNESDAY morning, Deke brought Lexie back to the hospital. When she had phoned earlier, she'd been told by a nurse that Alice was awake, and although being kept sedated for pain, she was responding to the staff.

"Dr. Harrelson wanted me to inform you that, as of this morning, Mrs. Kennedy's condition has been changed from critical to serious. And she will be allowed visitors during regular visiting hours, but only immediate family and close friends."

When they arrived in the waiting room, Lexie immediately recognized the blond twins sitting side by side. Amy's eyes widened when she saw Lexie. She punched her twin, Holly, who looked up and smiled. Simultaneously, the two girls got to the feet and rushed over to Lexie.

"Have you seen your mother?" Lexie asked.

"Just a few minutes ago," Amy said. "Oh, Lexie, she looks just awful."

"They have her lying facedown." Holly whimpered.

"And they have these tubes and wires connected to her, and she can't talk and… I can't understand why she didn't hear the fire alarm. If she had, she could have gotten out sooner."

"She probably took one of her sleeping pills," Holly said. "If she did, then a train could have roared through her bedroom without waking her."

"I'd like to go in and see her, just for a few minutes," Lexie said. "Unless y'all plan to go back—"

"No, we're going to Aunt Peg's to stay while we're here for the holidays. She's Dad's sister. She lives in Tiftonia. We came straight to the hospital as soon as we flew in this morning. We'll come back this afternoon and again tonight to see Mom," Amy said.

"You might need to wait until Mr. Lufti comes out." Holly nodded toward the ICU. "He just went back in. Of course, they did allow two of us to go in together, so they might not mind if you both see Mom at the same time."

"So Robert came back this morning?" Lexie asked.

"Actually, I got the impression Mr. Lufti had been here all night." Amy studied Lexie's reaction. "He said that he and Mom are good friends, but… Is it more than that? I mean, he seems really concerned about her."

"They *are* really good friends," Lexie said. It wasn't her place to explain to Alice's daughters that Alice and Robert had been lovers for months now. She gave both girls a hug and told them, "I think I'll go on back."

She turned to Deke, who was waiting patiently, and said, "I won't be long."

He nodded.

Lexie asked one of the ICU nurses which cubicle Mrs. Kennedy was in, and the nurse walked her to the correct unit. She hesitated when she looked in and saw

Robert kneeling by the hospital bed, his dark hands gripping the pristine white sheet on which Alice rested.

She took a step forward, then stopped again when she heard Robert talking in a soft, low voice. Apparently he was so lost in his one-sided conversation with Alice that he hadn't heard Lexie approach.

"You cannot die, Alice. You must live. Please live. For me. For your daughters. They are here, you know. And they are almost as beautiful as their mother."

Lexie felt like a voyeur, intruding this way on something so deeply personal. But she couldn't move, couldn't bring herself to turn and walk away.

"I love you, more than life itself. I cannot bear the thought of returning to Gadi without you. If only I could ask you to go with me. I should have asked you. I should have told you that I love you and want you to be my wife. But I was afraid you would reject me, that you would never give up your life here in America just to be with me. And I must return to Gadi. I am needed there."

Lexie swallowed a lump of emotion lodged in her throat, then stepped backward and out of the ICU unit, and all but ran back to the waiting room, her cane tapping loudly as she made her escape. She hurried straight into Deke's arms.

"What's wrong, honey? Are you all right?"

"Robert… He loves Alice. He wants to marry her. He's in there, on his knees by her bedside, and she can't respond to him. Oh, Deke…Deke…"

Deke stroked her back tenderly. "It's going to be all right, Lexie. Alice will recover, and if it's meant for Robert and her to be together, they will be."

CHAPTER TWENTY-SIX

DESPITE Deke's disapproval, Lexie went in to the office on Friday morning, knowing that not only did she need a distraction, but that she now had to find a temporary replacement for Alice. Either of Alice's young assistants could take over for a few weeks, but it would probably be months before Alice could even think about returning to work, so that meant hiring a professional PR person. And after the first of the year, she would have to hire an accountant. On top of that, with luck, Malik's younger siblings could come to American and work part-time at Helping Hands while both attended school here.

While Lexie settled in behind her desk, Deke took a seat across the room. She glanced up and smiled at him. "I promise we'll leave here at noon, and I won't return to work until after Christmas."

"I'm holding you to that promise."

Lexie considered her words carefully before she spoke. "I've been giving an idea some thought, and if you don't have any objections, I'd like to ask Cara to let us use the servants' cottage for as long as I have to stay at the estate."

Deke grinned. "Why would I object? I like the idea."

Before Lexie could respond, her office door flew

open and Toni breezed in, two large foam cups in her hands. "Morning, all."

Lexie's mouth flew open. "What are you doing here?"

"I'm still your assistant, aren't I? So if you're working, I'm working." Toni handed Deke one of the cups, then set the other on Lexie's desk. "Make sure I got those right. Fat-free mocha, no whipped cream for you." She glanced from Lexie to Deke. "Straight black coffee for you."

"Thanks," Deke said as he peeled back the flap on the lid.

"You didn't have to come in to work, and you certainly didn't have to bring us coffee," Lexie told her, "but I appreciate the help. I have about a dozen phone calls to make before I can get started on anything else. If you can take half those calls—"

"Just give me the list and I'll get right on it, just as soon as I tell Jafari you're going to let me stay and help."

"Where is Jafari?" Deke asked.

"Downstairs waiting," Toni replied. "He drove me here this morning. I'm staying at his place until I can find another apartment."

When Toni sailed out of the office, Lexie sipped her coffee and said, "Toni looks well, doesn't she?"

Deke nodded. "She looks great." He took several sips of his own coffee, then settled into the visitor's chair, crossing his legs.

Lexie continued drinking her coffee as she made the first two phone calls. She glanced over at Deke, catching him staring at her, and they exchanged smiles. Lovers' smiles that said "I know every inch of your body."

Lexie yawned. Her eyelids felt heavy. She hadn't been getting much sleep lately. "It sure is taking Toni a long time to say goodbye to Jafari."

"Lexie." Deke spoke her name, concern in his voice.

"Huh?" She glanced at him just as he started to stand, then quickly dropped back into the chair. "Deke, what's wrong? Are you sick?"

BAIN DESMOND called Geoff Monday on his way from police headquarters to the Helping Hands offices.

"Captain Cleveland just got a call from Rob Copeland," Bain said. "Today's the day. Homeland Security has agents on their way to Chattanooga and Spring City, here in Tennessee, and to Guntersville and Decatur in Alabama. The terrorists are planning to hit TVA dams in all four cities."

"Bloody hell! That means Lexie's stalker will go after her today."

"Yeah. I'm on my way over to Helping Hands now. I've been calling, but no one answers. I've also been trying Bronson's cell phone without any luck."

"I don't like the sound of that. I'll speak to Cara and turn her over to Bedell security, then I'll meet you at Helping Hands."

DISPOSING OF THE GUARD at the desk had been easy. He had simply walked up to him, smiling all the while, pulled out his semiautomatic and shot him in the head. He had just dragged the guard's body under the desk when the elevator opened and Toni emerged. Jafari quickly slipped his gun into his coat pocket.

"Hey, what are you doing? Where's the security guard?"

"He went to the restroom," Jafari lied. "He said he wasn't feeling well."

"Oh, I hope he doesn't have that stomach bug that's going around."

Jafari came out from behind the desk and walked slowly toward Toni. He had become fond of her during the past few months, and he would rather not harm her. When he had set fire first to Alice Kennedy's house and then to Toni's apartment building, he had considered the possibility of allowing Toni to die, but he had changed his mind and rushed in to save her at the last minute. Perhaps he owed her that much—her life.

"Lexie's going to let me stay and help her this morning, so you can pick me up around noon." Toni stood on tiptoe and kissed him.

While she was kissing him, Jafari though about how easy it would be to strangle her. When she ended the kiss and pulled away from him, he waved goodbye to her as she headed for the elevator. With Toni's back to him, Jafari pulled his gun from his pocket, held it by the muzzle and crept up behind her. Before she had a chance to react, he hit her over the head as hard as he could. He caught her unconscious body as she fell, dragged her across the lobby and placed her prone body next to the guard's under the desk.

Then he stepped into the elevator.

What if Deke Bronson had not drunk all of his doctored coffee? Jafari had been the one to suggest what a thoughtful thing it would be for Toni to take Lexie and her bodyguard fresh coffee this morning. He had even offered to go into the coffee shop and get it for her. Before returning to the car with the two cups, he had put a strong sedative in the black coffee and a mild sedative in the mocha latte. He didn't want Lexie Murrough unconscious, merely subdued.

Jafari approached Lexie's open office door cautiously. He stopped and listened. Silence. He walked in and saw her hovering over Deke Bronson, who was slumped in a chair in a seemingly comatose state.

"Ms. Murrough?" Jafari called to her as he entered her office.

She glanced up and looked at him, her eyes slightly glazed. "Help…me…"

Jafari hurried to her, lifted her to her feet and caught her about the waist when she staggered. "Are you all right?"

"Deke…help…Deke."

"Mr. Bronson will be all right," Jafari said. "He's just sleeping. If he drank all of his coffee, he will sleep for several hours. If he drank only part of it, he will probably wake in an hour or two."

"What…you…talking about…?"

"Are you feeling groggy?" Jafari asked. "If you are, it's just the result of the very mild sedative I put in your latte. You'll be feeling more alert soon, probably by the time we get to my boat."

"Boat?" She looked at him, blinking her eyes repeatedly.

"Come on, Ms. Murrough. We need to get you into your coat. We do not want you getting cold on our little boat ride, do we?"

"Toni?"

"Toni's staying here. She's downstairs with the guard. I'm sure Mr. Bronson will find them when he wakes up."

GEOFF MONDAY found Deke just as he was coming out of a deep fog, his brain addled and his head aching as if he'd been poleaxed.

"What the hell?" Geoff rushed over to Deke and helped him to his feet. "Are you okay?"

"Drugged," Deke said. "Coffee." He glanced down to where he'd set his cup on the floor.

"How much did you drink?"

"Enough. How long have I been out?" Deke rubbed his forehead, then tried to look at his watch. His vision blurred. "Where's Lexie?" He jerked his head up and searched the room for her.

"She's not here," Geoff said.

"What about Toni?"

"Lieutenant Desmond is downstairs with her," Geoff said. "When we arrived, the lobby was empty. No sign of the guard. We knew immediately that something was wrong."

"We've got to find Lexie." Deke staggered toward the door.

Geoff grabbed his arm to steady him. "We will. I promise."

"How is Toni? And the guard?"

"We found the guard under the desk. He'd been shot right between the eyes at close range. And Toni had been knocked unconscious and dumped there with him. Desmond's calling for backup and an ambulance. He's staying with Toni until the paramedics arrive."

Deke jerked away from Geoff and staggered to the door. "Gotta find Lexie."

"Go right ahead—if you have any idea where to start looking."

"He has her, doesn't he? Damn him! How the hell

did he manage to drug our coffee?" Deke spread his arms wide and grasped the door frame.

"Did Toni bring the coffee with her when she came in to work today?" Geoff asked.

"Yeah, why?" Deke lifted his head and glanced over his shoulder at Geoff.

"Chief Cleveland has the Chattanooga PD on alert. They're expecting a terrorist attack on the Chickamauga Dam sometime today. Rob Copeland's been in touch. Homeland Security is on their way here, and to three other areas with TVA dams that have been targeted."

"You get that dickhead on the phone and tell him we need to know who Babu Tum's son is, and if he's the terrorist assigned to Chattanooga."

"Sawyer was on the phone with him just as we pulled up out front." Geoff's eyes flared with anger. "Esayas Tum goes by his adopted father's name—Holston."

"Jafari!"

"Yeah, Toni's loverboy, Jafari, is Babu Tum's son."

"And he's taken Lexie with him to the dam. Good God, what if… The Majeed is known for its suicide bombers!"

JAFARI HAD BEEN RIGHT, Lexie thought. By the time they reached his boat, most of the sedative he'd put in her latte had begun wearing off. As he marched her straight to the shiny new speedboat, he kept the gun in his coat pocket pressed firmly against her ribs.

"If you do not cooperate fully, I will not only shoot you but anyone who tries to help you," Jafari told her, glancing around at the other people nearby. "You do not wish to cause another innocent person's death, do you?"

No, she did not.

When they boarded the boat, he forced her to sit in the cockpit at his side, in the double seat at the helm. He started the engine and guided the boat out into the Tennessee River. Once they were far enough from shore and the other craft in the area, Jafari tied her hands behind her and attached the rope to the seat.

"Where are you taking me?" she asked.

"You are going with me on an important journey that I take in the name of Allah. You will join me on my holy mission."

"What are you talking about, Jafari? What journey? Why—"

He reached down and slapped her. "Silence!"

Startled by his brutal attack, she stared up at him, seeing the real man for the first time.

He glowered at her. "My name is not Jafari Holston. I am Esayas Tum, the son of President Babu Tum."

Lexie gazed at him in disbelief.

"You will die today for the part you played in my father's assassination."

"But I—" When he lifted his hand to strike her again, she quieted instantly.

He withdrew his hand and turned his attention back to steering the boat north up the river.

Where was he taking her? What great mission for Allah was he going on?

Did it really matter? All she needed to know was that he intended to kill her. Today.

Had he already killed Toni? Was that why she had disappeared? And what about Deke? Had Jafari—no, Esayas Tum—only drugged him, or had he poisoned him?

Oh, God, please let Deke be all right. And Toni…I couldn't bear it if anything happened to them.

Rob Copeland and two other Homeland Security agents met Bain, Geoff and Deke at the River Park, where a bystander had reported seeing a woman who looked as if she were being forced aboard a speedboat. The CPD provided a cruiser, but civilians were prohibited from using it. Since Bain had forewarned Deke that he and Geoff wouldn't be allowed aboard, Deke had contacted Cara, who had immediately arranged for a power boat to meet them at the park.

"We believe Holston is headed directly to the Chickamauga Dam," Rob Copeland said. "Our information is that the terrorists intend to run speedboats into the powerhouses at the four dams, making a statement, letting us know that we aren't safe from them, that they can strike us whenever and wherever they want."

"You're talking about a suicide attack, aren't you?" Deke asked.

Copeland nodded. "Yes, I'm afraid that's exactly what I'm talking about." He looked right at Deke. "We've had word that two of the four terrorists have been stopped. One was killed in Decatur, Alabama, and the one at Watts Barr Dam in Spring City, Tennessee, has been captured."

While Copeland and Police Chief Douglas Cleveland boarded the police department's cruiser, Deke and Geoff boarded the sleek Sea Ray that Cara had provided. Without asking for instructions or being granted permission to pursue Jafari Holston, Geoff started the high-speed vessel's engine, and within seconds he and Deke were underway.

"I'll check and see if Cara had the proper provisions loaded onto the boat," Deke said, then went below to look for the semiautomatic rifle he had requested.

LEXIE PRAYED. She prayed for Toni and Deke and Alice, and all the people she loved. And she prayed for her own life.

Jafari/Esayas paid little attention to her, almost as if he had forgotten her presence. If she could manage to loosen the rope that bound her hands, maybe she could jump overboard. Or if she thought she had a chance of overpowering him...

Working tirelessly, trying to escape the ropes binding her wrists, she glanced left and right, then over her shoulder. She saw a boat behind them, and another one farther back down the river. If she could free herself and jump overboard, someone on the closest boat might see her. She would risk anything for the chance to get away from Jafari and save herself from whatever fate he had planned for them.

Lexie struggled with the ropes until her wrists were raw and probably bleeding. She knew one thing for sure, they burned like hell. But she had no intention of giving up. The boat directly behind them was fast approaching their left side. Was that port or starboard? As if it made any difference!

As Lexie scanned the river in every direction, she suddenly realized that they were traveling straight toward the Chickamauga Dam. Did Jafari intend to take them through the locks and go on up river?

Or was the dam itself their destination?

Oh, God, was it possible that this holy mission was in some way connected to the dam? She searched the deck for any sign of a machine gun or explosives and saw neither.

If only she could somehow signal the boat that was closing in on them and would in a few minutes probably pass them. She had a silk scarf in her coat pocket. If she could find a way to get it out and then… Then what? Even if the people in the other boat saw a purple silk scarf flying off the boat she was in, they would hardly take that as an SOS signal.

Suddenly, totally without warning, Jafari turned, leaned over and got down in her face. "Say your final prayers, infidel. Pray to your god. Today you will be sacrificed as atonement for my father's murder, and I will offer my life for Allah and the Majeed."

"What are you going to do?" She had to demand answers, even if it meant another brutal slap.

He smiled, showing his pearly white teeth. "We are approaching the dam from the south and will soon near the powerhouse on the east side. My boat is loaded with explosives. When I ram my boat into the powerhouse, it will be destroyed and the dam will be damaged, inter- rupting power and sending a message to America."

"And we'll be dead," Lexie said.

Jafari or Esayas or whatever he wanted to call him- self was insane, she realized. He was taking her along on his suicide mission!

"GET US A LITTLE NEARER," Deke instructed Geoff, who remained at the helm, guiding the Sea Ray closer and closer to the speedboat ahead of them. Deke peered through the binoculars hanging around his neck, then lifted the rifle, trying to get Jafari in his sights. "I'll be able to get a clean shot if you can come up alongside them. He's too damn close to Lexie for me to shoot from here."

Geoff didn't reply. He was concentrating fully on the task at hand, not once glancing back at the CPD cruiser fast approaching from behind. Homeland Security wanted Jafari alive. Deke had other plans.

LEXIE MANAGED to free one burning, aching wrist. But she kept her hand down, hidden behind her, in case Jafari glanced her way. Working as quickly as possible, she tugged on the rope around her other wrist, but the harder she tried to loosen it, the tighter it held.

She and Jafari noticed the other boat at almost the exact same moment, just as it came up alongside. Narrowing his gaze and squinting, Jafari glowered at the other vessel. Lexie noticed that sunlight was reflecting off something metallic in the hands of one of the other boat's occupants. Apparently Jafari noticed it, too, because he aimed his pistol and fired at the man. What the hell did he think he was doing?

Another shot rang out, but not from Jafari's pistol. It came from the other boat. A lone shot. Suddenly Jafari went stiff. Lexie gasped when she looked at him and saw the trickle of blood coming from his forehead as he slumped over and onto her lap, then slid down onto the deck. She screamed.

She thought she heard someone calling her name, but the rumble of the boat's engines and the roar of the frigid December wind deafened her to everything else.

Jafari lay dead at her feet. But one of her wrists was still tied to the seat, the boat was still racing straight ahead toward the dam, and there were still explosives on board.

GEOFF BROUGHT the Sea Ray as close to the speedboat as he could without ramming her, and Deke prepared to jump onto the deck of the other boat. He almost made it. Almost. He caught hold of the side and held on for dear life. As the waves hit him like giant watery fists, he struggled to climb aboard the speeding vessel.

Finally he hauled himself up, over and onto the deck, landing flat on his belly and knocking the air out of his lungs.

"Deke!" Lexie screamed, her voice blending with the engine's roar and the wind's merciless cry.

He forced himself up and onto his feet, and rushed to the cockpit.

"Are you all right?" he yelled.

"I am now," she told him. "You have to stop the boat. It's loaded with explosives. Jafari was going to ram it into the powerhouse at the dam."

Deke leaned down, untied her bloody wrist, jerked her up into his arms and, holding her close to his side, took over the helm and gradually slowed the boat, finally bringing it to a full stop less than a hundred feet from the towering wall of the south side of Chickamauga Dam.

LEXIE CLUNG to Deke, refusing to let him go, even after Bain, the Chattanooga PD chief and the Homeland Security agents arrived on the scene. Deke knew that he was going to have some major questions to answer, and that if Rob Copeland so chose, he could toss his ass in jail. Hell, he could bury him under the jail, if he felt like it. But he didn't give a damn. All that mattered to him was that Lexie was safe and the man who had tormented her for weeks on end, who had murdered so many innocent people and had intended to kill Lexie today, was dead.

"I thought I'd never see you again," Lexie murmured, her voice quivering.

He lifted her up and into his arms, carried her across the deck and handed her over from the speedboat to the waiting arms of Geoff Monday, who stood solidly on the Sea Ray's deck. Once she was safely aboard, Deke jumped onto the cruiser.

"Don't go too far," Rob Copeland called. "We've got some questions for you, Bronson. And you, too, Monday."

"He won't be hard to find," Lexie told the Homeland Security agent. "He'll be with me. For the rest of his life." As soon as Geoff set her on her feet, Deke pulled her into his arms. She stood on tiptoe, looked Deke square in the eyes and said, "If that's all right with you."

"You bet it is, honey. By the way, once we apply for a marriage license, what's the waiting period in Tennessee?"

"What makes you think I'll marry you?" She draped her arms around his neck.

"Isn't that what people who are in love with each other do—get married, have a couple of kids and live happily ever after?"

"You bet it is."

EPILOGUE

AT MIDNIGHT on New Year's Eve, the newly married Mr. and Mrs. Deke Bronson stood on the back porch of Deke's ramshackle old house on the lake in Alabama. Wrapped snugly in their heavy winter coats, they shot off fireworks to welcome in a brand-new year, and to celebrate the beginning of their life together as man and wife. Neither had wanted an engagement party or a fancy wedding or a honeymoon to some exotic destination. All they wanted was each other.

"We'd better get back inside," Deke said, right after they lit the last sparkler and watched it shimmer and fade away. "It's freezing cold out here."

He lifted her in his arms, kicked open the back door, walked into the kitchen, and then turned and kicked the door closed. He carried her through the kitchen and into the living room, which was the most habitable room in the house. A roaring fire burned in the old rock fireplace, and an air mattress awaited them in front of the flames.

He helped her off with her coat, then took off his own. Neither one of them had on a stitch of clothing underneath. Deke tumbled her onto the air mattress, reached down and pulled up the two heavy quilts to cover them, and snuggled close to his wife.

Lexie sighed with contentment.

"I wish everyone could be as happy as we are," she said.

"That's not possible. No other two people are as much in love as we are."

"Maybe Cara and Bain." She sighed. "I hope someday they find a way to be together." Lexie had spoken to both of her dear friends earlier in the evening. Bain was working tonight. His choice. And Cara was at a gala New Year's Eve party, her date a Chattanooga stockbroker.

"It was good to hear from Toni, wasn't it?" Deke said.

"I can't believe she called us all the way from Paris. She and her mother are hitting all the museums, and they're leaving next week for Switzerland."

"It'll take time, but eventually she'll be all right. If ever there was a survivor, it's our Toni."

"Speaking of survivors, I'm so happy that Alice got to go home from the hospital in time to spend New Year's Eve with Robert and her daughters."

"I can't believe that she's actually going to marry him and move to Gadi with him when she's fully recovered."

Lexie cuddled close to her husband. "Why do you find that so unbelievable? Don't you know that I'd follow you to the ends of the earth?"

"Look around you, honey. I think you already did."

She tickled him in the ribs. "Don't talk about our love nest by the lake that way. I love this place, and our children are going to love coming here for vacations."

"Our kids, huh? Just how many kids are we planning on having?"

Lexie laid her hand over her flat stomach. "Well,

before I decide for sure, let's have this one first and see how it goes."

Deke shot straight up, sending the quilts dropping to his waist and yanking them off Lexie's body. He stared down at her hand resting across her belly.

"Are you pregnant?" he asked.

"Well, I peed on a stick this morning, and it turned blue."

"And blue means you're pregnant?"

"Uh-huh." She crawled on top of him and kissed him. "Happy New Year…Daddy."